Praise f

The Undertaking of 1

T0358768

"A uniquely charming mixture of whimsy and the macabre that completely won me over. If you ever wished for an adult romance that felt like *Howl's Moving Castle*, THIS IS THAT BOOK."
—Helen Hoang, author of *The Kiss Quotient*

"Truly outstanding romantic fantasy. I loved both its kookiness and its deep authenticity. An instant favorite!"
—India Holton, author of
The Wisteria Society of Lady Scoundrels

"If Lewis Carroll and Nora Ephron teamed up to write a magical Western, this would be the result. An unabashedly offbeat adventure, *The Undertaking of Hart and Mercy* oozes romantic fun." —Freya Marske, author of *A Marvellous Light*

"A lovely, macabre fantasy romance about life, death, and Actually Living. I cried twice and smiled plenty."
—Olivia Atwater, author of *Half a Soul*

"This book is a gooey (and hot!) romance immersed in a tasty layer of quirky fantasy, like some decadent chocolate treat. A little sweet, a little spicy, a little sharp, and entirely moreish!"
—Davinia Evans, author of *Notorious Sorcerer*

"Perfect for readers who love enemies-to-lovers mashed up with a touch of secret pen pal romance. I showed up for the fantastic, fun fantasy setting but it was Hart and Mercy that kept me reading." —Ruby Dixon, author of *Ice Planet Barbarians*

"Full of sizzle and emotional turmoil, as well as plenty of sci-fi adventure and humor. Readers will be captivated."

—*Library Journal*

"Fans of the *Ask a Mortician* webseries and those who love gore and rom-coms in equal measure will find plenty to enjoy in this quirky outing." —*Publishers Weekly*

"A crispy, hot-fried, pastel-dipped piece of delicious fantasy fiction wrapped up in a ravenous rom-com. . . . This is a unique read!"

—*BuzzFeed*

THE
UNDERMINING
OF
TWYLA
AND
FRANK

By Megan Bannen

The Undertaking of Hart and Mercy
The Undermining of Twyla and Frank

THE UNDERMINING

OF

TWYLA

AND

FRANK

MEGAN BANNEN

Copyright © 2024 by Megan Bannen
Excerpt from *That Time I Got Drunk and Saved a Demon* copyright © 2021 by Kimberly Lemming
Excerpt from *The Hexologists* copyright © 2023 by Josiah Bancroft

Cover design by Lisa Marie Pompilio
Cover illustrations by Shutterstock
Cover copyright © 2024 by Hachette Book Group, Inc.
Author photograph by Brian Paulette

Orbit
Hachette Book Group
1290 Avenue of the Americas
New York, NY 10104
orbitbooks.net

First Edition: July 2024
Simultaneously published in Great Britain by Orbit

Orbit is an imprint of Hachette Book Group.
The Orbit name and logo are registered trademarks of Little, Brown Book Group Limited.

The publisher is not responsible for websites (or their content) that are not owned by the publisher.

The Hachette Speakers Bureau provides a wide range of authors for speaking events. To find out more, go to hachettespeakersbureau.com or email HachetteSpeakers@hbgusa.com.

Orbit books may be purchased in bulk for business, educational, or promotional use. For information, please contact your local bookseller or the Hachette Book Group Special Markets Department at special.markets@hbgusa.com.

Library of Congress Cataloging-in-Publication Data
Names: Bannen, Megan, author.
Title: The undermining of Twyla and Frank / Megan Bannen.
Description: First Edition. | New York : Orbit, 2024.
Identifiers: LCCN 2023043740 | ISBN 9780316568258 (trade paperback) | ISBN 9780316568265 (ebook)
Subjects: LCGFT: Fantasy fiction. | Romance fiction. | Novels.
Classification: LCC PS3602.A6664 U528 2024 | DDC 813/.6—dc23/eng/20231005
LC record available at https://lccn.loc.gov/2023043740

ISBNs: 9780316568258 (trade paperback), 9780316568265 (ebook)

Printed in the United States of America

CCR

10 9 8 7 6 5 4 3 2 1

To my WON-der-ful parents, Alan and Mary Kay Dillingham

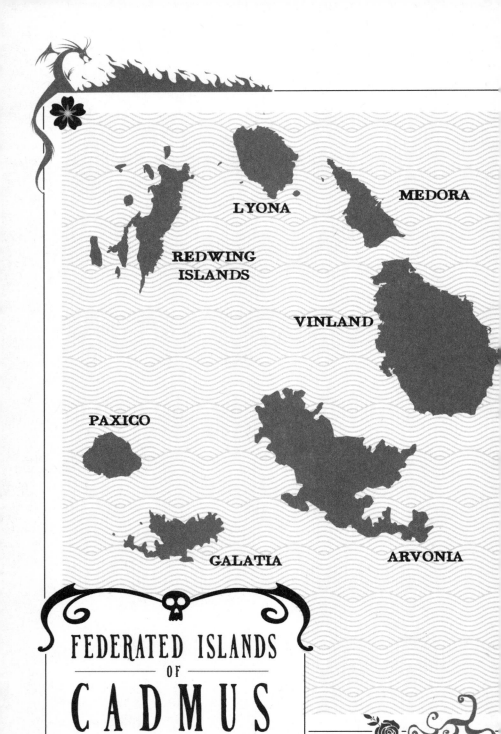

LYONA

MEDORA

REDWING
ISLANDS

VINLAND

PAXICO

GALATIA

ARVONIA

FEDERATED ISLANDS
OF
CADMUS

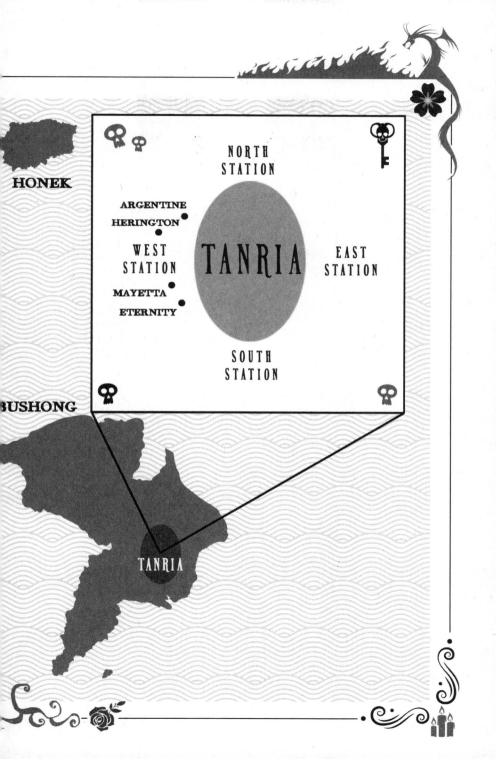

Chapter One

Twyla Banneker's unlikely career as a Tanrian Marshal began with a tuna casserole, which is to say, it began with Frank Ellis. She had presented him with the hot dish of starchy comfort the day that his wife left him. At the time, she could not have imagined that the casserole would lead to twelve years of friendship, eight years in law enforcement, and feeling perfectly at ease signing Frank up to run the miniature-equimaris rides with her at the county fair as part of the new Marshals in the Community initiative. Yet here she was, managing a line of over-sugared children and their exhausted parents and grandparents while her partner-cum-best-friend dragged the team around the water tank for four hours.

"I can't believe you did this to me," Frank muttered at Twyla after lifting yet another wet, screaming child off the scaly back of a miniature equimaris and handing him off to his mother. Oblivious to the young rider's shrieks of distress, the little purple water horse kept on swimming around the tank, nipping playfully at the kelp-like tail of the equally petite creature in front of her.

"Chief Maguire said we had to sign up to volunteer at the county fair, and you love equimares."

"Regular-sized ones. Without children on their backs."

"But you like kids."

"I like my kids. Who are fully grown. Other people's kids?" He shuddered.

"Pfft." Twyla gave him a dismissive wave before fetching the next round of riders. Years of whipping up cookies for temple bake sales, scrounging up costumes for school theatricals, and leading unruly scout troops had made her an expert at this sort of thing. Her late husband, Doug, used to joke that her middle name should be I'll Do It. *Twyla "I'll Do It" Banneker. That's you,* he would say with a fond shake of his head.

It's not like you're going to do it, she would think but never say aloud.

Frank, on the other hand, was here by her side, doing the thing that no one else wanted to do, gods bless him.

"Saddle up, Little Marshals," he declared in his deep southern Bushong drawl as he stood next to the sign that read "Little Marshals Miniature Equimaris Rides!"

Several adults in line tilted their heads to ogle Frank over Twyla's shoulder. Back in the day, when he and his family had moved in next door to her, he'd still had a bit of youthful roundness to his face, and his acne scars had pocked his skin like fresh craters. Now the crow's feet at the corners of his big brown eyes and the silver streaks in his shoulder-length black hair gave him an air of distinction. Even his old acne scars lent him a certain rugged pulchritude, as the lines of his face had grown firmer over the years. In his twenties and thirties, he had not turned heads; in middle age, he turned many.

Twyla's appearance, on the other hand, had always been bland and had only grown blander over the years. Her frizzy brown hair had dulled to a color resembling tepid dishwater. The freckles on her face and shoulders and arms and knees had faded into a barely there ruddy constellation across her softening body. The lashes that rimmed her brown eyes had thinned, as had her eyebrows, rendering her face washed out and forgettable. These days, whenever she felt inclined to study her reflection in the bathroom mirror, she cursed her past self, the young woman who had not appreciated her fresh-faced charm in her twenties and thirties.

Once she'd plunked the next eight kids onto eight colorful saddles, she bumped Frank in the hip. "Giddyup, Marshal Ellis."

"You owe me big time for this, Marshal Banneker."

"Please. You do it out of love."

He was reaching for the bridle of the lead equimaris when he stopped, put his hands on his hips, and bowed his head. He didn't stay that way for more than a few seconds, but it was long enough that the unmoving Little Marshals started to get restless, long enough that one of the miniature equimares blew water bubbles in annoyance, long enough for Twyla to consider panicking in that *Oh gods, is he having a heart attack?* kind of way.

"Frank?" She put a hand on his arm.

He shook himself. "I'm good," he told her before tugging on the bridle to lead the miniature equimares around the tank once more.

"Then stop being so grumpy."

"I am fifty-three years old. That officially makes me a grumpy old fart, doesn't it?"

Twyla fell into step beside him. "I'm two months older than you. If you're an old fart, what does that make me?"

"As smooth and mellow as a bottle of fine wine," he answered without missing a beat.

Twyla could both hear and feel her thighs rubbing together as she walked. "I think you mean 'full-bodied.'"

"That is a land mine, and I am not going anywhere near it."

They walked a few paces without needing to fill the conversational void. Frank stared off into the middle distance with his usual slow and steady deliberation before he spoke again. "Will you think less of me if I admit to some ingratitude?"

"As long as it's not about me."

"Never."

"What is it?"

"Don't you think the job has gotten sort of..." He glanced around furtively and lowered his voice. "Boring?"

"I have to admit, when you convinced me to join the Tanrian Marshals, this is not what I had in mind," Twyla conceded as she sidestepped a puddle.

Ever since the portals into Tanria were invented twenty-seven years ago, entrepreneurs and adventurers had poured into the former prison of the Old Gods to seek their fortunes. Many of them had been killed by the undead drudges that used to inhabit the place, hence the creation of the Tanrian Marshals. But a year ago, marshal-turned-sheriff-of-Eternity Hart Ralston had miraculously rid Tanria of its undead infestation, making Twyla and Frank's job much safer.

And less exciting.

"It's not just the community service stuff," said Frank. "Even when we're on patrol in Tanria, I'm bored out of my gourd. Don't get me wrong. I'm glad that the drudges are gone, but all we do these days is bust bird poachers or pimply teenagers sneaking in to bottle up ambrosia."

One of the miniature equimares gurgled in surprise as a child pulled on its mane, a sound that echoed the alarm bells going off in Twyla's head. "Are you wanting to retire sooner rather than later?"

"No, no. I'm happy to hold out for a couple more years until Hope's made it through med school and you're fully vested."

It was a relief to hear it, but then Twyla felt guilty for being the reason Frank was sticking with the marshals when he could walk into Chief Alma Maguire's office today and announce his retirement.

"You don't have to wait for me."

"What am I supposed to do in retirement without you?"

"You could get cracking on our master plan—find the property for the equimaris ranch, start building the bed-and-breakfast—and I could catch up in two years."

"Last lap!" he called to the riders before he looked at Twyla with a face full of warmth. "Nah, darlin', we're doing the ranch and the bed-and-breakfast together. I'll wait. At least busting poachers and pimply adolescents is easy. Your second child is trying to flag you down, by the way."

Twyla turned and spotted her son Wade in line holding two-year-old Teo while her other grandsons, Manny and Sal, bickered over who would get to ride the miniature equimaris with the glittery pink saddle. Wade motioned her over, nearly dropping Teo in the process.

"Hey, Mom, got a minute?"

"Not really, honey. I'm working."

"You're volunteering, actually."

"Chief Maguire has us on the clock for this."

Wade pulled Teo's hands away from his face as the toddler attempted to stick his drool-coated fingers into his father's mouth. "Okay, but what are you doing after?"

"Going to work, the not-volunteering kind."

"Well, shit, I guess that means you can't watch the kids for a bit?"

"Not unless they've decided to take up a career in law enforcement. And watch your mouth, will you? There are children all over the place here."

"Pfft," he said, the same dismissive sound she had directed at Frank. "As if they haven't heard it before."

"Some people's children haven't."

Teo grinned at her and said, "Shit." Twyla gave her son an *I told you so* look.

"Hi, Wade," Frank called as he guided the lead miniature equimaris past them.

"Hi, Frank," Wade answered with a wave, nearly dropping a squirming Teo again. He turned back to his mother. "Do you have to head straight to Tanria? Can't you fudge a little and take the kids off my hands for an hour or two?"

"I could, but I'd be defrauding the taxpayers of the Federated Islands of Cadmus, who pay my salary."

"So you'll do it?"

Twyla's right eye twitched. "No."

"You can take the boys on all the rides. Grandma-grandkids bonding time and all that. It'll be fun," Wade pleaded.

Twyla glanced at her son's two oldest children. Manny stuck his finger up his nose and wiped the results on Sal's bare arm, shouting, "No givebacks!" Sal shrieked in outrage as Manny darted behind Twyla to use her as a human shield.

"Hey, Twy, do we have a 4-29 on our hands?" Frank asked as he passed by them again.

She shook her head. "It's fine."

Wade's forehead crinkled in confusion. He'd inherited his overbite and brown eyes from Twyla, but his chestnut waves and broad shoulders and, most of all, that befuddled look on his face made it clear that he was Doug Banneker's son, through and through. "What's a 4-29?" he asked.

"Tanrian Marshal code. Don't worry about it." In fact, it was Twyla-and-Frank code for *Do you need me to rescue you from a socially awkward situation?* but she wasn't inclined to tell him that. "Honey, I'd love to help you, but I'm working."

"But Anita's volunteering in the crafts tent. How am I supposed to manage the kids all day on my own?"

"I thought she only had a three-hour shift."

"Same thing."

"One more lap," Frank told her as he passed by again, brushing her arm in moral support.

Twyla took a deep, calming breath as Wade begged, "Please, Mom? They wear me down to a nub, but you're a natural with them."

Echoes of her late husband drifted around her, this pernicious and lingering Old Gods notion that a uterus somehow endowed one with inherent childcare abilities. She put her hands on her son's shoulders and assured him, "You're a big boy. You can handle this, I promise you."

"End of the line, partners. Happy trails," Frank announced to a chorus of disappointed groans and only one sob of relief. Twyla gave Wade's shoulders one last pat of encouragement before helping Frank change out the riders. None of her grandkids got the equimaris with the sparkly pink saddle.

Once the ride was over, a couple of marshals whom Chief Maguire had also coerced into volunteering at the county fair came to relieve Twyla and Frank. Twyla kissed Wade and her grandkids goodbye before heading to the food vendors with her partner for a late lunch. Literally everything on offer was deep-fried and smelled divine, but Twyla forced herself to settle for the least bad-for-her option, which was, sadly, a corn dog. Food in hand, she and Frank walked past the delighted screeching of children on the Flying Dragon swings and sat at a picnic table on the fairgrounds. They were finishing up when Frank crumpled his paper napkin and uttered, "Aw, Salt Sea."

"What?" Twyla turned in her seat to see Liz Brimsby walking toward them, pie plate in hand.

"Yoo-hoo! Frank!" Liz sang.

"Hi, Liz." Ever polite, Frank put on a brave face, but several hours of working with small children had diminished his usually bottomless well of patience.

As a general rule, Twyla steered clear of Frank's romantic life unless he asked for her advice, but she could see plain as day that he wasn't interested. She chirped "Hi there, Liz" in a feeble attempt to run interference on his behalf.

It didn't work. Liz glanced at her only long enough to say "Hi" before returning her attention to Frank. "I saw you running the miniature-equimaris rides. I had no idea you were so good with children."

"Oh yes, Frank loves other people's children," Twyla agreed with an irony that sailed over Liz's head. Frank shot her a look that said *What are you doing to me?* and Twyla tried, once again, to deflect Liz's attention. "Do I spy a blue ribbon on your pie?"

Liz dimpled, a gesture somewhat undercut by the fact that she had pink lipstick on her two front teeth. "Yes! But I'm watching my figure, you know, so I thought Frank might like to have it."

"You're giving him your pie?" By the time Twyla got to the last word of her question, she could barely contain her mirth. She teared up with the effort of not laughing as Frank murdered her with his eyeballs from across the picnic table.

"My *prize-winning* pie."

Clearly making an exit, Frank rose and told her, "Thank you, but I'm afraid we're heading into Tanria, so..."

Now it was Twyla's turn to murder Frank with her eyeballs. Whether he wanted to date Liz Brimsby or not was irrelevant in this situation; the woman knew how to bake a good pie.

"What kind is it?" Twyla asked, praying *Don't be gooseberry* to the Bride of Fortune.

Liz gave her a flat stare. "Peach. For Frank."

Twyla nodded innocently, but she knew that any dessert of Frank's was essentially her dessert, too, no matter who baked it and for what seductive purpose.

"We need to get a move on," Frank insisted.

Liz leaned flirtatiously over the table as she slid the pie plate across the wooden boards toward Frank. "Stay safe in Tanria. I'll catch you when you get back."

Frank uttered a noncommittal sound, and she sauntered away. Twyla was of the opinion that Liz was shaking her hips rather excessively, and was, therefore, uncharitably gratified when the other woman tripped on the uneven ground. But honestly, who wore heels to the county fair?

"Don't say a word," Frank warned her as he reluctantly picked up the pie plate.

As if Twyla could resist that kind of temptation.

"Liz Brimsby, huh?"

"I am not dating her."

Liz turned around long enough to give Frank a coy finger wave. He scratched his eyebrow, pretending that he did not see the gesture.

"Does she know that?" asked Twyla.

"Apparently not, thanks to you." He headed for the autoduck in the parking lot, leaving Twyla to catch up.

"How is this my fault?"

"Ever since you made me dance with her at the Founders' Day party, Liz thinks I have a thing for her."

"I did not make you dance with her."

"You most certainly did."

"I would never make you dance with anyone."

"You would if Liz Brimsby was trying to corner Mercy Birdsall to make her recount the horrors of nearly being killed by a drudge on Main Street."

A vague memory tickled the back of Twyla's mind. "Oh wait, this is starting to ring a bell."

A drudge—one of the reanimated corpses that used to infest Tanria—had, in fact, found its way to Eternity's Main Street and lunged at Mercy Birdsall last Founders' Day, and Mercy had been rescued at the last minute by Hart Ralston, the former Tanrian Marshal who was now the town's sheriff (and Mercy's fiancé). Everyone and their mother had pestered poor Mercy that night at the party until Twyla and Frank ran interference for her so that she could escape for a bit of fresh air.

Frank treated Twyla to an uncomfortably accurate impression of her from that night. " 'Oh no. Liz Brimsby is heading this way. Ask her to dance, Frank, before she corners Mercy again.' "

By now, they had arrived at Frank's autoduck, a serviceable four-door model with a maroon-painted body. The duck was a good fifteen years old, but Frank washed and polished it religiously and changed out the tires long before the treads wore out. He unlocked the passenger-side door and opened it for Twyla.

"I guess I did make you dance with her," she admitted before she slid onto the bench.

She peeked under the foil covering the pie plate as her partner settled in behind the wheel, started up the duck, and drove them toward the road. The divine scent of butter, sugar, and peaches wafted over her. "You could do worse. Liz bakes a mean pastry crust."

"I do not want to go out with her, Twy."

"Suit yourself."

"She won't leave me alone. She's like a barnacle, and I'm the hull of the ship."

"You're too nice. It's time to start scraping, sailor."

She stared at the pie in her lap, her thighs spreading to either side of the plate, and thought, morosely, that Liz wasn't wrong about watching her figure. If Twyla indulged in a slice, all that butter and flour and sugar were sure to glue themselves to her hips for all eternity.

The pie.

In her lap.

She started to giggle.

"What?" asked Frank.

"She gave you a pie."

"So?"

"Her *award-winning* pie."

"Oh my gods—"

"Don't you want to eat her pie, Frank?" Twyla cackled without remorse.

"Ugh, Twy, stop it!"

She wiped away a tear of hilarity from the corner of her eye. "What, I can't make a pie joke?"

"No." He shook his head with vehemence. "Nooooooooo."

"Why not?"

"Because you're you. You mop your floors on a regular basis and bring cheesy potatoes to funerals."

"So because I do housework and cook comfort food, I'm not allowed to make mildly offensive jokes?"

"That sounds about right."

Twyla batted her eyes at him and imitated Liz. " 'I'm watching my figure, you know, so I thought you might like to have my pie.' Honestly, why go to the trouble of baking something delicious if you refuse to eat it? A man goes gray, and everyone thinks he's debonair. A woman gains a few pounds, and she may as well be dead."

Frank glanced at her, his eyes twinkling with mischief. "You know, that puts me in mind of a song."

"Oh no."

"*On the day we wed, you were as sweet as honey*," he sang. The word *honey* hit the bass notes of his impressively low register.

"No," Twyla groaned.

"Yes," Frank groaned back.

"That song is godsawful."

"Come on, darlin', you know the words. *And you . . .*"

Twyla relented. *"And you looked fine in your daddy's three-piece suit."*

"There she is. *Now you're old and drunk and spending all my money.*"

"Now your lying mouth ought to meet the pointy toe of my boot."

Early in their friendship, they had discovered a mutual tendency to burst into song whenever the lyrics to a particular ditty seemed relevant to the topic of conversation. Considering the fact that most of the records cranked out of the Bushong music scene over the past half century wailed about lost love and bitterness, it was pathetic how close to home some of those songs hit.

Twyla took a breath before belting out the first line of the refrain. *"Oh, your ass is draggin'."*

"And your ass is a-saggin'."

Together, they sang the song's title, in harmony no less. *"But no one else will have me, so I guess you'll have to do."*

Chapter Two

The chalkboard grid outside Chief Alma Maguire's office at the West Station informed them that *Ellis / Banneker* were slated to cover the day shift in Sector W-14 for the next ten days, with *Herd / Duckers* taking the night shift. On the corkboard next to it, someone had tacked a sign-up sheet for educational presentations at local retirement homes, another Marshals in the Community gig.

"Ugh," Frank grumbled an instant before their boss popped her head out of her office across the hall to ask, "Ellis, Banneker, what's this I hear about you bringing treats?"

Twyla froze, a statue dedicated to guilt, while Frank surreptitiously dusted flaky crumbs off the front of his blue work shirt.

Maguire narrowed her aquamarine demigod eyes, a pair of ice daggers in her brown face. "Salt Sea, seriously?"

"Pie doesn't last long in the commissary. You know how it goes, Chief."

"Humph." Maguire nodded toward the Marshals in the Community sheet on the corkboard, its blank spaces screaming at them in admonition. "Which one are you signing up for?"

Twyla and Frank caught each other's eyes in shared reluctance. Frank kicked off their hemming and hawing with a "Well now" that didn't go any further. Maguire jerked her head, indicating that they should follow her into the office, and they met each other's eyes again, this time in defeat.

"I'm going to be blunt," Maguire said as soon as she'd shut the door. She didn't even invite them to sit. "The Federal Assembly is breathing down our necks. They're saying that with the drudges gone, we don't need a force this size. Some are saying that we don't need the Tanrian Marshals at all."

"Maybe they should do a few tours busting poachers," Frank suggested acerbically.

"You don't have to convince me, but we all need to work together to convince the assembly. Feel free to find some serious criminal activity while you're on patrol, anything that could justify the taxpayer expense. The North Station got assigned a juicy smuggling case involving the illegal mining of Tanrian iuvenicite, lucky bastards."

"I thought the Doniphan Iuvenicite Mine had top-notch security," said Twyla.

"It does. That's why the case is such a big deal."

"Who would want a mineral that badly?" asked Frank.

"Tanria's the only place in the world where you can find iuvenicite. It's used in beauty products, the sort of stuff that's supposed to make women of a certain age look younger."

The old, familiar irritation at the ancient and unending double standard simmered in Twyla's stomach. "Wouldn't it be terrible if we let ourselves look our age?"

"Grandmother Wisdom forfend," agreed Maguire, who, like Twyla, was a woman of a certain age.

"Who's working the iuvenicite case?" asked Frank.

"Fox and Gomez."

"I thought Rosie Fox worked out of the East Station," said Twyla.

"She did, but she lost her seventeenth partner a few weeks ago. Gomez is the only one who'd take her, so now she's a Northie."

Frank motioned to the door or, more specifically, to the assignment board beyond it. "Looks like Duckers lost another partner, too. Wasn't he with Reese? Should have put him with Fox instead of Herd."

"And have Fox work out of the West Station? Thank you, no. I have enough headaches. And that's irrelevant. The West Station doesn't have a juicy iuvenicite case to work, so I'm having to get creative; hence, the Marshals in the Community initiative. You two are respected veterans. The younger ones look up to you, and I need you setting a good example. So let me ask you again: Which retirement home are you planning to educate about the work of the Tanrian Marshals?"

"Wisdom's Acres?" Twyla cheeped under her boss's brutal glare.

"Good choice."

Maguire opened the office door to dismiss them. As they shuffled past her, she asked, "What kind was it?"

"What kind was what?" asked Twyla.

"The pie."

"Um, peach." Her answer sounded more like a question than a statement.

Maguire sucked her teeth. "I love peach pie."

Twyla cringed under the weight of her boss's disapproval as Frank ushered her away from Maguire's Ire (as it was known among the Tanrian Marshals of the West Station).

They dutifully signed their names under *Wisdom's Acres* before making their way toward the weapons lockers. As they walked down the long hallway, Twyla had Rosie Fox on the brain. Fox was legendary among the marshals, the literal first person to sign up for the force, more than a quarter of a century ago, but Twyla had never met her personally. A lot of demigods, like Fox, joined the Tanrian Marshals—maybe as a way to feel closer to their divine ancestry. But Fox was the only one Twyla knew of who was actually immortal. She was more than a little curious about the woman.

"Do you know Rosie Fox?" Twyla asked Frank.

"Yeah. I used to run into her more often in the early days. She's...got a big personality."

"But you like her?"

One corner of Frank's mouth twitched upward. "I do. She's impulsive, which gets her into trouble sometimes. A lot of times. But that also makes her a great marshal. Your decision-making processes must work a little differently when you don't have to consider whether or not something is going to kill you."

By now, they had reached their destination, and it seemed rude to talk about another marshal where Fern, the registrar on duty, could drink in every word. They checked out their government-issued pistol crossbows and ammunition in short order. Twyla also requested a rapier, and Frank got his usual machete. While Tanria was much safer these days, old habits died hard, and after years of taking out drudges on Tanrian soil, neither Twyla nor Frank was ready to part ways with the weapons that had once separated corpses from the souls that had reanimated them.

After hitting the commissary to stock up on provisions, they headed to the stable to select their mounts. Twyla viewed equi-mares as merely practical, a means of getting around, so she didn't fuss about which one she chose. Frank, on the other hand, was far more particular. In his teens and twenties, he had worked on an equimaris ranch on the southern coast of Bushong, and he had the slightly bowed legs to show for it. He was one of the few mar-shals who was glad to find Saltlicker in one of the troughs. The Bride of Fortune was with him today, because there was Saltlicker in all his vivid violet glory, blowing churlish bubbles in the water.

"Hello, gorgeous," Frank greeted him.

Saltlicker lifted his huge head out of the water long enough to heave a disgruntled gargle in reply.

Twyla shook her head as she led her docile mare out of the trough. "Beauty is definitely in the eye of the beholder on this one, Frankie."

They toweled off the equimares' scales, saddled up, and ambled to the West Station's portal into Tanria. Millennia ago, the New Gods had defeated the Old Gods and imprisoned them here on the island of Bushong, inside a churning, impenetrable fog— the Mist. The Old Gods had long ago surrendered to become stars on the altar of the sky, but human beings had first entered Tanria only twenty-seven years ago, with the invention of the portals.

The metal archway, constructed directly into the Mist, emitted a gust of steam as the partners approached.

"Louis, you're back! How's the new baby?" Twyla asked the engineer on duty as he adjusted a couple of dials on the portal's frame.

"Real good! But no one's sleeping much at my house. You know how it is."

"That I do, three times over."

The engineer pulled on the crank, and a mystifying series of cogs and pistons whirred into action. The Mist within the portal's arch thinned to an opaque curtain, with the silhouette of Tanria's strange landscape barely visible on the other side. Twyla and Frank urged their mounts through, and in the few seconds it took to cross, the usual oppressive sense of wrongness squeezed Twyla's head, making her ears ring. She had grown used to the feeling, but it remained a loathsome aspect of an otherwise rewarding career.

Tanria came into focus, the bizarre otherworld of mismatched colors and landscapes and plants and animals, created by bored gods with nothing better to do. The Old Gods were not the gods of creation—the world and all that inhabited it were created by the New Gods—so Tanria looked more like a child's drawing of mountains and trees and flowers than actual mountains and trees and flowers. She used to marvel at the sight, but after eight years in the marshals, it had lost some of its wonder. Now this was simply the place where she worked.

They rode north-northeast to Sector W-14, where they were assigned for the duration of the ten-day tour. The landscape here was rugged and mountainous, a series of unnervingly triangular peaks known as the Dragon's Teeth, even though everyone knew the tales about Tanrian dragons were false.

According to legend, the Old Gods had ridden dragons into battle against the New Gods. When Tanria first opened to humanity, many hoped there might be a few left, hanging on to existence inside the Mist, but none had ever been found. That didn't stop big-game hunters and quack scientists from entering Tanria on a special license from time to time, hoping to be the first to find a Tanrian dragon. It never ceased to baffle Twyla that people would be willing to pay a ludicrous amount of money to go looking for something that clearly didn't exist and would in all likelihood kill them if it did.

They found Herd and Duckers saddling up for the night shift when they arrived at Sector W-14. Even in the dimness of the stable, the lurid violet of Herd's ostentatious equimaris-hide boots offended Twyla's eyes.

"Saltlicker!" cried Duckers when he spotted Twyla and Frank, or, more specifically, when he spotted Frank's mount. He patted the stallion's neck and got his hand out of the way as it tried to bite him. "I love this guy."

Saltlicker gurgled malevolently, and Frank's face split into an appreciative grin. "I knew I liked you, Duckers."

Herd's greeting was less charming. "If it isn't Mr. and Mrs. Banneker," he said as he led his mount out of the shadows of the stable, cackling at the same tired joke he'd trotted out countless times before.

"Men and women can be friends, and a man can take a woman's family name, but good to know you're still paying tribute to the misogyny of the Old Gods, thousands of years after their demise," Frank replied, his tone affable when Twyla was boiling on the inside. Her partner's magnificent unflappability was a reminder that Herd wasn't worth her time or temper, and she clamped her lips shut against an unhelpful retort.

That didn't stop Herd from winking at her and saying "If looks could kill, Mrs. Ellis" before he led his mount out of the stable and into the Tanrian gloaming.

"So wait, are you two married, or is Herd being a dick? Or both?" Duckers asked them.

"We're just friends," Twyla told him.

"And Herd's a dick," Frank added.

"Frank!"

"Well now, he *is* a dick, and that's a fact."

"We shouldn't say mean things behind a person's back, though."

"You were shooting figurative fireballs out your eye sockets at him seconds ago."

"You'd think the guy would retire," Duckers chimed in. "Not married. No kids. A good twenty years in the marshals. He must be rolling in it."

"Nah, he's broke," said Frank.

"I'm putting a kid through med school on this salary, and I'm not even fully vested yet," said Twyla, shocked. "How is he broke?"

"Gambling debts."

Twyla thought of the years she had worked and scrimped and saved to keep her family afloat, while this man had squandered what the Bride of Fortune had so generously bestowed upon him. Then again, a person who spent his time in gambling dens probably didn't have a lot to lose in terms of the important things in life: friends, family, a sense of belonging. So it was Twyla's charitable side that commented, "That's sad."

Duckers was less charitable. "What a dumbass."

"How did you wind up with Herd?" Twyla asked him. "I thought Reese was your partner."

"Reese quit a few weeks ago. Saltlicker kicked him in the nuts, and he wound up having to get a nut-ectomy. Vowed he'd never come back."

"Sounds like the work of a gorgeous equimaris," Twyla commented to Frank as he winced in sympathy.

Duckers laughed and reached around his equimaris's girth to tighten the saddle strap, revealing the green-blue lines of a stoppered bottle etched into his brown skin. A temple votary must have preserved his soul in the tattoo after his appendix burst. When drudges were still a problem, marshals like Duckers had been handy to have around, since the appendix, as the seat of the human soul, was where the lost spirits of Tanria would take up residence in order to reanimate a dead body.

Of course, now that the drudges were gone, it didn't matter where Duckers kept his soul.

"Not gonna lie: Herd isn't my favorite," Duckers said. "I mean, the guy wears purple equimaris-hide boots. Why would you want to wear something you ride? It's tacky."

Frank huffed in agreement as he coaxed a recalcitrant Saltlicker into one of the water troughs.

"But Maguire said she didn't want me working solo yet," Duckers continued, "so I got stuck with Herd."

"How many partners have you had?"

"Since Hart left? Only three."

Twyla sometimes forgot that Duckers had apprenticed under Hart Ralston, the savior of Tanria, a man so austere that it was jarring to hear anyone use his first name freely. "Who were you working with before Reese?" she asked.

"Paulson, but we only did two tours together before he left to follow after some lady on the Parcheesi tournament circuit."

"So you've had three different partners in one year?"

Frank slung his arm over Twyla's shoulders, the warm heft of it a comforting blanket around her. "Don't ever leave me, darlin'. They might stick me with this guy."

Duckers gestured toward Twyla's pack.

"Hey, Banneker, I didn't know you were a Gracie Goodfist fan."

"I've never read the comics, actually."

"But you have a Gracie Goodfist backpack."

"It belonged to one of my sons." She knew the bag was ridiculous, but she could never justify buying herself a new one when she had a perfectly serviceable (if slightly childish) option at hand.

"How old are your kids?"

She counted them off on her fingers. "DJ is thirty-three, Wade is thirty-two, and Hope is twenty-three."

"So they're old."

She leveled him with a stare.

Duckers put a hand over his heart, as if he'd been shot. "Dang. Fireballs."

Herd oozed into the wide doorframe of the stable and sucked all the fun out of the air. "You coming or not, kid?"

"I'm coming, I'm coming."

"That's what she said."

Twyla raised her eyes to the Unknown God in the Void Beyond the Sky. "Gods save us."

Ignoring her comment, Herd spat over his shoulder. Twyla could never understand a man's urge to spit. Doug used to do the same thing, and it drove her batty.

"I don't know why we bother riding out anymore," griped Herd. "We don't have shit to do, thanks to that sanctimonious twat Ralston."

Frank didn't rise to the bait, but Duckers clenched his fists, while Twyla snapped, "Yes, where does he get off, saving our lives?"

"Word is he gets off on Mercy Birdsall these days. Let's go, Duckers." With that, Herd walked away, leaving his partner to follow in his oily wake.

"If I murder him tonight, will you be my alibi?" Duckers asked them.

"Sure thing," said Frank.

Twyla was fairly sure that Duckers was joking, but on the off chance he wasn't, she said, "Maybe don't kill him tonight. Or ever. Please?"

"Fun-ruiner," Duckers told her amicably before he left the stable.

On Sorrowsday evening, Twyla and Frank returned to the barracks from their day shift to find Duckers leading his equimaris out of the stable, alone.

"Where's Herd?" asked Twyla.

"No idea. I thought he was taking a piss, but he stepped out an hour ago, and I haven't seen him since. If he doesn't get his ass back here in the next couple of minutes, I'm going to be working solo tonight. Again. He pulled this shit with me last week, too. Didn't catch up with me until two hours past sunset."

"Want me to ride out with you?" offered Frank.

"Don't worry about it. I'm sure he'll catch up. Eventually."

"Make sure you have your flare handy. We'll keep an eye out," Twyla called as he urged his mount out of the stables, and Duckers waved in thanks as he rode off.

An ominous roll of thunder echoed in the distance. There was only one storm inside Tanria, a giant angry cloud created by the imprisoned God of Wrath centuries ago, and it was never pleasant to be caught out in it. Twyla directed an uneasy glance at the sky before following Frank into the barracks. They left the door and windows open. If Duckers ran into trouble and sent up his flare, they'd be sure to see it.

They were sitting down to dinner when they heard a hesitant "Hello-o-o? Mail delivery?" from outside.

"Come on in," Twyla called, and a moment later, Hermia, the new nimkilim who delivered mail throughout Tanria, poked her upturned hedgehog nose into the barracks. Her predecessor had been a whiskey-swilling, foulmouthed, hard-bitten rabbit, so as far as Twyla was concerned, Hermia was a serious improvement, at least in terms of demeanor. While most nimkilim were shorter than humans, the top of Hermia's prickly head didn't even reach Twyla's hip, a diminutiveness that added to her bipedal charm. She wore an oversized Fair Isle cardigan, a red woolen scarf, and blue rubber boots with clouds printed all over them. Her spines jutted out of her sweater in odd patches, giving her a cozily rumpled air, and her beady black eyes looked enormous behind the perfect circles of her glasses. She was so ludicrously cute that Twyla had to resist the urge to say "Aw!" every time she saw her.

Hermia was digging around in her worn leather satchel when the barking of a stray dog in the distance made her startle. "Oh my goodness gracious!" she squeaked, sending a mini storm of undelivered letters fluttering out of her mailbag and onto the floor.

Frank gave a huff that was either laughter or exasperation—possibly both. Twyla got up from the table to help the hedgehog pick up the scattered mail, gathering as many letters as she could at one go, while Hermia picked up one missive at a time and blinked at each address before sliding the envelope carefully into her bag.

"This one's for you," she told Twyla as if she were surprised by the letter's existence.

"Thank you." Twyla dimpled when she saw that the letter was from her daughter, Hope.

"And this one. My goodness, two whole letters!"

Twyla took the second missive and went about digging around in her Gracie Goodfist backpack for a tip.

"I know there's one for you, too, Marshal Ellis." The nimkilim's little pink hedgehog tongue poked out the side of her cute little hedgehog mouth as she fished around inside her satchel.

And fished.

And fished.

She pulled out a letter, studied it, and said, "No." She pulled out another letter, studied it, and said, "No." She pulled out an enormous crate that was four times the size of the satchel, grunted under its weight, and said, "No." Visibly deflating, she dropped the crate into the satchel, retrieved what appeared to be a bottle of grape soda, and took a fortifying sip.

"Do you think it might be…there?" Frank pointed to Hermia's right shoulder, where a couple of letters had gotten stuck in the spines sticking out of her cardigan.

She set the soda bottle on the table and plucked one of the envelopes from her prickles with her tiny pink hand. "No, that isn't it." She stuck it to a separate set of spines poking out of the left side of her sweater.

Frank gave Twyla a long-suffering moue as another round of thunder rumbled through the Dragon's Teeth range.

"Be nice," she scolded him.

"I didn't say anything."

"You didn't have to."

Oblivious to this exchange, Hermia lifted a second letter off her spines, accompanied by a delicate rip. "Oh dear," she said with a tut before she straightened her glasses and studied the direction. "Oh! I found it."

Frank accepted his letter in its torn envelope as Twyla slipped the nimkilim a tip.

Hermia clutched the copper to her heart, her eyes growing misty behind her lenses. "Thank you ever so much. I'll be off, then."

She stuffed the coin into the cardigan's drooping pocket, adjusted her satchel, and nabbed her bottle of soda, an action that required both hands since her fingers were so tiny. "Have a good night."

"You, too. Thanks, Hermia," answered Twyla.

"Bye."

"Bye," said Twyla.

Frank gave a half-hearted wave from the table.

"Bye," Hermia repeated before she turned and walked out into the night.

Twyla hovered at the door as another clap of thunder shook the earth. "I hope she's safe out there."

Frank shrugged and took a bite of his burrito.

"You aren't worried about her?"

"She's immortal. What's there to worry about?" He stared into the distance before he spoke again. "You know, my mom used to collect hedgehogs—not real ones, but little statues and salt-shakers and stuff. She loved them." One corner of Frank's lips turned up. He always spoke fondly of his mother, who had passed away fifteen years ago. He did not recall his father or older brother with anything resembling affection. Twyla had long since learned not to press him on it, but she knew that, his mother aside, his childhood had not been a happy one.

Frank returned his attention to the present and to his letter, and Twyla followed suit, her heart blooming at the sight of her daughter's handwriting on the envelope. She opened the letter and read:

Dear Mom,
Frantically cramming, so this is just a quick note. I wanted to let you know that I'll be home by next Wisdomsday afternoon, if not sooner. Can't wait to see you!

Love,
Hope

P.S.—I hope it's okay that I'm bringing Everett!

Frank watched Twyla grin at her mail and guessed, "Hope?"

"She's coming home for the semester break. And she's bringing Everett with her."

"Who's Everett again?"

"You remember, Hope's friend. They've known each other since undergrad. He came for a visit last summer."

"Oh yeah. He's a good egg."

"He really is." Twyla was fond of funny, sweet-tempered Everett Simms. If her daughter had to go far from home to attend med school, Twyla took comfort in knowing that Hope had a good friend looking out for her.

"When are they getting in?" asked Frank.

"Next Wisdomsday."

"Then they'll be here in time for the wedding." He held up his own mail, and Twyla realized that she was holding a matching copy, an invitation in lovingly handwritten calligraphy on thick creamy paper.

With hearts full of joy we invite you to
the wedding of
Mercy Elizabeth Birdsall & Hartley James Ralston
On Wardensday, the 3rd of the Month of Painter
At five in the evening
All Gods Temple of Eternity, Bushong
Reception to follow

Twyla couldn't believe her eyes. "Hart Ralston, getting married. Who knew he had it in him?"

"Good for him," said Frank, and she could see that he was trying hard to mean it. Weddings were always an uncomfortable affair for Frank, a reminder of what he considered his greatest failure. But since that so-called failure had led, in a roundabout way, to the best friendship of Twyla's life, she couldn't bring herself to resent Cora for walking out on him twelve years ago.

The first time she met Frank was the day that he and Cora and Lu and Annie had moved in next door to her and Doug and DJ and Wade and Hope, twenty-two years ago. Their houses were mirror images of each other, a pair of three-bedroom ranches on small squares of lawn, facing west on Cottonwood Street in Eternity. But Twyla could barely remember shaking Frank's hand. It was Cora who became her friend first, that neighborly kinship born out of having children the same age. They would help each other in a pinch, watching the kids when one of them needed to run a quick errand, loaning an egg or a cup of sugar in a time of need—that sort of thing. Cora had been a lifesaver in those days, and Twyla liked to think she had been there for Cora, too. For a decade, the Ellis and Banneker children moved between

27

both houses and accompanying yards as if there were no fences between them, while Twyla and Cora sipped their coffee in the morning and the occasional glass of wine after dinner and talked about how exhausted they were all the time.

They also bitched about their husbands. Quite a lot.

Privately, Twyla didn't think Frank Ellis was that bad. True, he was gone much of the time on his tours of duty inside the Mist. But when he was home, he always seemed to be doing yard work or taking out the garbage or playing catch with Lu in the backyard or helping out with his kids' sea polo team. From what Twyla could tell, the real issue between Cora and Frank was the fact that Frank simply wasn't there. Yet sometimes, for that very reason, Twyla envied her neighbor.

The day Cora left, Twyla heard about it from Eugene Channing while she was ringing up his cabbage and bananas and digestive crackers during her shift at Wilner's Green Grocer. Eugene was a shameless gossip, but gods, if he wasn't accurate 99 percent of the time. In this case, he got wind of it from his buddy Bob Lowenstein, who had filled up Cora's tank for her at the Gas 'n' Save on her way out of town.

"Had the hold of the autoduck so full she had to tie it down. Trunks on the rack and everything. It weren't no vacation packing—that's what Bob said. You take my word for it: she's halfway to the southern coast by now. That's where she and Ellis come from, right?"

"I'm sure I don't know anything about it," Twyla told him, but guilt formed a hard, heavy lump in her gut as she thought of all the times she and Cora had complained about Doug and Frank, respectively. And now Doug was dead and the Ellises were splitsville.

When she got home that evening, she did what any self-respecting woman would do: she set about assembling a tuna casserole. A half hour later, with the glass dish in hand, she marched across the front yard and knocked on Frank Ellis's door. A long silence followed, but then she heard the shuffling of feet from within, and a moment later, Frank stood in the doorway.

It was as if Twyla were seeing him for the first time, not as Cora's husband or as Lu and Annie's father, but as a living, breathing person in need of a shower and some comfort food and a good hug.

His hair at the time was cropped short and stood up in irregular spikes around his head, more black than gray. His big brown eyes were bloodshot, his clothes wrinkled. He didn't look like he was wallowing in the depths of despair, per se. He simply looked lost. Twyla knew the feeling intimately, having experienced something similar the day the sheriff stopped by Wilner's a year earlier to let her know that Doug had wrecked their autoduck on Highway 4 and himself along with it.

She held up the casserole. "Have you eaten? I brought you dinner if you're hungry."

Frank gazed at her in confusion before nodding, as if to say *So I guess you know my life is in shambles* but also *That casserole sounds pretty good right about now.*

"Come on in," he said as he stepped aside. Twyla had never realized how deep his voice was until he uttered those three words. Had they ever spoken more than three words to each other in the ten years they'd shared a property line, she wondered? It was a lowering thought.

She went to the kitchen, turned on the gas sconce, and set the oven to preheat.

"It should take about fifteen minutes to get up to three hundred and seventy-five degrees. Put this in for forty minutes. When it's good and bubbly, take it out and give it five minutes to cool and firm up before you dig in. You should have plenty of leftovers to get you through the next couple of days. Do you want me to pick anything up for you? I've got a shift tomorrow at Wilner's, so it wouldn't be a problem."

"Aren't you having any dinner?"

"It's for you. I can rustle up something for myself."

"You made a whole casserole for me?"

"It's no trouble."

Frank started to blink furiously, and for one panicked moment, Twyla thought the poor man might crack like an egg. But then he gave a watery laugh and said, "I think there are a few bottles of beer in the fridge. Want one?"

She almost said no, but then it occurred to her that she hadn't had a beer in a long while. So she stayed for a bottle, followed by another, followed by a serving of tuna casserole and a side of carrots she had scrounged up from the back of the refrigerator.

From then on, they ate dinner together every now and again, whenever Frank was off duty and Twyla had an evening free from work or scouts or PTA meetings. Hope was in junior high at the time, and occasionally Wade and Anita would join them, too. Much to Twyla's surprise, Frank insisted on taking turns cooking and cleaning up the kitchen, which led to him fixing the pernicious leak under the sink that had plagued Twyla for ages. A few weeks later, while walking up the brick path to Frank's house, Twyla noticed his iris bed was overgrown, and she set about dividing the rhizomes for him when the weather cooled. The meals and the small neighborly acts snowballed into an unexpected friendship, leading inexorably to the day eight years ago when Frank, listening to Twyla agonize over the financial impossibility of sending Hope to college, suggested that she apply to work with him in the Tanrian Marshals when his partner retired.

"I'm not going to lie. It's dangerous work. But the money is good, and you know I'll watch your back every step of the way."

He wrote a letter of recommendation for her. She got the job. She put Hope through college and was now putting her through medical school, and she had enough left over each month to squirrel away a small college fund for each of her grandkids. Now here she was all these years later, eating dinner with Frank in Tanria.

Twyla lovingly tucked Hope's letter into its envelope and stacked it neatly with the wedding invitation. She wished that her eldest, DJ, wrote to her the way Hope did. Twyla's daughter-in-law sometimes sent her letters and photos of their kids, but Twyla knew that DJ's boys were much closer to their maternal grandparents than to her. It was only natural that they would visit their mother's parents more often, but it broke Twyla's heart all the same.

Frank was in a similar boat. Lu had been eleven and Annie had been only nine when Cora left him. Once a year, he took a long vacation to spend time with them at their ranch, and every summer Lu and Annie came to visit him for a couple of weeks in Eternity. He never said as much, but Twyla knew that the older they got, the more he feared they'd stop coming to see him.

A loud popping sound jolted Twyla out of her thoughts. She and Frank rushed outside to see a bright pink flare shooting into the sky, sizzling with alarm.

"Aw, shit," Frank said at the same moment Twyla said, "Duckers."

They abandoned their dinner plates, mounted up without bothering to dry off the equimares, and galloped off in the direction of the flare.

Chapter Three

By the time Twyla and Frank arrived on the scene, two miles from the barracks, the flare had landed. They found themselves on a flattened plain, nestled in the jagged foothills of the Dragon's Teeth mountain range. The flare's harsh light glared across the landscape, outshining their saddle lanterns and casting everything in bright pinks and dark shadows, rendering the area even more otherworldly than usual. Stranger still, a luminescent substance glistened in odd patches all over the rocky ground.

There was no sign of the person or persons who set off the flare.

"I don't like this," Frank whispered as he unclipped the pistol crossbow from his belt.

Their eyes met, the whites of Frank's glowing eerily pink by the light of the flare. Twyla nodded in response, not wanting to make any more noise than necessary. It had been some time since she had experienced true mortal fear on the job, but the continued hiss of the flare and the bizarre shining blotches on the earth made her insides twist up.

They dismounted as quietly as they could and walked toward the ring of the flare's light, with Frank scanning the landscape to their left and Twyla covering the right, their sidearms at the ready.

"See anyone?" she whispered as she squinted into the night.

"No. You?"

"No."

The plain wasn't wide, but Twyla felt exposed and vulnerable.

"This is not good," Frank murmured behind her.

Twyla was about to agree, but she tripped over something and went sprawling on the ground, landing painfully on her hip.

"Twy?" Frank was now having to cover both their flanks, but his eyes darted to her on the ground, and she could hear the worry in his voice.

"I'm good." She retrieved her pistol crossbow and got herself into a crouch to get a good look at what had sent her spilling.

"Boots," she declared. "And they have that weird, glittery stuff all over them. Crap, I got some on my pants. What in the name of the Unknown God?"

"Are the boots purple? Equimaris hide?"

"I can't tell in this light. You think these are Herd's?"

Twyla looked up. Frank's jaw was set, and he had his pistol crossbow trained straight ahead. He didn't glance at her, but he nodded toward something several feet in front of them. No, not something. Some*one*. A person lay unmoving on the ground, and it was clear they had sailed the Salt Sea. Like the boots, the remains were shimmering.

She scrambled to her feet, an action that took a humiliating amount of effort at her age. Back to back once more, she and Frank slowly approached the corpse to get a better look. The entire body was coated in a glittery residue, as were the soil, rocks, and scrub in a five-foot radius around it. The only things that rendered the victim identifiable were the outline of the ID key on a chain around his neck and the equimaris-leather boots he'd been blown out of.

"Mother of Sorrows," uttered Twyla.

"This is Old Hell and gone from boring," Frank agreed grimly. "I think I preferred boring."

The galloping slap of equimaris feet announced Duckers's

arrival in response to the flare. He pulled up to a stop and called "You all right?" as he slid out of the saddle.

"We're fine," answered Frank. "Herd, not so much."

Duckers joined them to stare at the disturbing remains of his now deceased partner.

"Well, fuck," he said.

A crack of lightning lit up the night sky, followed by a clash of thunder. The first fat raindrops pelted the ground and the marshals along with it. All three looked up in dismay.

"Well, fuck," Duckers said again.

Twyla stood at a window in the barracks, looking out, though there was nothing to see but deep darkness and blinding lightning beyond the glass. She listened to the sound of the rain lashing the pane and gushing down the roof.

"Think there'll be any evidence left after this thing blows over?" she asked without looking at Frank and Duckers, who were sitting at the table with steaming mugs of something Duckers called "medicine."

"Not much we can do about it now," said Frank. "Come and sit over here by the fire and get yourself warmed up."

They had done their best to wrap Herd in sailcloth without touching the glittery substance that coated him, while the storm poured the old God of Wrath's watery vindictiveness upon them. Now Herd's damp body was tucked away in the cellar until they could deliver the remains to the coroner.

Frank's voice came again from behind her, low and comforting, an audible hug. "Herd's beyond your help and your worry now, darlin'. Come have a seat."

Resigned, Twyla sat beside him, and Duckers pushed a third mug in front of her. Whatever it was, it smelled marvelous. She took a sip and felt the so-called medicine burn a path of warmth down her throat.

"Is that whiskey?" she half asked, half coughed.

"And black tea and honey. Lots of honey. It's better with lemon juice, but I'm not going to carry lemons around in Tanria, and the bottled stuff isn't the same."

Frank cupped his mug, letting it warm his fingers as he got down to business. "I'm sorry, Duckers, but we've got to ask you a few questions. Can you tell us your whereabouts this evening?"

Duckers had his own mug halfway to his mouth, but he set it down with a *thud*. "You don't think *I* killed Herd, do you?"

"No, but I think we need to cobble together a report to give Maguire. Who knows what kind of details might be important here. So, where were you between the time you left us at the stable and the moment you joined us at the . . . I guess we'll call it a crime scene?"

"I patrolled the northwest corner of the sector first, up there by the Alvarez Ambrosia Bottling Company in W-7."

Twyla calculated the time it would take to ride from the northwest corner of the sector to the place where they found Herd. It lined up with Duckers's arrival on the scene.

"How long had you and Herd been partners?" Frank asked him.

"Less than a month."

"You said he'd been ditching you on the job. Any clue where he was going or what he was doing?"

"No."

"And you didn't report him?"

"I'm not going to be the jerk who snitches on his coworker. Besides, I'm getting a reputation as the guy who can't keep a partner. I didn't want to cause trouble, for me or for him."

"Understandable. And very charitable of you, too," said Twyla. Already, Duckers's concoction was making her feel a bit muzzy.

"Anyone know what the glittery substance was? I'm worried the rain is going to wash it all away, and I'm not sure how to explain it to Maguire."

"If anyone wants a sample, there's plenty on Herd." Frank crossed his arms and leaned back in his chair, balancing precariously on two legs as he mulled everything over. "How do you think he died? Because I can't for the life of me figure out how you'd go about killing a man with glitter. Or why you'd want to."

Duckers leaned his elbows on the tabletop. "What if it wasn't a person who did Herd in? What if it was, you know, an animal? Ish?"

Twyla suspected Duckers was feeling muzzy himself. "What kind of animal-ish covers someone in gold sparkles?"

"Hear me out. What if it was a ——?" Duckers spoke the last word of his question so softly, no one could hear it.

"A what?"

"You know, a ——." Duckers shifted his eyes as, once again, he rendered the last word incomprehensible.

"Let it rip. There's no judgment here."

"A dragon."

Twyla gaped at him for a full five seconds before turning to Frank. They silently asked each other, *Did you hear that, too? Is that what he actually said?*

Frank brought the front two legs of his chair to the floor to give Duckers his full attention. "Well now, I don't mean to discourage a little thinking outside the box, but I've been working in Tanria for twenty-two years, and I've never seen a dragon or heard of anyone else seeing one."

"I get that, and Hart always said the same thing. But think about it: We found Herd in the middle of nowhere, covered in gold sparkles, with no MO, no weapon, no evidence, no suspect in sight, nothing. He was obviously scared enough to light his

flare to get our help. And there are all those old stories about dragons flying around in here. All I'm saying is, What if?"

"Seems pretty far-fetched," Twyla said doubtfully.

"I know, but..." Duckers took a fortifying gulp from his mug.
"Look, a couple of weeks ago, I thought I saw something flying
around that tall peak in the Dragon's Teeth. It was around sunset,
and I wasn't close up or anything, but dang, it looked big."

"It was probably an eagle or a vulture," said Frank.

"Maybe. But maybe not."

With that eager, earnest expression on his face, Duckers
reminded Twyla of her own kids, of all the times they had wanted
to believe that the world was far more magical than it was. She
softened. "Someone needs to bring in Herd's remains tomorrow.
I'm sure Maguire is going to want an autopsy. You could stop in
the station and float your dragon theory by her."

"Are you kidding? Maguire would laugh me out of the Tanrian
Marshals."

"So you want us to suggest it to her so that she can laugh *us* out
of the Tanrian Marshals?"

"She'll listen to you. You know, because you're old-timers."

The word *old* bludgeoned Twyla.

Frank barked with laughter. "If Twyla could shoot fiery balls of
glitter out of her eyes, Duckers, you'd look an awful lot like Herd
right about now."

"We shouldn't speak so irreverently of the dead," Twyla whispered as if Marshal Herd might hear her.

"You never had to listen to his Old Gods–level misogyny when
he discussed his supposed conquests. Didn't help that the guy
reminded me of Carl."

Carl could have referred to either Frank's father or his brother,
since they shared the same name. It didn't matter; he held them
both in the same contempt.

"I was not a fan," Duckers offered in support.

Frank gave Twyla a side hug. "You can bring cheesy potatoes to his funeral, if it makes you feel better."

The following morning, they were up with the sun, each of them the worse for wear, thanks to Duckers's medicine. They divided up, and for over an hour, they scoured the immediate environs around the site where Herd's body was found, but the area produced little evidence. Only a few remnants of gold glitter twinkled in the morning light, since most of the residue had been washed away with the rain. There were also traces of blood clinging to a rock, but no other signs of struggle. Twyla was about to call off the search when Duckers shouted, "Hey! Over here!"

The next thing Twyla knew, the rookie was on the ground. Alarmed, she sprinted as fast as her middle-aged legs and leaky bladder would allow. Out of the corner of her eye, she saw Frank hustle from the opposite direction. She reached Duckers a couple of seconds before he did.

"What's wrong?" she panted.

Duckers grinned up at her. "Nothing. I'm here for scale."

He was lying between two birdlike prints mirroring each other, each of them roughly half the length of one rookie Tanrian Marshal. The print on Duckers's left was more distinct than the one on the right, a foot with three long, skinny toes and a narrow heel.

"What do you think, Ellis? Eagle? Vulture? *Dragon?*"

Frank gave a long, low whistle.

"Is that your way of saying I was right?"

"I'm not saying a thing." Frank pulled a notebook, pencil, and measuring tape out of his pack.

Duckers made no move to help him and Twyla. He folded

his hands behind his head and crossed his ankles with a smug "Mm-hmm."

Twyla's hand was shaking as she moved toward the longest toe, unspooling the tape. "Is this creeping you out at all?" she asked Frank, who held the other end at the base of the heel.

"Yep. You?"

"Very much." She crouched on her end and pulled the tape taut. "The drudges were bad enough—thirty-four and five-eighths inches. I don't have a pressing need to come face-to-face with whatever this thing is."

"Dragon," Duckers coughed into his fist.

"Duckers thinks it was a dragon," Frank informed Chief Maguire at 11:43 in the morning, when the three marshals stood across the dinged-up desk from their boss.

"Thanks a lot, Ellis," grumbled Duckers.

"This is one of those best-to-rip-off-the-bandage situations."

Maguire opened a desk drawer, pulled out a bottle of aspirin, and helped herself before finally speaking. "So let me see if I have this right: Herd didn't show up for his shift. Duckers rode out alone. A flare went up, presumably set off by Herd. Ellis and Banneker, you two arrived on the scene first and found Herd dead, covered in glitter. Duckers arrived shortly thereafter, as did the storm. You wrapped the body and took cover. This morning, you returned to the scene to look for evidence and found a giant set of footprints that Duckers thinks belong to a dragon, even though dragons have been extinct for literal millennia."

"That about sums it up," said Frank, sliding the sketch of the prints he had made that morning with the accompanying measurements across the desk to her.

"We lost a twenty-plus-year veteran of the Tanrian Marshals, and the most likely theory is that he was killed by a glitter-breathing dragon?" Maguire got up and walked to her window with its view of the gravel parking lot and a sliver of the churning mist that shrouded Tanria. After a moment, she turned her blue-green demigod gaze on Twyla. "You're mighty silent, Banneker. What do you make of all this?"

"I'm not saying I think a dragon killed Herd, but I'm not *not* saying it either. Those prints were mighty big."

"Ellis, they're both saying dragon. What would you call it?"

Frank licked his lips. "I'm not sure what else it could have been."

Maguire threw up her hands. "Couldn't y'all have waited until the end of the day to dump this on my desk? It's not like I can knock one back before noon."

She began to pace the floor like a caged tiger. The three marshals watched her warily as if they were kids at a zoo, hoping the bars would hold.

"We won't know anything conclusive about the cause of death until the coroner's report arrives. For now, consider anything related to this case classified. Duckers, you're working with these two for the time being. I don't care how you all patrol Sector W-14 as long as no one goes out alone. And, Ellis?"

Frank stood at attention.

"Do you remember how to operate the old crossbows, the big ones?"

"I think so."

"Good. Check some out of the weapons lockers, and teach these two how to use them."

"Sure thing, Chief."

"If you come across anything else amiss out there, anything at all, report it to me as soon as you can. And let me be clear: If you see a—I can't believe I'm saying this. If you see a dragon, you shoot to kill. I don't care if it's the scientific discovery of the century. I'm not losing another marshal. Understood?"

"Understood," the three marshals answered, none of them with enthusiasm.

"Could've had a nice iuvenicite-smuggling case, but no—the Bride of Fortune has to dump dragons in my lap," Maguire muttered, and with that, she dismissed them, though not before popping another aspirin.

Maguire's shoot-to-kill order sat uneasily on Twyla's conscience. But then, she was the sort of person who was racked with guilt every time she heard the mousetrap under her kitchen sink snap. Reading her thoughts, Frank put his hand on her back as they walked toward the weapons lockers, and murmured, "If it comes to that, I'll do it."

"It isn't the same thing as taking out a drudge. The drudges were already dead. This..." Her voice trailed off.

"I gotta admit, I'm not feeling great about shooting down the scientific discovery of the century," said their new partner.

"We can cross that bridge if we come to it, Duckers," said Frank. "Try not to worry about it too much."

Twyla brought them to a halt. "If we're going to be working together, it seems to me we should be using first names. From now on, I'm Twyla, and this is Frank."

"Okay, but fair warning: my first name is ridiculous."

"Worse than Duckers?" Frank wondered aloud. Twyla swatted his arm.

"It's Penrose," he told them with chagrin. "But my friends call me Pen."

"I'm glad you're working with us, Pen," said Twyla.

"Back atcha."

At the weapons lockers, Frank scribbled their request on the requisition form and pushed it across the counter to Fern. The weapons registrar raised her pencil-thin eyebrows, but she returned a moment later with three full-sized crossbows.

"Fuck yeah," breathed Pen as he picked one up.

"Might want to oil the tiller and wax the strings," suggested Fern. "I don't think anyone has taken these things into the field in twenty years." She picked up one of the crossbows and blew on it, sending a dramatic cloud of dust whirling through the air. Pen caught it in the face and sneezed.

"Thanks, Fern." Frank picked up the crossbows and pushed one at Twyla. She took it, albeit reluctantly.

"Do you think this is necessary?"

"Maguire obviously thought it couldn't hurt, and I'd rather be embarrassed than dead."

"I am so here for this," said Pen.

Twyla gaped at him. "What were you just saying about the discovery of the century?"

"That still stands, but tell me it's not going to be fun as shit giving these things a whirl."

"Happy dragon hunting," Fern joked as they made to leave with their oversized weaponry. Twyla slapped on a fake smile and emitted an even faker laugh, not that Fern had the slightest suspicion that her words were absolutely on target.

Chapter Four

F uck yeah!" crowed Duckers as his bolt slammed into the tin can for the third time in a row.

Not even twenty-four hours had passed since they'd gotten the enormous weapons, but Duckers was already head over heels in love.

Frank gawked at the crook of a heartnut tree outside the barracks where seconds ago the can had perched. "Holy Three Mothers."

Duckers smoothed his thin mustache. "I'm a good shot."

"I'll say. Twy. You're up."

Twyla was enjoying crossbow practice far less than her compatriots were. She wasn't sure which was more unnerving: using the lever to heave the massive string into the nut or the terrifying power of pulling the trigger and unleashing the bolt. This was why she was relieved to hear Hermia's meek "Hello-o-o? Mail delivery?" from behind them.

"Ope, I guess we'd better pack this in," Twyla said, happy to hand her weapon to Frank.

It took a staggeringly long time for the diminutive hedgehog to cross the clearing in front of the barracks. Her oversized blue rubber boots didn't seem to help matters. She was puffing so hard by the time she reached the marshals that she had fogged up her glasses.

Twyla itched to pick her up and snuggle her. "Hello, Hermia. Good to see you," she said.

The nimkilim wheezed in reply, but it was a pleasant wheeze. "Report," she panted. "For you." She panted again. "From the." She panted. "Chief." She reached into her satchel and pulled out a letter. The envelope snagged on one of her quills, ripping open the flap as she handed it to Twyla. "Oh dear," she said sadly.

"It's all right."

Hermia nodded, but her eyes welled up all the same. She took a rumpled hankie from her pocket and blew her adorable upturned nose.

"Maybe tip her extra?" Twyla whispered to Frank.

"It's a ploy, I'm telling you," he whispered in reply, but he forked over two coppers anyway.

Hermia grasped the coins, one in each little hedgehog hand. "Thank you, Marshal Ellis. Oh!" Suddenly, the nimkilim began to look about frantically. "Oh no! Where did I put my mailbag?"

"You're wearing it," said Frank.

"Oh!" Hermia drooped in abject relief. "Thank goodness. Okay, bye then."

"Bye," said Twyla.

"Bye," Hermia said to Duckers.

"Bye," he replied.

"Bye," she told him, as if she hadn't already bid him adieu.

"Please don't say *bye* again," Frank begged his companions under his breath.

"Bye," Hermia said one last time before straightening her glasses and stumping away in her rubber boots.

"She's so pathetic," Duckers murmured as they watched her leave. "I love her."

"Not you, too," said Frank. He nodded toward the message in Twyla's hand. "What's it say?"

Twyla took the note out of the torn envelope and read it aloud:

Coroner's report states cause of death was traumatic brain injury, caused by a blow to the head when Herd fell. Lab results for substance found on Herd's body were inconclusive. Samples have been sent to the labs of the Federated Islands of Cadmus's Bureau of Investigation for further analysis. Since you three are the marshals of record on the coroner's report, at least one of you will need to take the body to the undertaker. I may be out of the office when you come through the station, so I want to make sure you're apprised of the situation. Reminder: this is classified information sent through secured nimkilim post. Destroy after reading. More from me soon.

—Maguire

"It doesn't help Herd, but at least his death was an accident," Twyla commented as Frank lit a match. She handed him the note so that he could burn it.

"Who wants to take in the body?" he asked.

"I'm in," said Duckers.

"Why don't we all go?" Twyla suggested. "It's not like we've seen criminal activity around here in weeks, and if a huge flying animal decides to stop by, I wouldn't mind not being here for that. Plus, we could grab lunch at the Salt and Key."

With everyone in agreement, they rode to the West Station, where Frank's autoduck was parked out front with a thin layer of Bushong dust coating it. But while many marshals used their own vehicles to transport a body, neither Twyla nor Frank relished sticking a corpse in the same hold where they put their groceries. Unfortunately, the only company autoduck available at the station was an old boneshaker with a single bench, so they wound up crammed together with Twyla at the wheel, Duckers on the hump seat in the middle, and Frank squeezed against the passenger-side door, all of them jouncing their way to Eternity. Twyla hoped poor Herd's remains survived the drive without further damage. By the time they arrived at the loading dock of Mercy's Undertakings, Twyla's teeth ached from all the rattling around.

Duckers rang the dock bell, and Mercy Birdsall herself, dressed in dungarees and a floral blouse knotted at her waist, hoisted up the gate and welcomed them with a wide smile.

"Pen!" she cried, pulling him in for a hug. "Hi, Twyla. Hi, Frank."

"These are my new partners," Duckers told her.

"That's wonderful! I hate to say it, but I didn't like seeing you with Marshal Herd."

"That makes two of us."

"Why did you split with him?"

"Um, well, he's in there." Duckers indicated the hold with a jerk of his thumb, and Twyla cringed in sympathy with Mercy's evident mortification.

"Oh," said the undertaker.

Twyla stepped in to change the subject to something far happier. "Getting excited about the wedding?"

Panic painted over Mercy's face. From the office down the hall, her sister, Lilian, shouted, "Do not say the *w*-word in Mercy's presence! She's stressed out about it enough as it is!"

Now it was Twyla's turn to say, "Oh."

It had been thirty-four years since she had gotten married, and her mom had been the one who had handled most of the planning. At the time, Twyla had bristled at her mother's meddling, especially since neither of her parents had been thrilled to marry off their nineteen-year-old daughter to her high school sweetheart. She felt a pang of remorse about that now. Poor Mercy—whose own mother had passed away many years ago—had to figure out the logistics of her wedding while running her own business.

"It's fine. I'm fine," said Mercy. She pushed her red cat-eye glasses up the bridge of her nose with an anxious giggle that bordered on hysteria. "You're in luck," she told Duckers. "Zeddie stopped by. He's in the kitchenette. Zeddie! Pen's here!"

A sound that could only be described as a squeal came from the direction of the aforementioned kitchenette, followed in short order by Mercy's brother. Zeddie Birdsall was a tall, golden-haired paragon of good fashion, but at the moment, he was little more than a blur as he raced to the loading dock to tackle Duckers in a hug.

"My dearest darling Ducky!" he cried jokingly before laying a loud smack on his boyfriend's cheek.

"You're ridiculous," Duckers informed him, although he was grinning like mad.

"You all catch up," said Twyla. "We'll take care of Herd."

"Are they friends or something?" Frank asked Twyla as they strapped Herd's sailcloth-wrapped body to a dolly and wheeled the remains toward the boatworks.

"They're dating."

"Really?"

Occasionally, Frank amazed Twyla with his utter cluelessness.

"Zeddie laid one on Duckers in front of your eyeballs. They've been together for ages. Where have you been?"

"Well now, how was I supposed to know?"

"By existing in the world?"

Frank grunted in annoyance.

By now, they had reached the boatworks, and Twyla helped Frank get the corpse onto the prep table. In the next day or two, Mercy would sing the incantations of the dead as she salted the body and rewrapped it in fresh sailcloth. She would build the boat that Herd had selected when he bought his funeral package at

Mercy's Undertakings, and she would place him inside and send him home to his loved ones.

They lingered at Herd's side, a pall falling over them. Frank doffed his hat and held it over his chest. "I hope there's someone to mourn him."

Twyla was suddenly worried that there might not be anyone to grieve for the man at all. He had been far from perfect in life, but it was unbearably sad to think of him being alone in death.

"Mercy will help his soul sail the Salt Sea to the House of the Unknown God," she said to comfort herself as much as Frank. He nodded, even though she knew he wasn't terribly religious. For her own part, Twyla was a praying woman who went to temple every Allgodsday (when she wasn't on tour), so she considered the dropping off of a body at an undertaker's a solemn, reverent part of her job, her way of helping souls move on to the next life beside the Unknown God in the Void Beyond the Sky.

Frank put his hat on. "We'd better be heading back."

They returned to the dock to bid their farewells to the Bird-salls. Zeddie took his boyfriend's arm, rolled up his sleeve, and kissed the stoppered bottle inked on his skin.

"Salt Sea, they're cute," rumbled Frank.

"He literally kissed Duckers's soul." Twyla clutched her heart. She had long since convinced herself that romance was something that occurred only in the pages of a book and in the imagination of the lonely. Yet deep down, she suspected that such affection might actually exist in reality for the lucky few.

Twyla was not one of the lucky few. She had come to terms with this years ago, but every now and again, she yearned for an arm to hold her in the night, a reminder that someone loved her and maybe even lived for her a little. If she lost her appendix, she wouldn't mind having someone kiss the tattoo that contained her immortal soul.

After a quick lunch, they bumped their way to the West Station in an autoduck with no shocks to speak of, and Twyla knew her aging body would feel the journey in spades tomorrow.

Frank drove this time, leaving Twyla free to notice that Duckers appeared less cheery than usual. "What's wrong?" she asked him.

He gave her a one-shoulder shrug, and she figured that leaving his boyfriend behind to hang out in Sector W-14 with boring middle-aged people must be disappointing. She patted his knee. "It's not easy having a love life with this job."

"Oh, yeah? Have you had a hard time dating?"

In fact, Twyla had not dated anyone in the past thirteen years. She'd had no love life at all since Doug died. Frank saved her from having to answer Duckers by grunting his own discontent with his love life.

"Stop grunting so much. You sound like a pig at a trough today."

He grunted again, this time with humorous theatricality.

Twyla gazed out the window, watching the arid Bushong landscape pass by. No one could see her grin as she sang, "*He leaves wet towels on the bathroom floor.*"

"Don't make me grunt again," threatened Frank.

"*And tracks in mud right through my door,*" she sang, louder, adding in extra twang for kicks.

"What is happening right now?" demanded Duckers.

Twyla reached across him to nudge Frank's shoulder until he relented and sang the next line.

"*But when I scold him—*"

Duckers put his hands over his ears. "Am I in Old Hell?"

"*I just want to hold him!*"

"Aaaaargh!" Duckers screamed as, together, Twyla and Frank sang, in full-throated glory, "*My man's a pig, but his heart is big.*"

"What in the House of the Unknown God was that shit?" asked Duckers in the aftermath of Twyla's and Frank's laughter and self-congratulatory clapping.

"The finest music in the history of the Federated Islands of Cadmus," answered Frank.

"No. Nuh-uh. New rule: that travesty to musickind can never happen again in my presence."

"All in favor of Duckers's new rule, say *aye*," said Twyla.

Duckers raised his hand and said, "Aye!" When he saw that he was the only aye, he raised both hands.

"All opposed, say *nay*," said Twyla, and Frank joined his strident "Nay!" to hers.

"You are overruled, Duckers," Frank declared smugly.

"Oh, wait. We're supposed to call him Pen now."

Frank shook his head. "Can't do it. He's clearly a Duckers."

Twyla realized that she had reverted to thinking of their new partner as Duckers roughly five seconds after he told them his name was Penrose. "Definitely a Duckers," Twyla had to agree.

Duckers snorted. "Told you."

By the time Twyla, Frank, and Duckers returned to Tanria, the sun was dipping below the horizon. As they approached Sector W-14, there was barely enough light to see a group of riders on the ridge to their northeast, silhouetted against the indigo sky as they dashed headlong in the direction of the Mist. The three marshals reined to a halt to assess the situation.

"Are they ours?" asked Duckers.

"Unknown," answered Frank.

Twyla squinted at the riders as the sounds of galloping began to drift toward her. "Think they need help?"

"I don't see a flare."

"Uh, guys?" Duckers aimed a shaking finger at a large creature that appeared to be following the riders.

At speed.

In the air.

Backlit by the dim twilight, the scene became a shadow puppet show playing out before their eyes. Twyla felt like a spectator, safe in her saddle, as a fantastical story unfolded in front of her.

"Tell me one of you has a reasonable explanation as to what that is," pleaded Frank. "And don't say *dragon*."

"I think it might be a dragon," Twyla heard herself answer.

"*Other* than a dragon."

The creature was a distant shadow in the sky, but that shadow had bat-like wings and a long serpentine body and the shimmer of scales that reflected what little light remained. And it was big. Salt Sea, was it big. Twyla was so stunned by the sight that she could swear her internal organs were disintegrating.

"Holy shit! That's a gods-fucking dragon!" cried Duckers, who was about to launch out of his saddle like a bottle rocket.

Frank barked an exultant laugh as a similar elation filled Twyla's chest, the kind of sensation a person experiences at the top of a Ferris wheel—a heady combination of terror and excitement.

"We should probably save those people," Twyla suggested. She turned to Frank, who shot her a wolfish grin, and she knew she wore the same expression. How long had it been since they'd seen this kind of action on the job? Months. Ages. Gods, it felt good.

Still grinning, Twyla took off, urging her mount to a gallop. Frank and Duckers each gave a whoop and bolted after her. She could barely make out the sound of her partners' equimares moving at full speed behind her over the sound of her own mare's webbed feet, slapping and sucking against the earth with each stride.

Why are you riding toward *a possible dragon?* Twyla's inner voice of reason wondered, but instincts honed through eight years' service with the Tanrian Marshals pressed her to help those riders any way she could. If she had to make a guess, she'd bet they were smugglers hoping to escape through a pirated portal in the Mist. An illegal portal was probably how they'd gotten into Tanria in the first place.

Luck was on the marshals' side when they hit an ambrosial runnel snaking its way south between a couple of foothills. The equimares' webbed feet were made for this, and the water horses surged north against the light current. Duckers let loose an exhilarated cheer at the increased speed as Frank, riding Saltlicker, took the lead.

This is why he loves that godsawful stallion so much, Twyla thought as she watched the equimaris and rider fly ahead of her through the ambrosia, outpacing her and Duckers by a good ten lengths. He was the first to catch up to the riders, about a mile from the Mist.

"Pull up!" he ordered them as he rode alongside them.

"Fuck you!" a man shouted back, his eyes wide with panic.

"You're going to break your necks!" Twyla hollered over the cacophony of equimaris feet as she and Duckers closed in on the galloping scrum. They were quickly running out of room to pull up before hitting the Mist. From outside, the Mist was a thick, churning cloud covering Tanria in an oblong dome. But from the inside, it was as clear as a windowpane, so that the Old Gods could look out at the world and see either what they had done to it or what they were missing. But invisible though it might be, it was as solid as granite, and smashing into it while riding full speed on an equimaris was sure to lead to injury or worse.

"There!" hollered Duckers, and now Twyla could see the illegal portal that had cut a temporary hole in the Mist to the world outside. Like most pirated portals, it was only large enough for one person to crawl through at a time, which meant the alleged smugglers would have to dismount to escape. If they made it that far to begin with.

They didn't make it that far.

The dragon was on them. It butted the first rider off his mount with what appeared to be antlers, scattering the rest of the equimares in all directions. The water horses gurgled with panic. Twyla's mount shied and reared, and it was all she could do to stay on. As soon as the equimaris's front feet hit the ground, she made the snap decision to slide out of the saddle rather than risk being thrown, a decision that proved wise when her mount fled pell-mell from the scene the second she was off. She could find Duckers nowhere in the chaos but caught sight of Frank astride Saltlicker, reining to a stop next to the portal and shouting, "Out! Out!"

It felt counterintuitive to Twyla to let a pack of smugglers escape the same way they'd illegally entered Tanria, but when it came to a choice between saving them or arresting them, the marshals needed to prioritize life. She ran to the rider who had been butted off his mount and helped him to his feet.

"Go, go, go!" she shouted as the goons converged on the exit. They didn't need to be told twice.

The dragon came tearing in again. Twyla thought it was going to crash into the Mist, the way songbirds sometimes tragically hurtled themselves against the glass of her picture window at home, but it seemed to sense the physical presence of the barrier and wheeled in a wide arc above them before it circled back again, a huge shadowy silhouette closing in on them against the purpling sky of dusk. It landed ten feet away from them, threw back its head, and . . .

Chirped.

It was not at all the sound Twyla would have expected to come out of something that big and that terrifying, and it was oddly more disturbing than a roar or growl.

Meep-meep-meep-meep-meep, chirrup! it cheeped as another criminal ran for the portal, clutching a strange round object to his chest.

Frank dismounted and ordered "Leave it!"

Twyla thought the man intended to barrel his way past Frank. Instead, he thrust his burden into Frank's arms, crying "We didn't know what they were!" before he hurled himself through the portal to safety.

Twyla saw two more of the strange objects on the ground where the goons must have left them, like a pair of marbled blue-green bowling balls. Except they weren't perfectly spherical. They were oblong. Egg shaped.

Eggs.

Her pulse thundered in her ears as she watched Frank help a crook through the portal with one hand while holding on to the egg with the other. The dragon cocked its wings and ran at him on its two enormous feet, calling a battle cry of *Meep-meep-meep-meep-meep!*

"Frank! Let it go!" yelled Twyla, but he either didn't hear her or wasn't listening.

Duckers ran up beside her. "Oh, shit!" he cried, echoing her own frantic thoughts. He tore the full-sized crossbow from his back and fumbled the bolt into the tiller.

The dragon pulled up, and its throat went sickeningly thick.

"Oh, shit! Oh, shit!" Duckers cursed as he tried and failed to lever the string into the nut.

"Drop it, Frank!" bellowed Twyla.

The last goon turned toward their shouting in time to see the dragon's threatening posture. With a squawk of terror, he dove for the portal and shut it down less than a second before the dragon hurled a jet of slimy glitter from its throat. The sparkly jettison smashed against Frank, a direct hit, knocking him spread-eagle against the Mist. The egg dropped to the ground with a sickening *crack*.

The dragon screeched in outrage and heartbreak at the damaged egg, matching the desperate scream that tore through Twyla's throat. Everything around her faded into oblivion, even the rampaging dragon. A whole future passed before Twyla's eyes, a life she'd have to get through without Frank Ellis by her side. No more equimaris ranch off the coast. No more bed-and-breakfast to run together. No more laughs or inside jokes. No more dinners made together or beers shared on their front steps. No more comfort in knowing him and being known. It was like standing on a beach, looking out on the vast gray ocean, only it was grief and loneliness and despair that made her feel small and useless rather than the sea.

"Shit! Shit! Shit!" Duckers chanted, even as the string finally clicked into place behind the nut.

Frank slid limply down the Mist until he landed on his knees.

And to Twyla's amazement, he held up one hand and called, "I'm good," even as he rubbed his sternum with the other hand.

Alive.

He was alive.

Duckers hoisted the crossbow up and took aim. Twyla's instincts moved her body before her brain had a chance to catch up. She pulled on Duckers's arm as he fired, sending the bolt plunging into the earth three feet from the dragon's feet.

"The fuck?"

"She's a mom. She's doing what moms do," Twyla said calmly, hoping her tone would somehow convey her meaning to the puffing beast before them. It was full dark now, and the creature was nothing more than a black smudge against the darkened sky. It shuffled past them, bent its head, and snuffled at one of the eggs left behind by the goons. A second later, it leaped into the air and spread its wings, covering the stars for a good ten feet to either side.

"Fuuuuuuuuck," said Duckers, fumbling for another bolt, but Twyla put a hand over his to stop him. The dragon reached down to pick up the egg with one foot, then swooped sideways to pick up a second. They both stared after it, Twyla nearly asphyxiating with her held breath until the creature faded out of view.

And then she realized that Frank had come to stand beside her on his own two feet to watch the dragon fly away with them.

"Frank?" she asked, so many questions wrapped into one syllable.

"I'm fine."

Twyla burst into tears. These were not softly falling, quiet tears. These were booming tears. Stentorian tears. The kind of tears that came with wheezing gasps for air. Her entire body sobbed. She'd thought this kind of weeping came only with grief. She had no idea a person could wail with relief.

"Aw, darlin'." Frank reached for her but seemed to think better of it, given his current state. "Duckers, care to do the honors?"

"Hugs, Banneker!" Duckers not only wrapped her in his arms but picked her an inch off the ground and jostled her. If there was one thing that could get her to stop crying, it was being picked up and rattled by an overly exuberant guy in his early twenties.

"Thanks, Duckers," she half cried and half laughed. "You can put me down now."

He dropped her and whooped. "Woo! Woooooo! Did you see that? Dragons! In Tanria! Who was right? I was right!"

"You were right," Frank agreed, bemused.

"In your face, Ellis! Haaaaaaa!"

"You're sure you're not injured?" Twyla asked Frank as Duckers danced to a song of his own devising, an entire ditty about dragons and being right and how everyone else could suck it.

"Not a scratch on me," he assured her.

He stood so close to her now that the heat of his living body drifted her way, making her heart turn over with gratitude.

"Hello-o-o? Mail delivery?" A familiar voice cut through the darkness—as much as a breathy, pathetic hedgehog voice could be said to cut through anything.

"Salt Sea, are you kidding me?" Frank groaned, and that was how Twyla knew he really was okay.

"Goodness me, it's dark." They could see Hermia's silhouette as she rummaged inside her bag. Seconds later, she pulled an already lit lantern out of its depths and held it up. "There, that's better. Oh!" Her black eyes went large when she caught sight of Frank. He looked bizarre—almost godlike—in his glittery state. "Did I come at a bad time?"

"No, perfect timing," Frank said with an irony that the nim-kilim wouldn't be able to catch with a ten-foot net.

"Let's get a good look at Captain Sparkles over here," declared Duckers. He swiped the lantern from the hedgehog—who yelped, "Oh dear!"—and held it up. Frank shimmered into focus. His back was relatively unscathed, but golden glitter covered every inch of his front hemisphere. Even his lips and hair were coated in glitter, and his eyes looked strange, peering out of all that brilliance.

"Dang," breathed Duckers.

"I could go for a bath," Frank admitted.

"Does it hurt?"

"No, just feels weird."

Duckers burst out laughing and gestured to Frank in all his sparkling glory. "I've been to clubs where you come home looking like this. Glitter cannons everywhere. You look like you've been having yourself a real good time tonight."

Frank's glitter-coated lips thinned. "I suspect the clubs are more fun."

"No way. That was the most fun I've had in a long time."

"Happy to amuse you," said Frank, but by now, he was laughing along with Duckers.

"Excuse me?" squeaked Hermia. She flapped a letter in the air. "Mail delivery?"

"Right." Twyla fished a coin out of her pocket and tipped the nimkilim. "Thanks, Hermia."

"Um, may I have my lantern, please?"

Duckers handed it to her, but the hedgehog didn't seem to be in a rush to leave. She set the lantern on the ground, rummaged once more inside her bag, and retrieved a bottle of grape soda.

"Do any of you have a bottle opener?"

"Not handy," said Twyla.

"Oh. Okay." The nimkilim set the bottle of grape soda next to the lantern and went about digging in her satchel yet again.

"Salt Sea," Frank muttered before stalking over to Saltlicker— the one and only equimaris that hadn't completely abandoned them—to light his saddle lantern and retrieve his own bottle opener. "Here," he said, thrusting the tool at the nimkilim.

"Thank you." Hermia blinked up at him in gratitude. She tried to open the bottle on her own, but her hands were too small to hold the bottle and open it at the same time.

"Mother of Sorrows," Frank breathed, and Twyla was fairly sure he wasn't praying. He snatched the bottle opener from Hermia, opened the bottle for her, and placed it into her hands. "Thank you. Goodbye."

"Okay, bye."

"Bye from all of us. Group goodbye." Frank was understandably at the end of his rope, so Twyla nudged Duckers, and they both bid Hermia their farewells before the nimkilim could prolong her exit.

"Bye," said the hedgehog one last time before disappearing into the night.

"We should have dashed off a quick note to the chief to send with her," Twyla said, staring in the direction the nimkilim had gone. And then she remembered that she was holding a note, probably from Maguire. She tore open the envelope and read aloud:

Will be coming by the barracks sometime tomorrow morning. Bringing an expert with me to assist with investigation.

—A.M.

Twyla folded the note and put it inside Frank's saddle lantern to burn. "I guess we don't need to send a report after all."

"Hey, look," said Duckers, squinting toward the Mist, where a splotch of glittery gold slime oozed downward toward an egg, the one that Frank had dropped when the dragon spat on him. Twyla grabbed the saddle lantern from its pole, and the three marshals cautiously surrounded the mottled blue-green shell. Frank bent over to get a better look as Twyla held the lantern over it.

"Be careful," she warned him.

"It's cracked," he observed.

Without warning, something launched itself out of the egg and latched on to Frank's torso, sending him toppling to the ground. He landed on his back with a pained "Oof!"

"Fuck me, Grandfather Bones!" exclaimed Duckers.

Twyla rushed over and fell to her knees beside him. "Frank! Are you hurt? Talk to me!"

"Not hurt," he grunted. "What... what is it?"

He gazed at Twyla, his eyes dark and pleading, as if he couldn't bring himself to look at the thing clinging to his front. The creature was a soft pastel pink in color and about eighteen inches in length from the tip of its tail to the top of its head. It had its limbs tucked against Frank's stomach and its face buried in his chest. Its wings wrapped around his trunk, the tips out of sight behind his back.

"Gonna go out on a limb and guess it's a baby dragon," said Duckers.

"Not helpful!" Twyla hissed at him.

"Them's the facts!"

"Can you get it off me?" asked Frank.

"We can try." Twyla knelt on one side of Frank, and Duckers crouched on the other. A discussion ensued about where exactly to grasp the baby and how much force to exert.

"Let's give it a go, folks," said Frank with a panicky edge to his voice.

Twyla took hold of the creature with one hand at its shoulder and the other under the lower flap of its wing. The hide felt cool and scaly to the touch, not entirely unpleasant. She looked at Duckers. "Count of three?"

He nodded.

"One...two...three."

They pulled gently but firmly, trying to dislodge the baby. Twyla felt it go tense beneath her grasp.

"Don't get it off! Don't get it off!" cried Frank.

Twyla and Duckers released the creature, and it appeared to relax its grip.

"Can you sit up?" Twyla asked Frank.

"I think so."

She and Duckers helped him get into a sitting position. The baby dragon gave a huff of annoyance, then nuzzled its face more firmly into Frank's sternum with a satisfied *chirp*.

Duckers shook his head. "Dang, Frank, this has got to be the worst day of your life."

"I've had worse." Frank finally let himself look at the pink baby latched on to the front of him. "But not by much."

Saltlicker cantered into their midst, tossing his huge head and snuffing the air. He turned a black eye on the cotton-candy-colored baby clinging to Frank and gave it a derisive snort. The baby puled softly into Frank's chest. The three marshals stared at it for several long seconds, but it didn't move or make another sound.

"Guess that's our cue to get out of here." Frank got to his feet, refusing a hand up from Twyla or Duckers. "Better not touch me, if you can help it. We don't know if this glitter stuff has any harmful effects."

Maybe he was right, but now more than ever, Twyla wanted to put a hand on him, to feel the reassuring solidity of him beneath her touch and to reassure him in turn.

Duckers took the lone equimaris by his bridle and hooked on the saddle lantern. "Saltlicker's the only mount we have left. Why don't you ride him, Frank. Twyla and I can walk."

Twyla could see that Frank was about to default to the gentlemanly manners his mother had instilled in him, but she cut him off. "Get in the saddle, for gods' sakes."

He acquiesced, but he insisted on mounting up without assistance, whether there was a baby dragon stuck to his torso or not. When he set Saltlicker moving east, Twyla called him to a halt.

"Where are you going? The portal's south."

"I think we should go back to the barracks."

Twyla and Duckers trotted to catch up to him.

"We need to get you to the infirmary," Twyla insisted.

He pointed at the dragon. "Pretty sure this is classified, which means the station is out. Going to W-14 is our best option." He clicked his tongue and got Saltlicker moving again.

Twyla looked to Duckers, who shrugged. "He seems fine. I

mean, as fine as a person can be with a glitter-barfing baby clinging to him."

"We need to get him some help."

"Maguire's coming in the morning. And, honestly, I think the sparkly guy with the baby dragon should get to call the shots on this one."

When they straggled into the barracks in W-14, Duckers took charge of Saltlicker, and Frank flopped face up on his cot, glitter and dragon and all. "Let me be unconscious for a while," he begged Twyla before she could say a word, and he closed his eyes.

She sat on the thin mattress by his side and took his hand in hers so that she could feel his warmth—his life—even through a layer of shiny dragon spit.

"You shouldn't touch me," he murmured, but it was halfhearted at best.

"Shut up," Twyla told him. An intense emotion that she could not name surged inside her as she watched his chest rise and fall, and she found it difficult to catch her own breath. Tears pooled in her eyes, but she brushed them away with her free hand before they could fall. Frank didn't need her going to pieces. He needed her solid. But that emotion—that confusing intensity— continued to roil in her stomach.

For a time, he held tight to her grasp, brushing the back of her hand as her heart kept time with the motion of his thumb over her knuckles. But then his fingers went slack and his thumb stilled, and she knew he'd conked out.

"This is so messed up," Duckers said when he returned from the stable. He busied himself at the stove, lighting a burner and setting down the kettle.

"Please tell me you're making some more of that medicine."

"Extra honey and extra whiskey."

"The Three Mothers bless you."

They spoke in low voices, like parents tiptoeing around a sleeping child.

"What are we going to do?" asked Duckers as he placed two mugs on the table.

Twyla came to join him, inhaling the medicinal scent while she waited for hers to cool. "I think we can assume that thing will eventually peel off him. Dragons don't spend their lives attached to other dragons."

"As evidenced by the big-ass dragon that just about made us shit ourselves."

"Let's hope this expert Maguire is bringing with her can help him."

"I'll drink to that."

They clinked their mugs together.

Chapter Five

The following morning, Twyla sat at the table with Frank to help him mop the golden shimmer off his face and hair and hands. Sparkles had buried themselves in the lines and grooves of his face, making him appear older than he was, and his eyes were extra hound-doggish.

"Thanks, darlin'," he said, managing a rueful grin that made Twyla's heart lurch. They'd seen each other raw and bruised countless times on the job, but the unguarded affection with which Frank regarded her now inspired that bewildering agitation within her to spike and flare. Twyla sent up another prayer of thanks to the Bride of Fortune that he was alive and seemingly well, and she snuffed out the disconcerting ripple in her rib cage with a joke.

"Look on the bright side. This is definitely going to get us out of the Marshals in the Community thing at Wisdom's Acres later this month."

"It's the little things."

When the distant gurgle of an equimaris heralded Maguire's arrival, Twyla and Duckers left Frank at the table to go outside and greet their boss.

As expected, Maguire had company, the expert she had notified them she was bringing. As the riders came into view, Twyla could see that the man wore a slouch hat, a khaki jacket cinched at the waist, a navy-blue scarf tied neatly at his throat, knee-high camping socks, and—the coup de grâce of the entire ensemble—a pair of khaki shorts that showed off several inches of bare masculine thighs.

Twyla marveled at the man's remarkable appearance. "Is that our expert?"

"And, more importantly, is he on safari?" asked Duckers.

"Don't you dare make me laugh."

"Those are the shortest shorts I have ever seen. I didn't know they made shorts that short."

"They're not *that* short."

"Short-shorts for thick thighs!" Duckers's voiced cracked with hilarity. "Now, there's a man who should be covered in glitter."

"Gods, I think he's wearing an ascot."

"You said *ass*!"

Twyla fought back a laugh. "Whoever he is, at least he can ride."

This would prove helpful in Tanria, where New Gods technology didn't work. With the growing predominance of autoducks on land and sea, at least half of all islanders under the age of fifty had never ridden a water horse in their lives.

Maguire and the human spectacle she brought with her dismounted and walked the last few paces to meet the marshals in front of the barracks.

"Banneker, Duckers, good morning. Let me introduce you to Dr. Quill Vanderlinden. He's a dracologist with the University of Quindaro. He should be able to shed some light on our situation."

Quindaro was the premier university of the Federated Islands of Cadmus, and mere mention of the institution made Twyla, who had only a high school diploma to her name, quail on the inside. The competition to get into Quindaro was fierce. She couldn't imagine how smart you'd have to be to work there.

Maguire continued the introductions. "Dr. Vanderlinden, these are Marshals Twyla Banneker and Penrose Duckers."

"Excellent." Dr. Vanderlinden shook their hands in turn,

reiterating each of their names in the smooth syllables of the very wealthy and highly educated. "Marshal Duckers. Marshal Banneker."

Even his handshake is posh, Twyla thought, noting the man's expensive wristwatch (which surely didn't work inside the Mist) as the strength and heft of his hand hugged hers. He appeared to be in his fifties, with the weathered face of a man who had spent time out of doors. His neatly trimmed beard was more gray than not, but a lock of hair curling at the nape of his neck hinted at a head of light brown hair under his slouch hat. He was not an obviously good-looking man, but self-assurance wafted from him like a spicy cologne, and the heat of his confident grasp crawled up Twyla's arm, all the way to her neck and then her face. She could feel herself go unflatteringly pink and blotchy and was, therefore, relieved when he relinquished her hand.

"This is all very exciting, but I don't want to get your hopes up—or mine—so I do feel that I ought to be honest with you up front," he told them in that resonant, plummy voice. "There are no known depositories of dragon fossils or prints on the island of Bushong that we know of. The climate simply wasn't amenable to dragons at the time, and so we tend to find their fossils in the northernmost islands and in parts of the continents. But then, one dares to hope that, perhaps, the Old Gods brought a handful of their battle dragons with them to their prison here on earth. I'm happy to take a look at this print you have found. No need to feel sheepish."

"Dang," Duckers whispered to Twyla, who was also taken aback by the man's lack of understanding of the situation.

"I'm sorry, Dr. Vanderlinden. You think we found a *fossilized* print?"

"I assume so, yes. Unless you've found a live dragon thousands of years after their extinction." He chortled the chortle of a man who assumed everyone was in on the joke. Twyla turned a questioning glance toward Chief Maguire.

"I may have been skimpy on the details for security purposes. Where's Ellis?"

"This should be fun," muttered Duckers.

"Is something the matter?"

Twyla valiantly kept a grimace from taking over her face. "You'd better come inside. There have been a few developments in the case since the last time we saw you. Dr. Vanderlinden, if you could wait for us here?"

"Er—"

"Great. Thank you." Twyla gave the professor a fake smile and a truly cringeworthy thumbs-up before she ushered Maguire into the barracks with Duckers bringing up the rear.

"Close the door!" Twyla hissed at him, and he fumbled to obey, slamming the splintery wood shut in Dr. Vanderlinden's face as the man sputtered, "I say, what—"

Frank stood at the stove, pouring himself a cup of coffee. He turned at the sound of their entrance, giving Alma Maguire a good look at the semi-glitter-coated veteran with a pink winged lizard clinging to his front. He raised his mug in greeting. "Hey, Chief."

Maguire stared at him, her face devoid of expression. Twyla wasn't sure she was breathing. After the silence stretched on for several uncomfortable seconds, Frank said, "Long story. Got a minute?"

"Mother of Sorrows, have mercy." Maguire went to the table, pulled out a chair, and collapsed onto the seat. She let her forehead smack the tabletop, and her hands came up to cup the back of her head as if she were taking shelter from a tornado.

"Uh, Chief? You good?" asked Duckers.

"Do I look good?"

"That sounds like a trick question," Duckers told Twyla, who set a freshly poured cup of coffee at her boss's elbow.

"Cream or sugar?" she offered.

"Whiskey."

Duckers coughed in alarm. "No, ma'am, no alcohol on these premises."

Maguire sat up in her chair and leveled him with a piercing glare. "You apprenticed under Hart Ralston, so don't tell me you don't have whiskey."

Duckers's shoulders drooped. "Coming right up."

"Any word from the FICBI labs on what this glittery stuff is?" Frank asked as Duckers dumped a generous glug of whiskey into his boss's mug.

"No, but it looks like it's not lethal, thank the Bride of Fortune."

There was a light rap at the door. "Hallo?"

"May as well let him come in," Alma said resignedly.

Upon hearing this, Duckers poured a dollop into his own mug and made an offering gesture to Frank.

"No, thanks."

"You haven't seen the man's *ass*-cot yet."

Frank tilted his head in confusion as Twyla opened the door and gestured for the dracologist in safari attire to come inside.

"I'm sorry to have kept you waiting. Come on in."

"Thank you." Dr. Vanderlinden doffed his slouch hat as he stepped into the barracks, revealing an expensive haircut, barely going gray at the temples. Frank, Duckers, and even Maguire raised their mugs in a gloomy greeting.

Twyla stepped in to make the introductions since Maguire didn't seem inclined. "Dr. Vanderlinden, this is my partner, Marshal Frank Ellis. Frank, this is Dr. Quill Vanderlinden. He's a dracologist from the University of Quindaro."

The professor squinted at the pink baby clinging to Frank's midsection, and then he froze, save for the rapid blinking of his eyes.

Frank extended his hand, revealing patches of gold sparkles that Twyla had yet to scrub off. "Nice to meet you."

Dr. Vanderlinden continued to gawp at the little dragon as he absently shook Frank's hand.

"Can I offer you some coffee?" asked Twyla.

The professor could not tear his eyes from the creature that continued to cling to Frank for dear life. "May I ask...what is that?"

"Baby dragon," said Duckers. "Latched on to Frank last night."

"Ah."

A pregnant pause filled the room.

"Yes. Yes, of course. I see," said Dr. Vanderlinden.

And then he passed out.

Twyla continued to help Frank get himself cleaned up while Maguire and Duckers tended to Dr. Vanderlinden. The professor was sitting up on one of the cots, holding an ice pack to the back of his head.

"I feel like I should avert my eyes from all that leg," Frank observed, pitching his voice extra low to make sure he wasn't overheard.

"Don't you start. Duckers has already had a field day. I mean, Pen. You're right. I can't not call him Duckers."

"First Pen, now Quill. We're surrounded by writing implements."

"I'm going to start calling you Pencil."

"Pencil? Are you casting aspersions on my manhood?"

"Hey now, if I can't make pie jokes, you don't get to make dick jokes."

"Fair enough, Chalk."

"I think I'm more of a Crayon."

She was glad to banter with Frank again. It lent an air of normalcy to the interaction, even if nothing about the current situation could be considered normal. Their jocular conversation came to an abrupt end, however, when the baby dragon suddenly popped up its head from Frank's sternum.

"Ope!" cried Twyla, startling, the cloth in her hand dripping glitter down her wrist and onto the floor.

Meep, said the baby, a softer, higher-pitched version of the dragon call they had heard the night before. It stared at Frank with huge tear-shaped green eyes. Although it was covered in abalone-pink scales, its face was more mammalian than reptilian, heart-shaped like that of a fox, with drooping scalloped ears, and two nubs on its forehead that hinted at horns to come. Duckers and Maguire left the dracologist to his own devices to come have a look.

"Is it me, or is that thing cute?" asked Duckers.

"I hate to say it, Ellis, but it is kind of cute," said Maguire, crouching with her hands on her knees to get a better look.

Frank reached out his hand, slowly, cautiously.

"Careful," Twyla murmured as his hand made contact. He stroked the baby's pink head once, twice, and the dragon closed its eyes and made a vibrating *chirp* reminiscent of a cat's purr.

"It's fucking adorable," cooed Duckers.

"It really is," agreed Maguire with an incredulous laugh.

Twyla pressed her hand to her heart. "Oh, Frank."

"By gods."

This last utterance came from Dr. Quill Vanderlinden of the University of Quindaro. The dracologist had recovered enough to come kneel beside Frank and examine the reptilian form curled around him.

"I assume you were present when it hatched?" he asked, his voice soft, as if he were speaking beside someone's sickbed.

"Yes."

"When was that?"

"Last night, shortly after sunset."

"And it latched on to you immediately?"

"Correct."

The baby looked at Vanderlinden and said, *Meep-meep-meep-meeeeeeep*, a call that was reminiscent of the sound its parent had made seconds before shooting a jettison of glitter out of its mouth. Twyla nearly took the professor by the shoulder to pull him away, but he was more than capable of flinching on his own. He scrambled to his feet and took several steps away from Frank and the dragon, frowning as he folded his arms and stroked his beard.

"Is something the matter?" asked Frank.

"I suspect that the hatchling has imprinted on you."

"Meaning?"

"It views you as its mother, as the adult who must teach it how to be a dragon."

Frank went green—at least, the parts of him that had been cleared of sparkles. "But I don't know how to be a dragon."

"The good news is that I do."

The dragon sneezed, spraying a fresh layer of glitter on Frank's neck.

"In theory," Vanderlinden added.

Frank smoothed his hand over the baby's head again, and it made the far less threatening chirping noises. "It hasn't eaten anything yet. Don't I need to feed it?"

"Absolutely. The sooner the better."

"What do dragons eat?"

"Well..." The professor didn't seem to know what to do with his hands. "People."

Maguire, who had been playing peekaboo with the baby, snapped to attention. "Salt Sea and all the gods of death, I need to evacuate Tanria."

"Well now, hold on," said Frank.

"I can't have dragons hunting people inside the Mist, Ellis. We're fish in a barrel in here."

"I understand, but Herd wasn't killed by a dragon, was he?"

"Technically, no."

"And the dragon we saw last night didn't kill anyone. Not us. Not even those people who took its eggs."

"What about this stuff all over you?"

"I'm fine."

"So far. We don't even know what it is."

Twyla asked Maguire, "Has anyone been reported missing in Tanria over the past, say, two weeks? Have any bodies turned up that have been . . . you know?"

"What? Like, chewed up?" offered Duckers.

"Thanks for the visual," said Twyla as the dracologist shuddered in her peripheral vision.

Maguire rubbed her forehead. "Not that I know of. I'd have to check with the Joint Chiefs to be sure."

"Let's play out what happens if you instigate the evacuation protocol," Frank suggested. "People are going to want to know why Tanria was evacuated. What happens when they find out there are dragons here?"

Twyla could already picture it. Big-game hunters would come pouring in, especially now that the drudges were out of the way. A hundred different dracologists and zoologists and the gods knew who else would go before the Federal Assembly, demanding their claim. Every crime ring in the Federated Islands would punch a hole in the Mist with their dicey, pirated portals to get their hands on a dragon. It would be chaos.

"We've got to do something," said Maguire. "We can't pretend these things don't pose a danger to anyone and everyone in Tanria."

"I'm only saying, whatever we do, let's do it slowly and thoughtfully and carefully."

"You're already completely in love with that thing, aren't you?"

"And you're not?"

Maguire ducked her head and sipped her coffee.

Dr. Vanderlinden cleared his throat from where he stood on the outskirts of the conversation. "I think it's safe to feed it a high-protein diet: mice, eggs, insects."

Maguire nodded. "I can take care of that. I'll have to bring it in myself since living things can't be delivered by nimkilim, and I don't want this information spreading any farther than it has already."

"If we could track down the adult dragon and observe it, we'd have a great deal more information to go on."

"I brought you in because you're supposed to be an expert on dragons. You *are* the information."

"Yes, well, the thing of it is, this little one does not fit neatly into any category of dragon species I can think of. We've found many fossils of young and juvenile dragons since the early days of dracology, including hatchlings, and we've reconstructed how they might have appeared in life. This..." He stroked his beard again. "I am afraid I don't know exactly what kind of dragon this may be. I certainly never imagined any of them would be pink. Or quite so comely in appearance."

Duckers nudged Twyla and whispered, " 'Comely'? Who talks like that?"

She nudged him in return to hush him.

"Are you saying this might not be a dragon?" asked Maguire.

"No, I do think we can all agree this is a dragon. A real one. A living, breathing dragon. Right here. Before our eyes."

Dr. Vanderlinden swooned and passed out yet again.

Maguire returned to the station to go about scrounging up a high-protein diet. Fortunately, the equimares that had spooked during the dragon encounter had eventually made their way back to the barracks' stable by the following morning, so Twyla, Duckers, and

Dr. Quill Vanderlinden were able to saddle up and set out to find a dragon, leaving Frank behind to babysit his reptilian infant.

"I'm not incapacitated here. I can walk," Frank argued as everyone left him.

"And you can also safeguard the greatest scientific discovery of the century," the dracologist pointed out cheerily, an argument no one could refute, least of all Frank.

Frank clamped his lips and sulked. Literally sulked. Twyla had never seen him sulk before, but as he sat in his chair at the table with a scowl on his face and a shell-pink baby curled around him, she felt a twinge of sympathy. How many times had she put her life on hold to take care of someone else?

"Sorry, Frankie. Hopefully we'll find something that makes all this easier."

He sighed in resignation as they departed, closing the barracks door behind them.

It didn't take long to reach the site of Herd's demise, even at the equimares' most placid pace.

"This is where the egg hatched?" Vanderlinden asked as he dismounted.

Twyla slid out of her saddle beside him. "No, this is where we found Marshal Herd's body. The egg hatched near the Mist, but that was after a chase of several miles across two sectors. It may be Herd ran a long distance before a dragon caught up to him, but since he seems to have been on foot, he can't have gotten far. I think this is the best spot to start looking for... What exactly are we looking for, Dr. Vanderlinden?"

"Dragons, of course, although I must admit that I am not eager to come face-to-face with a full-grown adult. The next best option would be scat."

"You mean, like, poop?" asked Duckers with distaste.

"For lack of a better word." The dracologist turned in a circle, taking in the lay of the land, a flat rocky plain with rosy grass and rosier scrub, nestled within the imposing magenta peaks of the Dragon's Teeth range. "To be perfectly honest, this is the last place I'd look for a dragon. They favored forested areas, apart from but adjacent to human populations for feeding purposes."

"That's not terrifying or anything," said Duckers, taking the crossbow from his back to have at the ready.

"Yes, do keep that handy, will you?"

"Don't have to tell me twice."

"Excellent. Let's have a look around."

They spent the next hour walking in a slow spiral outward from the spot where Herd's body had been discovered. Soon, they came across a small pile of pink pellets, and the professor gave Twyla a questioning look.

"Rabbit droppings," she explained. "It's pink instead of green since that's the color of the grass they eat here in Tanria."

"The Old Gods seemed to have had a penchant for the color pink. Rather surprising."

"Right?" said Duckers, his eyes on the sky above rather than the ground below. "You wouldn't think the Old Gods would be all 'Let fire and destruction rain from the skies and plagues decimate the land ... but make it pink!'"

"Indeed. The war dragons of old are rather bleak and gray in the history book illustrations."

"Except for all the blood."

By the time they happened upon a pile of bright blue pellets, Vanderlinden was pinching the bridge of his nose.

"Silksheep droppings," Twyla supplied. "Their wool is the same color."

"I'm sure it is," the dracologist muttered.

Twyla found the man's growing discomfort oddly charming, and as they scanned the ground on their slow, careful, circular

track, she sneaked glances at his profile to admire the long aqui-
line nose, resulting in her inadvertently stepping on his toe.

"Ope!" She grabbed his upper arm to steady him so that he
wouldn't plummet into an equimaris puddle, reeking of ammo-
nia. Twyla had thought him thin at first glance, but based on the
evidence of her accidental groping, there was a well-defined bicep
under the khaki safari jacket.

"Quite all right," he said, and she forced herself to relinquish
her hold on him. Her hands, however, did not soon forget the
feeling of muscle beneath the layers of cotton. When was the last
time her heart had fluttered over physical contact with a man?
Honestly, Twyla, she scolded herself, her internal voice sounding
like her mother. It came with a disapproving sniff.

They plodded along for another five minutes in silence until
Dr. Vanderlinden nearly stepped on a tripudium plant in full
bloom. The flower head snapped upright in alarm. The red petals
vibrated, and the yellow leaves unfurled wide as the orange center
split open to issue a threatening hiss. The professor startled away
several feet, as if a swarm of bees had attacked him.

"What in the name of the Unknown God?" His face was beet red
as he stared at the tripudium, its leaves unfurled as it shook its razzle-
dazzle warning meant to scare off anything that wanted to eat it.

"Everything all right, doc?" asked Duckers.

The dracologist placed a hand over his heart. "I don't mean to
be rude, but quite frankly, no, everything is *not* all right. Every-
thing is all wrong. This place is all wrong. That baby clinging to
Marshal Ellis is all wrong. Literally nothing in Tanria is right."
He sounded more overwhelmed than angry when he demanded,
"How do you do this?"

Twyla and Duckers looked to each other in mutual confusion
before Twyla asked, "How do we do what?"

"This! Tanria!" Dr. Vanderlinden gestured broadly, like an

actor onstage. "How can you carry on as if this place were normal? La-di-da, another day at the office with pink grass and bizarrely triangular mountains and flowers that breathe! And hiss! And..." For lack of words, he imitated the flower's threatening posture, making Duckers turn his head away to cover his laughter with a fake cough.

Twyla looked at the perfectly harmless tripudium and watched as it folded its leaves into place with a *humph*. "You get used to it after a while."

"I suppose one might, but for the time being, I find it deeply unsettling. I must say, you marshals earn every copper of your exorbitant salary."

"Fuck yeah, we do," said Duckers.

"How am I supposed to carry out any kind of rational research in a place where nothing makes sense?" His frustration spent at last, he put his hands on his hips and bowed his head. "My apologies. That tantrum was unscholarly and unprofessional. I shall refrain from such outbursts in the future."

A grap, one of the weird furry frog-like creatures of Tanria, hopped by in front of them.

"What is that?" Vanderlinden asked, his voice weary.

"It's a grap," said Twyla.

"They're called graps because graps say *grap*," added Duckers.

"Of course they do."

Grap, said the grap.

Duckers slung the crossbow over his back. It was so long that it jutted out a full foot over his head. "If I take a piss in those trees, what are the odds that a big-ass dragon is going to find me and off me?"

"Fairly low, I would guess," said Vanderlinden.

"My bladder will have to take those odds. Back in a sec."

Having eschewed the standard crossbow, Twyla pulled the pistol crossbow from the holster at her hip. It could not possibly do much damage to a grown dragon, but she felt confident in her ability to wield it, which was more than she could say about her skill with the large-scale version. The professor eyed it doubtfully.

An awkward silence filled the plain as Twyla continued to walk beside the dracologist. "So, Dr. Vanderlinden," she said brightly. "This is your first time in Tanria, I take it?"

"Please, do call me Quill. And yes, this is my first visit to Tanria—my first time on the island of Bushong, in fact."

"It must be overwhelming. You've spent your career studying creatures that have been extinct for centuries—"

"Millennia."

"—only to discover they're running around the former prison of the Old Gods. And feel free to call me Twyla."

"I must admit, it's all rather astonishing. Twyla."

"For what it's worth, we'll take good care of you while you're here," she assured him.

"Thank you," he said in a way that sounded both surprised and sincere.

The increasingly dashing dracologist stopped and considered her. She began to wonder if she had something stuck in her teeth, when Duckers emerged from a small copse of fire oaks and announced, "Don't be jealous, people, but I am the winner of today's Giant-Pile-of-Shit Scavenger Hunt."

Quill tore his gaze from Twyla's. "As in, you found unusual fecal matter?"

"Either that or a bunch of animals got together for a big old poop party in those trees."

They followed him into the copse to an impressive and sparkly pile near the base of a fire oak. Duckers held up his small collection scoop and a glass sample jar, both of which were dwarfed by the evidence. "Think it'll fit?"

Chapter Six

It was a two-hour ride to the portal at the North Station, the closest exit to the Center for Tanrian Biological Research, so Twyla, Duckers, and Dr. Vanderlinden set out first thing Wisdomsday morning. Quill was eager to have their fecal sample tested, but since Twyla was craving non-dragon-related conversation, she decided that some pleasant small talk was in order.

"Where are you from, Quill?" she asked, the name bringing to mind old-timey ink bottles and ruffly collars and those tight hose men wore in Ye Olden Days. Come to think of it, the hose would flatter the well-formed legs currently on display on either side of an equimaris saddle.

Keep your mind on the work, Twyla scolded herself.

"I'm from Stenland, as you may have deduced from my accent, but I haven't visited in five years at least."

The word *visited* stuck like a burr in her sock. A person *returned* to their home. They didn't *visit* it. DJ hadn't been home in three years, but Eternity would always be home to him, wouldn't it? What if Hope was beginning to think of Eternity as a place to visit, rather than as the place where she belonged? What if Twyla herself had ceased to be home enough for her children?

Then again, she sometimes wished that Wade didn't feel quite so at home in her house.

"Do you ever get homesick?" she asked Quill.

"Not at all. I'm the third child, and since I didn't stand to inherit much, it was up to me to find my own way in the world."

"Doesn't your family wish you'd come home more often?"

"My sister and brother are ten and twelve years older than I am, so they were already off at boarding school by the time I came along. My father passed away some years ago, and Mama would have preferred that I had studied the law. So I'm afraid that no one rolls out the red carpet when I pay a visit."

Twyla could not imagine cutting off her children. It would be like hacking off her own arm on purpose. Quill might be a tad ridiculous in his safari gear, but the idea that his own mother didn't want to see him filled her with pity.

"Dang. That sucks, man," said Duckers.

"It is what it is."

Quill had taken off the safari jacket with its many pockets, and now a Tanrian breeze buffeted the fabric of his shirt, blowing the man's scent in Twyla's direction. He smelled of good, clean sweat and bath soap with a classier, spicier scent than the basic bar of Honekian Springs most people used around here.

"Are you both from the Federated Islands?"

"I'm from Paxico," Duckers volunteered. "A town called Brookville. Ever heard of it?"

"I've been, actually. I gave a guest lecture at Brookville College. I seem to recall eating some excellent fried chicken at the hotel restaurant."

"Yes! Best fried chicken in the Federated Islands. How about you, Twyla? Where are you from?"

"I grew up on Medora in the suburbs of Diamond Springs, but I've lived on Bushong so long that this is home now."

"How long have you been with the Tanrian Marshals?" asked Quill.

"Eight years. Frank recruited me, actually."

"Ah."

That single syllable seemed to be weighted with meaning that eluded Twyla.

"Most people are surprised when they find out I'm a marshal, especially if they're not from around here. I don't exactly fit the stereotype."

"But in a good way," said Duckers.

"And what is the stereotype?" asked Quill.

"Rugged? Flinty? A man?"

"True, you don't strike me as any of those things."

"Most people don't expect to find a frumpy middle-aged mom patrolling the western sectors, is all I'm saying."

"*Frumpy* is not the word I would use to describe you."

"Agreed," said Duckers.

"And for what it's worth, I don't exactly fit the stereotype either. The continental toff: privileged, self-superior, clinging for dear life to the ways of the Old Gods thousands of years after their downfall."

She bit her lip and met Duckers's eyes as they rode. He clearly agreed with her that considering the man's getup, Dr. Quill Vanderlinden might as well have worn a shiny badge that proclaimed him *A Continental Toff.* She decided to steer the conversation in a safer direction.

"It sounds like you've traveled a lot, Quill. Where all have you been?"

"Where *haven't* I been?"

"I've never even left the Federated Islands. We must seem pretty provincial to you, out here in the sticks."

"*Provincial* is another word I would not use to describe you."

He might not have been the handsomest man in the world, but that much self-assurance came with a heaping dose of masculine allure. Duckers must have sensed her growing attraction to the professor, because he grinned at her and fanned himself. "It's getting hot out here, isn't it?"

She cleared her throat in warning at him before saying, "Duckers, did you know that this is Quill's first time in Tanria?"

"Oh? So how do you like Tanria, Quill?" Duckers made the dracologist's given name sound positively lascivious.

"It's unsettling yet magnificent," answered Quill, but something in Twyla's face made him add, "You don't think so?"

"Tanria stops being magnificent after a while, especially when you spend most of your time arresting bird poachers, or busting farm boys sneaking in to shear silksheep, or trying to convince arrogant big-game hunters that there are no dragons in Tanria and that their shiny new rifles are not going to work inside the Mist anyway."

"Except there *are* dragons," Duckers pointed out.

"You know what I mean."

"And what about the drudges?" asked Quill. "You did face the undead, I assume, before they disappeared?"

"Of course. Many times."

"You have no idea," added Duckers.

"And?"

"I never got used to the drudges," said Twyla. "I didn't *want* to get used to them. So many people came to Tanria looking for an opportunity, a way to improve their lives, only to be killed and possessed by a lost soul. But that's one of the reasons why I've always found this job satisfying, too. I could rid bodies of those lost souls and help send their remains home to the people who loved them most. It was a service and an honor."

"Aw, that's poetic and shit, Twyla," said Duckers. Only Penrose Duckers could make that statement sound genuinely admiring.

Sheepishly, she sneaked a glance at Quill and found him studying her with hooded gray-blue eyes.

"What?" she asked, returning her gaze to the road but feeling his eyes on her all the same.

"Marshal Twyla Banneker, you are quite extraordinary," he pronounced, his plummy accent making the proclamation all the more stunning.

Twyla couldn't bring herself to accept the compliment. "*Extraordinary* is not the word I would use to describe me."

"We shall have to agree to disagree on that."

She wasn't sure if the sudden heat prickling her skin was due to the summer sun, a hot flash, or the palpable manliness of a dracologist in short-shorts riding beside her.

"Mm-hmm," Duckers hummed smugly.

This is the longest equimaris ride of my life, Twyla thought and continued to think until they reached the portal at the North Station and set about finding a government autoduck to take them to the Center for Tanrian Biological Research.

In the lobby of the center, Quill leaned on the front desk and smiled at the receptionist, who blinked at him, unimpressed. Twyla got the sense that Dr. Quill Vanderlinden was not the first professor in safari attire who had crossed her path.

"Can I help you?"

"Might I have a word with Dr. Sellet?"

"Do you have an appointment?"

"No."

"Dr. Sellet is the director of the institute. I'm afraid you'll need to make an appointment."

Twyla thought that this woman was not in the least bit afraid, certainly not of the unaccountably attractive continental toff leaning on her desk.

Quill winked at her. "Tell him Alcomworth has come to say hello."

She pursed her lips, but she rose and said "If you'll wait here, please?" before stepping through the door behind her desk.

"Alcomworth?" Twyla asked Quill.

"The name of my family's estate. My father was the seventh Earl of Alcomworth."

He said this the way one might say, *My father was a plumber*, as if earls could be found under every bush in Stenland. Each article of clothing on his body suddenly looked five times more expensive.

A balding man in a green-and-maroon striped waistcoat came striding through the door. "Alcomworth!" he cried, shaking Quill's hand. "I had no idea of your being on Bushong."

"I only arrived yesterday evening."

"Come in, come in." The head of the institute motioned for Quill to follow him into his office. When Twyla and Duckers made to follow, he asked, "And these are…?"

"How rude of me. May I present Marshals Twyla Banneker and Penrose Duckers, my escorts during my stay here."

"Ah."

Did all the Stenish use this single syllable to speak volumes? wondered Twyla.

"Come along, then. Can I offer you a brandy?" Dr. Sellet asked as soon as he'd escorted them into a light-filled, wood-paneled office.

"I must confess, this is not entirely a social visit," said Quill.

By now, Sellet was holding the cut-glass decanter of brandy as if it were a foregone conclusion. "Oh?"

"We've come across some interesting scat. Thought you might have a look at it under the microscope?"

"Wonderful!"

Twyla hadn't heard the word *wonderful* associated with excrement since the day four-year-old Wade finally used the potty-chair in the hall bathroom of their old house on Medora decades ago.

Sellet set down the decanter and reached for his white lab coat, which hung on a hook in his office. "Let's have a look, shall we?"

He led them through a maze of corridors, chatting the whole way.

"Didn't know you were doing research in Tanria, Alcomworth. Didn't think there were any old dragon bones moldering around these parts at all."

"It's a new line of research," Quill told him in an affably vague way.

Sellet stepped into a laboratory where five scientists at different lab tables leaped to attention as he and Quill and the marshals entered the room.

"As you were, as you were," he said cheerily. "Lawson, might we borrow your microscope for a tick?"

"Of course, sir." The young man nearly tripped in his excitement to get out of his boss's way.

Quill and Dr. Sellet chatted about old schoolfellows as the director went about setting up a glass slide with the sample they had collected in Sector W-14. He hummed as he slid the glass under a lens and positioned himself over the eyepiece. "Lots of vegetable matter, grass mostly, the marshy sort. Some cattails. A very soggy diet. No idea what the sparkly bits are, but I'd say you have an herbivore here."

"An herbivore?" Twyla exclaimed.

Duckers was equally taken aback. "You mean this thing is a vegetarian?"

"For the most part, although I do detect some insect matter. Probably tangled in the plants as they were ingested." Sellet looked up at both of them. "Were you expecting different results?"

Realizing that they might be giving away too much information, Twyla said, "Nope."

"This was collected in Tanria?"

"I'm afraid that's classified information, old boy," said Quill. He crossed his arms and leaned against the wall beside the microscope. The man had perfected the art of casual leaning. "If you had to place a bet on what kind of animal created this sample, what would you guess?"

"I'd say something in the Anatidae family. A goose, perhaps? Possibly a swan? A bird who has gotten into a vial of children's craft glitter?"

Duckers burst out laughing. "Shut up! A goose?"

Dr. Sellet looked up but directed his answer to his old schoolfellow, not to Twyla or Duckers. "I was unaware of any species of waterfowl inside the Mist. If this sample did originate from Tanria, I suspect that someone secreted a goose or a swan through a portal."

"Seems an odd thing to smuggle in," said Quill.

"People do bring the oddest things into Tanria."

"True," Twyla agreed, thinking of a marshal's apprentice who'd kept sneaking his pet guinea pig into Tanria. He hadn't made it past his probationary period.

"Capital. You've been a great help, old fellow." Dr. Quill Vanderlinden, son of the seventh Earl of Alcomworth, clapped his friend on the shoulder, refused one last invitation for a glass of brandy, and made his dashing exit with Twyla and Duckers in tow.

A quick jaunt to the Zeandale branch of the Bushong Public Library produced nothing helpful on the subject of the Anatidae family, save a children's nonfiction picture book on swans titled, simply, *Swans*. A half hour later, they found themselves in a line of marshals and workers atop a veritable herd of equimares, waiting to get through the North Station's portal.

"This is the day that will not end," Twyla muttered.

"Tell me about it," said the marshal in front of them in line. "The portal's been acting up all week. Chief Mitchell just sent for Dr. Lee."

Adam Lee was the inventor of the portals. If he had been called in to fix the North Station's entry point, the situation must be serious.

"I wonder if we should take an autoduck to the West Station," Twyla suggested to Duckers, when the tall marshal in line behind them dismounted, handed her reins to Twyla, and strode to the front of the line as if there were no line at all.

"I say!" exclaimed Quill.

Twyla was equally put out until she got a good look at the person in question.

"Who is that?" asked Duckers.

"Rosie Fox, I think, though I've never met her." But Twyla couldn't imagine who else on the island of Bushong—or anywhere in the Federated Islands—stood over six feet tall and had a pair of red demigod eyes glaring out of a pale elven face. Even cast in the shadow of a wide-brimmed hat, those eyes were impossible to miss. Two carrot-colored plaits dangled down her back from beneath her hat, adding to her vivid appearance.

"Dang," breathed Duckers. Twyla wasn't sure if this was in response to Fox's demigod looks or her legendary reputation in the Tanrian Marshals.

"That's Fox, all right," said the chatty marshal in front of them. "Ever met her?"

"No."

"Do not party with her. You will never survive."

"Good to know," said Duckers in a way that indicated he was now extremely interested in partying with her. They'd probably wind up at a dance club with Zeddie Birdsall, all of them covered in glitter.

By now, Fox had reached the portal, where she asked the engineer, "Mind if I have a look?"

"Uh..."

Without waiting for permission, she began to fiddle with the knobs and dials on the portal's arch.

The engineer's eyes bugged. "Um, you probably shouldn't—"

Fox pounded her fist against the frame with a *thwack*, and the portal whirred to life, the Mist within thinning as it ought to.

"You're welcome," she told the nonplussed engineer before returning to the end of the line behind Twyla, Duckers, and Quill.

"I don't think we've met. I'm Rosie."

Duckers shook her hand. "Penrose Duckers, and this is Twyla Banneker and Dr. Quill Vanderlinden, who's doing research stuff in Tanria."

"Banneker? I've heard of you. I thought you worked with Frank Ellis."

"I do. Duckers recently lost his partner, so he's teaming up with us for now."

"No worries, Duckers. I go through partners like there's no tomorrow, and they haven't fired me yet."

Duckers beamed at her. "I can't keep a partner to save my life!"

"Twinsies! We can start our own club!"

Twyla spoke up before they could invent a secret handshake. "You're working the iuvenicite case, aren't you?"

Fox rolled her red eyes. "Ugh, it's a hot mess. We can't find any connection between the miners at the Doniphan Iuvenicite Mine and the stuff that's making its way to the black market. But there's nowhere else the iuvenicite could be coming from, unless some rando has found a vein outside of Tanria, which I doubt. The only clue we have to go on is that the miners have been hearing 'weird booming sounds' from time to time when they're in the shafts. Great. Super helpful. And the Feds are up my ass because, apparently, the Galatian mob is involved. Plus, the mob put a hit out on my latest partner, so he quit a couple of days ago. Technically, they put a hit out on me, too, but you know, good luck with that."

By now, they'd reached the portal, and Rosie nodded at it. "You'd better go on through before it breaks again. Catch you later."

Once the trio was through the Mist, Quill asked Twyla, "What did she mean, 'Good luck with that'? Shouldn't she be worried that the Galatian mob wants to kill her?"

"She's immortal."

He glanced back and regarded the towering, red-eyed, ginger-haired demigod. "By gods."

"So then Twyla reaches into her pack, and—I kid you not—pulls out a FireTires," Frank told Duckers over plates of hot dogs, carrot sticks, and canned pears in the barracks that evening. He hadn't eaten much yet; he was too busy stuffing strips of wilted lettuce into the baby dragon's eager mouth.

"A FireTires? Like, one of those toy autoducks?"

"Yes, sir, and that little girl went from hollering to smiling in two seconds flat."

"I used to love FireTires! Do you seriously keep toys in your Gracie Goodfist bag, Twyla?"

"I always had a couple of FireTires rolling around my purse when my kids were little, to keep them occupied if I had to bag my own groceries or if we had to wait for food at a restaurant—not that we ate out much. These days, I keep them around to entertain the grandkids. Although that particular autoduck was left over from the days my bag belonged to one of my sons."

"Vintage!" crowed Duckers.

"I'm telling you," said Frank, "Twyla's backpack is magical. I can't believe the things she's pulled out of it."

"Such as?"

"Here we go," Twyla said under her breath, pretending to be annoyed when, in fact, she loved the way Frank relished telling a good Twyla story. She worried that Quill, who sat at the far end of the table, studying the children's book on swans, might feel left out of the conversation. She almost asked him to join them before Frank launched into his tale, but he turned a page without looking up, so she thought better of it.

"So this one time—it would have been a good six or seven years ago—we arrived on the scene of a flare to find a woman in labor at the Alvarez Ambrosia Bottling Company and a whole bunch of panicked coworkers. Apparently, she thought she had another month to go, but the little one showed up early. So the two of us helped deliver the first baby ever birthed on Tanrian soil—"

"The *only* baby ever delivered in Tanria," Twyla added.

"And there's Marshal Banneker, pulling a *diaper* out of her trusty Gracie Goodfist backpack."

"You had a fucking diaper in there?" Duckers hit a couple of impressively high notes at the end of his question.

"It was one of those flat-fold diapers. I always keep one on hand, because they're great for cleaning up spills." She got up from her seat, dug around in her pack, and pulled out a diaper to demonstrate. "They come in handy."

Duckers hooted and clapped his hands. "Your bag is your superpower."

"Nope," said Frank. "Twyla's true superpower is making grown adults sob with her guilt-laden I Know You're Better Than This speech."

"They actually cry?"

"She can lay the Mom Guilt on you faster than you can say *Grandfather Bones*."

"Dang, Twyla, you're a badass."

"Be sure to mention that to my sons. They're unimpressed with me."

"But their mom's a Tanrian Marshal. How cool is that?"

Twyla shrugged. To say that DJ and Wade had been unimpressed when she joined up was the understatement of the year.

Wade had laughed at her, as if the mere idea of his mother's becoming a Tanrian Marshal was the most ridiculous thing he'd ever heard. But that was preferable to DJ's reaction. Her eldest had actually taken the trouble to write her a letter full of grave concern.

Mom, I love you, but what in the Salt Sea are you thinking? A woman your age, joining the Tanrian Marshals? You don't know what you're getting into. I'm in law enforcement, and I can tell you right now, you're going to get yourself killed. Please don't do this.

DJ's complete lack of faith in her had cut her to the quick, as had Wade's dismissive laughter. Frank knew all of this, and he surreptitiously rubbed her back in understanding, a gesture that lessened the dull ache of her memory. Twyla caught movement out of the corner of her eye and noticed Quill finally looking up from his book to watch Frank's hand at her back. The moment was short-lived, because the dracologist's eyes immediately darted to his book again.

"Hey, there are four of us. How about a game of Gods and Heroes?" suggested Duckers.

Frank fed the dragon another piece of lettuce. "Why not? I'm in. Twyla?"

"Sure."

"Vanderlinden, want to play Gods and Heroes?" Frank asked over the dragon's pink head.

"I'm afraid I never learned."

"We can teach you," Twyla offered.

Quill glanced at her and then at Frank. "No, thank you. I should bring myself up to speed on animals of the Anatidae family."

Twyla couldn't imagine a children's nonfiction picture book

was going to be incredibly helpful, but since he didn't seem inclined to play, she let it go.

"Hello-o-o? Mail delivery?" came Hermia's uncertain call as she stepped into the barracks.

"Hey, Hermia, do you know how to play Gods and Heroes?" asked Duckers.

"Ooh, I love Gods and Heroes! But I always lose."

Twyla could almost hear the sad trombones that accompanied this statement as the hedgehog rummaged in her satchel for today's mail.

"One for you, Marshal El—oh!" Hermia spied the dragon wrapped around Frank's torso and startled so violently that the missives went sailing through the air like paper airplanes. "Oh my goodness gracious with sprinkles on top, what is that?"

"A baby dragon," said Duckers before taking another bite of his hot dog.

Quill looked up from his book. "I thought that was classified."

Duckers jerked a thumb at the hedgehog. "Privacy laws and shit. She literally can't tell anyone about this."

"Ah." He returned his attention to his illustrated swans.

Hermia clasped her hands as she smiled sweetly at the baby. "That's a neat dragon you've got there, Marshal Ellis."

"Thanks."

"I hope it doesn't eat you someday."

Frank gave Twyla his most long-suffering Hermia Look.

The nimkilim picked up a missive that had fallen to the floor, but she paused before delivering it to anyone present. Her tiny eyes gleamed as she held the letter under her darling nose and inhaled, and inhaled again, and then inhaled so deeply that she swooned and staggered.

"Everything okay?" asked Frank.

"It's for you, Marshal Duckers," said the nimkilim as she

crossed the room on unsteady feet to deliver the letter. "Oh my stars and garters, it smells wonderful!"

"From Zeddie," Duckers explained to his human companions. "He sometimes sprays his letters with vanilla extract to remind me of his baking."

"Aw," cooed Twyla.

"Yeah," said Duckers, clearly embarrassed, but Twyla thought it was precious. She remembered what it was like to be young and in love.

"Bye, then," said Hermia.

Frank held up a finger. "Can I get my letter?"

"Goodness, I nearly forgot. Oh dear, where did it go?"

"It's stuck to your sleeve," said Twyla.

Hermia held up the wrong arm for investigation under the huge round lenses of her glasses.

"Other sleeve," said Twyla.

"Oh, here it is!" She ripped the envelope from her spines and handed the slightly torn letter to Frank.

"Have a good night, Hermia," said Twyla, pressing a coin into the hedgehog's tiny hand.

Hermia stuffed it into the drooping pocket of her Fair Isle cardigan. "Bye."

"Bye," three marshals and a dracologist said in chorus. Even the dragon said, *Meep.*

"'Kay, bye," the nimkilim said one last time before making her exit.

"And there go your hopes for Gods and Heroes, Duckers," said Frank as he opened his letter.

Twyla recognized Lu Ellis's bubbly print on the envelope. "What's Lu got to say?" she asked him.

A relieved smile spread across his face. "Lu and Annie are planning to visit next month."

"That's great."

His smile fell as he recalled one slight problem. "I have a baby dragon attached to me."

"I'm sure it'll be off by then."

"Gods, I hope so." Frank rubbed his knuckles between the knobs of the baby's future horns. "You're sweet, Mary Georgina, but I need you to detach in the next couple of weeks."

"Her name is Mary Georgina?" asked Duckers.

"Thought she needed a name."

"Aw," Twyla sighed again as Duckers said through a half-chewed bite of hot dog, "That's a mouthful."

"His mom was Mary, and his grandma was named Georgina," Twyla explained.

"Aw," said Duckers, easily converted to the merits of the name Mary Georgina. "Do we know if it's a girl, though?"

"No idea," said Frank.

"Too early to tell, but I doubt the dragon will take offense at human notions of gender," Quill put in without looking up from his book.

Someone rapped on the barracks' door, and a moment later, Chief Maguire stepped inside, carrying a waxed paper sack. "Okay, I've got snails and crickets from the pet store in Zeandale and eggs from Wilner's Green Grocer. Best I could do on short notice."

Twyla cringed an apology at Maguire as Frank fed Mary Georgina another shred of lettuce.

"What is that? Are you giving it veggies? I thought this thing ate animals."

"There's been an interesting development today in our understanding of dracological dietary needs," said Quill, gesturing to the vacant chair next to Frank. She sat on the seat in a tired droop, but by the time they were finished filling her in on everything, she had perked up significantly.

"So, to be clear, these things do not eat people?"

"It appears that they do not," Quill confirmed.

"Thank gods."

"So no evacuation of Tanria?" asked Frank.

"Not yet, at any rate. We need to figure out what to do about these dragons, though, especially this one."

"You mean Mary Georgina?" asked Duckers.

Maguire stroked the dragon's back. "We probably shouldn't be naming it or getting too attached."

Frank gave her a dubious look as she petted the pink scales.

"Oh, be quiet," she huffed at him.

Duckers went to his cot and pulled a deck of cards from his pack. "Hey, Chief, want to play Gods and Heroes since you're here?"

"You're on. I already told my wife I wouldn't make it home tonight."

"No offense, Boss, but I'm about to own you."

"Challenge accepted."

In the end, it was Twyla who owned all three of them—Frank, Duckers, and Maguire—while Quill remained glued to the book on swans and jotted notes in his journal. She kept getting the Trickster, the wild card of the Old Gods suit, and the Briar Thief, the wild card of the Heroes suit. So even though Duckers dealt her the Unknown God—the strongest card in the deck—only one time over the course of the five hands they played, she managed to win three games easily. Despite her victories, she hated playing the Briar Thief card. No matter the deck, his illustration was always gruesome, the hero who had tried to steal the Thorn of Eternal Life from the garden of the Old Gods, only to be captured by the God of Wrath and impaled on the briar, the long thorn piercing his heart.

A flatulent sound from Frank's direction jolted Twyla from her contemplation of the tragic hero. She looked at her best friend in time to see a semisolid stream of slimy glitter ooze out of Mary Georgina's backside. Utterly resigned, Frank glanced at the baby-dragon poo in his lap, then turned his woebegone eyes to Twyla.

"Still got that diaper handy?"

Maguire left the following morning to acquire a more vegetarian-friendly diet and to scrounge up some diapers for Mary Georgina, who continued to cling to Frank through Wardensday and Allgodsday. Most of the time, the dragon appeared to be sleeping with its face pressed against its foster father's warm bulk, but its periods of alertness were growing longer. Quill took advantage of the time to take measurements of the scaly baby and to observe the sounds it made—mostly variations of meeping. He had Frank feed the dragon different Tanrian plants and then studied the aftermath of each type of food in the diapers that Twyla had fashioned from a standard-issue cot cover. Because of course the diapering had fallen to Twyla.

For the most part, Twyla didn't mind. She had diapered so many babies in her life that it held no horror for her. She would never forget the time that DJ and Wade had picked up a stomach bug when they were babies. She'd dealt with unbelievable blowouts for two straight weeks, and all the baths and laundry that came along for the ride. Compared to that, sparkly dragon poo was nothing. In fact, she was fairly proud of herself for figuring out how to fold and wrap her makeshift diapers around the dragon's tail.

"Thank the Three Mothers for you," Frank murmured as she pinned yet another diaper in place late Allgodsday evening.

"You say that to all the girls who diaper your baby dragon."

"I mean it, Twy."

Exhaustion lined his face. He was still wearing the shirt he'd worn three days ago, since the baby was cinching it to his torso, and he looked far more rumpled than she'd ever seen him before. More than anything, his demeanor screamed a vulnerability he did not often show the world or even his best friend.

Frank was like a house with many rooms. The places inside him to which Twyla was allowed access were bright and interesting, but she knew there were dark closets and cobwebby cellars where he kept the difficult things locked away. He never spoke of the pain of losing Lu and Annie when Cora left him. He had stayed behind in Eternity because it was the only way he could earn enough money to support his family, even if it meant he got to see them only a few times a year.

Which was why she knew his kids' impending visit was weighing on him now. If he couldn't get Mary Georgina to dislodge, he might miss them, and who knew when or if they'd be back again? There was little Twyla could do to comfort him on that front, so she offered what she could.

"Duckers," she called over her shoulder to the young marshal brushing his teeth.

"Yeah?"

"Think you could help Frank get his shirt off tomorrow and maybe run him a bath?"

"Yeah, sure thing, Frank."

Frank narrowed his eyes at Twyla. "Is this your way of telling me I stink?"

"I would never."

Duckers spat out his toothpaste. "But you are getting mighty fragrant over there, Ellis."

"And a good night to you, too," Frank called back to him wearily.

Chapter Seven

Banneker, your tour is over as of this afternoon, correct?" asked
Maguire the following morning, when she showed up with market bags full of lettuce and greens and two dozen flat-fold diapers.

Twyla didn't bother to glance up from the dry sink where she
was scraping the remnants of a pancake off an iron skillet. "Yes,
but…"

"But what?"

"Obviously, I can't leave Frank." She gestured toward the
northwest corner of the barracks, where, on the other side of the
walls, Frank was attempting to bathe himself in the small bathhouse while a no-longer-extinct creature clung to him.

"You can leave him and you will leave him. Marshall Ellis is
going to pick up overtime this week, while you and Duckers go
home to your loved ones and behave as if everything's normal."
Twyla was about to protest, but the chief cut her off. "He already
knows this is what we're doing. He's the one who suggested it."

Twyla threw her dish towel on the counter. "If that isn't just
like him! Infuriating man."

"I'll check in on him this week. And I'll bring him more diapers, too."

Checking in with Frank wasn't the same as being there for
him. Twyla looked hopefully to the dracologist. "Quill, are you
staying?"

"In fact, I am departing with Chief Maguire this morning. My plan is to return to Quindaro on the earliest ferry out tomorrow to carry out a bit of research at the university library. If we can identify the exact species of dragon we're dealing with here, it would be most helpful, especially for Marshal Ellis."

Did Maguire—or Frank, for that matter—actually expect Twyla to leave her best friend alone under these circumstances? "I don't like this."

"I'm sure you don't," said Maguire. "To be honest, I don't like it either, but we need to keep this dragon business on the down-low for as long as possible. Go home, Twyla. Get some rest. You've earned it. Dr. Vanderlinden, I'll meet you at the stable."

The words were uttered with finality, and Maguire took up her overnight pack and departed before Twyla could make any further arguments. She was about to storm to the bathhouse to protest Frank's heavy-handedness (without actually going inside, of course) when Quill stopped her at the barracks door.

"Marshal Banneker—er, Twyla—might I have a quick word?"

She wanted to talk things over with Frank, but she also didn't want to be rude. "What's up?" she asked with as much patience as she could muster.

"I wanted to express my gratitude. You've been most helpful these past two days, and I have enjoyed working with you."

"Thank you. I've enjoyed working with you, too."

"If you don't mind my asking a rather delicate question, is Marshal Ellis your partner, or is he...your *partner*?"

It had not occurred to Twyla until that moment that a highly educated man in an ascot might find her demeanor with her best friend unprofessional on the job, a thought that mortified her. "Me and Frank? No!" She tittered involuntarily, sounding ridiculous even to her own ears. "We've known each other for ages, but there's never been anything romantic between us."

"I see."

"I know that we might come across as casual, but I promise you, we take our work seriously."

"In that case, would you care to have dinner with me tonight?"

A pregnant pause filled with the grapping of graps and the strange call of exotic Tanrian birds followed the question as Twyla attempted to make sense of the words.

"You want to have dinner with me?"

"I would, yes."

"As in, a...date?"

"If that is amenable to you?"

Twyla knew she needed to say something, but her mind was a blank. She couldn't make herself believe this was really happening.

"Ah. I see," Quill said after an agonizingly long pause. "Forgive me. I misread this situation."

True, he had misread the situation, but more in the sense that it had never occurred to Twyla that a reasonably attractive man her own age with years of education and worldly experience might want to have dinner with her. Several locals had asked her out in the years since Doug had sailed the Salt Sea, but those men had had personal agendas that Twyla had not found appealing. One was on the hunt for a stepmother for his three children. Another had wanted a woman to keep house for him while he tried to get a new business up and running. Not that any of these men were consciously thinking, *I need a wife so that I don't have to pay someone for all the things a married woman does for free*, but Twyla could see the quiet motivations lurking beneath the surface.

Quill, on the other hand, didn't live here. He would stay for as long as it took him to carry out his work, and then he would go home to Quindaro. He wasn't looking for someone to take care of him. He was looking for a little company to pass the time on Bushong. And why shouldn't his company be Twyla?

"I haven't been on a date in so long, I've forgotten how to do this," she said. "Yes, I'd like to go out to dinner. With you. Tonight."

He beamed at her. "Excellent."

"Where are you staying?"

"The Sunny Hill Hotel in Eternity."

"I live in Eternity. I can pick you up, if you want?"

"Nonsense. I have my own duck with me, and since I'm the one inviting you, I should be the one picking you up. Say, six o'clock?"

As Twyla dug out a small notebook from her supplies, she saw his eyes land on the Gracie Goodfist backpack and thought that perhaps the time had come to invest in a bag designed for an adult. Blushing furiously, she scrawled her address, tore out the page, and handed it to Quill. "See you then."

"Indeed."

Indeed. The Stenish accent was making the knee socks and ascot more endearing by the second. She hoped he found her son's old backpack equally charming.

Twyla walked him out the door and saw him off to the stables as Duckers returned from helping Frank.

"How is he?" she asked him.

"Not bad, all things considered. I think the bath cheered him up."

"You were able to get his shirt off?"

"Yeah, but I doubt he can get another one on. He's glad to be wearing clean underwear and pants, though."

"Oh, the indignities of motherhood," she commiserated. "Did you hear Maguire ordered the two of us to go home this afternoon?"

"I knew *I* was leaving, but you are, too?"

Twyla nodded.

"So we're all ditching Dragon Daddy?"

"Yep."

"Sucks to be Frank, although I gotta say, I'm looking forward to my time off. This tour has been batshit."

"No kidding. I'm about to ride out on rounds. Want to come with?"

"Sure. I'll meet you at the stable in fifteen?"

Twyla patted him on the shoulder in agreement and went to check on Frank. He was behind the bathhouse by the clothesline, hanging up his old shirt, which he had tried to scrub clean in his bathwater. He had plaited his wet hair into a braid to keep it out of his way, and, of course, he had a small shell-pink dragon attached to his now naked torso. The only other item he wore from the waist up was his silver ID key on a chain around his neck, a holdover from more dangerous times when everyone entering Tanria was required to have a prepaid funeral package on file should they die inside the Mist.

Twyla had seen Frank's bare chest and arms and shoulders and legs—pretty much everything but his privates—countless times, mostly to patch him up after a particularly nasty drudge fight, and he'd seen quite a bit of her unclad skin, too, for the same reason. And yet it was jarring to behold so much exposed Frank-ness in the peaceful morning sunlight. He was in his fifties, and his physique had softened with age, but Twyla sometimes forgot that despite his slightly below-average height, he had a powerful frame.

Built like a battering ram, and I mean that in the best possible way, one of his ex-lady-friends had once slurred over margaritas at a party in Twyla's backyard years ago.

She did not want to think of Frank as a battering ram, but as he stood there before her, damp and sun bronzed, the phrase *battering ram* and all that went with it burned itself into her brain. Her cheeks went hot, and she was certain that her face had turned the color of a vine-ripe tomato.

"Don't lay into me, darlin'," pleaded a blessedly oblivious Frank as he hung his pants on the line beside his shirt. "There's no point in both of us being stuck here."

Yes, that's right. I'm supposed to yell at him, Twyla reminded herself. "You could have asked me for my opinion before you made decisions on my behalf."

"And you would have insisted on staying."

"Because you're my best friend."

"And you're mine."

She couldn't argue with that, especially not when he picked up his clean shirt from where it sat neatly folded on the fence and struggled into the sleeves as a baby dragon meeped in protest.

"Need help?"

"Please."

She walked around him, surveying the situation from every angle. "There's only six inches of space between the wing tips, but I can maybe make this work if I stand behind you."

"Do what you can do. I'd rather not walk around Tanria half-naked if I don't have to."

Twyla suspected that there were a few marshals who would love nothing more than to see Frank Ellis traipse about half-naked, but she kept that opinion to herself.

Battering ram, her traitorous brain whispered. She crammed that thought into the recesses of her mind, like a railroad worker tamping dynamite into a hole before blowing up the side of a mountain. Which, come to think of it, was another extremely unhelpful analogy.

Frank had already struggled into each sleeve up to his elbows, so Twyla stood behind him to work the shirt's front panels under the wings. Mary Georgina huffed in annoyance at her efforts, but Twyla was able to slide several inches of cotton canvas past the baby's clutch, all the way to Frank's sides, allowing her to pull the collar up and cover his shoulders, which were much bigger than she remembered them being. The struggle now was to get the placket to meet the buttons in front underneath the dragon's belly. The only way Twyla could pull it off was via a full-body hug. She had to press her chest flat against Frank's back and her pelvis against his butt. His body was a pleasing combination of hard and soft and comforting warmth.

Not alarming. Not alarming at all.

"Good thing I took a bath," he joked, but his voice sounded strangely husky. And since his speaking register was so deep, Twyla felt the words vibrate all down her front.

"Your baby had better not bite me," she told him, praying to the Mother of Sorrows that he didn't notice her fluster as she did up two more buttons.

And then it occurred to her that Mary Georgina really might bite her, and that sounded fairly awful.

"Want to hear something nutty?" she asked, as much to distract herself as to deliver interesting news.

"Sure."

She got another button through a buttonhole. "Dr. Vanderlinden asked me out."

"He..." Frank went very still. "He did what, now?"

"He asked me to go out to dinner with him." She got another button through its corresponding hole. "On a date." Another successful buttoning. "Tonight."

She stepped aside to assess her work and smooth the fabric over his shoulders. They were broad and strong. Romance-hero shoulders. Twyla snatched her hands back at the disconcerting thought.

"I am so sorry that happened to you, Twy. Are you filing a complaint?"

This was not going as planned. Not that she had planned it.

She stepped to his front side and pulled down on his sleeves. "No, I'm not filing a complaint."

"I think you should. It's unprofessional of him."

This was awkward.

Why was this awkward?

"The thing is, I said yes."

"You did *what?*"

His shock and surprise were beginning to offend her.

"I said I'd go out with him."

"Are you pulling my leg?"

Twyla moved from offense to anger. "Do I sound like I'm joking?"

"You're going out with Professor Vanderlegs?"

"Yes, and his name is Vanderlinden."

"On a date?"

"It's been a few decades since I've done this sort of thing, but yes, that's my understanding."

"What in the Salt Sea are you thinking?" burst Frank, and now Twyla wasn't mad; she was *hopping* mad.

"What is the problem? He's not my boss, and I'm not his. There's no ethical dilemma here."

"But you're working together."

"So? You've dated other marshals in the past, haven't you?"

He clamped his lips, because he couldn't deny it.

Meep? said Mary Georgina, looking first at Frank and then at Twyla.

"How many people have you dated since you and Cora split up?" Twyla pressed, hands on hips.

"Well now, I don't rightly know."

"Exactly. Too many to count. Do you know how many men I've dated since Doug died?"

Frank hunched his shoulders. "None."

"That's right. None. Zero. In thirteen years. Why can't I be the one having fun for a change?"

"What are you saying? You think I'm some kind of womanizer?"

"Of course not."

"When was the last time *I* went on a date with anyone, Twy? Do you even know? Or care?"

Mary Georgina buried her face in the crisp blue cotton of Frank's clean shirt.

Twyla hadn't seen Frank this worked up... possibly ever. But she was too livid to concern herself with him when he was awfully busy not being happy for her.

"That's beside the point. A nice, attractive man asked me out, and I said yes."

"So he's attractive now, is he?"

"As a matter of fact, yes, he is. You know what? Forget it. My love life doesn't have a thing to do with you." She turned on her heel and marched toward the stable, but Frank matched her, stride for stride.

"Forgive me for looking out for you."

"I am a grown woman. I can look out for myself."

"You can look all you want. You sure as shit don't see much."

"What's that supposed to mean?"

"Nothing," he growled.

Twyla urged her mare out of the water trough and began to towel off her scales as Frank glowered at the stable door. "I'm going out on rounds."

He remained where he was, watching as she got the equimaris saddled up. He finally spoke when Duckers arrived to get his own mount saddled.

"Take the big crossbows with you."

Twyla led her equimaris to where Frank stood by the large stable door. "I. Can look out for. Myself."

"Whew, you could cut the tension here with a knife," Duckers whispered none too subtly to his gelding before he mounted up.

Several hours in the saddle did nothing to assuage Twyla's fury at Frank. It didn't help that Duckers spent half the circuit prying into what had happened in the time between when he left Twyla to stuff some breakfast down his gullet and the moment fifteen minutes later when he'd come out to the stable to find the friends at each other's throats.

"Everything's fine," she told him through gritted teeth.

"Obviously."

Twyla was tempted to confide in Duckers, if only to vent her frustration with Frank, but she decided it was best to keep the details of her love life—if it could be called a love life—to herself for the time being.

Frank was sitting in one of the deck chairs outside the barracks, waiting for them, when they returned.

"Can we talk?"

Twyla nodded.

"Mm-hmm," Duckers hummed as Twyla and Frank walked away from the barracks together.

"Can it, rookie," Twyla told him, making him snicker.

They walked in silence for several yards, long enough for Twyla to realize that she was now taking it as a given that Frank had a baby dragon stuck to him.

"I'm sorry," he said abruptly. "I don't know why I . . . I was taken off guard, is all."

It was his shock that bruised her, the fact that he apparently could not fathom anyone finding her attractive. Which meant that *he* didn't find her attractive. Not that she wanted anything beyond friendship from Frank, but his complete lack of interest cut her all the same.

"Is it so surprising that someone would ask me out?"

"Of course not."

She thought she was doing a creditable job hiding her hurt feelings, but of course Frank saw right through her.

"Twyla Jo." He tilted her chin up, forcing her to look him in the eye. "It does not surprise me in the least."

She could see that he meant it, and the big, unwieldy, weepy feeling she'd been experiencing ever since she witnessed his near death by dragon spit bubbled inside her. His fingertips pressed a drugging warmth against her chin, and all she could think to do was bat his hand away with an affectionate swat. "Pfft. I'm not exactly hot stuff over here."

"Darlin', what you don't know on this subject is a lot." He addressed this comment to the toes of his boots rather than to Twyla directly, a lack of eye contact that ratcheted up Twyla's anxiety for reasons she could not identify.

"Meaning?"

"Meaning I wasn't surprised that the professor asked you to dinner. I was surprised that you said yes. I can think of at least four men who have asked you out over the years, and you turned them all down. I kind of assumed that you'd taken yourself out of the game, but I guess not."

He picked the head off a gray tuft flower and rubbed it with his thumb, sending the seedlings billowing through the air.

"In your defense," said Twyla, "the whole thing has taken me by surprise, too."

He stopped suddenly, took her hand in his, and stared at their joined hands as he spoke.

"I don't say this often enough, but your friendship means the world to me. I wouldn't do anything to jeopardize what we have. I hope you know that."

"I do. And I feel the same way."

He finally met her eye. "That was my long-winded way of saying I'm sorry, by the way."

"And I forgave you before you even opened your mouth."

Frank released her hand, draped an arm over her shoulders, and began to haul her toward the barracks. "You'd better move along. Rumor has it you have a hot date tonight."

"I don't know about that. I'm going to have to take your duck to get home, since you drove this time. I hope that's okay."

"Of course. The keys are in my pack."

She touched his fingertips, which dangled from her shoulder. "I hate leaving you alone like this."

"I'm not alone. I have Mary Georgina. Right, darlin'?"

It took Twyla a minute to realize that he had called the dragon *darlin'*, not her, and she was mildly offended. Then again, she, of all people, knew how easy it was to be lonely, even with a baby clinging to you.

Since there were no nimkilim boxes inside Tanria, Twyla offered to take Frank's response to Lu and Annie's letter and slide it into the nimkilim box at the station for him.

She also offered to give Duckers a ride to his apartment since their tours ended at the same time, but Zeddie Birdsall was waiting for him in the parking lot. The youngest of the Birdsall siblings leaned against the family's old autoduck, his golden curls and pretty green eyes and poreless tawny skin screaming, *I am young and beautiful!*

It was for the best that Zeddie had come to pick up Duckers; Twyla needed the solo drive to Eternity to process all that had happened on this tour. Dragons and romance were two things she had not envisioned in her future ten days ago, and now both had fallen into her lap. She felt a twinge of remorse for leaving

Frank—and driving his duck home without him—but she was also looking forward to a peaceful several days in her quiet house. After her date that evening.

Home at last, she put her key in the lock, but there was no answering *click* of the bolt when she turned it, which meant the door was already unlocked. She heard a familiar commotion coming from inside the house—*her* house—and she sent a silent prayer to the Mother of Sorrows before opening the door. Her grandson Sal was singing a full-throated rendition of the children's song "Now I Know My New Gods" while jumping on her sofa, which had been denuded of its cushions. Each time his bare feet hit the springs, she swore she could hear her sofa cry for mercy. Wade's oldest son, Manny, was lying on the aforementioned cushions, which had been cast to the floor and were now surrounded by a sea of spilled Cheezykin crackers, some intact, some pulverized into orange crumbs. Manny's face was hidden behind, of all things, one of Twyla's more salacious romance novels, which, at age nine, he could neither understand nor appreciate (or so she hoped). He shouted "Would you shut up, Sal? I'm trying to read!" to which Sal retorted, rather predictably, "*You* shut up!" From somewhere deeper inside the house, possibly her bedroom, Twyla could hear Teo pitching a fit and Wade's helpless pleading with him to "Stop touching the poo! Don't touch! Poopy no-no!"

Twyla hoped she would not have to wash toddler poo out of her coverlet. She turned to the family altar beside the front door, dipped her fingers in the teal-colored porcelain dish that had once belonged to her late husband's grandmother, and touched salt water to Doug's key. "It's just like old times, honey," she told him before tackling the uphill battle that was getting Sal Banneker Padilla in line. By the time Wade emerged from her bedroom with a tear-damp Teo in his arms, Twyla had marshaled Sal into putting her sofa back together, while Manny clumsily swept the floor.

"Mom! You're finally home!"

"Hi, honey." She went to hug her son, but he mistook the gesture as an offering of help and dumped the child into her outstretched arms.

"Wammy," said Teo with a tiny-toothed smile. Manny had called her Wammy in his infancy, and the name stuck. All the grandkids called her Wammy now.

She kissed Teo's big black curls with a loud *mwah-mwah-mwah* and inhaled his milky scent. "How's my sweet Teo?"

In reply, he sucked the middle two fingers of his left hand and mouth-breathed on her neck as he lodged the fingers of his right hand into her hair above her forehead. His diaper was already loose beneath the soaker, and since Twyla did not want Teo to leak on her person or on her floor, she took him to the guest room, where she had a changing station already set up and had for years, and why didn't Wade know this?

"Not that I'm not thrilled to see all of you," she lied to her son as he followed her, "but why are you here?"

"Anita's grandma isn't doing so hot. Her mom said she needed to come home to say goodbye."

"Oh no!" Twyla exclaimed in all sincerity, but in the privacy of her mind, she fretted over the fact that Wade referred to Herington as his wife's hometown when they had been married for eleven years, and Anita had been living in Eternity for twelve.

"The guys and I are going on a camping trip. The duck's already packed and everything. We've had it planned for weeks. Can you watch the kids today and tomorrow?"

The fact that he was packed and ready to go indicated that he took her affirmative answer as a foregone conclusion.

"But I can't tonight," she said, even as she felt herself caving.

Setting boundaries had never been her strong suit, an unfortunate truth that bit her in the butt with frequency.

Speaking of butts, she thought as she regarded Wade's shoddy handiwork in cleaning up Teo. She reached for one of the washcloths she kept by the changing area and sent her son off to get it damp.

"Mom, please?" Wade begged from the bathroom. "The guys are waiting for me. We're supposed to get to the lake before sundown to set up camp, and then we're fishing first thing in the morning."

Wade returned with the washcloth, which was dripping wet and cold. Teo squealed in surprise when Twyla touched the cloth to his poor bum.

"Honey, I have plans."

"What plans could you possibly have that you couldn't cancel?"

"For your information, I have a date."

He burst out laughing, clapping his hands as if he were applauding a particularly good performance. When Twyla did not join him in his mirth and when her typically clueless second child finally noticed that she was pissed off, he said, "Wait, you're not kidding?"

"Why does everyone think I am incapable of dating?"

"Because it's unnatural. Fifty-five-year-old ladies with grandkids don't date." He shuddered.

"I'm only fifty-three, and last time I checked, I'm not dead yet."

She pinned the diaper, pulled up the wool soaker, and handed Wade his child so that she could wring out the washcloth in the bathroom sink and put it in the laundry. She returned to the parlor in time to see her son set down his youngest to toddle on the floor. Teo made a beeline for a stray Cheezykin. Twyla lunged and snatched him up before he could stuff the dirty orange cracker in his mouth.

Sal and Manny burst into the parlor through the kitchen door, Manny holding the box of snack cakes that Twyla kept on the top shelf of her pantry. There was no way they could have reached it without standing on a chair, so she sent up a prayer of thanks to the Bride of Fortune that neither of them had broken their necks in their attempts to retrieve the sugary loot.

"Wammy! Can we have one?"

"Yeah, go ahead," Wade answered for her.

"Can I have two?" asked Sal, a master of angling for more than was on offer.

Once again, Wade beat Twyla to the punch. "Sure," he said, blissfully unaware of sugar's effect on the children, whom he persevered in assuming Twyla would babysit that evening.

Manny and Sal looked at each other, their eyes wide in disbelief. Twyla barely had enough time to holler "Eat them in the kitchen!" before they took off running with the unopened box of snack cakes, knowing that what Dad giveth, Wammy might taketh away. Twyla was about to follow after them to limit them to one each, when Wade spied the novel Manny had been reading on the lamp table. He gaped at the half-clothed couple in old-fashioned clothes who were clinched together in a passionate embrace on the cover, and read the title aloud in a stilted voice.

"*The Rogue of Redwing Ruins*. Salt Sea, Mom, is this the sort of thing you leave out when the kids are around?"

"Give me that!" She snatched the paperback from his hands, feeling ashamed of herself both for enjoying a good, sexy romance and for letting her offspring scold her about it in her own house.

Pivoting like the professional callow fellow he was, Wade asked, "Can I have a snack cake, too?"

"Go ahead. At least that way the kids won't wolf down the entire box."

"Thanks!"

He followed his two oldest sons into the kitchen, leaving Twyla in the parlor with an armful of toddler and the urge to cry. She tried to wrest *The Rogue of Redwing Ruins* from her grandson, but Teo had a death grip on it and squawked like an angry parrot when she tried to tug it free of his grasp. Giving up, she went to her bedroom to check on the state of her coverlet.

"Did you get poo on Wammy's bed?"

"Wammy!" he answered, and gnawed on the corner of the book as Twyla inspected the damage.

"It's not as bad as I thought it would be, but ick."

Making a mental note to chuck the coverlet into the hamper at the earliest opportunity, she returned to the parlor in time to see Sal wrestling Manny to the floor and smashing a frosting-filled snack cake into the side of his face, with Wade nowhere in sight.

"Boys!" shouted Twyla. "Where is your father?"

Wade appeared in the kitchen doorframe, shoving a cake into his mouth. "Mom, they're fine. See? They're laughing."

"And making a wreck of my house!"

"Calm down."

Maybe it was the exhaustion of coming off a difficult tour; or maybe it was a middle-aged woman's lack of sleep; or maybe it was the way everyone seemed to dismiss her hopes and dreams and needs as if she were barely human at all; or maybe it was the sensation that no matter how much she gave to her family, it would never be enough, and that every time she thought she was empty, she'd dig a little deeper and find a little more of herself to fork over. Whatever the reason, her patience snapped like a worn pistol crossbow string, and she fired a seething retort at her son before her better judgment could stop her. "Do not tell me to calm down in my own fucking home!"

Twyla was not one to drop an f-bomb—certainly not in the presence of children—as evidenced by the shock waves that ensued. Wade coughed so hard on his snack cake, he launched half-masticated doughy bits in a three-foot radius, and Manny and Sal dissolved into giggling fits, squealing "Wammy said *f*!" to each other in unadulterated delight.

Into this chaos walked Hope Banneker, stepping through the front door with a mustard-yellow hard-shell suitcase in hand and blue eyes alight with amusement.

"Hi," she said, humor bubbling in her throat as she took in the pandemonium of the parlor. Her friend Everett peeked his head in, as if he were a turtle that might duck into his shell if the environment proved too dangerous.

"Honey!" Twyla surged forward and extended her free arm to hug her daughter. Everett hovered on the doorstep behind her, a bespectacled man in his midtwenties wearing his Allgodsday best. He smoothed the front of his jacket with one long, graceful hand and clutched a bouquet of daisies in the other.

"Hi, Twyla," he said with a wave. An uncertain smile plastered itself across his face as he peered over Hope's shoulder to watch Manny and Sal roll with laughter on the floor, screeching, "Wammy said *f*!"

"Everett! So good to see you. And my, don't you look dashing today." Twyla smiled at him, even as her mind whirred into a hostess's panic. If she put the boys in DJ and Wade's old room, she could borrow Frank's inflatable mattress and have Hope and Everett sleep in the same room, if neither of them minded. Or maybe Twyla could sleep on the couch and let Everett have her room? Could she spot clean the coverlet in time?

She realized that she was smiling blankly at Hope's friend, whose own smile was beginning to show signs of panic.

"What am I doing? Come in! Come in!" She stepped aside to let Everett through the door. Teo remained in her arms, contentedly sucking on the book. Twyla looked to her son, who was shoving yet another cake into his mouth. "Wade, come get the luggage."

"I need to get going."

"If you have time for snack cakes, you have time to be helpful."

He rolled his eyes but obeyed. "Hey, Sis. Hey, man." He hugged Hope and shook Everett's hand before he took their suitcases.

"You're early. I thought you weren't coming until Wisdomsday."

"I know, but we were both finished with finals, and it's cheaper to take the Sorrowsday ferry. I thought you wouldn't mind."

"Of course I don't mind. I'm so glad you're home. And that you brought Everett with you."

"That's good, because, as it turns out..." Hope's eyes went soft as she touched Everett's arm, and he smiled shyly at her. "We're getting married."

Twyla blinked at her daughter in stunned silence.

Married.

She blinked again.

Married?

Married?

"I know this is sudden, but I hope it's good news?" said Everett, his voice cracking, and Twyla realized that she was being unpardonably rude, when Hope was the one who had failed to inform her of the most important thing going on in her life.

"Don't be silly!" She hugged Everett. "Welcome to the family!"

"Thank you," he breathed in relief.

"I couldn't be more thrilled!"

But Twyla was not thrilled, although she had no idea why. She loved Everett. She ought to be thrilled.

She stood back and squeezed his hand to make him real, to make all of this real, but she couldn't seem to get her bearings. How could Hope be getting married? She glanced at the family altar, where Doug's key glinted, damp from the salt water she had pressed against the metal.

"Congrats, Sis," Wade told Hope, granting her a rare, brotherly hug.

"Thank you." Hope turned to Twyla, expectant.

"This is wonderful!" said Twyla, trying to sound convincing as she hugged her daughter.

Hope beamed at her mother before leaning down to kiss Teo's curls with a loud *mwah-mwah-mwah*. She raised an eyebrow when she saw the book in his hands. "*The Rogue of Redwing Ruins*, huh? You must be a very advanced reader, kiddo."

"Don't get your brother started," muttered Twyla.

There was a rapping at the open front door. Quill, dressed in a dapper tweed suit, peeked into the parlor.

"Hallo? Am I too early?"

Twyla hung her head. "Mother of Sorrows."

Teo grinned at Quill and repeated, loudly, the one new word he had acquired that day: "Fucking!"

Chapter Eight

Throughout dinner, Quill and Everett kept up a steady stream of conversation with each other, and only with each other, in the way that nervous men who have no idea how to interact with children cling to one another like mutual rescue buoys on the open sea. Meanwhile, Twyla spent the meal begging Manny to eat something, anything; trying to get Sal to stop shooting meatballs at his older brother via his spoon trebuchet; and wiping spaghetti sauce off Teo's face and hands (and the wall). But once the older two boys got wind of the fact that Wammy's dinner guest with the funny accent studied dragon fossils for a living, they lost their ever-loving minds and peppered him with questions for the rest of dinner, all of which Quill answered with growing pleasure.

With Quill and the boys deep in discussion, Twyla studied Hope and Everett, who were in an oblivious lovers' bubble across the table. She tried to remember what it was like, the first flush of love, when all you could see was everything that was good and right about the other person.

The couple looked great together, that was certain. Hope had grown into a lovely young woman. She had inherited Doug's height, with the slim athletic build of a person who enjoyed running. Her blond hair, a gift from her paternal grandmother, framed a pretty oval face that went tan in the summer. Of all Twyla's children, Hope was the one who most resembled Doug, for which Twyla was oddly grateful. Hope's loveliness was a reminder of Doug's golden youth, of the time when he had been young and handsome and full of promise.

Everett Simms was tall and wiry, with the sharp jawline of the young and fit. With his clean good looks and his polite demeanor, he had the makings of a classy, competent doctor. He was Twyla's favorite of all the friends Hope had made since leaving home. So why did she feel anything less than happy that her daughter was marrying this truly decent young man?

She wanted to ask what had happened, how and when they had gone from being friends to being ready to link their lives together permanently. But she didn't want to cause any awkwardness for Hope by revealing she had known nothing of their romance until shortly before six o'clock this evening.

Then again, whose fault was that?

"So, Dr. Vanderlinden," Hope said conversationally, dragging Twyla out of her moody thoughts.

"Do call me Quill. No need to stand upon ceremony among friends."

"Is that what you and my mom are? Friends?"

Quill's polite smile showed signs of trepidation. "I'd like to think so. We've only known each other a short time."

"And how long is that exactly?"

Twyla did not fail to notice Everett's hand tighten on her daughter's. His own smile also showed signs of trepidation.

What was this? Had Hope decided it was her place to grill Twyla's date? That was rich. Suddenly, Twyla did not care whether she made things awkward for her daughter or not.

"Quill is carrying out research inside Tanria. We met last week. So, honey, when did you get engaged?"

"Last Wardensday. He asked me under the altar of the sky in the park where we first realized we were perfect for each other."

Hope and Everett shared a gooey look that should have warmed Twyla's heart.

It did not.

"And how long ago was that exactly?" Twyla pressed, deliberately mirroring her daughter's question to Quill.

Now it was Hope's turn to squeeze Everett's hand. Her expression was more gritted teeth than smile. "A few weeks ago."

A few weeks? A few weeks was nothing. It certainly wasn't the basis for marriage. Twyla nearly said as much, but then she caught sight of poor Everett, who appeared to be sweating bullets. He ran a finger under his collar as if the bow tie were choking him. She decided her best option was to shut her mouth and excuse herself and put Teo to bed, after which she could get to work on the dinner dishes. Manny and Sal took this as permission to get into the hall closet where Twyla kept the board games. By the time she had a sink full of sudsy water, Quill's and Everett's respective competitive streaks had come roaring to life, as evidenced by the cacophony in the next room. Given Quill's cutthroat approach to Candy Cane Mystery, Twyla wondered why he'd been so hesitant to play Gods and Heroes with her and Frank and Duckers when, clearly, he was game. Literally.

Alone in the kitchen, Twyla took a beer out of the fridge and raised a toast to herself, the woman who had had to scrounge up enough food in her bare-bones pantry to cook spaghetti dinner for a large crowd when she had not anticipated having to make dinner at all that evening, the one who had to change Teo's diapers and make sure the kids were eating decently and behaving themselves, the one who was now cleaning up the kitchen while everyone else was laughing in the next room.

She could hear the dulcet tones of Quill's voice as he, in the role of Miss Meringue, accused Professor Chocolate Chip of stealing cookies in the dining room, to which Hope—a.k.a. Professor

Chocolate Chip—shouted in mock outrage, to the amusement of Everett and Manny and Sal—a.k.a. Princess Jelly Bean, Mr. Pudding, and Captain Jack Jam Tarts. As Twyla took another swig of beer, she thought of Frank, stuck in Sector W-14 with Mary Georgina. Frank had always been good about rallying the troops to help clean up before the board games came out, even in the days when Doug was alive and Frank and Cora were married and the Bannekers and the Ellises would sometimes have cookouts together. Without him, it was too much effort for Twyla to oversee everyone else's cleaning up while doing a huge chunk of what needed doing herself.

As if in answer to her prayer to the Mother of Sorrows, Hope appeared in the kitchen doorway.

"Need help?"

Normally, Twyla would have been thrilled with the offer of assistance, but for the first time in twenty-three years, she had no idea what to say to her daughter. She couldn't sort out her own feelings at all, and she was certain that Hope would not appreciate her lack of enthusiasm. No, it was best if they didn't talk about the engagement tonight. She held up a soapy plate and said, "I've got this. You should go spend time with Everett."

"I'm afraid Princess Jelly Bean teamed up with your *friend* to defeat Professor Chocolate Chip, so I'm available to dry dishes."

Twyla did not miss the snarky emphasis on the word *friend*. She clamped her lips shut before she said something biting in return.

Hope grabbed an ancient dish towel from the drawer where the ancient dish towels had lived since they were brand-new and took her place beside her mother at the kitchen sink. But Twyla could sense that the dish drying was a front. Hope wanted to press the issue, while Twyla was too hurt and annoyed and tired to talk about it.

"Quill seems nice."

"He is."

"So he's your... what? Boyfriend? Man friend?"

"No. We were supposed to go out to dinner tonight, that's all." She handed Hope a clean plate to dry.

"Why didn't you?"

Twyla gave Hope a flat stare before motioning to the dining room in answer.

Hope shook her head as she dried. "You could have gone, you know? Everett and I are adults. We can handle the kids."

"I'm not going to make a guest babysit the second he walks in the door."

"Everett isn't a guest. He's family now."

"Right. Since last Wardensday. Or are we counting the handful of weeks you've been dating without mentioning it to me?" Twyla was about to hand the next plate to her daughter, but it slipped out of her hand and landed in the sink, sending a spray of water all over Twyla's apron.

"Is that too little time or too much?"

"Both? Neither? I don't know."

"Mom," Hope said in a warning tone.

Twyla did not appreciate the warning tone.

"What?"

"Why are you being weird about this?"

"I'm not!" She handed Hope the clean plate, or it might be more accurate to say that she shoved the plate into her daughter's waiting dish towel.

"Everett's the one."

"I didn't say he wasn't."

"You're implying it."

"I am not implying anything. Stop putting words in my mouth."

"Then put your own words in your mouth instead of hiding out in the kitchen so you don't have to talk to me."

"It took me by surprise. That's all." It was an echo of the words Frank had said to her a few hours ago when she'd told him about the date with Quill. The memory softened her. Hope was sharing good news with her; she ought to celebrate, not pitch a fit like a selfish child. She grabbed another dish towel out of the drawer and dried her hands so that she could give her daughter a proper hug. Hope sniffled over her shoulder, and Twyla squeezed her harder.

"I'm happy for you," she said, and she did her best to mean it.

"Are you sure?"

"Of course I'm sure."

"Because you don't sound happy."

"I am. You know I love Everett to bits." That much was true. That much she could say with complete honesty. Twyla had absolutely nothing against the lovely young man her daughter had decided to marry.

"He's wonderful."

"I completely agree." Twyla gave Hope one more squeeze and relinquished her. "I hate to be awkward here, but since you're staying in the same room, I have to ask: You're using protection, aren't you?"

"Mom!"

"Well?"

"Yes."

"Thank you."

Hope narrowed her eyes, and a sly smile crossed her face. "What about you and your cute, tweedy new boyfriend? Are you using protection?"

Twyla blushed so hard it was a wonder the town's fire marshal didn't knock on her door. "He's not my...! We're not...! Oh my gods, go back to the dining room before your nephews upend the place."

"Okay, but you do realize that you completely undermined your own date tonight to be all freaky-deaky about my engagement, right?"

"I did not!"

"You did too!"

Twyla all but pushed her smirking daughter into the next room while she finished up in the kitchen. An hour later, she ushered Manny and Sal into her boys' old bedroom to go to sleep, a process that took an inordinate amount of time and glasses of water and stories, while Quill sat with Hope and Everett in the parlor, waiting for her.

Frank would have helped, she thought, words that popped into her head unbidden. But of course Frank would have helped put the boys to bed; he'd known them since birth. Hope had, too, obviously, but it would have been rude of her to leave Everett alone. And why should Quill help when he was her guest, not a babysitter?

Quill. What must he think of her after the debacle that was their first date?

She went to the kitchen before heading to the parlor to see what kind of drinks she could scrounge up for the adults. They had already polished off a dusty bottle of wine, which was the classiest option she had had on hand. She remembered Dr. Sellet offering Quill a brandy, and Quill did strike her as a brandy drinker, but Twyla didn't have any. She was fairly sure she'd never had brandy in her life. What she had was half a bottle of whiskey, a fairly new bottle of gin, and three bottles of beer. Hope and Everett took her up on the beer, and to her surprise, so did Quill.

"Aren't you having any?" he asked her when she handed him the last bottle and sat in the chair next to his. Hope and Everett had taken the sofa, which meant that Twyla didn't have to face the dilemma of figuring out where to sit on a sofa in relation to Quill.

"I had a beer when I was washing dishes," she admitted.

He raised his bottle to her. "Much deserved."

"To Twyla," said Everett, raising his own beer.

"To Twyla," Hope and Quill agreed, causing the recipient of the toast to squirm with pleased embarrassment.

"And to the happy couple," Quill toasted Hope and Everett, and Twyla forced herself to sound overjoyed as she repeated "To the happy couple!" with no drink in her hand.

As the evening drew to a close, Quill stood to make his exit. Twyla walked him out to his autoduck—an autoduck that, upon further inspection, revealed itself to be a staggeringly expensive make and model. Twyla had never stood so close to a duck that swanky, and she was struck speechless.

"I had a lovely evening," Quill said, holding his tweed jacket casually over his shoulder.

"Too bad our dinner plans turned into a night at the zoo. You handled the dramatic change in itinerary with good grace. Thank you."

"I assure you, it was my pleasure. Twyla." He added her name at the end, giving it its own weight and importance in a way that made Twyla's face heat. She had blushed more in the past twenty-four hours than she had in the past five years.

Quill draped his jacket over his arm and took a step closer, gazing at Twyla through his long eyelashes. It had been a long, long time since a man had looked at her like that.

"Twyla?"

"Yes?"

"May I kiss you?"

"I'm a little out of practice."

"I suspect that will not make a bit of difference." He leaned in close, so close, and Twyla stopped breathing. "May I?"

"Yes," she whispered.

And he kissed her.

And it was nice.

Not life altering or earth shattering. But pleasant.

"Perhaps we could take a rain check on that dinner," he said when the kiss was done.

"Yes, please."

"I'm leaving first thing in the morning, but I hope to return by Wardensday. Are you free that evening?"

"As long as my family doesn't descend upon me unannounced again, yes."

"Excellent."

He kissed her again—a sweet peck this time—got into his ludicrously fancy duck, and drove away.

Everett stayed for two nights before leaving for a summer internship near his home in the Redwing Islands. During his one full day in town, Hope took him to all her old haunts around Eternity, which meant that Twyla didn't have much opportunity to talk with him. Part of her wanted to get to know him better, while another part of her wanted to stick her head in the sand and pretend he wasn't there.

She wished she could figure out why Hope's engagement news had thrown her for such a loop. She hadn't reacted this way when her sons got engaged.

Once Everett departed, Hope started picking up hours at Wilner's Green Grocer, where she had worked every summer since she was sixteen, and she and Twyla fell into their old routine in the house on Cottonwood Street. Twyla did the housework and all the usual errands she ran when she was off duty, and made sure there was dinner on the table when Hope got home from work. In the evening, they read in the parlor. One night, they walked to Main Street to get ice cream. Another night, they painted each other's toenails.

And yet tension hung in the air. Twyla's inarticulate and unarticulated worries about Hope swirled inside her head at all times. She wished she could put into words this gnawing concern and anger—yes, anger—but she didn't understand it herself yet. And so it festered.

On Wardensday evening, Hope got home from Wilner's as Twyla was dithering over what to wear on her date.

"No and no," Hope declared upon seeing the two options Twyla had laid out on the bed. "And also no," she added, pointing at the blue sheath dress Twyla was wearing.

Twyla looked in the full-length mirror on her closet door. "What's wrong with this?"

"It's perfect if you're going to a tea party or a funeral."

"All of these outfits are perfectly fine," said Twyla, even though she herself had been agonizing over them all of three minutes ago.

"Mom. Fine ain't gonna cut it tonight. Show some skin, for gods' sakes." By now, Hope was half-buried in Twyla's closet, examining each article of clothing in turn with a *screech, screech, screech* of hangers on the metal rail.

"My skin has seen better days, honey. No one wants to see more of it."

"Says you. Here." She tossed Twyla's one and only pair of dressy black pants over her shoulder. Twyla caught them in the nick of time before they hit the floor.

"Hold on. I've got the perfect blouse." Hope zipped out of the room as Twyla took off the offending outfit and put on the pants, which were too snug in her opinion. Hope returned with a slinky, silky, sleeveless white top. She pulled up short when she saw Twyla standing there in the pair of black pants and her brassiere.

"Mom, no. No."

"What?"

"Your brassiere."

Twyla looked down at the serviceable boob-colored cups. "What's wrong with it?"

"The gods have blessed you with cleavage. Let's lift those girls up!" Hope clapped her hands twice, as if the sound would cause Twyla's breasts to stand to perky attention.

"I'd need a crane to lift these girls. When you're my age, you'll understand that comfort is so much more important than cleavage."

"I will only understand that when I am dead." Hope began rifling through Twyla's lingerie drawer, uttering squeaks of scandalized horror. Twyla was also uttering squeaks of scandalized horror, mostly because her daughter was making a giant mess of her carefully folded underwear.

"This!" cried Hope, holding up a brassiere whose existence Twyla had forgotten, a pretty underwire confection with lace that she had bought in a moment of low self-esteem after coming to terms with the fact that the twenty-five pounds she had put on since age forty weren't going anywhere.

"I'm not even sure that fits."

"It is the only acceptable option here. I don't make the rules. Dare I ask what panties you're wearing?"

"What does it matter?"

"A woman is only as sexy as her underwear."

"That is a disgusting double standard. Would you say any of this to a man? Why am I sending you to college?"

"You're wearing cotton granny panties, aren't you?"

Twyla sniffed. "Every woman should wear cotton granny

panties. Wedgies are unacceptable. Comfortable underwear is our gods-given right."

"Thank Grandmother Wisdom you were smart enough to buy the matching panties when you got the brassiere. Put these on. Do not argue with me." Hope shot the panties at Twyla like a slingshot.

Twyla couldn't believe she was putting up with such abuse from her own daughter, but then again, Hope knew a lot more about dating than Twyla did. Obediently, she changed into the lacy bra and panties and pulled on the blouse.

"Look who's sexy sexy-pants now!" crowed Hope as Twyla gaped at her reflection. Her hips were way too bumpy under the fabric of the black pants, and her underwear was already going up her ass crack. The underwire of her impractical brassiere cut into the flesh under her boobs, and the cowl neck of the slinky top revealed far more cleavage than Twyla was comfortable with.

"Honey, I don't know about this," she said doubtfully.

"Trust me. And you're wearing heels, by the way."

"I only wear heels to weddings and funerals."

"And now you also wear them on hot dates."

Twyla owned only one pair of dress shoes: tan leather Mary Janes with sensible two-inch heels. When she had bought them— gods, how many years ago was it?—she had thought them comfortable. Now they were torture devices strapped to her feet.

"Do these even match this outfit?" she asked Hope dubiously.

"The tan leather with the black pants? Super classy."

Hope dragged Twyla into the hall bathroom and made her mother sit on the toilet while she got to work on her makeup.

"My gods, woman, do you have any idea how foxy you look when you actually put on eyeliner?"

"I've always been terrible at makeup," said Twyla, who didn't love the sensation of having a pointy object poking around her face so close to her eyeballs.

"Fortunately, you have me, a self-taught artist, since my mother never bothered to teach me how to do this stuff."

"You don't need it. You're perfect without it."

"Says the woman who is not biased at all."

"I'm not. My daughter is beautiful."

Hope kissed the tip of Twyla's nose and commanded her to close her eyes. Twyla obeyed and felt the complex maneuvers of her daughter's makeup brush feathering over her eyelids.

"So, out of curiosity, how does Frank feel about you dating?"

"Why should Frank care about my love life?"

The motions of the brush stopped, and when Hope didn't answer her, Twyla opened her eyes. Her daughter stared at her with a skeptical pursing of her lips.

"What's that look about?"

"I don't mean to pry, but I always assumed you and Frank were good friends."

"We are."

"*Really* good friends."

"We are."

"With benefits."

"With...? What? No!"

"If you say so. Close your eyes."

"I do say so," Twyla huffed, but she closed her eyes obediently.

She didn't know what to make of Hope's line of questioning. Obviously, she and Frank had taken romance off the table from day one. That sort of thing ruined friendships, which was the last thing either of them wanted. And yet even now, Twyla could hear the shock and anger in his voice when she'd told him about the date, the way he'd taken offense to the very idea before he'd calmed down and apologized. But he had been surprised, not jealous.

Hadn't he?

Twyla was relieved when, several minutes and many products later, Hope said, "There. Have a look."

She stepped aside so that Twyla could stand up and study her reflection in the mirror. The makeup made her look younger and prettier than she was. And yet that face did not look right to her, did not resemble the person she was in reality. The smoky eyes and black lashes and dark lips belonged to a woman who was not her.

"Do you think the lipstick is too much?" she asked, watching her maroon lips form the words in the mirror.

"No, I think the lipstick is sexy as all get-out, and I'm putting it in your purse—that cute clutch, not your worn-out Mom Bag."

Twyla wrung her hands as she turned to her daughter. "I never know where to put the clutch."

"Set it on an empty chair."

"And nothing fits in the clutch."

"Except for your compact and a tube of lipstick, which is all you need tonight, because you can't tell me Professor Hot Tweed isn't paying."

"I don't know how I feel about that."

"I think you should feel pretty great about that." Hope put her arm around Twyla's waist and gave her an affectionate shake.

"But—"

"Mom, let this classy man take you out in style and treat you like the god you are. And feel free to bring him home."

"Bring him—oh! How can you...? I am not bringing a man home on our first real date."

"Why not?"

"Because!"

"When was the last time you got it on with a living, breathing human being?"

Twyla was mortified to be having this conversation with her

daughter. Hope might be twenty-three years old, but she was still Twyla's baby. "I am not answering that."

"If the answer is thirteen years, that is a crying shame." Hope turned Twyla toward the mirror, forcing her mother to look at her made-up self. "You deserve sexy times, Twyla Banneker."

"Even if I was going to have 'sexy times' with a man on our first date—second date?—I wouldn't bring him home with my daughter in the house."

"He's got a hotel room, doesn't he?"

"Hope!"

"I'm not waiting up for you. That's all I'm saying."

A knock came at the front door.

"Good, there he is!" Hope pushed her mother out of the bathroom and into the parlor and opened the front door before Twyla had so much as a second to mentally prepare herself.

"Quill, hello!" said Hope too ebulliently. "Come in!"

Once again, he was dressed in a way only a truly rich and dapper man could pull off. He wore a tweed sports coat over a camel sweater vest over a gray-and-white striped shirt. The dark gray tie knotted at his neck and the brown pocket square with a red-and-gold pattern on it should not have matched the jacket and shirt and vest, and yet they did. His hair was neatly pomaded, his beard trimmed. She had never stood so close to a man who was this well groomed, much less gone on a date with one. She felt positively shabby in her aging prêt-à-porter pants and her daughter's borrowed top.

"You look marvelous." He leaned in to kiss her cheek and handed her a bouquet of lilies of the valley and delphiniums and peonies.

"How lovely!" said Twyla. She had never received such an expensive bouquet of flowers, the sort that came from an actual florist's shop. Doug used to pick up a ready-made bunch of daisies for their anniversary, but since he bought the flowers at Wilner's Green Grocer, usually from Twyla at the checkout counter, they had never seemed terribly romantic.

"I'll put them in a vase. You kids scoot along and have fun." Hope plucked the bouquet from Twyla and disappeared into the kitchen, leaving Twyla alone with Quill and her own fraught nerves.

"Shall we?" said Quill, gesturing for her to cross in front of him out the front door. He put his hand at the small of her back to walk her to his waiting autoduck, and it all felt incredibly gentlemanly.

The duck looked even more intimidatingly luxurious in the evening sunlight, a compact model with a polished olive-green exterior composed of aesthetically glorious lines and curves. When he opened the passenger-side door for her, she saw that there were two bucket seats upholstered in tan leather rather than the typical bench found in more economical models. She was so impressed by the fact that a man had opened a door for her that she sank into the seat without thinking much of it. It wasn't until the leather had enveloped her in sumptuousness and Quill had shut the door that she worried that she might accidentally sully the interior of the duck with her mere presence.

You didn't roll in mud to get ready, she reminded herself. She deserved to have some fun tonight. She had earned a little pampering, for gods' sakes.

Quill came around to his side and sat behind the wheel. The leather of his seat made a satisfying leathery *poof* as it hugged his posterior, and his door shut with an expensive, muted *whump* rather than the thunderous slam of Twyla's autoduck doors. "I have been informed that Proserpina's is the place to take a beautiful woman to dinner," he said as he started up the engine, which purred to life.

Twyla experienced two knee-jerk responses to this statement:

1. *I'm not beautiful.*
2. *Proserpina's is way too expensive.*

She bit her lip against both of these assertions. Quill must find her at least moderately attractive, or he would not have asked her out. And if he wanted to spend money on a fancy dinner, she would not stop him.

"Is that all right?" he asked her.

"Proserpina's? I've never been."

"Then this will be a culinary adventure for both of us." He looked boyish as he grinned at her and put the duck in gear.

Proserpina's was located on Main Street in Argentine, the northernmost of the border towns that had popped up like mushrooms around the West Station over the past quarter century. The drive took only twenty-five minutes, but twenty-five minutes was an awfully long time when one was riding in a spotless and expensive vehicle with a man one barely knew. Somehow, Quill didn't strike her as someone who would burst into a campy song.

"So, Twyla Banneker," he said as he merged onto the highway. "What is your story?"

"Me? I don't have a story."

"Everyone has a story."

"If that's the case, mine is more like a children's picture book than a great work of literature."

"I doubt that. You said you were from Medora originally?"

"Yes, my parents are in Diamond Springs—Nancy and Chip Memford—and so is my brother, Greg."

"How long have you lived on Bushong?"

"Twenty-seven years, ever since the portals into Tanria opened."

"You've been with the marshals for twenty-seven years?"

"No, not even close. My husband moved us here. Wade—you

met Wade the other day—he was five at the time, and my oldest, Doug Jr., was six."

He kept his eyes on the road, but he raised his eyebrows. "I didn't realize you were married."

"Not anymore."

"I should hope not. That would make our dinner plans rather awkward."

She giggled nervously and inwardly berated herself for tittering like a green girl rather than behaving like a grown woman. "I'm widowed. My husband, Doug, sailed the Salt Sea thirteen years ago."

"I'm sorry to hear that."

"It is what it is."

"Why did he want to move to Bushong?"

"He had hoped to set up shop selling life insurance to the people pouring into Tanria."

"That makes sense, given the undead problem."

"I thought so, too, at the time. Unfortunately, Doug's ideas were better than his follow-through. He never made a go of it."

"Is that when you joined the marshals?"

"No, I worked nights and weekends at the local green grocer. By the time Doug passed away, my boys were mostly grown. DJ had already graduated high school and joined the Naval Guard, and Wade was working his way through trade school—he's a mechanic. But Hope was only ten years old, so it was tough for a few years. By the time she was in high school, she had started talking about going to college. I didn't know how I was going to afford it, until Frank came to my rescue."

"Marshal Ellis?"

"We've been friends for a long time and next-door neighbors for even longer. He knew my predicament, so when his partner retired from the force eight years ago, he recruited me. Now I make a decent salary, and Hope is in her second year of med school. In two years, I'll be fully vested, my daughter will be Dr. Banneker, and Frank and I can retire and open up a bed-and-breakfast on an equimaris ranch somewhere on the coast."

"Ah."

Quill truly had a knack for making the word *ah* say so much and yet so little. Even so, her muscles slowly began to unclench as she grew more comfortable in Quill's presence. She melted into the plush leather of the seat as they continued to chat, and soon enough, they arrived at Proserpina's.

Twyla nearly let herself out of the car, when she recalled that she was dating an actual gentleman this evening. She waited until he came around to the passenger side, opened the door for her, and handed her out of the duck. She couldn't decide if she liked this sort of formality. On the one hand, she enjoyed being treated as if she were a precious, worthwhile human being. On the other hand, she did not require assistance to open her own door and get out of the duck. In either case, she was not here to pass judgment; she was here to have a good time. And so far, she was, in fact, having a good time.

Twyla had no idea what to expect from a posh restaurant, as she had never been to one. The interior of Proserpina's was at once intimidating and comforting. The walls were painted dark blue, and the chairs were wood with plush green seats. Each table had a votive candle and a dark gold tablecloth draped over its surface. There were potted palms near the large windows on the east side of the building and old landscape paintings and vintage portraits of people and horses and dogs in ornate frames on the wall.

"Vanderlinden, party of two," Quill informed the maître d' at the front podium, a pale woman dressed in black with straight brown hair pulled into a tight ponytail. She consulted the notebook on the podium.

"Yes, this way, please," she said, leading them to a table near one of the windows. Quill held out Twyla's chair for her and helped her scoot close to the table. No one had ever held a chair for her, and she wasn't terribly sure how to navigate this social nicety. She managed to be seated without falling face-first onto the tabletop, so she decided to call that a win. The maître d' placed a small cardstock menu before each of them and left a black folder that turned out to be the drinks menu to the side.

Twyla had never been to a restaurant that featured only five items on the menu, and while she didn't know what half the ingredients were—*Girolles? Caciocavallo?*—she could read the price tag attached to each meal. She had spent most of her adult life clipping coupons and stretching her food budget in creative ways to feed her family, and here she was, ordering one plate of food that was equivalent in price to an entire week's worth of groceries.

It's too expensive, she thought in a panic, and a smaller, more insidious voice whispered, *You don't belong here.*

There, she stopped her spiraling thoughts. Why didn't she belong here? Why couldn't she have an extravagant meal? What if it were Frank sitting across the table from her? Would she feel out of place then? Was this really about food, or was it about the fact that she had no idea how to go about having a love life in her fifties? And why should she hide her nerves, when she could be perfectly...well...*frank* with the dashing dracologist having dinner with her?

"I'm very nervous," Twyla blurted out after the server brought her a glass of wine she couldn't pronounce and set a snifter of brandy in front of Quill. "I haven't been on a date since my husband died, and I don't know what I'm doing."

Quill took a fortifying gulp of brandy. "Is it barbaric of me to admit that I am glad to hear it? You seem so poised, and here I am, an absolute wreck."

Twyla grasped the stem of her wineglass as if it were a lifeline. "No kidding? You're nervous, too?"

"Incandescently so."

"*I* make *you* nervous?"

"You have no idea."

"But I'm only me."

"Exactly. You are you, a whip-smart Tanrian Marshal with a kind heart and a sense of humor who manages to balance a challenging career with a full and busy family life."

It was stunning to hear herself described this way, and by a man who had seen more of the world than she had. Most of the people Twyla regularly encountered thought of her as Doug's wife, the mother of three children, the sort of town matron who dutifully supplied cheesy potatoes at every funeral. But Quill knew her only as she was in the here and now, and he saw her as an independent woman who had her act together. She sat taller in her chair, feeling a tiny bit sexy in her slinky blouse and vivid lipstick.

She picked up her wineglass and studied him across the rim. "You seem so at ease. I assumed you were used to dating."

"I must admit that I have dated my fair share of women over the years. But as I have gotten older, I have found it all so much more difficult and tiring."

"Have you ever been married, if you don't mind my asking?"

"I don't mind at all, and no, I have not. Never found the right person to settle down with. And if I am being perfectly honest, marriage has not been at the top of my priorities. I often travel in my line of work, and my scholarly pursuits keep me busy for much of the time. It seemed unfair to inflict that life on another, and so I never put my mind to it—marriage, that is."

That was the swooniest statement Twyla had ever heard a man utter. Imagine giving consideration to how one's actions might affect another human being. Twyla resisted the urge to fan herself. And since he was speaking so openly, she thought it only fair to reciprocate.

"I've never been to college, you know," she admitted, bracing herself in case this was a deal-breaker for him. In the microsecond before he answered, she imagined him wincing and trying to hide the fact that he was wincing as she shriveled in shame on the inside.

"And you think that should matter to me?" he asked her.

Twyla saw no sign of wincing.

"You're a professor. At the best university in the Federated Islands."

"If you don't mind my saying so, it seems to me that you do not give yourself enough credit."

She thought of herself standing before the mirror in a sexy outfit, wearing makeup and worrying that she was not enough. "Maybe," she conceded.

"There are many kinds of learning. Tanria itself is an education, and a daunting one at that. I imagine motherhood is an education as well, and if it were a doctoral program, you would no doubt be dean of the department."

"You say that like I know what I'm doing."

"You do. I've met two of your children and three of your grandchildren. They are far more impressive than any article or book I have ever written."

This time, she really did fan herself, and Quill chuckled. He looked handsome by the votive's warm, flickering light. Maybe the candlelight flattered her, too. She began to enjoy herself. This was what she wanted, a lovely evening out with an interesting man who found her equally interesting. She asked him about his schooling and about dragons and how he came to study fossils and ancient texts recounting tales of the Old Gods' battle dragons.

They had finished most of the meal when Zeddie Birdsall came out from the kitchen to stop by their table and say hello.

"You must be Dr. Vanderlinden. Pen said I might see you this—Twyla?" Zeddie looked askance at her. "What are you doing here?"

"Having dinner?"

"Wait. *You're* the big date?"

Twyla laughed and turned to Quill. "So when you said you had been informed that Proserpina's was the place to take a beautiful woman to dinner, I'm guessing that Duckers was the one doing the informing?"

Quill raised his snifter. "Perhaps."

Zeddie extended a hand to the dracologist. "I'm Pen Duckers's boyfriend, Zeddie Birdsall, one of the sous-chefs here. He told me to keep an eye out for you."

There was a glint in his eye as he spoke, and Twyla was certain that Duckers had told him all about Professor Short-Shorts.

"Pleasure to make your acquaintance," said Quill.

"Likewise. So, Twyla, when did you and Frank break up?"

Quill's snifter froze halfway between the table and his mouth. Twyla stared at Zeddie in horror. "I think you have to date someone in order to break up with them."

"Weren't you two a thing?"

"No. Never. At any point in time."

"Huh. This is awkward." Zeddie coughed into his fist. "Would either of you like to see the dessert menu?"

"I think we'll take the check," said Quill.

"Righty-o." Zeddie grimaced an apology at Twyla and fled to the kitchen.

Feeling a need to salvage the situation, Twyla slid her hand across the table and was gratified when Quill placed his own over hers. "You know, Frank and I really are just friends."

"I don't imagine I would get to enjoy a lovely evening with you if you two were anything other than friends."

"Eh, if we were mortal enemies, you and I could probably go out for a couple of beers."

Quill laughed, the fine lines around his eyes and mouth crinkling with amusement.

Honesty had served Twyla well this evening, so after Quill helped her into his duck and took his place behind the wheel, Twyla admitted, "Your autoduck is so high-class, I was terrified to set foot in it when you came to pick me up."

"What is a duck for but to transport a person from one place to another?"

"Okay, but this is an amazing way to transport a person. How is it on the waterways? I bet it cuts through the sea like butter."

He cocked one roguish eyebrow at her. "Care to find out?"

"It's an hour's drive to the coast."

"I'm game if you are."

She was about to say no. The word hovered on the tip of her tongue. But then a voice in her head, one that sounded an awful lot like Hope, asked, *Why not?*

"All right."

"You're sure?"

"Let's do it."

He took the nearest exit heading west, the motor purring as the duck ate up the miles between land and sea. They talked of all sorts of things as they headed to the coast, the windows rolled down, the air growing saltier with each passing minute until Quill merged onto the waterway an hour later. The ocean stretched out before them, as vast as the sky above. They drove south, parallel to the coast, feeling the sea spray mist their arms as the duck plowed through the gentle waves.

When was the last time Twyla had driven on the sea, she

wondered? Not since she and Frank had decided to take a day trip to one of the outer islands when the kids were all in town. They had taken both of their ducks and Wade's besides, and they had packed them full of sandwiches and sodas and beer and bathing suits and floaties.

Why on earth didn't she come this way more often? The ocean was only an hour away from Eternity, and yet she always stayed where she was, living the same life she'd always lived.

Quill pulled off to the side of the waterway and cranked down the convertible roof, and they floated there on the sea, staring up at the stars—at all the gods who had come and gone before and ended their lives on the altar of the sky. The waves rolled beneath the duck, rocking them like children in a bassinet. Quill kissed her then, a soft beginning that grew hot and sharp. She knew he'd ask her to come to his hotel room, and she was prepared to tell him no. She thought about her extra pounds that weren't going anywhere, the flesh of her body that seemed to be oozing downward like a lava flow, the way her skin was becoming crepey, the incomprehensibility of any man finding her sexy. But then he kissed her again, kissed her with passion and with wanting, and for the second time that evening, she thought, *Why not?*

Chapter Nine

The second Quill drove her home the following morning, Twyla took off the torture devices that were her heels, but any aspirations she had of sneaking into her own house first thing Allgodsday morning without her daughter catching her were dashed when she found Hope waiting for her in the parlor, sipping a cup of coffee and smiling smugly. "Good morning, you lucky bitch."

"Language! Why do you kids think you can talk that way around me? I'm your mother, no matter how old you are."

"You're my mother, who was out all night with Professor Cute Accent. How was your walk of shame this morning?"

Twyla sniffed. "It's not a walk if someone drives you."

"Oh? Did he *drive* you?"

"I am not going to dignify that with a response."

"I hate to be awkward here, but since you're getting it on with Dr. Vanderlinden, I have to ask: You're using protection, aren't you?"

Twyla had never thought she'd have these particular words thrown back in her face. She needed an aspirin.

"You do realize I'm postmenopausal, right?"

"You do realize you can catch a venereal disease, right?"

"Fine! I was careful, Dr. Banneker! Happy now?"

"Yes. Was it good? Was it great?"

"Pfft. I am not discussing this with you." Twyla waved a hand through the air as if she could erase the entire conversation. "Are you coming with me to temple?"

"No. I have a shift at eleven, and also I don't want to."

"It wouldn't kill you to thank the gods of creation every now and again."

"Thank you, gods of creation!" Hope shouted at the ceiling.

"Heathen."

With that parting shot, one that did not affect her daughter in the least, Twyla went to her bedroom to get ready for temple. How different was her reflection in the closet mirror this morning compared to last night? Her black pants and borrowed top were wrinkled from having spent the night on a hotel room floor. Last night's eye makeup formed a pair of black half-moon smudges under her eyes, even though she had tried to wash off the mascara in Quill's bathroom at the hotel. Her hair, frizzy at the best of times, looked like she'd spent a couple of hours driving along the waterway with the top down, which, come to think of it, she had. And she was more than thrilled to remove the bra, which had made ruddy marks on her skin where it had dug into her middle-aged softness, not to mention the supposedly sexy underwear that was taking a ride in her crack. The miracle of it was that Dr. Quill Vanderlinden, professor of dracology at the University of Quindaro and son of the seventh Earl of Alcomworth, wanted this. And she had willingly given it. And she found that she did not regret it one single bit.

That would be fodder for meditation at the altar of a god.

She made herself presentable as quickly as she could and walked to All Gods Temple, where the devout population of Eternity filed in with their weekly offerings to the New Gods.

Twyla meandered down the center aisle, contemplating to which god she would make an offering today. The ceiling arching above her was painted deep black, with all the constellations depicted in soft white, a replica of the altar of the sky with the gods that had come and gone long before. It reminded her of riding in Quill's autoduck under the stars. In the center of the ceiling was the skylight that represented the Unknown God, the first of all the gods, their life the only life that would truly last forever in the Void Beyond the Sky.

Although the temple was crowded today, it was also quiet. Friends and neighbors might murmur hello to each other, but temple was a place for quiet reflection, not socializing.

There were many alcoves lining the long aisle of the building. The six largest were dedicated to the gods of life and death. Twyla usually prayed at the altar of the Mother of Sorrows, the god to whom one went to let go of one's hardships and be reminded of one's joys. But there were good reasons to pray to any and all of the gods.

After Doug died, Twyla had done the requisite mourning in the death gods' alcoves, but the gods of death had other qualities, too. As the god of doorways, the Warden was the deity of introspection and change, of looking to the past and the future. As the divine being who separated body and soul, Grandfather Bones was the god of peace and acceptance, of the fleetingness of all things. The Salt Sea was the god of journeys, of treading new paths and trying new things.

Even so, the faithful tended to drift toward the alcoves of the gods of life. In addition to the Mother of Sorrows, there were the Bride of Fortune and Grandmother Wisdom. The Bride of Fortune was the god of hope but also the god of balance, of finding positive in the negative. As the god of aging with grace and dignity, Grandmother Wisdom also guided the faithful through life's moral dilemmas, helping a person untie the knotty problems that kept them awake at night.

Twyla decided to pray in the alcove of Grandmother Wisdom

this morning. The marble-topped altar stood in front of a floor-to-ceiling mosaic depicting the god, an old woman who sat at a loom. Her many-colored threads snarled together in a tapestry of living complexity, a symbol of the beauty that could be found in facing life's complications. Twyla placed her offering—a cream cheese pastry she had picked up at the bakery on the way over—on the god's altar, then sat in one of the pews in the alcove to pray.

She had intended to mull over her evening with Quill, but instead, it was her daughter who came to the forefront of her mind. She thought of Hope, sitting on the couch with her cup of coffee, home for a few weeks before returning to the grind of medical school. Would she and Everett wait two years, when the world would know her as Dr. Banneker, before they tied the knot, or would they get married sooner?

Tying a knot. What an apt metaphor it was, to commit oneself to something that was easily done and extremely difficult to undo, especially once children were involved. Yes, Everett was kind and considerate, but he was also a man.

Speaking of men, Twyla said to Grandmother Wisdom in the privacy of her mind, turning her thoughts to Quill. She contemplated what had transpired in his hotel room, her self-consciousness in removing her clothes in front of someone who was not her husband, and his delicate and generous appreciation of her middle-aged body. She'd been so worried about what he would think of her that she had not concerned herself overly much with what she thought of him. In hindsight, she could better admire how his body had felt under her hands, lean muscles and coarse hair, so different from what she was used to, an entirely new landscape to explore.

And yet.

He had certainly demonstrated a finesse and self-assurance that were markedly different from Doug's style, which, over the course of two decades of married life, had not evolved much past their first high school fumblings. But while Quill's touch had been welcome, it hadn't gotten her where she needed to go. This was not entirely his fault. It was much more difficult for her to find release at her age. But she had ended up faking it last night, which didn't sit well with her.

She did not regret having sex with Quill, but if she was being perfectly honest, she was disappointed. She had never been intimate with anyone other than Doug, and she had long suspected that sex was overrated. No one really had the life-altering sex that fictional characters experienced in the romance novels she devoured. Wasn't that why people—mostly women—read romance novels in the first place, to experience the kind of love and desire that existed only in the imagination?

And yet there was a tiny part of her that had hoped she was wrong, that men who could make love to her in a way that made her toes curl existed in reality. Sex with Quill wasn't bad, but it wasn't great either, and Twyla was now facing the unfortunate truth that she would never have sex with another human being that couldn't be outdone by a smutty book and a good vibrator.

I know, I know, Twyla prayed to Grandmother Wisdom. *This is not a real problem, and I should get over myself. Please look after my Hope and make sure she doesn't get pregnant before age thirty at the earliest.*

Twyla had nothing left to pray for, but she stayed where she was, her butt growing numb on the wooden seat. Quill was already heading into Tanria, which meant that he was going to see Frank before she did. Surely, he wouldn't tell him the specifics about what had transpired last night. She realized then that she had no intention of telling Frank the specifics either, which whiffed of lying to her best friend. But then again, Frank had never divulged the details of his own sex life to her, and he had most definitely had plenty of sex since his divorce. It had never bothered her, so why would it bother him that she was finally having sex again, too?

Why am I even worried about this? she asked Grandmother Wisdom.

Sunlight shone in from the Unknown God's skylight and struck the mosaic in such a way that it looked like Grandmother Wisdom's eyes were twinkling, as if she were laughing at Twyla.

Twyla pulled up outside Duckers's apartment building first thing Sorrowsday. He was waiting for her out front, holding hands with Zeddie Birdsall, who was pouting mightily.

"I can take you," Zeddie told Duckers as Twyla put the autoduck in park. "I don't have to be at Proserpina's until this afternoon."

"I know, but Twyla and I are working together. We're going to the same place at the same time. And she's already here."

Zeddie gave Duckers's hand a sulky yet affectionate shake. "Gods' tits, Pen, we barely get to spend time together as it is. Why are you making it so that we're spending even less time together?"

Twyla cringed. She did not want to overhear such a personal conversation, but there was no escape. She sank into the bench in a feeble attempt to disappear.

"Twyla offered to give me a ride. Don't read weird shit into it."

"But you're going to be gone for two whole weeks," Zeddie whined, although he somehow made it sound endearing. "Is it wrong that I'd like to spend twenty extra minutes with you?"

Twyla sank lower.

"I've got time off in the middle of this tour for the wedding.

You'll see me in four days." Duckers relinquished his boy-friend's hand to chuck his pack into the hold. "I gotta go, Z. I love you."

"I love you, too, jerk face."

They kissed one last time before Duckers got into the cab and Twyla drove off, with Zeddie shrinking in her rearview mirror. The rookie stared out the passenger-side window, sulking.

Twyla nudged him. "Want to talk about it?"

"It's complicated."

"Try me. If you want. No pressure."

Duckers sat up straighter. "So, I love Zeddie, but he's driving me fucking nuts. I know I'm being a dick, but...here's the deal: I have my own place now, for the first time ever. I've never even had my own room before, and now I have a whole-ass apartment. And I like it. And sometimes when I come home from work, I want everyone—including my boyfriend—to leave me the fuck alone, and I mean that in the nicest possible way."

Twyla sympathized with this sentiment to her bones. "Have you told him that?"

"No. How am I supposed to tell my boyfriend to leave me the fuck alone?"

"There are probably better ways to put it," she conceded.

She assumed he would spend the trip staring out the window and stewing. Instead, he flashed her a strong side-eye.

"What is that look about?"

"I heard a certain someone went out to a fancy-ass restaurant with Dr. Vanderluscious?"

"Mother of Sorrows, have mercy. I've already been grilled by my daughter."

Duckers steepled his fingers. "Did he wear fancy shorts and a fancy *ass*-cot for his fancy dinner out with his fancy lady?"

"I am not discussing my love life with you."

"No fair. You know all about my love life."

"And whose choice was that?"

"Cruel woman."

Twyla thought about Quill, the impish look in his eyes when he said they should take his glorious autoduck out on the waterway. He had looked handsome last night.

"He wore a suit, for your information," she informed Duckers. "It was very dapper."

"Was tweed involved? Because I heard tweed was involved."

"Yes."

"Were there corduroy patches on the elbows?"

"Maybe."

Duckers gasped and clutched his non-existent pearls. "Twyla Middle Name Banneker, did you remove Professor Vander-elbow-patches's jacket?"

Twyla kept her eyes on the road and willed her blush from blooming across her cheeks. "Have you met my daughter yet? I think you two would get along like gangbusters. And it's Josephine."

"Who's Josephine? Are you telling me that Dr. Vanderlucky is into threesomes?"

"What? No! That's my middle name: Josephine."

"Throuples are a thing, Twyla. There's no shame here."

"We're not a throuple. We're hardly a couple. It was one dinner out. Good gods."

"I've seen his legs, and all I can say is, good on you, ma'am." He gave her a congratulatory salute.

"Did I just get ma'am-ed?"

"Yes, ma'am."

"Don't make me sing at you, Duckers."

He mimed locking his lips and throwing away the key.

When they arrived at the West Station, they found *Ellis,*

Banneker & Duckers written in the slot next to *W-14* for a two-week tour on the assignment board, as expected. Maguire pounced on them two seconds later.

"Banneker, Duckers, in my office."

They both jumped.

"I know we're not in trouble, but she always makes it sound like we're in trouble," Duckers whispered before they walked through the office door.

"We're probably not in trouble."

"Probably?"

"Close the door," Maguire ordered the moment they crossed the threshold.

" 'Close the door,' " Duckers mimicked under his breath for Twyla's benefit. " 'The spanking shall commence.' "

Twyla twisted her mouth to contain a guffaw.

Maguire leaned on her desk. "Lots to fill you in on, but not here. Provision yourselves for camping out. You're not staying at the barracks."

"Provision ourselves to camp out for the full two weeks?" asked Duckers.

"Affirmative."

Twyla understood her young partner's misgivings. It wasn't unusual for marshals to camp out for a few nights, but for two full weeks? That did not sound pleasant. "Where are we going?" she asked.

"I'll take you there myself and fill you in on the way."

Duckers raised his hand. "Chief? Aren't we all taking time off to go to Hart and Mercy's wedding this weekend?"

"Shit. Banneker, are you and Ellis going?"

"We've both RSVP'd, and you approved our time-off requests. But, of course, Frank can't attend in his current...situation."

"I'll get to that in a minute. Shit. Duckers and I are *in* the wedding. Let me think on this. For now, go get your gear, and that includes full-sized crossbows."

"Fuck yeah." Duckers did a fist pump.

"I'll meet you at the stables in half an hour."

Loading up a pair of equimares for an extended camping trip in Tanria would be a chore under any circumstances. Loading up a pair of equimares for an extended camping trip in Tanria in under a half hour was a feat worthy of a New Year's bonus, in Twyla's humble opinion. They were strapping the packs of supplies onto their saddles when Maguire met them exactly a half hour later, selected her own mount, and led them through the portal into Tanria. She waited until they were a good fifteen minutes into the journey before finally speaking.

"Two major developments have happened since you left. One: Mary Georgina has dislodged. Frank is a free man, in a manner of speaking."

"That's wonderful news!" said Twyla.

"It is, but she follows Ellis wherever he goes. Poor guy can't go to the bathroom without a baby dragon following him into the privy."

Twyla was sympathetic to his plight. She could recall entire years of her adult life when all she wanted to do was poop in peace.

"Two, and this one is big," continued Maguire, "when I went to one of the small lakes in the Dragon's Teeth range, looking for the kind of food one of these dragons might eat, according to Vanderlinden's scientist friend, I found a dragon hangout of sorts. There was an adult and two young ones swimming on the water, so apparently swimming is a thing they do. Makes sense, given their dietary needs. I didn't feel like getting eaten, so I left, but Frank and I came back the following day with Mary Georgina in the hopes that we could move her into a new family, and there they were again."

"Did it work? Did they take Mary Georgina?"

"No, but we're camping out by the lake, not staying in the barracks. So far, the adult has left us alone. Can't say I love the close proximity, though."

"Understandable. How's Frank holding up?"

"You know Ellis. He's pretty unflappable."

"That he is."

"Vanderlinden arrived yesterday, and he's over the moon about getting to observe live dragons in the wild. He's leery, though. All that research he's done on the diet of ancient dragons isn't doing him any favors. I think the man prefers bones to living, breathing animals."

"Living, *glitter*-breathing animals," Duckers corrected.

"Did he faint again?" asked Twyla.

"Only the one time."

"Dr. Vanderswoony—am I right, Twyla?" said Duckers.

The chief cowed him with her aquamarine demigod glare. The rest of the ride was uneventful.

Twyla had never been to the lake to which they traveled. It was located so deep in the Dragon's Teeth that she would never have known of its existence if not for Maguire leading them there. The terrain was daunting in this area of the mountains, so it wasn't a regular stop on the marshals' rounds.

They made it to the campsite shortly before noon, but neither Frank nor Quill was there. Maguire, Twyla, and Duckers found them both at the lake—or, in Frank's case, *in* the lake. He sat atop Saltlicker's back as the equimaris swam in large, looping circles, the stallion's powerful legs and webbed feet churning gracefully through the water. Mary Georgina followed in his wake, paddling awkwardly with wings and feet. She was remarkably cute, reminding Twyla of her kids when they were young, wearing water wings and splashing around the public swimming pool in Mayetta.

"Aw, look at Dragon Daddy. Isn't that sweet?" said Duckers, and Twyla didn't think he was kidding. There was something positively adorable about Frank Ellis, oblivious to their presence, riding the world's surliest stallion in circles, teaching his baby how to swim, grinning and laughing and giving words of encouragement to his adopted dragon child. When he finally caught sight of them, his whole face lit up, which did something achingly pleasant to Twyla's heart. She couldn't remember the last time she'd seen her friend this carefree and happy.

He rode toward them, even though both Saltlicker and Mary Georgina were clearly annoyed to have to leave the water for dry land. By the time Frank dismounted, he was smiling so hard Twyla could see both his top and bottom teeth. "Hey, darlin'," he said as he gave her a side hug. He dripped all over her, but she didn't care. She was glad to see him looking so contented.

Mary Georgina came clambering after him and sat up alertly to study the newcomers. She had grown noticeably in the past week, and the scales along her back and sides had darkened to a rosy watermelon hue. The small nubbins on each side of her head protruded further. She blinked at them with those sweet, tear-shaped green eyes, which seemed to have grown larger and more devastatingly innocent over the past several days. Twyla had held tiny puppies and kittens that weren't as cute as Mary Georgina.

"Wow, things are coming along here, huh?" she said.

"They really are. Mary Georgina's learning to do all sorts of stuff. She's swimming, and she's figuring out how to feed herself—"

"And she's no longer latched on to you," Twyla added.

"Yeah, but whew, she gets into everything. She started playing with my lamp the second my back was turned last night and about burned down the tent. Isn't that right, baby girl?"

The dragon wagged her tail like an eager spaniel and climbed into Frank's arms.

"Do we actually know for sure whether she's a girl dragon or a boy dragon?" asked Duckers.

"According to Vanderlinden, they're all female," answered Maguire.

Twyla craned her neck, looking around for the dracologist in question. "Where is Quill?"

Frank's broad smile dimmed a fraction. He nodded toward a different section of the lake. "He's behind some cover to the north, observing the family, taking notes, that kind of thing."

He guided them around the edge of the lake until the northernmost section came into view, and indicated the Tanrian willow tree whose leaves maintained a buttery yellow shade year-round. "He's inside the canopy of that willow."

But neither Quill nor the willow was what caught Twyla's interest—or Duckers's, for that matter. They gaped instead at the full-grown dragon swanning around the lake in all her magenta-colored glory, with two pink babies paddling in her wake.

Twyla didn't know if this was the same dragon they had encountered the night Mary Georgina latched on to Frank, but her gut told her it was. In the light of day, she seemed less terrifying. Her scales shone like richly hued garnets in the noon sun. Her wings were less bat-like than Twyla would have expected, and instead reminded her of the billowing sails of a ship at sea, darker at the shoulder and lightening to a pale pink at the tips, like the petals of an exotic tulip. The dragon was quite lovely, in fact, save for the bizarre antlers atop her head, which were covered in coral-colored fur. Twyla got the sense that they would be soft and silky to the touch rather than rigid. Like the babies, the mother also had gorgeous green eyes. In fact, the only thing terrifying about her was her size. It made Twyla think of the times Frank had teased her for being afraid of cows; she knew they were harmless, but when you got up close, they were awfully big.

The babies were every bit as cute as Mary Georgina, and Twyla couldn't help but laugh indulgently as they frolicked together on the water, one of them splashing and trying to dunk the other. They reminded her of kittens pouncing on their litter mates.

"And they're all female?" Twyla asked Frank, but it was Quill who answered, popping his head out of the drooping willow branches like an actor sticking his head out of velvet theater curtains.

"I believe so, yes. Hallo, darling." He sauntered over to her and kissed her, nothing over the top, but she wasn't sure how she felt about being called *darling* or receiving a kiss while she was on the clock. Frank gave a start, his face a mask of revulsion, as if both Twyla and Quill had broken out into seeping boils. She could not specifically recall having seen Frank kiss one of his lady friends, but she was certain she must have at some point, and she was equally certain she hadn't responded with a look of sheer horror. Now she was annoyed with both men, one for mixing work and romance, the other for behaving as if her having a love life was revolting to behold.

"In answer to your question," said Quill, oblivious to Frank's disgust and Twyla's irritation, "I cannot say that I have gotten up close and personal with our *Draconis* family here, but as far as I can tell, none of them present demonstrable hemipenile bulges at the base of their tails."

"Is that your way of saying they don't have nuts?" asked Duckers. "Because all I heard from that was *penile*."

"Lizards do not have the same genital presentation as mammals, but you are correct in that they do not have the reproductive organs one might expect to find on a male dragon."

"So, where are all these babies coming from?" asked Twyla.

"That is the question that I have been discussing with Marshal Ellis and Chief Maguire. This particular family spends a significant amount of time here at the lake, but they do not seem to be nesting here. To better understand dragon behavior and reproduction, we must discover their nesting site."

"Which will also help us figure out next steps," said Maguire.

"Precisely. And, hopefully, we will be able to rehome Marshal Ellis's young dragon friend."

Meep, said Mary Georgina, as if she could sense that they were discussing her. What remained of Frank's smile disappeared entirely.

"On that note." Maguire dusted off the brim of her hat and put it on her head. "I miss my wife, and I'm going home. I'll check in with you soon. In the meantime, send a message with Hermia if anything comes up."

Chapter Ten

"This is the longest they've stayed by the lake," Frank observed as he and Twyla sat on a couple of fallen logs around the campsite that afternoon. Since they were in the mountains, the sun was already setting behind a peak. The dragons lounged in the cattails on the lake's edge, sunning themselves in the last rays of daylight. Mary Georgina sat at Frank's feet, her head resting atop his thigh as she stared up at him adoringly.

Hoo boy, this is going to be a problem, thought Twyla. If the baby dragon had bonded this strongly to a human, how were they going to get her to live with other dragons? And if they did manage to successfully release her into the wild, what effect would losing her have on Frank? She didn't even want to think of that.

Twenty yards away, Quill appeared to be taking elaborate measurements with a compass and a ruler. He had two reference books open beside him, as well as a journal in which he scribbled notes. They could hear Duckers rather than see him. Bored to tears after a couple of hours of watching dragons, he had taken off some time ago to practice shooting with his crossbow. The occasional "Fuck yeah" made its way to their ears.

"How was the date?" Frank asked Twyla as she set up kindling for the fire they'd light later in the evening.

"*Dates*, plural, and the first one was as unromantic as it is possible to be." She filled him in on finding Wade and the kids waiting for her when she got home, finishing with "And then Hope showed up a day early."

"That's good, right?"

"With Everett."

"Who you like."

"Who is now her fiancé."

Frank blinked. "I didn't know she was engaged."

"That makes two of us." Twyla sat and began to worry at a piece of loose bark on the log beneath her. "It's all so sudden. She showed up with him on my doorstep and basically said, 'You remember Everett. Hey, by the way, I'm going to marry him.' I feel bad, because I know my response was less than enthusiastic. I wish I could figure out why this is throwing me for a loop."

"Did Hope notice your less than enthusiastic response?"

"Yes, but I think I managed to gloss over it."

"This is maybe not the best thing to gloss over. This is maybe something you need to hash out with her."

"Hashing out: not my strong suit."

"I'm not winning any awards there either."

A prickle of concern poked Twyla's conscience. She'd been so wrapped up in her own dilemmas that she hadn't given Frank adequate thought lately—Frank, who'd been covered in glitter and who now found himself the parent of a baby dragon.

"What are you needing to hash out these days?"

"Nothing," he told her, brushing it off. "Listen, it's not wrong to have concerns about your daughter getting hitched, but at the end of the day, she's in love. She's happy. That's good news, isn't it?"

"I suppose it is. I suppose it'll have to be."

They both sank into a ruminative silence. As she suspected, talking to Frank had helped lessen her anger and her worry. But there was something peculiar lingering under the surface of their conversation, a subtext she didn't grasp. As she watched him pet

Mary Georgina, she wondered if, with all her talk about Hope and marriage, she had inadvertently stumbled across one of the closed doors in the house that was Frank Ellis.

"You said you had dates, plural, with Vanderlinden. How was the second one?"

"His name is Quill, you know. And it was fine. We went to Proserpina's."

A torrent of words she couldn't and wouldn't say to Frank gushed through her mind: *Dinner was amazing, and I enjoyed talking with him, and we drove on the ocean, and then I went to his hotel room, and we had sex, and it was decent, but I wish it had been better, as in an orgasm would have been welcome, but I wound up faking it, and now I feel guilty for faking it, but maybe he could have tried a tiny bit harder.*

"Nice," said Frank, the exact word she had thought in the aftermath of it all. The kiss, the sex—they had been nice.

"It was."

Frank had never gone into extensive detail with her regarding his love life, and Twyla decided that she was equally reticent regarding her own. She didn't want to say any more on the subject, and Frank didn't ask. *Thank you, Grandmother Wisdom,* thought Twyla.

Meep chirr-chirr-chirrup, the adult dragon trumpeted from the lake, but it lacked the menace of her call the night she'd chased the goons to retrieve her eggs. The two babies obediently climbed onto her back and, with a wonderous unfurling of her wings, the mother lifted herself above the surface. She ran, skimming across the water on feet that were clawed at the tips and webbed between the toes. Her wings threshed the air with a *whump whump whump* as she took to the sky, soaring five, ten, fifteen feet overhead.

Twyla stood and walked toward the shore to get a better view.

"Wow," she whispered as the lovely creature glided across the horizon and blotted out the setting sun for one breathless moment.

Frank came to stand beside her with Mary Georgina clinging to his back the way the other babies clung to their mother. "It's something, isn't it?" he said in hushed tones. "Watch. She'll circle around and head south-southwest."

She did exactly as he said, careening through the air in a graceful arc on wings tinted orange by the sunset. Awe expanded inside Twyla as she watched the dragon soar through the amber sky, the babies sweetly chirping on her back.

"Maguire and I tried heading that direction to see if we could find the nest, but that terrain doesn't lend itself to hiking. By the time we crested the peak, they were out of sight."

"Holy shit! Did you see that?" cried Duckers as he returned to camp. "Okay, real talk: Who's riding one of those things, and when can we make it happen? And please tell me the answers are 'Penrose Duckers' and 'soon.'"

Every maternal nerve ending in Twyla's body twanged with alarm. "The answers are 'no one' and 'never.'"

Duckers sucked his teeth at Twyla. "Frank, help me out. What about Mary Georgina? She's going to be that big someday. Are you trying to tell me you're not going to take her out for a spin?"

"She's not an autoduck, and I don't know how I'm going to teach her to fly when I have every intention of keeping my boots on the ground the way the Three Mothers intended."

"Come the fuck on! These things were made to ride! Why wouldn't we ride them?"

"Because we're not gods?" suggested Twyla.

"This sounds rather heated," said Quill as he returned to the campsite and set his pack by his tent. "What are we discussing?"

"Duckers wants to ride a dragon," Twyla told him.

"Ah."

She wondered how Quill's *ah* could sound so different from Frank's *oh* that there seemed to be an ocean between them. She wished she could put her finger on what it was, and why Frank's *oh* was full of comfort and understanding, while Quill's *ah* was... not. The latter joined them at the lake and wrapped his arm around her shoulders. Frank's eyes followed the line of the other man's arm before he disentangled himself from Mary Georgina and went to light the campfire.

Meep, the dragon whined at having been abandoned by her human parent. Duckers scooped her up, an action to which she gave a semi-mollified *chirp*.

Quill regarded Duckers as he nuzzled the scales between her growing horns with his nose. "I think we should refrain from saddling up any and all dragons until we are quite certain that they do not wish to kill us."

"They eat grass and frolic in the water, and they're cute as fuck. Even their horn things are soft and fuzzy." Duckers rubbed his cheek against one of Mary Georgina's nubbins. "Who's a cute baby dragon? Is it Mary Georgina? Is Mary Georgina the cutest fucking dragon of all time?"

"I'm not sure which one of them is cuter," Twyla commented to no one in particular as she shrugged out from underneath Quill's arm and returned to her log.

Quill reached into his pocket, pulled out a pipe, and lit it before following Twyla to sit beside her. "First of all, it would not be a great feat to be the cutest dragon of all time when, given our reconstructions of ancient dragons based on the fossil record, most if not all of them were hideous and rather terrifying. Secondly, cute does not equal friendly. Although I have developed a theory about the apparent docility of these Tanrian dragons."

"Which is?" asked Frank. He glanced at the pipe and narrowed his eyes, as if to say, *Of course Dr. Vanderlegs smokes a pipe.* The dracologist didn't notice, but Twyla did, and she shot him a look that said, *Cut it out.* Frank pretended he didn't see it.

"It is entirely untested. I should not speak of a hypothesis until I have more evidence to support it."

"We're not scientists, Vanderlinden. Tell us what you think. It's why you're here, to advise us."

"I suppose there is no harm in mentioning it in present company." Quill puffed on his pipe and released a plume of sweet-smelling smoke. "These dragons have much of what we consider dracological physiology, and yet I can find no description from any contemporary text nor reconstruction deduced from the fossil evidence that matches what we see here. Not even a close proximation. I begin to wonder if the Old Gods created this species with a new purpose in mind once they were imprisoned inside the Mist."

"What purpose?" Frank asked Quill.

"I hesitate to say something so ridiculous aloud, but I am tempted to postulate that the Tanrian dragons might have been created as companions rather than as weapons."

Duckers perked up. "You mean they're pets?"

"That doesn't sound too far off, actually," said Frank as Mary Georgina crawled into his lap.

"Think of it this way: if the war dragons of the Old Gods were analogous to wolves, these dragons are more like..." He looked at Mary Georgina, who snuggled her snout under Frank's chin. "Poodles."

Duckers, who'd been taking a drink of water from his tin cup, choked with laughter before he coughed out, "Poodles?"

"*Toy* poodles might be a more accurate analogy."

"Like, put-a-sweater-on-them-and-carry-them-around-in-a-purse toy poodles?"

"Yes, I believe it is entirely possible—although far from

proven—that the imprisoned Old Gods created these dragons to be their pets, to keep them company in Tanria."

"And then they abandoned them like stray dogs," said Frank, drawing Mary Georgina more closely to him. Twyla wondered if he was aware of the cuddling or if it was unconscious. In either case, it was obvious to anyone with eyes that he was growing more attached to the dragon by the second, which was going to make it all the more painful when he had to give her up. Which he inevitably would.

"The gods' leaving might also explain why no one has seen dragons inside the Mist until now," Quill went on, warming to his topic, in full lecture mode as he punctuated important points with his pipe. "According to Bendel of Brackridge in *The Chronicles of Lathford*, the ancient battle dragons of the Old Gods would go dormant if they were injured or simply not in use. Of course, that particular source is a translation of the original, thought to have been penned by Woollven Hearthmaker in the second century ante-aspera, and it is considered apocryphal by many scholars, myself included. Until recently."

"Wake me up if he says anything good," Duckers whispered to Frank but not softly enough.

Frank waved him off. "So you're saying they hibernate?"

"Yes. It's the only way I can think to explain why no one has seen them since the portals opened."

"How does something hibernate for centuries?"

"Look around you, Marshal Ellis. Nothing about Tanria makes sense according to the laws of nature as we understand them."

"Do you think there are more?"

"I would be surprised if there were not more. I suspect it is only a matter of time before the dragon population of Tanria grows exponentially, at which time we will no longer be able to keep it a secret."

"How much longer do you think we have?"

"We've already seen a mother and three babies, including Mary Georgina. I can't imagine we won't see more within the next week or two. That is why Chief Maguire has asked me to prepare a report on my findings and to make recommendations therein by the end of next week."

"What are you going to recommend?" Frank asked warily as he stroked a hand along Mary Georgina's scales.

"I wish I knew. It would be most helpful if we could find the nesting site for at least one mating pair, if not more. That would be informative."

"Why now?" asked Twyla. "If the dragons have hibernated this long, why are they coming out now? Why not before? Why not ten years from now?"

"Something must have woken them."

"What can wake up a dragon?" Duckers asked.

"I don't know, nor do I care to find out. I'll leave answering that question to the Tanrian Marshals. Because whatever it was, it must have been extraordinarily disruptive."

The rest of the evening passed uncomfortably, at least from Twyla's perspective. As they discussed the best way to go about finding the dragon's nest, Quill toyed with a lock of her hair, which was distracting in the extreme, and not in a pleasant, sexy way. Her eyes flicked to Frank, who appeared to be looking everywhere but at her and Quill. Given the fact that Quill was practically sitting in her lap, Frank could hardly glance her direction without getting an eyeful of leggy dracologist at the same time.

When they turned in for the evening, Quill wrapped his arm around her waist and jokingly murmured in her ear, "Your tent or mine?" Joking in that he was substituting the word *tent* for *place*, but he clearly had every intention of getting her naked within the next ten minutes.

"There's not much privacy here," she hedged.

"It isn't a secret that we are seeing each other."

"I know, but I'm not comfortable sharing a tent with you—or with anyone—in this situation. Our private lives are...well, private. There's nothing private about a pup tent."

He frowned at the tents in question, four triangles of canvas lined up in a row. "I suppose you are right, but I have already been forced to miss you desperately for twenty-four hours. How shall I manage an entire tour?"

Missed her desperately? She could hear the humor that laced his words, and yet there was an alarming ring of truth under the surface. Surely, he hadn't really missed her. Then again, he was a man, and if there was one thing a man knew how to miss desperately, it was sex, no matter how recently he'd had it.

Frank and Duckers were milling about the fire, close enough to catch a whiff of what they were discussing.

"Take a walk with me." Twyla took him by the arm, robbing him of the option to refuse, not that he would. When they'd made it safely out of earshot, she turned to him. "Quill, I had a nice time with you the other night."

There was that word again: *nice*.

"As did I, darling."

And there was *that* word again: *darling*. A gag reflex pulsed in her throat, and she had no idea why.

"But I am at work. You are at work. We are both at work. And while we are working, I don't think we should..." She twirled her hand in the air, a vague gesture meant to contain multitudes.

Quill repeated the gesture, his eyes lit with mirth. "Is this your way of saying *enjoy carnal bliss*?"

The distance between *nice* and *bliss* opened up in Twyla's mind, as if she stood on one side of a vast canyon and Quill on the other. But having starved herself of male companionship for the past thirteen years, at least in the physical sense, she was interested in exploring the valley between those two points, especially when Quill rewarded her with the boyish grin he gave her now.

She performed the twirling gesture again. "This is my way of saying that I don't think we should be romantic with each other while we're on the job."

A pair of tragic crevices creased his forehead. "You are on a two-week tour."

"I am, and I'd prefer to behave professionally while I'm on this tour."

"I understand that, but..." The tragic crevices sank deeper. "Two weeks."

"Actually, I have Wardensday off for a wedding—"

"A wedding?"

"But it amounts to the same thing. It's only two weeks."

He heaved a theatrical sigh and took her hand in his. "Fortunately for me, you are worth the wait."

As he kissed her good night, she thought it was gratifying to be worth something to a man as smart and accomplished as Quill Vanderlinden, even if it was only a wait.

"Hold up," Twyla begged. She bent double, put her hands on her knees, and panted. She was not as young or fit as she had once been, and hiking at a high elevation was about to give her a coronary.

Duckers, on the other hand, had barely broken a sweat. His taking off his hat and fanning his face was the only indication that their search for a dragon's nest was bothering him in the least.

They'd found a silksheep trail, which had led them up to this wide ridge, giving them a good view of the surrounding mountains. So far, they'd seen no signs of dragon nests, not that they knew what they were looking for.

"I don't mean to be a whiner, but how are we supposed to find a dragon's nest in a whole-ass mountain range? We don't even know where to begin looking. In a cave? Under a tree? On a cliff?"

"Better than doing nothing," said Twyla. "Hold on. Give me a sec to catch my breath."

"Take your time," Duckers told her, adjusting the strap of his ridiculously enormous crossbow.

"You're not really going to shoot a dragon with that, are you?"

"Probably not. But we know they don't appreciate people fucking with their nests, and I'd rather not die today."

"So no glitter for you?"

"The glitter could be fun. Accidentally becoming a dragon daddy? Not so much. I'm not ready for parenthood."

"Good for you."

Duckers shot her a suspicious side-eye.

"That wasn't sarcasm. I meant it literally. Good for you for knowing that you're not ready to be a parent."

"Definitely not. Now, Frank? Frank is daddy material."

"That he is."

Frank and Quill had remained at the campsite to continue observing the dragons on the lake and to teach Mary Georgina how to be one of them, although Twyla was beginning to doubt their ability to incorporate the baby into larger dragon society. She already said *Meep-meep* in the exact same tone and manner Frank used when he started off a sentence with "Well now."

"Are you worried about that?" Duckers asked Twyla.

"About what?"

"Frank being daddy material for a dragon?"

"Are you a mind reader?"

"You don't need to read minds to see disaster written all over this. He loves that little fucker, and frankly, she loves him, too. Ha! *Frank*ly."

"He hates that."

"I bet he does. But the point is, what's he going to do with a baby dragon that's going to be a full-grown dragon someday? Keep her in his backyard swimming pool?"

"He doesn't have a swimming pool."

"This is what I'm saying." Duckers surveyed the rocky incline sloping away from them to the east. "You take a breather. I'm going to climb up there for a better view and look for something dragon-y."

"Be careful."

"Okay, Mom," he said in a dopey voice before scrambling up.

As Twyla scanned the mountainous landscape from the ridge, she considered Frank's dragon conundrum. She was certain that he had no intention of keeping Mary Georgina, but then again, they were planning to run their own bed-and-breakfast on an equimaris ranch on the coast once they retired. She knew he cherished a hope that at least one of his kids would come work at the ranch with him once they got it up and running. Surely he didn't believe that he could keep this new child with him as well, swimming among the equimares.

Did he?

She made a mental note to pull him aside at their earliest convenience for a heart-to-heart. This would not prove easy, since it was challenging to have any privacy while camping out, and she had the distinct sense that he was avoiding her, probably because Quill had a tendency to stick to her side like chewing gum under a school desk whenever they weren't actively working. She enjoyed having Quill around, but she wasn't a fan of not having Frank around. More fodder for that heart-to-heart, she thought.

"Uh, Twyla?" Duckers called to her.

She turned her attention upward to where he sat on a huge

bolder twenty feet above her. His attention was focused on something below her position on the ridge, which she couldn't see.

"What is it?"

Her stomach dropped to her knees when Duckers's response was a worrisome "Uh."

She turned in time to see the mother dragon's head clear the ridge.

"Ope!" she cried, a ridiculous sound in the face of something so large and wild and majestic and frightful.

The dragon hovered, flapping her vast wings so that Twyla's hat blew off her head and strands of her frizzy hair came out of her ponytail to buffet her cheeks. She could hear the creature's breath, in and out like a bellows, and watch the thin line of her nostrils pulse with each respiration.

"Don't move," said Duckers.

This went without saying, since Twyla was pinioned to the spot by the dragon's piercing green eyes. True, she had spent the better part of the past several days watching this particular dragon swim and eat and doze, but that had been from many yards away. Now that Twyla was within glittery spitting distance of the enormous being, she pissed herself. A little.

With a dramatic upward surge, the dragon arced away from the ridge.

"Thank fucking gods," breathed Duckers from above, but he spoke too soon. Twyla's spine had barely had time to collapse with relief when the dragon looped back and landed on the rocky slope halfway between her and Duckers.

She yelped a much louder and higher-pitched "Ope!" this time, and when the dragon crawled toward her, she pissed herself again. More than a little.

"Fuck, fuck, fuck, fuck, fuck." Duckers fumbled for his crossbow.

Twyla put her hands up, as if the dragon could understand

the gesture as surrender. The babies clinging to her back chirped, a delightful, happy chatter that contrasted brutally with what appeared to Twyla to be their mother's threatening approach. She had no way to escape, unless she jumped off the ridge into the valley below.

Behind the dragon, Twyla saw Duckers pull the string into the nut. She saw him hoist the crossbow up and take aim. She thought of the way he hit the target every time with a "Fuck yeah."

The dragon slowed to a halt three feet in front of Twyla, a mother with two babies, who had tolerated the humans' presence by the lake without so much as a threatening spit, who as far as Twyla knew, hadn't hurt a soul.

"Duckers, don't shoot," she said, loudly enough to be heard but calmly enough to (hopefully) not alarm the dragon.

"Fuck that!"

"She's not going to hurt me. I don't think."

"You don't *think?*"

The dragon stretched out her neck and snuffled Twyla's knees, then her torso, then her neck, her hot breath steaming Twyla's clothes and making her break out into a cold sweat.

"O-o-okay. A-a-all right," Twyla half sang, trying to keep her panic at bay as the dragon sniffed her.

Chirr-chirrup, it cheeped in her face. And then the dragon wagged her tail, swishing its length through tall pink grass on one side and sending pebbles tumbling off the ridge on the other. The babies on her back broke out into sweet chirps that echoed their mother's, as if they were serenading the marshal.

The dragon turned and settled herself in the sunlight splashing the ridge. The babies climbed off and began to tussle in the nearby grass.

Twyla stayed where she was, her hands still held in the air, as her brain tried to soak in what had happened.

"What do we do?" asked Duckers from his boulder.

"I guess we're lounging with dragons?" Twyla suggested slowly.

"Right. Okay. Did you piss yourself?"

Twyla put her hands on her hips and glared at him. "You give birth to three babies, and then come talk to me after you find yourself face-to-face with a twelve-foot dragon."

Duckers considered this. "My lips are sealed," he said. "So, picnic?"

They sat on a couple of boulders near the dragons and ate sandwiches while the babies chased grasshoppers, their mother calling chidingly whenever they got too close to the ridge. Twyla nodded in solidarity. She remembered this, the constant diligence required to keep small children alive when they seemed determined to get themselves killed. These days, she was experiencing it all over again with her grandkids, especially Sal.

"This is wild," said Duckers through a bite full of turkey sandwich as a baby clung to Twyla's leg, which didn't appear to bother her mother in the slightest. Twyla patted the little one on the head.

"I wonder if we're failing to integrate Mary Georgina with this bunch because we've been hanging back. Maybe Frank needs to get up close and personal with this lot."

"They're awfully cuddly for monsters. I'm kind of a dick for almost shooting one."

"But you didn't. No harm, no foul."

The baby climbed onto Twyla's knees, flapped her wings, and went airborne.

Meep! she squealed in surprise. *Meep! Meep!*

Her mother lifted her head and meeped approvingly. Twyla applauded until the baby pooped a slimy, glittery drizzle down the front of her dungarees.

Duckers held up his canteen in a toast. "To the purse dogs of the Old Gods."

"Twy, you up?" Frank called softly outside Twyla's tent at dawn.

"Be out in a minute," she mumbled. Sleeping in a pup tent with nothing but a thin pad between her and the ground wasn't doing her any favors. Getting dressed inside a pup tent was also a challenge. Twyla was glad that Quill couldn't see her wrestle her no-longer-limber body into a pair of dungarees and a work shirt that needed washing.

"Bless you," she told Frank when he handed her a cup of coffee as she emerged.

"I know better than to make you face the day without your caffeine, darlin'."

"It's too early for joking."

"Who's joking?"

"Why am I up this early?"

"I'll show you."

He guided her north along the lakeshore. She tried not to slosh coffee all over herself as she sipped and walked at the same time, but she was too groggy to pay much attention to her surroundings, until Frank came to a sudden stop. He stood behind her, pointed over her shoulder, and murmured in her ear, "There."

She blinked, taking in the sight of not one, not two, but three adult dragons on the water, each with their own young. She recognized the mother who'd joined her and Duckers for a picnic yesterday, but the other two adults were distinctly different. One was smaller and leaner, the color of her scales a fuchsia pink that leaned toward purple. The other was rounder, her coloring closer to a salmon hue. The babies showed even more variation. While all of them were pale, their coloring covered an array from orangey coral to bluer violets. They were here, and they were real, and they were breathtaking.

"Oh, Frank," Twyla whispered, clutching the warm mug to her heart with both hands. Sentimental slob that she was, she teared up as she watched the dragons swim on the lake with the solid comfort of Frank's physical presence at her back. Out of long habit, she melted against him, her back to his chest, her head leaning on his shoulder. His arm came around her waist, and he rested his chin against her hair. They stayed that way for some time, simply watching and breathing and living in the moment. Twyla sensed that this would become a perfect memory someday, one of those rare gems a person stored up in their heart over the years. She was glad that, of all people, she was sharing it with Frank.

As the sun rose higher in the sky and burned off the dew, her thoughts turned to the dragon expert sleeping in his lonely pup tent, whom she had completely forgotten in the magic of the moment.

"We should probably get Quill up to see this," she said. She had spoken softly, but her words seemed too loud, as if she had banged a gong.

Frank's hand slid off her waist. "Probably. Duckers, too."

Reluctantly, Twyla led the way to the campsite, where they found Quill already up, brushing his teeth. He spit and rinsed in the most delicate and polite way possible when he saw them, and came forward to greet Twyla while Frank went to wake up Duckers.

"Good morning, darling."

"Quill."

"Yes?"

Twyla pulled him to the side. "Remember what I said about being professional?"

"Of course."

"Calling me *darling* is in the same vein as kissing me, don't you think?"

"Marshal Ellis called you *darling*."

"No, he didn't."

"He most certainly did."

"When?"

"Literal moments ago."

Had he? Frank hadn't spoken a word since they'd returned to the campsite, so Quill must have overheard them speaking outside the tents before Frank took her to see the new dragons. What had he said? A twinge of panic mixed with guilt pinched Twyla until she remembered what it was Frank had actually said to her.

I know better than to make you face the day without your caffeine, darlin'.

For gods' sakes, how innocuous could you get?

"That's different," she told Quill.

"How?"

"He doesn't mean it romantically."

"Are you quite sure about that?"

"Yes."

"Well, I am not. I think his calling you *darlin'*"—here he imitated Frank's drawl—"is also in the same vein as kissing you, and I don't like it."

"You're being ridiculous, but you're cute when you're jealous." In fact, he did look adorable, pouting there in his safari jacket and ascot and shorts and knee socks, resembling an overgrown scout. She peered over her shoulder to make sure they were unobserved, then she kissed him on the nose.

A grudging smile pulled at the corners of his mouth. "Who's unprofessional now?"

Twyla laughed. She liked that he was affectionate, even if she wanted him to save that affection for her for off hours.

"How much longer until we don't have to be professional?" he murmured.

"Behave."

Duckers sliced through the romantic mood when he danced

up to them—literally danced—singing, "Dragons, dragons, more fucking dragons, oooooh!"

A divot of confusion formed between Quill's eyebrows. "I beg your pardon?"

"There are more dragons on the lake," explained Twyla. "Frank and I saw them this morning. I was just coming to get you."

"This is excellent news! Let me...I shall get my...Wait for me!" He plunged into his tent to grab his notebook and a pencil and other scientific paraphernalia.

Frank joined Twyla and Duckers outside Quill's tent. "He's like a kid on New Year's morning."

Duckers performed a few more dance moves, singing, "More fucking dragons!"

"And you're like a kid on New Year's morning, too."

"I take that as a compliment."

They spent the rest of the morning watching the dragons on the north side of the lake. Frank, riding Saltlicker, led Mary Georgina closer to the group than he had before, but she stuck to her human parent and seemed shy of the others. As far as Twyla could tell, nothing terribly new or exciting was happening—the dragons ate grass and cattails, swam, meeped, pooped—but there was something riveting about the scene all the same, something calming and domestic. She felt at peace, even when her magenta friend from yesterday swam close to her and sniffed her where she sat on the bank.

"Do be careful, darl—Twyla," Quill fretted.

"It's fine. Duckers and I had lunch with her yesterday."

The dragon stretched her long neck across the water and pressed her snout to Twyla's forehead, knocking off her hat. Twyla's heart raced with exhilaration at the touch. The dragon gave her a chirp before swimming to her babies, who were now holding their own in the water.

"Salt Sea, Banneker, you're going to give me a heart attack."

Twyla turned to see Alma Maguire approaching them. "Hi, Chief."

"Don't *Hi, Chief* me as if you're not over here cavorting with battle dragons. Get away from the water."

"It's okay, Chief. They're purse dogs," said Duckers.

Maguire gave him a nonplussed look before turning to Quill. "What is he talking about?"

"Ah, yes, he is referring to my theory regarding this particular breed of dragon, which I am tentatively calling *Draconis tanrias*, but I am not comfortable stating it as fact—"

Frank, who by now had ridden ashore with Mary Georgina in tow, insinuated himself into the conversation. "The professor thinks these dragons were created by the Old Gods to be pets, so they're not going to kill us. They're likely to cause more damage wagging their tails."

Quill scowled at the interruption. "Yes, but it is only a theory."

Twyla could have cut the mutual animosity between Frank and Quill with a knife.

Men. Honestly.

A series of playful *meeps* caught Maguire's attention, and she staggered when she saw what was happening on the water. "There are more of them?"

"Yes, and their interactions are fascinating," said Quill, launching into a lengthy report of his observations since she'd been gone. When he was done, she nodded and addressed the group.

"I came here to check up on things, but I also wanted to let you know, in person, that the Joint Chiefs of the Tanrian Marshals have drafted a report for the Natural Resources and Environment Committee of the Federal Assembly."

"Saying what?" asked Frank, his voice edged with alarm as Mary Georgina climbed onto his back.

"That there are dragons in Tanria. I can't sit on that, Ellis. We're on federal land here, and the government needs to be made aware."

"What are they going to do?"

"I don't know. I'll be passing along Dr. Vanderlinden's recommendation as soon as it's ready. In the meantime, we're under orders to keep this a secret as long as possible. Although, I wonder how long we can pull it off." She said this last part while gazing doubtfully at the increasing dragon population swanning on the lake.

Maguire spent the next two hours with them, watching the newcomers and playing with Mary Georgina while trying to pretend that she wasn't playing with Mary Georgina. She sounded almost reluctant when she said, "I need to go. I'm off for a few days for the wedding. Duckers, I'll see you on Wisdomsday. Banneker, I'll see you on Wardensday. Ellis, do you feel comfortable leaving Mary Georgina here with Vanderlinden overnight? I think it would look odd if you didn't come to the wedding, and I want to raise as little suspicion as possible about anything strange going on in Tanria."

"I had thought I might accompany Twyla to the wedding," said Quill, to the shock of Twyla, who had not invited him.

"But you don't know the people getting married," she said.

"I know *you*."

Maguire intervened. "I'm sorry to put you out, Dr. Vanderlinden, but Ellis has RSVP'd to the wedding, and the man hasn't left Tanria in two weeks. It would do him good to get a night off. I'm sure you understand."

"Ah." There it was, the *ah* that said so much, but he caved to Maguire's request. "Yes, naturally, he should go. I shall stay here with our dragon compatriots, then."

Maguire shook his hand. "Much appreciated. Ellis, I hope you enjoy your weekend off. Weddings are always a good time."

"Speak for yourself," he muttered, but Maguire didn't hear

him, or if she did, she showed no sign of it. She left them to return to her equimaris, and Quill returned to his dragon study spot. With nothing much to do, the three remaining marshals sat by the lakeshore with Mary Georgina scampering among them.

"What are you doing in the wedding?" Frank asked Duckers.

"I'm Hart's offer-bearer."

"Aw, that's sweet," said Twyla.

"I'm a sweet guy."

"That you are. How are you feeling about…things?" She animated her eyebrows in a way that said *I know you're trying to navigate the Zeddie issue* without actually saying it aloud, in case he didn't want anyone else to know.

"What's wrong with your eyebrows?"

"I'm being subtle."

"Frank's cool. He can know about what a shit boyfriend I am."

"You're not a shit boyfriend," Twyla and Frank said in unison.

"I need space," Duckers explained to Frank.

"That's understandable. Everyone needs breathing room sometimes, although I'm not the best person to advise anyone on matters of the heart."

"As long as you don't burst into song again, we're good."

Frank looked past Duckers to Twyla. "Did that sound like an invitation to you, darlin'?"

"It sure did."

"No," said Duckers.

"What are we in the mood for?" asked Frank.

"A love song, obviously."

"Please, no," begged Duckers.

Happily ignoring Duckers's protests, Frank launched into a classic. *"I've drunk down half the bottle by the quarter chimes of nine."*

"Good choice!" cheered Twyla.

"No," whined Duckers, but Frank kept singing.

"You're marrying a good man, but I wish that you were mine."
Twyla joined in with gusto. *"I know it's wrong to love you—"*
"Fuck, no."
"I'm a scoundrel through and through."
Mary Georgina began to chirp along with the song over
Frank's shoulder.
"You hate me for my lawless ways, but bad boys need lovin', too."
"You call this a love song?" demanded Duckers.
Frank paused his singing long enough to comment to Twyla,
"He misses the point of this entire genre of music."
"At least Mary Georgina gets it," she said before busting out
the refrain, with Frank jumping in.

> *Dear, I need your lovin',*
> *My heart is warm and true.*
> *Sure, I cuss and fight and gamble,*
> *But bad boys need lovin', too.*

Twyla had screwed her eyes shut tight as she belted out the lyrics. When she opened them again, she found that Quill was standing over her, blinking in astonishment. "That was, er, something."
"If by *something* you mean *the worst song ever*, then yes, I agree,"
said Duckers.
"The Bushong classics are an acquired taste," Twyla conceded,
embarrassed that Quill had caught her crooning a ridiculous
love song at the top of her lungs. What on earth had she been
thinking?
At least he hadn't caught Frank calling her *darlin'* this time.

Chapter Eleven

"Have fun tonight," Frank told Duckers as he watched him zip up his pack on Wisdomsday morning.

"Thanks." Duckers plastered on his usual upbeat exterior, but Twyla could see the way his worries over his relationship with Zeddie hung on him like a wet wool sweater. She walked him out to his equimaris to offer him what little encouragement she could.

"Get through the wedding. Be there for Hart and Mercy. When it's over, you can decide if you need to ask for some breathing room."

He shook out his shoulders, trying to release the tension building inside him. "You're right."

"You're a good person. If you weren't as kind and thoughtful as you are, you wouldn't be tied up in knots."

"Thanks for being my mom away from home."

"It's a privilege and an honor." Twyla patted him on the shoulder. "I bet your mom is so proud of you."

"She kind of is."

"Have a good time. Eat some cake. Drink some adult beverages. Everything's going to work out."

"See you tomorrow?"

"You bet."

Maybe she was overestimating her encouragement abilities, but she thought he seemed lighter when he mounted up and rode off.

She returned to the campfire, where Frank had already poured her a cup of coffee. He handed it to her when she sat beside him on the log. In the distance, Quill crouched in the marsh grass, observing the adult dragons and their young on the water, tearing his eyes away from time to time to jot a few notes in his journal.

Frank indicated Quill with his cup of coffee. "He's all right, your fella."

"Yeah, he is," Twyla agreed, but her mind went to the moment when Frank saw them kissing and the look on his face and the uncomfortable feeling of having been caught, as if she weren't supposed to be kissing anyone.

She didn't want to think about Quill or Frank or romance, so she watched the dragons instead, the way they serenely glided through the water as they cared for their young. "They're so peaceful. I don't get it."

"What?"

"Why did a dragon attack Herd that night? He set off his flare, so he was clearly scared. He was covered in glitter, and we found that footprint, so we know a dragon was involved. Why would a dragon have gone after him? What was he doing?"

"Maybe he got too close to the nest?"

They both startled, each of them realizing what he'd said.

Twyla spoke her thought process out loud. "We know those goons we saw by the Mist somehow got into the dragons' eggs, but we had no idea where they came from. What if Herd got too close? And what were those people doing in a dragon's nest in the first place? They didn't seem to know what they'd found until the dragon came after them, so why were they there?"

"I can't believe we didn't think of this until now."

They rose and tossed their coffee. All this time, they had been looking for the nest in the mountains near the lake, when they should have been looking in the area where they had found Herd's body.

Frank jerked his head toward the place where Quill sat on the north side of the lake. "Think we should tell him where we're going?"

"I think we should at least leave Mary Georgina with him. Give him a practice run for tomorrow."

"Well now, I don't know if that's a good idea."

Twyla pointed at the dragon, who was now clinging to Frank's leg. "Barnacle." She pointed to Frank. "Hull. Time to start scraping, sailor."

He put the dragon on his shoulders and followed after her, but he dawdled so much on the brief trek to the north side of the lake that Twyla had to take him by the arm and drag him. "Quill is an adult. Better yet, he's a literal dragon expert. He is more than capable of taking care of Mary Georgina for a few hours, and he's going to have to handle this all day tomorrow and part of Allgodsday anyway."

"I know, but—"

"Quill!" Twyla waved her hand to get his attention before Frank could back out. He was worse than she had been the first day she dropped DJ off at kindergarten.

Quill sprang to his feet—an impressive achievement for a man of his age—and approached them with eagerness. He didn't kiss her or call her *darling*, but he brushed his hand down her arm, a gesture that made Twyla bristle, even as she felt herself to be unreasonable. She'd had sex with this man. They were dating. Of course it was appropriate for him to touch her. And yet there was a certain stamp of ownership in that brush of his hand, as if he were stating to the world—or at least to Frank—*This is* my *woman*.

It made Twyla less than forthcoming when she removed the dragon from Frank's shoulders and handed her to Quill. "We need to check out a lead. We'll only be a few hours. Please keep an eye on Mary Georgina for us."

"I hadn't planned on—"

"Thank you so much. You're a huge help."

Never give a man a choice, her grandma Eloise had advised her a few days before her wedding. *Never ask. Always tell him what he's going to do. If you ask, you give him a choice, and if you give him a choice, he won't do it.* It had taken Twyla twenty years of marriage to figure that out. And then Doug went and sailed the Salt Sea, so it didn't matter anymore. Today, she put her grandma Eloise's words of wisdom to good use and left Quill stammering behind her.

She and Frank mounted up and rode south to the rocky plain where Herd had sent up his flare weeks ago. There were no longer any signs of what had happened here, no glitter, no blood, no evidence that a man had died on this spot. The indifference of time sent a shiver up Twyla's spine. They picketed the equimares, and Twyla brought Frank up to speed on how much of the site she and Quill and Duckers had already searched, looking for scat or a living dragon rather than a nest.

"Quill said the terrain didn't scream dragon habitat, although maybe he's got some new theories now that he's seen them in the flesh."

Frank gave her a sage nod. "Dragon poodles."

"Dragon poodles," she agreed. "Duckers found the scat in those trees over there, so I think that's where we should start. We can keep circling outward from there."

"Makes sense."

It felt good to be working together again, Frank and Twyla, Twyla and Frank, partners in the Tanrian Marshals. But their first flush of excitement slowly dwindled as the day wore on and produced no sign of a dragon's nest. It was hotter here than it was by the lake, and the fine hairs that had escaped Twyla's low ponytail stuck uncomfortably to her neck. She took off her hat to fan herself.

"There's a pebble in my boot," she told Frank. She sat on a nearby rock to pull off her boot and shake it out. Without warning her seat lurched beneath her, and the next thing she knew, she was falling, down and down, darkness closing in around her until she hit dirt.

"Twyla!" Frank's voice came from a distance that didn't make sense.

She was stunned. Her entire body rang with the impact of hitting the ground. And then she realized, *I can't breathe.*

"Twyla? Can you hear me?"

She wanted to call to him. She wanted him to lift her up and make her breathe. She couldn't draw air.

"Fuck! I'm coming!"

She clutched at her chest and throat, panic setting in.

You've had the wind knocked out of you, the voice of reason in her brain begged her to understand. *You're going to be okay in a minute. Calm down.*

She willed her muscles to go lax before she drew in a quick, sharp breath. It wasn't enough.

"Twyla?"

She wanted to answer him, but she couldn't.

"Hang in there! Fuck!" He sounded as panicked as she felt.

She tried to breathe again and choked in a little more air. It was dim where she was, but not dark. She could see light overhead, a large hole sending down a shaft of sunlight. She could hear Frank clambering down to her—down, because somehow, someway, she had ended up underground. There was the sound of his boots hitting earth, and then he was kneeling beside her, brushing her hair away from her face, his hands moving along the length of her body, searching for injury.

"Where are you hurt?"

She wheezed for air.

"Fuck!" he spat, his hands trying to find a problem that wasn't there.

She took another wheezing breath. It was getting easier.

"Come on, darlin'. Stay with me." Frank leaned over her and put his hand over her heart. She felt something wet drop onto her face, and she understood that he was crying.

"I'm fine," she gasped.

"You're not fine!"

She pulled in another painful, juddering breath and choked out a few more words. "Got the wind knocked out of me."

His hands scanned again, feeling around her rib cage, frantic.

"I'm fine." She put a hand over his wrist and forced herself to sit up, grunting with ache and effort. She sucked in air until her lungs finally sorted themselves out.

In the faint sunlight filtering in from the hole above, she saw tears streaking down Frank's face. Horrible, strangled sobs caught in his throat. Her chest throbbed at the sight of his anguish, and she took his face in her hands and wiped at his tears with her thumbs.

"I'm fine. I promise."

Frank closed his eyes, his face a rictus, as if he were in physical pain. He grasped her shoulders and pressed his forehead to hers, and they stayed that way for a long, long time, and all the while Twyla repeated, softly, "I'm fine. I'm fine."

"Merciful Mother of Sorrows," Frank uttered at last. He wasn't a religious man, but it sounded like a prayer coming from his mouth. He wrapped his arms around her and pulled her against his barrel chest. They clung to each other, and Twyla couldn't imagine anything she would rather do less than let go.

Eventually, they had to put their minds to the task of getting out of wherever they were. They appeared to be in a sizable underground cavern with tunnels leading off to the left and the right. The hole through which she had fallen was an uneven circle of daylight roughly ten feet above them.

"Is that a ladder?" Frank asked, shuffling toward the cave wall to investigate.

"Bride of Fortune, seriously?"

"Definitely a ladder. I bet you knocked it over when you fell in. Someone's been here before, that's for sure. Can you stand?"

"Yeah, but oof, I'm too old to be falling like that."

He helped her to her feet but kept a hand on her arm, as if he needed to touch her to be sure she was alive and not about to crumple into a dead heap at his feet. "Gods, you scared the shit out of me."

"Sorry."

"No *sorry* about it. I'm just glad you're okay." He turned away to pick up the fallen ladder and prop it against the entrance.

"Think Herd put this here?"

"That's my guess. Probably marked the opening with that big rock you sat on. The mouth is wide, but it's in a depression, so it's hard to see unless you're on top of it. Maybe he found this tunnel on rounds and decided to go poking around on his downtime."

Twyla had taken several exploratory steps toward what appeared to be the mouth of a tunnel leading off to their right when she tripped on a pile of cylindrical objects and went spilling onto the ground again, this time bruising her knee.

"I'm okay!" she assured Frank before he had the chance to worry again.

"Salt Sea, woman, are you trying to kill me today? My heart can't take it."

She held up one of the tubes she'd sent scattering all over the place. She must have kicked a hole in its pasteboard casing, because a fine powder smelling of rotten eggs tickled her hand.

Frank bent over, hands on his knees, to squint at the object before shouting, "Put it down!"

Startled, Twyla dropped it immediately.

"Don't drop it, Twy!"

"You told me to put it down!"

"Gently!"

"You didn't say gently!"

Frank rubbed his chest. "This is how I'm going to die."

"Well, what is it?"

"It smells like gunpowder," he said as he gave her a hand up.

"Ope!" Twyla startled again, hopping away from the explosives and nearly knocking Frank over in the process.

He wrapped his arms around her to steady her, and here they were again, all wrapped up in each other. Her heart pounding for a variety of reasons, Twyla extricated herself.

"Does gunpowder work inside the Mist?" she wondered aloud. "Is that an Old Gods thing?"

"If it is, it's yet another reason to get out of here."

The connection between the tubes and the marshals' reason for investigating this area in the first place snapped together in Twyla's mind, like pieces of a puzzle revealing one corner of a larger picture. "Holy Three Mothers," she breathed.

"What's wrong?"

"Think about it. What could wake up a hibernating dragon?"

The blood drained out of Frank's face as he looked first at the pile of gunpowder-filled tubes and then toward one of the tunnels leading away from the main cavern.

"That's it. We're done here. And we need to get you to the infirmary."

"Are we sure this ladder is solid?" she asked him, staring up at the splintery wooden rungs.

"About to find out."

Frank held the bottom steady as she climbed up and out of the wide hole and into the light of day, her muscles aching the entire way.

There was no one on duty at the infirmary.

"How can no one be on duty at the infirmary?" an outraged Frank demanded of Fern at the weapons lockers.

"Hiring freeze. Maguire can't get permission to fill the opening, and there aren't enough doctors on staff to cover all the hours. You'll have to go to the hospital in Herington or wait until tomorrow morning. Are you hurt, Marshal Banneker?"

"I'm fine," she said, and she repeated herself, emphatically, to Frank. "I'm fine."

"You're limping."

"Hardly."

"We're at least getting an ice pack. Come on."

He strode off to the infirmary, and Twyla followed, because honestly, her right hip and butt cheek were mighty sore, and that ice pack sounded pretty good. And maybe some aspirin. He held the door for her, turned on the gas sconce, and patted the top of the exam table. She hopped up as he got an ice pack out of the icebox and handed it to her. When she pressed it to her lower back, he said, "Let's have a look."

"At what?"

"Your back, where you are clearly injured, because that's where you slapped that ice pack on."

"You sneaky bastard." She sighed and pulled her shirt up to the line of her brassiere with no embarrassment to speak of. Frank had seen a fair amount of her skin after eight years partnered up in the marshals, and he had doctored her in the field more times than she could count.

But then he touched her, softly, carefully, his fingers sliding across her ribs, feeling along the length of each bone, his fingertips dry and warm against her skin.

And Twyla wanted to purr.

Had she been so sex starved that messing around with Quill had awoken some randy beast within her? Or maybe it was the fact that sex with Quill had left her wanting? Why else would she be enjoying this completely innocuous contact with Frank as much as she was?

"Does it hurt when you breathe? Any sharp pain when you inhale?"

"No, I don't have any broken ribs," she said tetchily, eager to draw the examination to a close.

"That was not a short fall, Twy. Pull away the ice pack for a second so I can have a look."

His hand was smoothing slowly over her back, palm flattened against her, and Bride of Fortune, it felt good. Why did it feel good? And now he wanted her to take away the ice pack? When she was about to combust?

"Sure," she said casually, as if the man who was her best friend in the world wasn't presently waking up what she had considered her faltering libido all of five minutes ago.

I need to get this out of my system, she thought. *It's* The Rogue of Redwing Ruins *and the fluorescent green vibrator for me tonight.*

She set the ice pack on the exam table beside her and held her breath as Frank stared at her back and gently ran his fingertips toward her hip, which, as it happened, was located in close proximity to her butt cheek. So she was now inflicting on him a traumatic peek at her staggeringly not sexy granny panties. She felt the moment his fingers brushed the elastic waistband in her soul.

"Sorry, Twy, but I'm going to have to pull this down an inch or two. Is that okay?" he asked, indicating her underwear.

"Of course! Why wouldn't it be okay?" she shrilled.

He pulled on the elastic with one hand and gently smoothed over the tender flesh where her hip met her ass.

If he goes one inch lower, I'm not sure what's going to happen, she thought. As surreptitiously as she could, she picked up the ice pack and held it to her neck.

His hand went one inch lower.

She yelped, more from mortification than from pain, but Frank startled away in response. When she looked over her shoulder at him, he had his hands in the air, as if Twyla were arresting him.

"It doesn't hurt that badly, I swear," she assured him.

His eyes were wide, and his hands were still in the air. "You're going to have a nasty bruise, but as long as you're not pissing blood, I think you're okay."

"Hello-o-o? Mail delivery?"

Frank's hands fell to his sides, and he hung his head. "Salt Sea," he cursed as Hermia opened the infirmary door a crack, just wide enough to poke her black button nose into the room. "I have a letter for you, Marshal Banneker."

"Come on in," Twyla said in welcome to the nimkilim, who had unwittingly come to her rescue.

"I like your underwear," Hermia told Twyla as she handed over the envelope with Hope's handwriting on the front.

"Thank you," Twyla answered in humiliation as she opened the letter and read:

Hey, Mom, I know Wardensday is Mercy Birdsall's wedding, but Everett got a few days off and we're taking a quick trip to Halifax Island off the coast of Lyona with friends. Ms. Wilner is giving me some time off so I can go. Be back Sorrowsday. Love you! —Hope

Twyla loved having her daughter home, but she was thrilled to have the house all to herself for the next couple of days.

Frank had grabbed the prescription pad off the counter and was scrawling a note on it. "Hermia, can you take a message to Dr. Vanderlinden in Sector W-14? He's expecting us this evening, but as you can see, Twyla is hurt."

"I'm not hurt," Twyla protested.

"I'll write a quick note for Maguire, too. If she gets it before the wedding, great, but if not, that cave's not going anywhere."

"Aren't we abandoning our post, though?"

"You fell a good ten feet into an underground cave. I'm sure Maguire won't mind. We have the day off tomorrow anyway. It makes more sense for you to rest up at home than to ride back to W-14 for one night."

And with Hope gone, Twyla would be blessedly alone in her own house. As long as Wade didn't invade this evening.

"I suppose," she said, brought nearly to tears by the force of her wanting to be home right now, right this very minute.

"That's settled, then."

Frank took his wallet from his pocket and pulled out a twenty.

Twyla blinked at the biggest tip any nimkilim had ever received. "What are you doing?"

"Tipping this hedgehog to say goodbye one time and only one time and leave immediately to deliver these messages to Vanderlinden and Maguire."

Hermia snatched the crisp bill out of his hand and held it in front of her glasses, her black eyes gleaming. "Ooooooooooooooooooh! Do you know how many Lulu's Grape Fizzies I can buy with this? But oh dear, Chief Maguire isn't on duty, and I can only deliver on my mail route."

"I'm sure you'll find a way."

The nimkilim slid the bill into her pocket, which seemed to

have grown droopier since the last time they saw her. "I'll put it in the nimkilim box for you."

"Fine. Bye, Hermia."

"Bye," she said once and only once and made a beeline for the door, her rubber rain boots squeaking on the linoleum. That was as far as she got, however, because the door stymied her. She pulled and pulled on the handle to no avail, until bone-weary Frank had to push it open for her.

Hermia turned and raised her tiny hand in a wave.

"Don't," Frank warned her.

She slapped the hand over her mouth and walked away.

Twyla's disconcertingly heated response to Frank's examination continued to fluster her during the car ride home. The front bench of her autoduck felt unusually small and cramped as Frank drove along the empty country road. Desperate to quash the unwanted pants feelings for the man behind the wheel, Twyla dragged her attention away from his disturbingly appealing forearms and directed it toward the investigation. "Why do you think Herd needed explosives? And how has no one heard them going off? Except the dragons, I guess."

"I've been thinking about that. Remember the night we found his body? We heard thunder."

"That's because the storm came in."

"I know, but we were hearing thunder a while before the rain started. We assumed it was the storm. But what if it wasn't? What if everyone who's heard something go *boom* in Tanria assumed the same thing?"

"That makes sense, but it doesn't tell us why he wanted to blow stuff up in the first place."

Another piece of the puzzle tickled the back of Twyla's mind, but her tired brain couldn't remember what it was or figure out where it fit. And then everything that had happened over the past few hours caught up to her all at once, and she wound up conking out for the remainder of the ride home. She didn't wake up until Frank opened the passenger-side door.

"We're home, darlin'."

The weirdness of the infirmary dissolved like magic as he half carried her into her house. He offered to draw her a bath, and it wasn't weird, because Frank was her best friend, and he was trying to help her. That was all. That was all he was trying to do in the infirmary, too.

She said no to the bath and thank you for the friendship, and she fell asleep in her own bed in her own house without the assistance of *The Rogue of Redwing Ruins* or the fluorescent green vibrator.

Chapter Twelve

The tan pumps stared at Twyla from the floor of her closet.

The "sensible" tan pumps that weren't actually sensible, because they mangled her feet, Mary Jane straps or no.

You're going to a wedding, Twyla, they seemed to say to her. *You're supposed to wear heels to a wedding. Weddings and funerals. Everyone knows this.*

She closed the closet door and stared at her reflection in the full-length mirror, wearing nothing but her most comfortable pair of granny panties and her least uncomfortable brassiere. A fifty-three-year-old post-menopausal woman stared back at her in all her imperfect glory. This woman was more than a sum of her faults, wasn't she? She had the wisdom and competence that came only with age and experience. Her body—which had given birth to three children, saved lives in Tanria, and housed her soul every day of her life—was worth something, especially when she thought of how close she had come to losing it.

She turned to the side, pulled down the elastic waistband of her underpants, and tried to get a look at the multicolored bruise taking up significant real estate along her right hip and butt cheek. It was ugly, but it was also a reminder that she was alive.

And life was too short to wear shoes that wanted to kill her.

She opened the closet door, glared at the heels, and said, "You can go to Old Hell." She reached instead for a pair of flats, after which she slipped into the simple blue sheath dress that her daughter had found inadequately sexy, and put her pretty beaded cardigan over it. After dabbing on tinted moisturizer and giving her lashes a few swipes of mascara, Twyla decided that her simple style lent her an air of elegance and grace.

"You look good, Twyla," she told herself, and she actually meant it.

She was twisting her hair up with a sparkly clip when Frank gave a perfunctory knock on her front door and let himself in. "Hey, darlin', I'm here," he called.

"Almost ready." She tucked her favorite lip-colored lipstick and a roll of mints into the small satin clutch that passed as her fancy purse, then met Frank in her parlor. She pulled up short when she saw him.

"You cut your hair!"

"Good afternoon to you, too."

"Good afternoon, but oh my!"

He gazed bashfully at his freshly polished loafers and gave a self-conscious laugh as she made a show of examining his new haircut from every angle. He had grown out his hair in the aftermath of his divorce, and at the time, privately, Twyla had thought it had the whiff of midlife crisis about it. But he had kept up the length for twelve years now, so the new look was a shock to Twyla's system. He was still Frank, and yet it was as if she were seeing him for the first time.

"What made you do it?"

"Liz Brimsby stopped by yesterday all of five minutes after I got home. And I got to thinking that a lot of ladies I've dated over the years seem to like my hair more than they like me."

"So you decided to see if you could scrape off the barnacle with a haircut?"

"It worked."

"No, it didn't!"

"She stopped by a while ago with cinnamon rolls. I think she was angling for me to take her to the wedding, but she took one look at the hair, set down the cinnamon rolls, and said her goodbyes."

Twyla was outraged and oddly relieved at the same time. "Shallow! Poor Frank—it's terrible to be objectified."

"Eh, who cares what she thinks? What do *you* think?"

She took a long, assessing look at him with his new haircut. He wore his good suit, the one she'd helped him pick out five years ago, when they'd been invited to three different weddings in one summer and his old suit no longer fit him. At the time, she'd thought he should have paired the dark gray jacket and pants with a white or light gray shirt—and he did buy the white and light gray shirts—but he had also picked out a dress shirt in the same dark gray as the suit. Now he stood before her in all that monochromatic gray with nothing but a tie with thin pale gray stripes against a field of anthracite to add a pop of pattern to the ensemble. She smoothed his lapels (which did not need smoothing) and declared in complete honesty, "Franklin Timothy Ellis, you look good, sir."

"You have to say that because you're my best friend."

"And yet I'm correct."

"You usually are."

He offered her his arm, and together they set off for the temple on foot since it was only four blocks away and the weather was clement. Best of all, Twyla didn't have to take mincing steps, because she was wearing shoes that weren't designed to torment her.

"Aren't you going to ask me how you look?" said Frank.

"I know how I look: fifty-three and not too shabby."

"You look beautiful."

Twyla knew that she was a reasonably decent-looking human being, but she could count on one hand the number of times anyone had referred to her as *beautiful*. *Invisible* was more accurate. And yet Frank had never blown smoke up her ass a day in their lives together, so she knew he was being not only kind but sincere, a notion that made her flush with embarrassed pleasure. "Thank you," she said.

"You don't have to thank a man for the truth. How's your back?"

"Ugly and a little tender. Nothing aspirin and some champagne toasts can't cure. I wonder if we should pull Maguire aside and fill her in on what we found?"

"I vote no. If she got my note and wants to ask questions, fine. But otherwise, I say we take the day off. I haven't had a real day off since..." He made a vague gesture, but Twyla could fill in the blank.

"How are you holding up without you-know-who?"

"It feels like I cut out a vital organ and left it in Tanria, but other than that, I'm good." Frank patted her hand in the crook of his elbow.

"Oh, Frank."

"No worries. Getting to sleep in my own bed more than makes up for it."

When they arrived at temple, Twyla was surprised to learn that the ceremony was being held at the Warden's altar. Any god, even minor ones, could witness wedding vows, but most people shied away from having their union blessed by one of the death gods. Twyla had no idea who Hart Ralston's divine parent was, but given the fact that he had managed to save them all from the undead of Tanria, it would make sense for him to be literally related to death.

That would be rough, she thought. Then again, he looked happier than she had ever seen the man as he moved through the crowd, greeting wedding guests at Mercy's side. He was certainly difficult to miss, since he stood at least a head taller than every single person present. Mercy's father, Roy Birdsall, stood by the Warden's altar, chatting with the key-keepers and offer-bearers— Alma Maguire and Duckers for Hart Ralston, and Mercy's siblings, Lilian and Zeddie, for their sister. Zeddie held a covered cake plate, while Duckers carried a rectangular bundle wrapped in brown paper and tied with twine. He looked nervous, and Twyla wondered if he was anxious about the wedding or his boyfriend or both. She caught his eye and gave him an encouraging smile. He gave her a surreptitious thumbs-up in reply.

"Twyla! Frank!" Anita Banneker whisper-shouted when she saw them, and she waved them over to come sit with her and Wade. She looked lovely with her ink-black hair in a chignon and her lips painted the perfect shade of red. Anita was one of the only people Twyla knew who really could carry off red lipstick.

"You look divine. Are you getting a night out without the kids?" Twyla asked as she and Frank took the seats her daughter-in-law had saved for them.

Anita bubbled with unfettered joy. "We got a sitter."

Twyla patted her knee. "Good for you."

A low but happy buzz of murmuring voices filled the Warden's alcove, the accompaniment to one of those rare occasions in life when people gathered together in unapologetic merriment. The long marble slab that served as the Warden's altar at the front of the alcove hosted vases of flowers and so many lit candles it looked like Grandfather Bones's birthday cake. All that candlelight glinted off the mosaic behind the altar, an enormous image of the death god with two faces: one for looking inward, and one for looking outward. Now that Twyla thought on it, the Warden was the perfect choice to witness a wedding ceremony; he was, after all, the god of doorways and of new beginnings.

"If everyone could take a seat, I think we're ready to begin," announced the temple votary. Twyla was pleased to see that Votary Asebedo was running the show today. She was a retired schoolteacher, and she knew how to keep a wedding ceremony moving along at a nice clip.

Roy kissed Mercy's cheek when she arrived at the altar, and then he gave Hart Ralston a bear hug. Roy was not a small man, but the sheriff had to bend over to hug him in return.

"Good gods, he's tall," Anita marveled to Twyla out of the side of her mouth.

The wedding party took their places at the altar, with Lilian and Zeddie facing the bride and groom from Mercy's side and Maguire and Duckers facing inward from Ralston's side. Roy Birdsall stood at the center, the only parent left living, unless one counted the groom's divine parent. Hart Ralston, towering and blond and handsome in a three-piece navy suit, stood to Roy's left, while Mercy stood to his right, nervously adjusting her new chunky tortoiseshell glasses. She was a human ray of sunshine in her lemon-yellow dress, so flattering to her full figure and olive skin and brown curls. Twyla put a sentimental hand over her sentimental heart when she noticed that the groom wore a yellow pocket square and a navy-blue tie with yellow paisleys to match his bride's sunny dress. And then Twyla saw the way they looked at each other, so disgustingly and perfectly in love, and she pressed her hand even harder against her aching breastbone.

Gods, she loved weddings.

Votary Asebedo invited Roy to kick things off with the ritual of the parents' keys.

Every child was given a key at birth, a reminder that they would always have a home in the House of the Unknown God in the Void Beyond the Sky. At death, Grandfather Bones would free the soul from their body. They would sail the Salt Sea to the House of the Unknown God, and the Warden would open the door to them to welcome them home. When a person died, their family placed their birth key on the family altar to remind the people who loved them most of the good life they had lived. And so this key was a symbol of the death that gave everyone life.

The votary handed Roy the ceremonial tray with three keys spread across its velvet surface: the birth keys of the bride's and groom's mothers, who had already sailed the Salt Sea, as well as Roy Birdsall's own birth key. Beside them was a small dish of salt water. He presented the tray first to Mercy, who dipped her fingers into the salt water and touched each key.

"From water we come, and from water we shall return," Roy repeated after the votary, the same words Twyla had spoken at DJ's wedding and at Wade's. "The Salt Sea reminds my child that life is precious, and my child, in turn, honors those who gave her life."

Since the groom had no parents present, Roy offered the tray to him in their stead and intoned the same words as Hart Ralston dipped his fingers into the salt water and touched the keys. He looked up when Roy called him *my child*, his eyes glistening with unshed tears, making Twyla's own waterworks kick into gear. She sniffed as she opened her tiny purse, only to realize with a deep sense of nose-dripping dread that she had forgotten to stuff a tissue therein.

As if by magic, a square of clean, freshly pressed linen appeared before her eyes.

Thank you, she mouthed at Frank. He winked in acknowledgment and returned his attention to the wedding.

Roy sat in the place of honor at the front of the guests, and the votary called for the offerings to the Warden. Zeddie Birdsall stepped forward first, handing Mercy the cake plate, which she set on the altar.

"What offering does the bride bring to thank the Warden for blessing this union?" asked Votary Asebedo.

Mercy lifted the dome off the cake plate to reveal the gorgeous confection beneath, iced to precise perfection with white frosting. "A coconut cake baked by my brother, Zeddie Birdsall." The answer was intended for the Warden, but she directed her words to Hart. Twyla sensed an inside joke in the form of a coconut cake, because Hart Ralston bit his cheek, trying not to laugh as Mercy returned to her place beside the votary.

Duckers, as the groom's offer-bearer, handed the brown paper parcel to his friend and breathed a sigh of relief once his main duty had been carried out successfully. Ralston set the package on the Warden's altar and unwrapped it, revealing a stack of colorful paper.

"What offering does the groom bring to thank the Warden for blessing this union?" the votary asked him.

"Every issue of the *Old Gods* comic series that I could get my hands on." Unlike Mercy, Hart addressed the mosaic of the Warden and his two faces that covered the wall behind the altar. He cleared his throat, a man on the verge of tears. The Hart Ralston whom Twyla had worked with for nearly seven years before he became sheriff was not a man she would have described as warm or emotional—but she had always suspected hidden depths there, and now she was seeing them.

She blew her nose as quietly as she could into Frank's handkerchief. He gave her a soft nudge, one that said, fondly, *You are a sap, Twyla Banneker.*

Hart returned to his place to the left of the votary. Mercy dimpled at him. She obviously knew why he was giving the Warden a stack of comic books rather than the typical offering of food.

Votary Asebedo addressed the gathering once more. "In the days before the New Gods triumphed over those who came before them, the Old Gods bought humanity's devotion with fear: fear of war, fear of grief, fear of pain, fear of loneliness. These cursed gifts are with us today. Knowing that life is difficult, those who choose to marry must understand and accept the challenges that come with sharing one's life with another. For this reason, Mercy and Hart will now make the Promises of Marriage to each other. Mercy, will you take Hart's hands in yours and repeat after me?"

Mercy reached out her hands across the votary, and Hart placed his long hands in hers.

"Hart," she repeated, her voice firm and steady, "I promise to walk this life beside you. I will shoulder your burdens. I will consider your hopes and dreams and needs in all my decisions. I will show you acts of kindness, large and small. I will hold you in the dark of night. And I will find joy in this world with you at my side."

"Hart, will you take Mercy's hands in yours and repeat after me?" asked the votary. The couple changed the positions of their hands so that Hart's were beneath Mercy's.

"Mercy," he repeated after the votary, his voice quiet, as if no one else were in the alcove but the woman standing across from him. "I promise to walk this life beside you. I will shoulder your burdens. I will consider your hopes and dreams and needs in all my decisions. I will show you acts of kindness, large and small. I will hold you in the dark of night. And I will find joy in this world with you at my side."

This was one of Twyla's favorite parts of a wedding, when the vows were complete and that wonderful frisson of relief and happiness passed between two people pledging their lives to each other. She could see Mercy's fingers curl over Hart's hands and the way he squeezed her hands in return, the acknowledgment that together they were doing something bigger than themselves.

"We will now have the exchange of the birth keys," declared Votary Asebedo.

Mercy's sister, Lilian, handed her the key on a silver chain. Mercy clutched the chain with both hands over her heart, looking her groom in the eye as she repeated after the votary.

"I, Mercy Elizabeth Birdsall, entrust you, Hartley James Ralston, with my life and all that I have made of it. I give you my happiness and my sorrow, my fortunes and my failures, my wisdom and my foolishness. Do you accept me as I am?"

"I cherish all that you are, now and always," Hart Ralston answered without needing to be prompted, his voice soft and gruff.

He leaned down so that Mercy could put her key around his neck. Fortunately, she was tall herself, and she was wearing the cutest pair of yellow-and-white spectator pumps Twyla had ever seen outside of a fashion magazine. When Hart stood straight, Mercy's birth key hung over his heart. A watery laugh escaped Mercy's lips as she gave it a happy tap with her fingertips, which made her groom crack a rare smile.

"Repeat after me," Votary Asebedo instructed Hart after Alma Maguire handed him his own birth key on a chain.

"I, Hartley James Ralston, entrust you, Mercy Elizabeth Birdsall, with my life," the groom began dutifully, fighting tears with the same ferocity he'd once used to take out the undead.

It was at this dramatic moment that Mercy's toddler niece escaped from her father in the front row, sprinted to the groom like a runaway equimaris, and wrapped herself around Hart Ralston's left leg.

"Danny!" Lilian hissed at her husband, a ginger-haired man who turned beet red.

"Sorry!" he whispered, hustling to retrieve the errant baby, who squawked in protest as Danny tried to pull her off the groom's leg.

"Emma Jane," Lilian sighed in maternal exhaustion as she joined the fray.

"Up!" cried the toddler, a single sharp syllable that echoed off the domed roof of the temple and the skylight that represented the Unknown God at its center. "Up! Up!"

"Come here, Emma Jane Little Bottom," said Hart Ralston as he caved to the child's demands and lifted her into his arms. She patted him on the cheeks and grinned in triumph, and given the way he grinned back at her, Twyla got the distinct sense that he didn't mind in the slightest. She would never in a million years have pegged him as the sort of person who liked children, but here he was, full of surprises on his wedding day.

He looked at Mercy and shrugged. She laughed and shrugged in return, and the ceremony continued, with the groom holding a young child as he repeated after the votary and held his birth key out of the toddler's reach.

"I, Hartley James Ralston, entrust you, Mercy Elizabeth Birdsall, with my life and all that I have made of it."

He smiled as he spoke the words, and Twyla thought it was sweeter this way, rather than him bawling all over the altar. She, on the other hand, was bawling all over Frank's hankie.

"I give you my happiness and my sorrow, my fortunes and my failures, my wisdom and my foolishness. Do you accept me as I am?"

"I cherish all that you are, now and always," answered Mercy, beaming beatifically up at him as he placed his birth key around her neck with one hand.

The votary spoke again. "You have offered gifts to the Warden in thanks for his blessing. You have made the Promises of Marriage to each other. You have each offered the other your life, and you have each accepted the life of the other in return through the Exchange of Keys. Before the Warden and all the witnesses assembled here today to celebrate your union, I pronounce you married in the eyes of gods and law. You may now seal your union with a kiss."

Hart leaned down to give Mercy a gentle kiss on the lips, careful not to tip the baby over in the process.

"No. Nope. Let's try that again." Mercy snatched Emma Jane from Hart's arms and dumped the toddler on her sister. She grabbed the groom by the lapels and brought his mouth down to hers in a much more impressive kiss to seal the deal, to the approving applause and catcalls of the wedding guests. When the kiss ended, Hart was as pink as Mary Georgina and clearly thrilled, while Mercy laughed in giddy joy.

The votary brought their hands together and had them face the wedding guests. "I present to you the newlyweds!"

"The Bride of Fortune favor you!" cheered the crowd.

"Fucking beautiful," sobbed a deep voice behind Twyla. She turned in her seat to see Tanria's former nimkilim, a crass rabbit named Bassareus, sobbing into a red handkerchief. "Isn't it fucking beautiful?" he asked Horatio, the nattily dressed owl who used to deliver Eternity's mail before the two nimkilim went to work for Mercy's Undertakings. They now delivered dead bodies all over the Federated Islands of Cadmus.

"Do get ahold of yourself, Bassie," said Horatio. "I had this waistcoat made especially for the occasion, and here you are, *leaking* all over it."

"Fuck you," wailed the rabbit.

The owl patted his shoulder consolingly. "There, there, you mawkish lummox."

Like every other couple married in the town of Eternity, Bushong, Hart Ralston and Mercy Birdsall held their reception in the city hall community room. Unlike every other wedding reception held in the community room of Eternity's city hall, this one was catered by Proserpina's, featuring the most elegant buffet Twyla had ever seen as well as a three-tier chocolate wedding cake (baked by Zeddie Birdsall) and three blueberry pies (also baked by Zeddie Birdsall) artistically arranged on small risers of different heights.

"I have walked this earth for over half a century without ever stepping foot inside the swankiest restaurant on the island, and now I've managed to stuff my face full of Proserpina's twice in one month. How is this my life?" Twyla commented to her daughter-in-law as the band was setting up. They were the only two left at the round table with its yellow tablecloth. Everyone else who had been sitting with them was milling about the room or getting more dessert.

"When do I get to meet this new boyfriend of yours? I'm surprised you didn't bring him to the wedding."

Twyla tried to imagine Quill sitting on a metal folding chair in the city hall community room, wearing tweed and sipping brandy. She was glad that she wasn't having to fret about whether or not he would be having a good time at this gathering. She hoped he'd received their note via Hermia; she didn't want him worrying about the fact that she and Frank hadn't returned to camp yesterday. "Quill and I have only gone on one real date. He definitely hasn't qualified for bring-to-a-wedding status."

"You came with Frank, so has he reached bring-to-a-wedding status? Or did he bring you?" Anita sipped her wine, her eyes twinkling with a combination of mischievousness and tipsiness.

"Pfft. You know it's not like that."

"Haven't you ever been the teeniest, tiniest bit curious?"

"About dating Frank? No." Her answer was the same knee-jerk response she'd given dozens of times over the years, but then she remembered his face in the mineshaft when he thought she was hurt or worse. She thought of his hands stroking her bare skin in the infirmary.

Stop that! she scolded herself.

"Not even when he wears that suit?" pressed Anita.

"Nope."

"He looks good in that suit."

"All men look good in suits."

Twyla scanned the room and found Frank chatting with Duckers and Zeddie by the double doors, which had been thrown open to let in the cool evening air.

He looked good in that suit.

"He looks really good in that suit," said Anita.

Wade came to sit beside his wife with his third slice of chocolate cake. "Who, me?"

"Yes, you." Anita leaned over to kiss his cheek, leaving red lipstick on his skin, and it made Twyla's heart swell to see them in love and happy. She often worried that Wade was too oblivious to the needs of others to be a good husband to his wife, but maybe she wasn't giving him enough credit. Something about this small window into his married life made her think he and Anita would be fine. And it probably helped that her second child did, in fact, look handsome in his suit this evening.

"All right, all right!" shouted the bandleader over the din. A few of the wedding guests clinked their silverware against their wineglasses to help him get the room's attention. "It's time for the newlyweds to have their first married dance together. Let's have some applause for Hart and Mercy!"

The whooping and clapping were thunderous as Mercy and Hart took to the dance floor. Mercy had exchanged her gorgeous spectators for a pair of red canvas high-tops, while Hart had taken off his jacket and rolled up his shirtsleeves, although he still wore his waistcoat and tie.

"Speaking of men looking good in suits," Twyla commented to Anita.

"Mom!" Wade chastised her.

Anita patted his hand. "Honey, your mother has eyes in her head and a pulse."

The band kicked off an unusually up-tempo song for the first dance, but when Hart Ralston led his bride into a perfect pair of turns and a shoulder slide, Twyla understood the choice of music. Most couples opted for the safe Sway in a Circle, and here were the town undertaker and all six feet, nine inches of her demigod husband showing the town of Eternity how it was done.

"Look at those moves!" Anita whooped.

"You want moves? I'll show you moves," said Wade, offering her his hand once the first dance was finished. She took it eagerly, and they joined the other couples on the dance floor.

Twyla glanced toward the doors, but no one was standing there now. She spotted Duckers and Zeddie dancing together beside Alma Maguire and her wife, Diane, but she didn't see Frank anywhere.

She made a circuit of the room, stopping to catch up with friends and neighbors, and she danced one song with Wade, but after a half hour had passed with no sign of Frank, she stepped outside in search of him, carrying with her two bottles of beer from the bar. She found him gazing up at the stars in the park behind city hall. He had his jacket off and carried it over his shoulder by two hooked fingers. Twyla came up quietly beside him and offered him one of the beers. He took the proffered drink and clinked his bottleneck to hers.

"What are you doing out here?" she asked him.

"Getting some air."

"Are you doing okay?"

"Yep."

Twyla sensed she'd bumped up against the Cora-shaped door in Frank's internal house that he wasn't eager to open up to anyone, not even to her. She had decided not to jiggle the proverbial doorknob when Frank surprised her by admitting, "Nah, that's a lie. I'm not okay. I'm out here thinking about lots of not-okay stuff."

"Such as?"

"Such as the fact that I fucked up my marriage, and to this day, I'm not sure how."

With those words, Frank had flung open a door, and Twyla hovered silently on the threshold, waiting to see if he would invite her in.

He did.

"The only things I knew when I tied the knot were that I loved Cora and I wasn't going to be to her what my daddy was to my mama. That man was useless. Worse than useless. He didn't provide for his family a day in his life, not one copper and not a single ounce of love. Didn't seem to think it was his responsibility to take care of anyone but himself. Everything fell to Mama, and even then that asshole drank away the money she didn't manage to hide from him. I thought, if that's what marriage is, I don't want it. But then I met Cora and changed my mind real quick. We were happy in those days, I swear we were, even if her family never thought I was good enough for her."

"They were wrong if that's what they thought."

"I was a stable hand at her daddy's ranch. I was definitely not good enough for her. Seemed like getting away from both of our families would do us good. I thought it was—good, I mean. I thought we had a good life. The money I was making as a marshal was more than enough to provide for our family. But Cora seemed less and less satisfied as time went on, and I couldn't understand it. I was doing everything I could to make it all work. I know I was gone a lot on the job, but when I was home, I spent time with the kids every second I got, and I was careful to clean up after myself and do the things around the house that needed doing. I tried to make her life easier, but it never seemed to be what she wanted."

"I imagine what she wanted was you."

He huffed a bitter laugh. "Imagine that."

"It wasn't your fault, or Cora's. Sometimes these things don't work out."

"I know, and I don't blame Cora. But gods, I've missed my kids. Twelve years, and it's the same fucking hole in my heart that it's always been."

Frank had let Twyla into his most private room, and all the sorrow and regret she found there was putting a hole in her own heart.

"Look at me, because I need you to understand this." She waited until his eyes met hers, the whites reflecting the dim light of the distant gas lamps along Main Street. "You are a great dad. Even when you had to be far away, you've always been there for Lu and Annie in the ways that mattered most, and they know that. That's why they come every summer, even now that they're grown. They love you as much as you love them."

A wet trickle gleamed on his cheek. This was the second time Twyla had seen him cry in as many days. Everything was coming in pairs lately: dinners and dates and weddings and a good friend's tears.

He dabbed at his eye with his shirtsleeve. "Sorry. Weddings dredge up this crap for me."

"You have nothing to be sorry for."

"I don't know what I'd do without you. I really don't." He spoke the words so softly, it was almost as if they were only half-said.

"The feeling's mutual." She wiped a tear away for him with her fingertips. "I'd offer you your own handkerchief, but I've snotted all over it."

That earned her a wet laugh.

"I'll wash it and get it back to you," she promised him.

He pulled her into a side hug. "Yes, I know. I'm familiar with this routine by now."

"I have a hankie routine?"

"You always cry at weddings—always—and you never remember to bring a tissue, you slob." He jostled her teasingly before letting her go.

"I don't know why weddings turn me into a sentimental sap. I think it's all that promise for the future. A new beginning. The hopefulness of it all."

As she stargazed beside her friend, she was glad to be looking at the sky and not at Frank—Frank, who could read her like a book—because they were bumping up against one of her own closed doors now.

"I'm going to have to bring a bedsheet instead of a handkerchief when Hope gets married."

"I don't know if I should laugh or cry about that comment."

"It's messing with you, isn't it? This business with Hope?"

And now he was knocking on that closed door. "Yes, it is."

"Want to talk about it?"

"Not particularly."

"Fair enough."

Twyla's gratitude for the friend who knew when to let something drop nearly overwhelmed her in her emotional postwedding state.

"Can I ask you something?" he said, speaking to the stars above.

"Sure."

"Why Vanderlinden?"

She didn't know what question she'd been expecting, but that wasn't it. The air seemed to thin. Every breath, every rustle of clothing, the tracing of Frank's finger along the sweating glass of his beer bottle roared between them. It was a simple question, but Twyla sensed that her answer carried weight, and it irritated her that something so small should matter to Frank. Because it shouldn't matter to him, the way his own parade of girlfriends in the wake of his divorce had never mattered to her. Why did it bother him so much that she was finally moving on with her love life when he'd done nothing but move on since the day Cora left him?

"Why *not* Vanderlinden?" she said. "He's fun. I'm having fun. Don't I deserve that?"

"Of course you do, but that's not what I'm asking." Frank deliberated his next words carefully. "I know you never got over losing Doug. You two had something special, and when he died, I thought—I *assumed*—there'd never be anyone else for you."

How could Frank, who knew her so well, also know her so little? He was banging up against her most guarded locked door, and he had no clue what was on the other side.

"You think I've spent the past thirteen years pining for Doug?"

"Haven't you?"

She'd already had two glasses of champagne, but she was going to need to be more buzzed to have this conversation, so she gulped down half her bottle of beer. "What if the answer to that question is no? What would you think of me?"

"Nothing could change my opinion of you," said the man who had just informed her that she and Doug had had *something special*.

"Ha!" Twyla barked, and she chugged the rest of her beer.

"Are you mad at me?" he asked her cautiously.

"Am I mad at you?" She contemplated the question. "I don't know. And I don't know why I'm so crabby either. I love weddings. Why do I love weddings?" She flung the question at the Old Gods and the even older gods that had come and gone before them, and the gods who had blinked out of time and memory before that, all of them cold and silent on the altar of the sky.

"I always assumed it was because you loved being married."

"There's that word again. Lots of assuming tonight." She went to take another drink before she realized the bottle was empty. It was dark, but she could see well enough to know that Frank was making a baffled face at her.

"What's that look about?"

"I feel like I'm seeing a part of you for the first time tonight."

"The part that isn't the dedicated wife and mother you thought she was?"

He floundered like a fish flopping around in a boat.

"You want the truth, Frank? The godsawful, ugly truth about me? I don't miss Doug. And do you want to know why I don't miss him?"

"I want to know anything you're willing to tell me," he answered delicately.

The anger she rarely acknowledged simmered in her guts. She didn't want that rage anymore—she was so tired of that rage— but as she spoke her truth to Frank, it got hotter, bubbling under her skin, and now it came frothing out of her mouth like a pot boiling over.

"You heard those wedding vows today. You've spoken those vows, and so have I, and we both meant them when we stood at the altar of our gods. 'I cherish all that you are, now and always.' That's what we said. And that's what Doug said to me. But a few years into our marriage, I looked around and I realized that I was his cook, his maid, his children's nanny, his secretary, his whore. My whole life was in service to that man and to our family. I cherished everyone, but who cherished me? I wasn't a cherished wife. I wasn't his equal. I was invisible to him, that's what! I was no different from a...a...a *chair*. I was useful. I was there when he needed me or wanted me and insignificant when he didn't. There was never a question that I wouldn't be ever present, never an understanding of how hard his life would be if, one day, his chair simply wasn't there, and he no longer had anywhere to sit. I was a chair, Frank. For twenty-one years. So when Doug up and died on me, I got my life back, and gods help me, I have been so much happier on my own."

She had never said this to anyone, had never so much as hinted at it, and as she stood there shaking before Frank—the person whose opinion mattered most to her—she felt hollow. It was as if the words and all the heartbreak and loneliness and anger that came with them had left nothing behind when they emptied out of her.

Frank stood motionless at her side. "I had no idea. Why'd you stay with him?"

"I almost left. Once. I had it all planned out. I was going to swallow my pride and go home to Medora and let my mom tell me 'I told you so.' The boys were both in school by then, so I wouldn't have to worry as much about childcare. I'd set aside enough money from the pittance I made at Wilner's to put down a deposit on an apartment. And then I realized I was pregnant again. There was no way I could work and be the kind of parent the boys needed while taking care of a baby, not unless I stayed. So I stayed. Besides, I vowed to take Doug as he was, and in the end, that's exactly what I did."

There. It was done. All the ugliness inside her was laid bare for Frank Ellis. She waited for him to say something as a cold pit of dread opened up inside her.

"Aw, darlin', come here." He pulled her into one of his perfect Frank hugs, and Twyla lost it. She sobbed against the shoulder of his dress shirt.

"I loved him. I did, I swear. And he loved me, in his way. He wasn't a bad man. He didn't hurt me. He didn't cheat on me. He didn't do anything wrong. He didn't deserve to have a wife who almost walked out on him."

Frank said nothing, only stroked her gently on the back.

"Do you think I'm a terrible person now?"

"How could I ever think that?"

"That wasn't an unequivocal no."

"It is an unequivocal no. You're a gem, and no one can convince me otherwise. Not even you."

Twyla did not want to tear herself away from his arms and his warmth and the comforting hum of his voice in his chest, but she was getting mascara all over his shirt, so she extricated herself. "Sorry. I turned a conversation about you into a conversation about me."

"Nah, we had a conversation about both of us. Thirteen years is too long for either of us to hold on to this stuff. It's good we got it all out in the open. You don't judge me, do you? You're not saying to yourself, *Cora had it right. Frank was a shit husband.*"

"Of course not."

"Exactly."

Now it was his turn to wipe tears from her face.

"I left your hankie in my crappy tiny purse," she told him apologetically.

"Which is where?"

"In the community room."

"I'll remember to bring two to the next wedding."

"Thank you, Frankie. For everything."

His poor shirt was done for, so she hugged him again, pressing her face against the comforting rumble of his voice as he said, "That's what friends are for."

Chapter Thirteen

That night, a hot flash hit Twyla shortly before three o'clock in the morning. She didn't know it was happening until she woke up in a puddle of her own sweat. She cast off the coverlet and the sheets and lay there steaming on the mattress, her face so hot she was certain she could cook an egg on her forehead. It finally passed, but she knew from experience that she would not be able to get back to sleep anytime soon.

Deeply annoyed, she turned on the bedside lamp and reached for *The Rogue of Redwing Ruins* and her reading glasses. The latter she knocked off the table, and since she couldn't read without them, she was forced to get out of bed and crawl around on her hands and knees to retrieve them.

Which was when she spotted the bomb attached to the underside of her bed frame.

It took her about three minutes to arrive at the word *bomb*. At first she thought, simply, *What is that?* Having been the person who put together the bed frame twenty-seven years ago, she tried to remember if this odd protuberance was some kind of support she had simply forgotten about and failed to notice ever again. That seemed improbable. But she was tired and didn't feel like dealing with it, so she grabbed her glasses and crawled into bed and cracked open *The Rogue of Redwing Ruins*. It was a boring section between sex scenes, and the presence of that inexplicable thing under her bed nagged at her. So she threw off the covers once again, grabbed the small flashlight out of her bedside drawer, gave it a crank, and turned it on. She directed the light underneath the bed and squinted at the strange object. There were curling wires coming out of it, and there appeared to be a watch involved and a clump of long tubes.

Those look like the tubes Frank and I saw in the cave, Twyla thought.

Oh, this is a bomb, she realized a second later, absurdly proud of herself for figuring it out.

And then it hit her: *This is a* bomb.

She had no idea why there was a bomb under her bed, and it didn't matter why, because it was there, and she needed to get out of her house in order to not die. Dazed with shock, she stumbled for the bedroom door, and by the time she hit the hallway, she was running. In the three seconds it took her to traverse the parlor, she had convinced herself that she would find a bomb under Frank's bed, too. She didn't know how or why she had come to this conclusion, and again, it didn't matter. There was a bomb under Frank's bed, so she needed to save Frank.

Twyla grabbed his house key off the hook in her entryway and flew across their respective lawns. She unlocked Frank's front door, let herself in, and sprinted down the hall.

"Salt Sea!" he shouted as she crashed into his bedroom. "Twyla, you scared the daylights out of me! What are you doing?"

She did not have time to explain. She flattened herself onto the floor, and sure enough, there was the bomb. Had she been thinking clearly, she would have calmly ushered him out of his house and alerted the local sheriff's office to the extremely dangerous situation. But she was not thinking clearly. All she could think of was the fact that she needed to save Frank, and for some reason, the most logical way that presented itself to her mind was to rip the bomb off the bottom of his bed frame, run it to his front door, and hurl it onto his lawn. This was precisely what she did, with Frank dogging her heels, asking "What the fuck, Twyla?" and "What is that?" and "What in the Salt Sea is going on?"

The second she chucked the bomb outside, she slammed the door shut, which was a good thing since it exploded when it hit the ground, shaking the entire house and half the neighborhood with it.

"Was that a bomb?" he asked in the silence that followed.

Twyla was rattling from head to toe, but her voice sounded calm and detached when she answered. "Yes."

"That was a bomb."

"Yes."

"That was a *bomb*? You held a bomb *in your hands*?"

By now, Frank was so worked up he was practically frothing at the mouth. But he was alive, so she didn't care that he was mad. She could watch him fume and rage at her every day for the rest of her life.

"Have you lost your ever-loving mind, woman? You could have blown yourself up!"

He's alive, she thought, and that was all that mattered.

"What were you thinking? I have half a mind to—"

And she was so unspeakably glad that he was alive that her knees gave out, and she collapsed on him, and he tried to catch her, but they wound up tangled against the parlor wall, and then she was kissing him. She was kissing him because he was alive, and so was she, and there were too many emotions to put into words. And his lips moved against hers as she thrust her fingers into his newly shorn hair to pull him closer, and the kiss deepened and slowed and turned tender, and then it was done.

It wasn't until Twyla came up for air that she truly understood what she had done. The horror of it sank in. She backed off, untangling her limbs from his.

"I...I...," she began, but what could she possibly say that would make what she had done to him okay? Because she was definitely the one who had initiated that kiss, even if Frank hadn't stopped her.

And now that she was looking at Frank, she saw that there was something more than shock playing across his face. He gaped at her as he remained flattened against the wall. Because she had flattened him there. He was breathing hard, and his pupils were blown wide with heat. She'd never seen him like this, with a bald hunger traced in every line of his face and coiled in each tensed muscle.

And before she could think or act or speak, they were kissing again, and she couldn't say who had started it this time. The next thing she knew, she was the one flattened against a wall, beside the front door, and even in all that heat, Frank pressed himself against her so that the right side of her back, the part that was bruised, wasn't touching the wall behind her.

She wanted to grab him by his new haircut and shout, *I don't give a shit about my back right now!* But she was too busy kissing him, and he was too busy pulling her closer. She ran her hands over his chest, his shoulders, his arms, and marveled at the way his body was familiar and unfamiliar at the same time—his living body, softened with time and age but solid beneath her touch. And he was deliciously warm and smelled like Honekian Springs soap and the laundry detergent they both used and a faint spicy-sweet scent that was all his.

She pressed her chest against his chest, her want against his want. And he wanted her. She could feel how much he wanted her. His hand slid along her left side, heading for the curve of her unbruised hip and on to the swell of her generous hind end. His lips broke away from hers, kissing a hot line across her jaw.

"Stop me," he told her, a ragged whisper in her ear before he bit her earlobe.

That bite sent shivering sparks straight down her spine. "Don't stop."

His left hand palmed her breast, and his right hand slid under her hind end to pull her into him. She ground against him in approval, and he growled, a sound that made the tightening pleasure of her core ring like a bell.

Somewhere in the farthest corner of her mind, the voice of good sense screamed, *What under the Void Beyond the Sky are you doing?* But that voice was so small and insignificant and far away that it was nothing more than a tinny echo drowned out by a much louder *Yes! This!*

She stroked his back, savoring the breadth and strength of his body.

"Stop me," he snarled into the sensitive skin of her neck.

"Keep going."

He cupped her breasts over the fabric of her nightshirt with both hands, squeezing with the perfect pressure, his thumbs playing over her nipples. He scraped his teeth across her collarbone as he unbuttoned her pajama top.

"Salt Sea, stop me, Twy," he begged her, and she could have eaten his desperation with a knife and fork.

"Don't stop! Do *not* stop!" she begged him in return, and the shreds of his self-control snapped. He ripped apart the flaps of her pajama top, popping off the last two buttons and sending them skittering across the floor. And then he was smoothing his hands over her bare breasts and latching on to one pebbled tip with his mouth.

"Yes!" gasped Twyla.

There was a pounding at the front door.

"No!" Frank moaned, as if his saying this would inspire the Unknown God to make whoever it was disappear.

"Ellis? Ellis, you in there? Ellis!"

"Go away!"

"Open this fucking door, or I'm opening it for you," said a voice that was alarmingly familiar.

Frank stopped.

Twyla stopped.

The weight of what they had done hovered over them, but it hadn't fallen yet.

"Salt Sea." Frank artfully draped his white T-shirt over his pajama bottoms and opened the door.

"Evening, Ellis," said a rusty voice. Oh gods, it was...

"Sheriff Ralston," said Frank.

"Were you aware that there's a smoking hole in your front yard?"

"I am aware."

"Care to elucidate?"

"Well now, you'll have to ask Twyla about that." Frank glanced at her as she frantically did up her pajama top with the but- that remained. "In a minute."

Salt fucking Sea," Hart Ralston uttered in outraged disbelief.

By the time Twyla stood in the doorframe, clutching the bot- om of her pajama top closed, a crowd of onlookers had gathered in the street in their bathrobes, including Wade.

"Mom! Are you all right?" he shouted while a sheriff's deputy held the crowd at bay.

She waved at him. "I'm fine, honey!"

"Banneker," said the sheriff in a tight-lipped greeting.

She grimaced. "Oh, Sheriff, it's your wedding night."

"Yes, I know." He gave her a withering glare with his gray demigod eyes before indicating the damage to Frank's lawn. "Smoking hole?"

Duckers came sprinting up the front walkway, leaving Zeddie to stand with Wade in the street.

"What the fuck is going on?"

Twyla opened her mouth to answer, but the bomb under her own bed detonated, blowing a hole in her roof. A quick series of fireworks shot out of Twyla's bedroom and exploded into the night sky.

"Gods' tits and testicles," Zeddie Birdsall uttered from the street in a voice full of awe.

Resigned, Twyla turned to Hart Ralston. "Why don't you come inside, Sheriff?"

"I'll brew some coffee," said Frank, equally resigned as he let in Ralston and Duckers and headed for his kitchen.

Chapter Fourteen

Wade stood in Twyla's front yard with his mother, thanking a buddy who served in the local fire brigade, while Twyla, who was now drowning in Frank's bathrobe, tried not to cry on the fire chief.

"What do you mean, I can't stay here?" she asked him.

"There's a hole in your roof, Twyla."

"I could use one of the other bedrooms until I have it fixed."

"You're going to have to replace the wall of the adjoining bedroom, and the whole house has extensive smoke damage. You need to stay somewhere else until it's fixed, and that's going to take weeks, if not months."

"But I'm heading to Tanria tomorrow morning."

"Today, actually," said Wade as he came to stand beside her.

"How am I supposed to get someone to fix this while I'm gone?"

"I'll take care of it," Wade volunteered.

Wade.

Actually volunteered to help her.

Her eyes went wide with wonder as she looked at him. "You will?"

"Yeah, I'll take a couple of days off and find a contractor and everything. You've got insurance, don't you?"

"I . . . Yes?"

"With Cadmus Family Insurance, right? You're the one who

helped me and Anita set up homeowner's insurance when we got our place, so I'm assuming it's the same."

Twyla couldn't believe what she was seeing and hearing. Wade—her Wade—was an adult who knew about homeowner's insurance.

"That's right," she said.

"Okay. I'll take care of it."

"You will?"

"Of course. You're my mom. You've taken care of me my whole life. I can handle getting someone out here to fix your house."

Speechless, Twyla hugged her little boy (who was six inches taller than she was).

"That's settled, then," said the fire chief. "Good luck, Twyla. Thanks, Wade."

Wade gave the man a wave goodbye as Twyla continued to squeeze the life out of him. And then Twyla jolted in her son's arms, remembering that her daughter was going to come home to an uninhabitable house. "Oh no! Hope!"

Wade patted his mother on the back. "She can stay with me and Anita. I'll try to head her off at the train station before she shows up here."

"Really?"

"Mom, it's no big deal."

"It's a big deal to me," she cried against his chest.

"Least I can do."

She gathered her dignity, since some of the neighbors were rubbernecking by the curb, and let him go.

And then he completely did her in when he said, "Love you, Mom."

Once Twyla stopped crying all over her son, she sent him home and girded herself to return to Frank's house. The idea occurred to her that she could grab the shovel out of the garden shed and dig a big hole in her backyard and hide there forever, but she knew she would have to face Frank sooner or later.

He's your friend, Twyla, she reminded herself. *You're going to get through this.*

With those faint words of encouragement, she crossed the lawn and stepped through his front door.

Frank was setting a carafe and several mugs on his coffee table so he didn't look up when she came inside. Now that they were in the same room together, she swore she could feel the memory of his touch radiating from her skin like a furnace. She wanted to grab the sports magazine off the coffee table and fan herself with it, but that would put her in close proximity to the man whose kiss had made her abandon plain good sense but a mere half hour ago.

Hart Ralston eyed the coffee with distate. "Any chance I could get a cup of tea?"

Frank shook his head. "Don't have any."

"I might have some tea bags next door," Twyla offered, eager to be anywhere else but in Frank's presence.

"You also have a hole in your roof, Banneker. Never mind."

"How is it next door?" Frank asked, barely looking at her, which was just as well, since she could barely look at him either.

"The good news is that they put the fire out quickly. The bad news is that the fire chief said I can't live in the house at all until someone repairs the roof and the smoke damage."

Under any other circumstance, this would not have been a huge problem, since she could have camped out in one of Frank's kids' rooms until her home was habitable again. Now? That seemed like the worst possible idea, and Frank, notably, did not make the offer.

A knock at the door rescued her from the elephant in the room, if only briefly. The sheriff took the liberty of opening Frank's door and letting Alma Maguire into the parlor.

"Rumor has it exciting things are afoot on Cottonwood Street."

"Sorry to drag you into this, Alma, but since two of your marshals were targeted, it seemed like the appropriate thing to do."

"Agreed. Fun way to kick off married life." She gave him a friendly slap on the arm, and Twyla remembered that long before he mentored Penrose Duckers and long before Maguire was the chief marshal of the West Station, Hart Ralston and Alma Maguire had been partners in the field for years.

"Are you two all right?" she asked Twyla and Frank.

A hysterical giggle bubbled up Twyla's throat before she could stop it, and though she couldn't bring herself to look at Frank, she heard his edgy snort from across the room.

"Yeah, that was a bad question," said Maguire. "Obviously, you're not all right."

If only she knew.

Wrong, wrong, wrong, thought Twyla. *Everything about this night is a giant pile of wrong.*

Maybe she could ask Maguire for vacation time. Effective immediately. Hadn't she recently read something in the newspaper about cruise ships that went to the polar ice caps? Going somewhere cold sounded like an excellent plan.

The memory of Frank's erection pressing against her hot want flared and burned in her memory.

Somewhere extremely cold, she thought.

Through all of this silent drama, Duckers was arguing in whispers with Zeddie Birdsall near the dining table.

"Go home, Z."

"No."

"This doesn't involve you."

"You're my boyfriend. If it involves you, it involves me."

"I'm doing my job. Does a problem at Proserpina's involve me?"

"If the place burns down with me in it, then yeah, it does. What if there's a bomb under *your* bed?"

"Then you'd better stay at your dad's place tonight."

The sheriff held up a hand to get their attention. "You think there might be a bomb under Duckers's bed?"

Zeddie reluctantly tore his furious glare away from his boyfriend to answer his brother-in-law. "He's been working with Twyla and Frank, so yeah, it's a concern."

"Shit." The sheriff opened the door to speak to one of the deputies milling around the smoking hole in Frank's lawn. "We need to evacuate the apartment building on Denniston Street immediately. Duckers, give him the address. And actually, we'd better clear my father-in-law's house, too, to be on the safe side."

"Yes, sir," said both the deputy and Duckers.

"You call him *sir*?" Alma asked the latter.

He shrugged. "Old habits and all that."

"Guess I'll have to stay with Pen," Zeddie said smugly while his boyfriend talked to the deputies outside.

"No," Hart told him. "I've got an investigation going on here, and you're not part of it. You can go to my place. Mercy's up. My wedding night, ladies and gentlemen." He muttered the last bit to himself before he turned to Twyla and Frank. "Anyone else working closely with you?"

Maguire answered for them. "These three are working a special case. Anyone else involved is currently inside the Mist and under my jurisdiction. I'll check on them."

Hart nodded and turned to Twyla. "So, you dropped your glasses, and when you picked them off the floor, you noticed the bomb underneath your bed. What I don't understand is how you knew Ellis also had a bomb planted under his bed."

"It was a gut instinct. My body reacted before my brain could catch up." Yes, holy Three Mothers, her body had reacted and then some. Surely, everyone present could discern from the flush of her skin that she and Frank had gotten hot and heavy in this very room. She was tempted to hide behind the couch until everyone went home, except this was Frank's house, and if she hid behind his couch until everyone left, that would leave her alone with Frank again, and if she was alone with him again, who in the Salt Sea knew what would happen next?

"Your gut was right," Ralston told her. "You saved a man's life tonight."

That, at least, was good. She had forgotten that part.

"Theories? Thoughts?" asked Maguire.

Frank spoke up from where he leaned against the wall, as far away from Twyla as he could get considering the small size of the parlor. It happened to be the same spot where Twyla had first kissed him, though, so his location didn't assuage the tension between them at all. "I don't think there's anything under Duckers's bed or anywhere else in his apartment, or at the Birdsalls' house either. The bombs would have gone off at the same time."

"That makes sense," Twyla agreed, relieved to focus on her job rather than her personal life, which had gone up in flames, both literally and metaphorically. "Whoever did this wouldn't assassinate us at intervals. The only reason Frank's bomb went off early was because it detonated when I threw it out the door."

Frank heaved an angry huff from across the room. She wondered how mad he was at her and for how many reasons, and if he was also furious with himself for his part in the happenings *after* the bomb exploded.

"Why would someone try to silence you two and not Duckers? Maybe this isn't related to the job," said Maguire.

The sheriff rubbed the morning stubble on his jaw. "The question is, What do you two know that no one else knows?"

Twyla's gaze snapped to Frank's in a moment of understanding, and they both looked away from each other as quickly.

"I think the answer to that question is classified," answered Twyla.

Maguire turned to her old partner. "Can I get a minute alone with Banneker and Ellis?"

"Seriously, Alma?"

"What?"

"I've got a bomb case on my hands, on my fucking wedding night, and you're cutting me out?"

"It's classified, and you are no longer a Tanrian Marshal, Sheriff."

"Fine. Great, actually. I'm going to let you sort this out. In the meantime, there are two deputies stationed outside. Banneker and Ellis, don't go anywhere in town without an escort until the marshals get to the bottom of this. When do you head back to Tanria?"

"Tomorrow morning," said Twyla.

"Also known as today," grumbled Frank.

"Probably for the best. Whoever wanted you dead thought it was easier to get to you in Eternity rather than Tanria."

"Thanks, Hart. I'll take it from here," Maguire told him.

"If anyone needs something, feel free to call on a person who is not me, because I'm leaving on my fucking honeymoon in"—he checked his pocket watch—"three fucking hours." He took his newly acquired brother-in-law by the arm and hauled him out the door with him.

"Hey!" Zeddie protested, but if he had more to say, Twyla didn't hear it, since Hart shut the door behind him.

A second later, Duckers scared the crap out of her when he came up behind her and asked, "What's cooking?"

"Salt Sea! Where did you come from?"

"I snuck in the back door. Didn't feel like having it out with the boyfriend tonight."

"So you're hiding from him?" asked Maguire, unimpressed. Twyla, on the other hand, was sympathetic to his plight.

"Don't knock it, Chief. So, what's the scoop?"

"These two apparently know something we don't."

"It happened on Wisdomsday," Twyla explained. "We accidentally discovered some kind of cave system under the Dragon's Teeth."

"Twyla literally fell into it, almost broke her neck."

"For real?" said Duckers. "And you're only mentioning this now?"

"You were in a wedding. What were we supposed to do, stop the ceremony to report?"

"Maybe."

Alma poured herself a generous cup of coffee. "Unlike your young partner here, I care about your well-being. Banneker, are you hurt?"

"Only bruised. We found tubes of gunpowder down there, too—just like the ones I saw under our beds tonight—but Frank wanted to take me to the infirmary, so we left. We sent a report—"

"A note. Nothing formal," added Frank.

"But we weren't sure if you'd see it before the wedding."

"I had a pause set on delivery. I won't get the report until Sorrowsday. This is weird. Obviously, you stumbled onto something. You said you found this cave Wisdomsday afternoon, went to the infirmary, and sent me a note. What did you do after that?"

"I thought Twyla ought to rest up, and since we had today off, I didn't think you'd mind if we went home."

"I don't mind at all. Did either of you talk to anyone about this between then and now?"

"I haven't," said Twyla.

"Neither have I," Frank concurred.

"What about Vanderlinden?"

Quill. Somewhere in all of this, Twyla had completely forgotten about him. Guilt pinged around her insides like a pinball.

"Dr. Vanderlinden wasn't with us," she told Maguire.

"I sent a message to him letting him know we wouldn't be returning to camp, but that's it. No details," said Frank.

"So how would anyone know what you found? You two don't even seem to know what you found."

"We know they found fireworks, thanks to the pyrotechnics coming out of Twyla's house tonight," said Duckers.

"True," Maguire mused. "Why would someone need fireworks in Tanria?"

Frank topped off his mug. "If you want to blow something up in a place where New Gods technology doesn't work, you're going to need explosives that were around during the Old Gods era. Anyone know when fireworks were invented?"

"I'm guessing a long, long time ago," Maguire replied dryly. "That doesn't answer our original question: How could anyone know you two found that cave?"

"Maybe someone got their hands on the note Frank sent you?" suggested Duckers.

"Nimkilim post is the most secure delivery system in the world. That report is probably hanging out in an immortal plane even as we speak."

"Okay, but have you met Hermia?"

"Adorable but incompetent," agreed Maguire. "Given a lack of better theories to go from, let's assume Hermia was...being Hermia, and someone managed to intercept the message Frank sent me. Whoever it was must not want anyone to know about that cave, and they tried to get rid of you to keep you quiet."

"I guess we better lie low in Tanria for our own safety," said Duckers, eager to avoid Zeddie.

"You can't stay in Tanria forever, but I do think it's a good idea to lie low for now. Be on guard, though. We know the wrong sort of people can get in and out of Tanria without going through the official portals. I won't consider you safe until we get this case figured out. We'll have to communicate through Hermia, so be cautious about what kind of information you include in your reports. I'll check in with you in person as soon as I can."

"Understood," Twyla said.

"I don't have authority over Dr. Vanderlinden, but I highly recommend that he stay with you in Tanria for his own safety, at least for now."

Again, Twyla caught Frank's eye, and again, they both looked away quickly, as if eye contact could scorch them.

"We'll let him know," said Frank. "Want us to check out the tunnels?"

"Not yet. I'll make that call when I meet up with you later."

Duckers helped himself to the carafe on the coffee table. "What about you, Chief? Aren't you in danger now, too?"

"That's what I get paid the big bucks for. I'm going to bring in the FICBI since two of my marshals were threatened outside the Mist. Pretty sure bombs going off anywhere in the Federated Islands other than Tanria fall under their jurisdiction, and that way, we can get it off Hart's plate." She clapped her hands. "Pack up what you need for at least the next week. Let's get you to Tanria while we've got these deputies to escort you."

Duckers raised his hand like a kid in a schoolroom.

"What is it, Duckers?"

"My bag is in my apartment, the one Hart had evacuated."

"My bag's in my house," said Twyla as the realization sank in that the entire contents of her bedroom and beyond were either scorched or sopping wet.

Maguire rubbed her temples and looked to Frank.

"I'm packed and ready."

"There's that at least. Duckers, have one of those deputies escort you to your apartment to see if they've finished looking for bombs. If you can't get in, we'll figure out a way to get your clothes to you."

Duckers gave her a good-natured salute and left.

"Banneker, I'll have the other deputy go next door with you. See if you can salvage some clothes and supplies and whatnot to take with you."

"I'll go with Twyla," Frank volunteered. "Might be better to leave the deputy out front, looking out for both our houses."

"Good idea, Ellis."

Twyla froze, and since she wasn't moving, Frank wasn't going anywhere either.

"Move along," ordered Maguire, the edge in her voice lighting a fire under Twyla.

"On it," she told the chief, trying to sound and move like a real person instead of an animated puddle of mortification (which was what she felt like) as she walked out the door with Frank following behind her.

"Twy?" Frank called softly to her once they had crossed the property line between their houses.

She marched steadily ahead of him. "Mm-hmm?"

"Are we going to talk about it?"

"Oh. Uh." Apparently, she was capable of emitting only high-pitched vowel sounds out of her mouth.

"I know this is hard. It's hard for me, too."

Did he have to use the word hard*?* wondered Twyla as her intestines shriveled up and died inside her. She unlocked her soggy front door and went inside her soggier house.

Undaunted, Frank kept at it. "There's only so long we can put it off, and this might be our only ten minutes alone together for a while."

The dam of pent-up, unidentifiable emotions burst. She turned toward him long enough to yell "Yeah, and look what happened the last time we were alone together!" before she fled to her bedroom, with Frank uttering a defeated "Fuck" in her wake.

Did he have to use the word fuck?

By the time her bedroom rug was squishing wetly beneath her bare feet—because she hadn't bothered to put on shoes before she removed the bomb from under Frank's bed—she understood that there was no running away from the fact that she and Frank had kissed and done significantly more than kiss, nor was she going to be able to weasel out of a conversation about the kissing and the more-than-kissing. Exhausted and overwhelmed, she leaned her forehead against the closet mirror as Frank's reflection moved into her peripheral vision. A torrent of words gushed out of her, steaming up the mirror as she spoke.

"I'm so sorry, Frank. I can't believe I...I don't know what happened. There was the bomb, and you were standing there in your parlor, and you were alive, and I was so glad you were alive that I..."

She took a breath and forced herself to face him. There he stood on her sodden bedroom rug, looking as lost and miserable as she felt in the predawn light that had begun to seep in through the curtains. She couldn't bear to see him lost and miserable, not when she could put on her big-girl pants and simply talk things through with him. She crossed the room, took his hands in hers, and said what needed to be said.

"It was a mistake. I know it was a mistake. I own it, and I'm sorry, and believe me, it will never happen again."

"A mistake." His voice was flat. It wasn't a question so much as a simple repeating of her words.

She nodded emphatically. "A huge, horrible mistake."

"A mistake. Right." His gaze dropped to their joined hands. He cleared his throat. "I'm sorry, too."

"We're both to blame. Or, no, neither of us is to blame. There were bombs, and we're friends, and we care about each other, and things got out of hand. That's all. It's not a disaster unless we choose to make a disaster of it. So let's decide to put this past us and move on. We can do that, can't we?"

He nodded, but a few more uncomfortable seconds passed before he spoke. "Well now, I guess that's settled, then."

Relief flooded through Twyla's veins. "We're good?"

"We're good." He squeezed her hands before letting them drop. "We'd better get moving before Maguire sends the FICBI after us. Where's your bag?"

For the first time, Twyla took a good look at her bedroom. Even in the dim light, she could see what a disaster it was. What had once been her bed was now a scorched pile of broken wood and bedsprings and charred bedding. The hole in her roof was four feet in diameter, and several roof tiles had dropped onto the floor. The walls were blotchy with smoke stains and water. Everything was wet, from floor to ceiling.

Her Gracie Goodfist backpack was where she had left it on her dresser, packed and ready to go. She unzipped it and checked the contents, and to her amazement, everything inside was dry as a bone. "I will never doubt you again," she told her child's ancient backpack.

"I'll wait in the parlor while you get changed."

It wasn't until he left and shut the bedroom door behind him that she remembered she was still wearing his bathrobe over her pajamas, which were now missing a few buttons. The robe was too large for her, but she was reluctant to take it off. It was soft and warm and it smelled like Frank. Before she could think better of it, she pulled the front over her nose and inhaled the familiar scent of him.

A scent that would now be associated with his warm hands on her skin and the ragged whisper of the words *Stop me.*

Doing her best to push the memory aside, she took off the robe and hung it in her closet, the only moderately dry place in the bedroom. Although she knew it was wrong, she privately hoped it would still smell this good when she got back from Tanria.

Not that she'd be able to stay in her own home by then.

She dressed in her work clothes and went to meet Frank in the parlor. He was standing at the family altar by the front door. To her surprise, he dipped his fingers into the dish of salt water and touched Doug's key. Twyla didn't know what exactly he meant by the gesture, but she was moved by it, this honoring of the husband who had been integral to her life, for better or for worse. Reluctant to puncture the moment but aware that they were running out of time, she said, "I'm ready if you are."

Without turning around, Frank asked, "What are you going to tell Vanderlinden?"

Once again, she had forgotten about Quill, but now that Frank had reminded her of his existence, she panicked. "Nothing! I mean, there's nothing to tell, right?"

"Right."

"Because we're good now, right?"

"Right."

Frank had yet to turn around, and talking to his broad back was beginning to unnerve her.

"You're not going to tell him, are you?" she asked him hesitantly.

"No. I'm not going to tell him." He finally turned to her, but she could read nothing in his face. He was a closed door. He was an entire house, locked up tight, and Twyla didn't know what to do about it. Surely one tiny mistake could be overcome. Surely their friendship couldn't and wouldn't end over one kiss.

Slightly more than a kiss.

"We'd better go," he said. This time, he led the way, walking so quickly she had to jog to keep up. Everything about his body language sent up a fiery flare of concern in her stomach. She put a hand on his arm to stop him, precisely on the line where their properties met.

"Frank."

His eyes skated near her face, but he wouldn't look at her full on. *This is not good*, she thought. How had they completely changed positions in the course of ten minutes? He was the one who had chased her into her home, pressing her to talk about the difficult thing between them, while she had wanted to scurry away like a terrified mouse. Now she was the one who wanted to keep talking, while he buried his head in the sand.

"I know things are weird between us right now, and they're probably going to be weird for a while, but we're better than this. We're going to be okay."

He licked his lips as if he were gearing up to speak, but he said nothing.

The familiar warmth of his arm seeped into her fingers, and she pressed her hand more firmly against him. "Tell me you believe that."

He put his hand over her hand, and then, without preamble or warning, he pulled her into a hug, pressing his face into her hair. When he released her, he forced his mouth into a brave closed-lip smile, and he gave her a reassuring nod that failed to reassure her in the slightest.

Maguire poked her head out of Frank's front door and called, "There you are. Come on. The deputy is giving you all a lift to the station. You'll pick up Duckers on the way. Are you both ready to go?"

"Yep," said Twyla. By now, they'd reached Frank's front steps.

He went inside, presumably to get his pack, but instead, he looked to Maguire and asked, "Can I get a quick word, Chief?"

"Sure."

"Alone." Frank didn't wait for an answer. He walked to the kitchen without so much as glancing Twyla's way.

Maguire raised her eyebrows at Twyla, whose Oh Shit Meter ratcheted several notches higher. "If you'll excuse me, Marshal Banneker," she said before following Frank to the kitchen to talk about the gods knew what.

And for the first time in twelve years, Twyla wasn't in any position to ask Frank what was going on.

Chapter Fifteen

Duckers, who did not have a bomb under his bed, bitched about Zeddie the entire drive from Eternity to the West Station, which was great, since Twyla far preferred to deal with his problems than her own.

"I get it. He loves me. And I love him. And I know it freaks him out when my job gets dangerous. But dang, give me some breathing room, you know?"

Twyla, who sat beside him on the back bench of the sheriff's department's autoduck, patted his knee in sympathy. "It's a tough situation."

"And that's not all. He told me he wants us to move in together. Which isn't a terrible idea. His internship is unpaid, so he's having to live at home. Don't get me wrong. I love his family, but it can get awkward, getting busy in his bedroom when his dad is taking a nap in the parlor."

Twyla did not need the words *getting busy* marching across her brain with Frank only two feet away from her. So she latched on to the most salient point of the conversation, one she understood in her bones. "But you'd prefer to keep your own space to yourself."

"Yeah, as a matter of fact, I would. Especially since, like I said, he's not getting paid. I'm sending money to my mom every month. One of my little sisters wants to go to college next fall.

They need my help. Zeddie doesn't. Ugh, I sound like such an asshole."

"You don't sound like an asshole. You sound like an adult with adult problems."

"Adulting sucks."

"Yes, it does," Twyla and Frank said in unison. Even though Twyla had said the same thing, the fact that Frank had agreed so readily made her wonder if what he was really saying was *Kissing Twyla sucks*, or simply *Twyla sucks*.

"This is the kind of thing I'd usually talk through with Hart," Duckers continued. "But what am I supposed to tell him? *Your new brother-in-law is driving me nuts*? That's not awkward or anything."

"Maybe you and Zeddie need a break from each other."

"Yeah, maybe. But Zeddie already bitches that we don't spend enough time together. What's he going to say when I tell him I want my space?"

"There's only one way to find out," Twyla said as gently as possible.

Duckers groaned piteously.

"How old are you, Duckers?" Frank asked, directing his question at the windshield so that he wouldn't run the risk of looking at Twyla.

"Twenty-one."

"Twenty-one? Salt Sea, you do not have to commit your life to someone at twenty-one."

"You are awfully young, if you don't mind my putting in my two coppers," agreed the deputy who was driving them to the station.

"Go ahead," said Twyla, glaring at the back of Frank's new haircut. He knew that she had been only nineteen years old when she had married Doug, and DJ had come along hardly a year later. She was a wife and a mother twice over by the time she was Duckers's age. Last night, she had told Frank the truth about her marriage, and this barb about not committing your life to someone at twenty-one felt like it was aimed directly at her, a knife to the heart.

Maybe she should be asking the sheriff's deputy for advice. Maybe the sheriff's deputy should be advising them all.

At the West Station, Duckers and Frank bickered over equimares.

"You always get Saltlicker," Duckers whined in the stables.

"For gods' sake," muttered Twyla, worn to a nub. She stomped up to the grouchy stallion and claimed him for herself to shut the other two up.

"Dang, Twyla, is my mom away from home a little grumpy today?" Duckers asked her.

"Someone tried to assassinate me a few hours ago, and now there's a hole in my roof and smoke and water damage all over my house. Why would I be grumpy?"

Duckers cocked a thumb at Frank. "And this one's grumpy as fuck, too."

Frank grunted and took out a gelding to towel off and saddle up.

"Why don't you two burst into song or something? That should cheer you up."

"Duckers?" said Frank.

"Yeah?"

"No offense, but shut up."

Duckers frowned at the last remaining equimaris in the stable, more filly than adult. She dipped her head in the trough and blew playful bubbles, splashing Duckers's shirt in the process. "This is going to be a fun week."

The ride to Sector W-14 was anything but fun. It was silent, save for the calls of exotic Tanrian birds and the occasional grapping of graps. It was almost a relief to reach the campsite by the lake, even if Twyla was dreading facing Quill after kissing Frank.

Mary Georgina either heard them or sniffed them out before Quill was aware of their presence. She came tearing down the slope toward them, so excited to see Frank that she opened her wings and sailed through the air, straight into his chest, knocking him flat on his back.

"Hey, she flew, kind of!" said Duckers.

"It's a start," Twyla agreed.

Frank was too busy patting the dragon and reassuring her with "Yes, yes, I'm here" to comment on Mary Georgina's encouraging movement toward flight.

Quill caught up to his ward, looking more rumpled and exhausted than Twyla had ever seen him. "Thank gods, you have returned."

"Rough night?"

"You have no idea. Mary Georgina cried for three hours after Marshal Ellis departed Wisdomsday morning. Did you know dragons could cry? She made a mewling sound, and golden tears streamed out of her eyes and nostrils. She was inconsolable. I was completely unable to carry out my research under the circumstances."

Quill's griping reminded Twyla of the time she had left Doug alone with the boys before Hope was born. She'd gone home to Diamond Springs on Medora to help her parents out when her mother had broken her leg. She had cooked and cleaned for them for a week, until her mother was better able to hobble around the house on crutches. When she came home, the house was a wreck, and the first thing Doug asked her was "What's for dinner?" after which he complained about how hard it had been to "babysit" his own children for a whole week. Twyla was surprised to discover that even now, it filled her with rage, a rage Quill did not deserve but that rubbed off on him to a certain extent anyway.

"Did you get Frank's note?"

"I did. Are you quite well?"

If he had received the note, that meant he knew she had been hurt, but he'd opened with *Thank gods, you have returned*? It seemed at odds with Quill's otherwise thoughtful behavior up to now, but Twyla knew better than anyone how childcare could reduce a grown man to a toddler in seconds.

"I'm banged up, but I'm fine. Listen, Quill—"

"Ah, good," he said, leaning in for a kiss before he remembered that he wasn't supposed to kiss her on the job. He settled for a quick touch of her arm, a gesture that pummeled Twyla with guilt. The memory of Frank's voice punched her right in the conscience.

What are you going to tell Vanderlinden?

"Nothing!" she said aloud. "I mean, nothing happened. At the wedding. Meaning you didn't miss much."

The words spewed out of her like glittery dragon spit, minus the sparkles. Every single part of her body that Frank had touched with his hands or his mouth seemed to light up, as if Quill could see the evidence of her wrongdoing in neon yellow.

"Nothing?" repeated Duckers with offended incredulity. "Someone tried to kill you and Frank, and you call that *nothing*?"

"He asked about the wedding. The assassination attempt was *after* the wedding."

"In fact, I didn't ask about the wedding," said Quill. "What was that bit about someone trying to kill you? Did I hear that correctly?"

"Well, yes."

"Someone tried to kill you?"

"And Frank."

"I don't give a rat's arse about Ellis!" exclaimed Quill.

As if summoned, Frank loomed behind Twyla, his mere presence scorching her back. "Feeling's mutual, Vander—"

"Don't." Twyla cut him off. How differently last night would have played out if she had said *Don't* instead of *Don't stop*. Now she couldn't stop thinking about Frank's hands on her body, his mouth on hers, the hungry way he had growled *Stop me* against her skin.

"Don't," she said again, this time to herself, as she stood between two men, one of whom she was dating for the fun of it, and one of whom she absolutely could not be with romantically.

Except, apparently, she could.

"Salt Sea," she moaned, and she fled toward the campsite, leaving Quill and Frank and Duckers and Mary Georgina to catch up.

Quill dogged her steps like a puppy begging for scraps. "I am sorry, darl—Twyla. I didn't mean to be snappish. I was simply distressed to learn that you were in danger. Please, do tell me what happened."

And now guilt beat Twyla over the head again. But what did she owe this man anyway? Was kissing Frank cheating if she and Quill had been on only two dates, one of which was spent with her grandchildren? No, she decided, it wasn't. What had happened with Frank was Twyla's problem, but it wasn't Quill's. She turned to him and told him what he needed to know, nothing more.

"Frank and I happened upon an underground cavern and some tunnels. I literally fell into the cavern, hence the giant bruise on my backside. We sent a report about our discovery and went to the wedding, but as it turns out, there must be something important about the cavern and tunnels, because someone found out that we discovered them, and put bombs under our beds last night. We located the bombs before they detonated, so we are alive, and now we are here to find out what's so important about the tunnels. It was and is very upsetting. That is all."

"Ah."

"Yes. Ah."

By now, they had reached the camp, with its four pup tents lined up in a row. Twyla was glad to have one all to herself, because an uncomfortable realization reared up and bit her on the ass (or *arse*, as Quill would put it): if someone put a pistol crossbow to her temple, and she had to choose between sleeping in Quill's tent and sleeping in Frank's, she knew which she would pick.

And it would be another mistake.

Duckers caught up to her and nudged her in the ribs with his elbow. "I don't know what in Old Hell is going on with all of you, but I think your love life might be more fucked up than mine."

"Thanks, Duckers."

He gave her a friendly salute. "Misery loves company."

Maguire arrived one day later, but it was a brutally long day for Twyla. She kept trying to catch Frank alone to talk to him, but Frank avoided her so they couldn't talk about anything. In the meantime, she was avoiding Quill for reasons she couldn't pinpoint, and Quill was now growing increasingly concerned about Twyla's reticence. And all the while, Duckers informed everyone, repeatedly, "This sucks."

Twyla had never been so happy to see her boss. Now Alma Maguire sat across from her and Quill at the makeshift firepit, filling them in on what was going on outside of Tanria as Duckers sat beside the chief and Frank stood, playing jungle gym to a growing dragon.

"The FICBI is on the bomb case, which means we'll have

to share information across agencies, since, presumably, the assassination attempt was linked to something going on here in Tanria."

"Any idea who wants us dead?" asked Twyla.

"No. I wish we did. I'll let you know as soon as I hear of any leads."

"So what now?" asked Duckers.

"Now we have a look at the cave and tunnels Banneker and Ellis found."

"Is that a good idea?" wondered Twyla. "There are explosives down there. And if that's where the dragons are nesting, we already suspect they defend their young, like geese."

"Except a goose only comes up to my kneecaps, while a dragon could pound me into a flat little pancake," Duckers said cheerily, as if being pounded into a flat little pancake would be a lark.

Quill stroked his beard. "Is that the theory? Do you think that the dragons are nesting in these caves?"

"It's what Frank and I went to check out," explained Twyla. "We thought the dragons might be nesting near the place where we found Herd's body rather than here by the lake."

"And you didn't think to mention that at the time?"

"It was only a hunch. We had no idea I'd be falling ass-first into a cave that day."

Quill stroked his beard more forcefully, and Twyla knew he was stewing. One more thing she would have to deal with later.

Maguire got down to business. "So, here's the plan. Banneker, Duckers, and I will check out this cave and the tunnels that go with it. Do you two feel comfortable with full-sized crossbows?"

"No," Twyla answered at the same time Duckers said, "Fuck yeah."

"It's been a long time since I used one, and I was never a good shot with them anyway, so I'm bringing my pistol crossbow and a machete with me. Ellis, you'll stay behind with Mary Georgina. No use endangering the baby."

Frank balked at the command. "I think I should go."

"And I'm ordering you to stay."

"What about me?" asked Quill.

"What about you?"

"I'd like to go."

"Negative. I'm not putting a civilian in harm's way."

"You are looking for dragon nests. I am a dracologist. And..." Here, he eyed Twyla. "I think I should accompany you and provide you with my expertise."

"The dragons haven't hurt anyone yet, Chief," said Duckers. "If he wants to go, I say let him."

"I'll allow it, but the marshals won't be held accountable should anything happen to you, Dr. Vanderlinden."

"Understood."

Now it was Frank's turn to stew as the party left him at the campsite with Mary Georgina to set out for the cave entrance.

Maguire checked the steadiness of the ladder before going in first, followed by Twyla, then Duckers, then Quill. They were better prepared than Twyla and Frank had been a couple of days ago, and with four lanterns pushing away the darkness belowground, the cavern looked far less ominous.

The chief busied herself with stacking the explosives into a neat pile off to the side.

"Is it safe to be handling that stuff?" Twyla asked her.

"Safer than one of us tripping over them while holding a lantern. I can't believe these fools thought it was a good idea to set off fireworks underground." Maguire dusted off her hands on her pants and gestured for Twyla to lead them into the tunnel to the right. "After you. Duckers, I want you behind Banneker with your crossbow. Dr. Vanderlinden, you'll come next. I'll bring up the rear."

In this order, they made their way along the tunnel until, a few minutes later, Twyla kicked something heavy and metallic with the reinforced toe of her boot. She picked it up, and Duckers looked over her shoulder so they could examine it together in the lamplight. The object was about a foot long, maybe less, a narrow piece of iron, curved at the top, with a triangular point on each side of the center.

"What is it?" he asked.

"I don't know. A tool of some kind?"

"It's heavy," said Duckers when Twyla handed it to him.

Quill, in turn, took it from Duckers. "Of course it's heavy. It's made of iron."

"Do you know what it is?" asked Maguire.

"It's a pickaxe. You can see here where the handle should go."

"A pickaxe? You're sure?"

"Yes. I own at least ten of these myself. It's one of the most important tools dracologists use when exhuming fossils."

"Is that why this is here?" Twyla asked. "Was someone digging up dragon bones?"

"Perhaps, although I'm not sure the price they'd fetch on the black market would be worth the effort of digging them out." Quill traced a series of gouges in the wall next to him with his fingertips. "These grooves don't match the excavation patterns one would see at a dracological site."

"Let's put a pin in this and keep moving," said Alma.

As Twyla shuffled ahead, she couldn't help but recall the last time she'd been down here, with Frank. For the past couple of days, she'd been able to think about only the kiss and the fallout of that kiss, but now she remembered how distraught he'd been when he had thought she was hurt or possibly even dead, the way he'd cried, the way he'd held her so tightly against him when he'd realized she was fine. She remembered the warmth of his body, the comfort of a friendship that ran deep and true.

A friendship that could surely weather one measly kiss.

Although there was nothing measly about it.

The tunnel opened up into another cavernous space—though not as large as the cave at the entrance—with several more tunnels leading off in different directions. The extra space allowed the group to gather and confer.

"What do you think?" asked Twyla, mostly to Maguire.

"Pick one and go with it. If it branches off into more directions, we'll reassess. I don't want to be getting lost down here."

"Agreed," said Quill.

They had made it only a few feet into the new tunnel when Duckers called, "Wait a sec." He held his lantern close to the wall, its light illuminating rivers of glistening gold running in horizontal layers through the rock.

Quill leaned in for a closer look. "Whoever was messing about here before, they weren't digging up dragon bones. They were mining whatever this substance is."

"Gold?" suggested Duckers.

"No. Gold is found primarily in rivers and streams. I don't know what this is. Copper, perhaps, although the color is off."

Maguire leaned her head away from Duckers and Quill to give Twyla a self-satisfied grin. "Banneker, this sector shares a border with N-8, correct?"

Twyla pictured a map of the Tanrian sectors in her brain. "I think so."

"Where the Doniphan Iuvenicite Mine happens to be located?"

Twyla gasped. "This is linked to the case that Rosie Fox is working on! The iuvenicite-smuggling ring!"

"What is iuvenicite again?" asked Duckers.

"A mineral, a very valuable one," Maguire told him.

Twyla's eyes widened as another piece of the puzzle clicked into place. "Duckers! Quill! Remember when Fox was telling us about her investigation? She said the workers at the Doniphan mine had been hearing booming sounds."

Duckers nodded slowly, catching on. "Someone has been down here trying to blow new mine shafts with fireworks."

"Because modern explosives won't work in Tanria," Quill filled in. "I highly doubt fireworks would be effective for that purpose, but they would certainly be loud enough to rouse hibernating dragons."

"The smugglers aren't stealing iuvenicite from the Doniphan mine," said Twyla. "They've found another vein right here in Sector W-14."

"And it looks like Herd was in on it," Maguire said grimly.

"That's why we found him covered in glitter," said Duckers, his own excitement ratcheting up. "He woke up a dragon or got too close to the nest. Or both."

"And it explains why someone wanted to kill me and Frank—to shut us up before we could tell anyone about the entrance to the illegal mine."

Duckers's smile fell. "Uh, Twyla?"

"What?"

"Dragon."

"Ope!" She whirled on her heel and found herself face-to-face with a giant reptile, glaring at her with gleaming green eyes. She knew, instinctively, that she had never encountered this one before, that there was something different and unfamiliar about it. Beyond the dragon, in the weak lantern light, she could barely make out a ring of rubble with three eggs sitting inside.

A nest.

"Everyone back away, very slowly," said Maguire.

It was easier said than done. In the confines of the tunnel, they trod on one another's toes as they shuffled backward in reverse order.

The dragon moved with them, maneuvering fluidly through the short tunnel.

Meeeeeep, said the dragon, and while the call was high-pitched, there was a rasp of menace in it.

Quill broke. He shoved past Maguire and made a dash for the exit, only to bump straight into another dragon. He shrieked in terror as the second beast cried, *Meeeeeep, chirp-chirp-chirp-chirp*. Twyla knew what was coming, but was powerless to do anything about it. She looked to the first dragon to see that it was doing the same, and before she could attempt to get out of the way, it unleashed a blast of glittery slime from its maw, pushing her against Duckers, as the second dragon's sparkling spume squeezed Quill and Maguire against them from the opposite direction.

Someone screamed—Quill, she thought—and whoever it was choked and coughed on dragon spit, silencing them. Twyla squeezed her eyes shut, closed her mouth, and held her breath to avoid breathing in the spit or getting it in her eyes. As the golden onslaught continued, her lungs burned, and the first twinges of panic, of thinking she might die of asphyxiation, began to spasm inside her. Slime filled her ears and wormed its way up her nostrils.

And then it stopped.

She fell to her hands and knees and sucked air into her lungs, coughing on the bitter-tasting spit as she blew it out of her nose. She pulled a clean corner of her undershirt out of the waist of her pants to wipe her face, at which point she could finally open her eyes. The dragon before her was shrinking meekly into the tunnel from which it had come. It was more difficult to make out what was happening on the other end of the line. She could hear multiple dragons, one whose meeping rang of authority and another whose chirps carried a cowed tone.

"Everyone all right? Duckers?" She pounded him on the back to help him cough up the glitter in his lungs.

"Holy shit!" he sputtered.

"Quill? Chief?"

The light was dim, and Twyla realized that all but one of their lanterns had been extinguished in the sparkling onslaught. She snatched up the one that remained lit before it could succumb to the slime crawling up its sides, and she held it aloft, trying to get a better look past Duckers. The halo of light revealed Alma Maguire with her arms wrapped around Quill from behind. She jerked up and back, forcing Quill's lungs to eject dragon spit. Glittery slime burst from his mouth and splattered Duckers, who whined, "Ew!"

Quill hung from Maguire's arms, heaving and gasping. She carefully helped him get into a seated position, murmuring, "Easy now. Easy."

Twyla crawled over Duckers to help Maguire with Quill.

"Oof!" cried Duckers as Twyla's knee crunched into his shin. "Would you all stop kicking the shit out of me, please?"

"Ope, sorry."

Twyla knelt on one side of Quill while her boss knelt on the other. She touched his sparkling cheek with her equally sparkling fingers. "Quill?"

He moaned in answer.

The light grew brighter in the corridor as Maguire held up a glowing lantern.

"Where did that come from? I thought the other lamps blew out."

The chief shrugged. "My demigod gift. I can light fires with my bare hands."

"For real?" said Duckers. "How cool is that?"

Quill moaned again, slightly less piteously. Twyla was about to cosset him when Maguire spat, "Shit!"

Another dragon loomed over them in the close tunnel. With

her free hand, she reached for her pistol crossbow and, finding the holster empty, tried to draw her machete. But the ceiling was too low, and slime was dripping down the handle, coating the blade and clogging up the scabbard.

"It's okay, Chief," Twyla told her, staying her hand.

"Okay, my ass."

"Please tell me that's our picnic friend, Twyla," said Duckers.

"I'm pretty sure that's our picnic friend."

"How sure?"

"Eighty-five percent."

"Fuuuuuuck."

"Ninety percent. Ninety-two."

Maguire got as far as asking "Is our picnic friend going to—" before the dragon leaned past her to snuffle Twyla's head. The chief squeezed herself against the wall. "Shit!"

"Good gods," whispered Quill, following suit.

With a shaking hand, Twyla patted the dragon on the head between her fuzzy antlers. "Hi, friend." She hoped she sounded a thousand times more confident than she felt. The dragon closed her eyes and chirped in a way that sounded happy rather than murderous, which Twyla took as a good sign.

Meep? squeaked the dragon that had attacked them from the rear.

The friendly dragon opened her eyes, glared over her folded wings, and uttered a menacing *Chirp-chirp-chirp*. The other dragon skulked off. Satisfied, Twyla's picnic friend returned for more pets.

Quill rested his head against the cave wall in evident relief. "I don't know why this dragon has taken a particular liking to you, darling, but I am glad of it."

Given the circumstances, Twyla decided not to harp on his calling her *darling* again.

"This dragon is definitely on Team Twyla," said Duckers. "You know what I think it is? Mom vibes. She's vibing on your mom-ness."

"My mom-ness?"

Duckers held up one hand. "You're a mom." He held up his other hand. "She's a mom." He brought his hands together, lacing the fingers. "Mom-ness. You're the one who protected her and her eggs that time by the Mist. I think she gets that. I think she's grateful."

"Mom-ness," Twyla mused, stroking the dragon's head with growing confidence.

"She certainly came to our rescue," observed Quill, weak but somewhat recovered. "Do you think she might allow us to vacate this tunnel?"

Twyla detected hints of barely contained panic in his voice. "Of course," she said, but she wasn't sure how to signal to the dragon that she was finished petting her. She smoothed a hand over one of the antlers. "That's enough? Thank you?"

To her amazement, the dragon retreated out of the tunnel, allowing the humans to scrabble out of the slime-filled corridor. With only two working lanterns to light their way, it was more difficult to see in the larger space, but as her eyes adjusted to the dimness, Twyla was able to make out two more dragons coming in from the direction of the main entrance. One bore babies on her back while the other did not, but they both carried masses of vegetation in their mouths. The one without babies entered the tunnel that the marshals and Quill had vacated seconds ago.

"What is going on?" asked Duckers.

"My guess is that they are feeding the dragons who are sitting on the eggs," said Quill.

Twyla's friend picked up the mass of plants she had deposited on the floor when she came to their rescue, and she carried it into one of the other tunnels, with her babies waddling behind her.

"But two of them have clutches that have already hatched," said Twyla. "Maybe they laid more eggs? Think it's safe to look around? Or should we get out of here?"

"I think it best that we leave," Quill replied at the same time Duckers said, "Let's look around."

Maguire tried to wipe off the glitter around her eyes with the inside of her shirt collar, to little effect. "I'm deferring to the professional dracologist on this one."

"But the dragons were only guarding their nests," said Twyla. "The danger has passed."

"I'm not convinced of that. We're leaving."

"But, Chief—" began Duckers.

"Out."

Reluctantly, Twyla and Duckers followed Maguire and Quill the way they'd come. The sun was setting by the time they climbed to the surface, with the sounds of baby dragons chirping in the nests below.

"Hello-o-o? Mail delivery?" came Hermia's tentative call as the last of the expedition party emerged from the cave entrance. "Goodness gracious me, you're all very shiny this evening. Are you having a party?"

"Sure," Maguire answered flatly. "What do you have for us, Hermia?"

The hedgehog looked at her blankly, then startled. "Oh, that's right. You have a letter." She reached into her satchel, pulled out an envelope, held it before her glasses, and blinked at the direction. "Ooh, I got it on the first try. Here it is."

The nimkilim delivered the mail, preening over the fact that she was doing her job with an iota of competence.

"Who's it from?" asked Twyla as Maguire tore into the envelope.

"The FICBI. This should be the lab results identifying the substance found on Herd's body."

"And on us," added Duckers, spreading out his arms and gazing down on his newly glittery appearance.

As Maguire's luminous demigod eyes scanned the message, an incredulous expression took over her face. "Well, I'll be the Warden's doormat."

"What does it say?"

The chief glanced at the hedgehog. "Duckers, tip the nimkilim."

"Why do I have to?"

"I don't have any change."

Duckers sucked his teeth, but he handed the hedgehog a copper from his pocket.

Hermia held it up, as if she were toasting them with a beer. "Okay, thanks. Bye."

"Bye," said the four humans.

"Bye, then."

"Goodbye," said Quill.

"Stop. Trust me," Twyla whispered at him.

"Bye."

With that, Hermia hiked off in her blue rubber boots, which made a squeak with each step she took.

"So what is this stuff?" asked Duckers once the nimkilim disappeared from view.

Maguire held up the lab results from the FICBI. "It's a resin."

"No kidding." Duckers wrinkled his nose at the thick golden slime dripping off his hand.

"That, when combined with sediment and geological pressure over time, turns into iuvenicite."

"By gods!" cried Quill. "These dragons are the source of iuvenicite?"

"Yep. Dragon spit, sediment, and time." Maguire frowned at the report in her hand. "I need to get a message to Chief Mitchell and Rosie Fox posthaste. They're going to want to know about this connection to their smuggling case."

"That's intra-agency. You could have sent a note with Hermia," said Twyla, trying to wrap her brain around the fact that the dragon spit coating her from head to toe could one day turn into one of the most valuable minerals in the world.

"I don't trust that hedgehog to find the nose on her own face. Best to tell Mitchell about it in person anyway. I'm riding back now. You three stay at the lake and keep your heads down until you hear from me."

With that command, Maguire mounted up and galloped southwest toward the portal at the West Station, leaving Twyla, Duckers, and Quill to make their way to the campsite. It wasn't a long ride, but Twyla spent the entirety of it longing to jump in the lake to get the glitter off.

"How much do you think we're worth right now?" asked Duckers, examining his spit-covered arms.

"I'd like to think we're priceless," said Twyla.

"All I know is that I'm scraping as much of this shit as I can into a jar before I get cleaned up. Money, money, money!" He sang the last three words in a soulful falsetto.

"I doubt it is worth more than a few coppers until millennia have turned it into iuvenicite for you. I, for one, shall be happy to bathe as soon as humanly possible," griped Quill.

"Suit yourself," Duckers told him, but Twyla planned to follow Quill's lead. The slimy resin had made its way into the various crevices of her body, and it was not pleasant.

Frank leaped to his feet when they made their way into camp, his eyes goggling as Mary Georgina approached them for a better look.

"What in the Salt Sea happened to you?"

"What do you think?" replied Duckers.

"Where's Maguire?"

"She rode to the station."

"Is everyone all right?"

"Yes," Twyla said at the same time Duckers said "Never been better" and Quill said "Define 'all right.'"

Frank burst out laughing, a deep familiar rumble that Twyla was more than relieved to hear again. Kiss schmiss. They were going to be okay; she just knew it.

"You look like you've been having yourself a real good time, Duckers. Did y'all go clubbing?" he asked before he threw back his head and laughed even harder.

Chapter Sixteen

By the following morning, there were more dragons of both sexes gathering on the lake. Whenever Duckers spotted a male flying overhead, he took great delight in shouting, "Look, Dr. V., hemipenile bulges!" To his credit, Quill smiled indulgently every time.

Frank was less enthusiastic about the growing dragon population. "It's only a matter of time before someone spots one flying around in a neighboring sector—someone who's not us," he murmured to Twyla as they watched Mary Georgina dip her head into the water to pull up a bite of swampy grass. A truce had formed between them, and slowly, carefully, they were finding their way back to their pre-wedding, pre-bombs, pre-kiss friendship.

"And you're worried about what that means for Mary Georgina," Twyla surmised.

"Eventually, the wrong sort of person is going to find out she can spit the world's most expensive mineral."

"No, she spits a resin."

"That turns into money."

"It sounds like there's a lengthy geological process involved before it becomes iuvenicite, though."

"I don't know, Twy. I've got a bad feeling in my guts about this. If someone can figure out how to make a portal into an impenetrable mist created by gods, I'm pretty sure people can figure out how to use these dragons to make iuvenicite. Or, Salt Sea, they'll just steal them and breed them and turn them into pets, same as graps."

Five days ago, Twyla would have wrapped her arm around his waist to comfort him. She wouldn't have thought twice about it. Now she thought it through three times before deciding to keep her hands to herself.

"I'm here for you. I've got your back. And Mary Georgina's," she told him, words that sounded limp and helpless the second they passed her lips.

"I know."

Five days ago, he would have slung his arm over her shoulders or at least have given her a rueful grin. Today, he kept his eyes on his adopted baby, who had already grown so much that she stood at his hip now.

"I have a theory," Quill announced as he and Duckers joined them beside the lake. He stood so close to Twyla that he squished the side of her thigh.

She subtly eased away from him. "Let's hear it."

"Mind you, it is only a theory and would need to hold up to rigorous scientific testing—"

Frank interrupted him. "We understand. What's the theory?"

Twyla resisted the urge to give him a scolding look. Their friendship was on the mend, and she didn't want to do anything to upset their delicate truce.

Unaware of Frank's terseness, Quill held forth. "Given the anatomy that we have observed in *Draconis tanrias*, I think it safe to say that the males of the species fertilize the eggs, and the females lay them, exactly as you would expect in most reptiles. What is interesting, based on our observations here at the lake and at the nesting site, is that it appears that while mothers lay the eggs, the fathers sit on them. The females bring food to the males as they incubate the eggs. But when the babies hatch, the mothers are the ones who care for the young, while continuing to feed the males of the species. We do, on occasion, see male dragons in and around the lake, and they do feed themselves whilst they are here, but they do not participate in the raising of the young, and the females continue to bring them food at the nesting site. It's fascinating."

Twyla stared at him. *Fascinating* was not the word she would have chosen to describe this behavior. *Infuriating* seemed more apt.

"So what's up with those two?" asked Duckers, waving his hat at a pair of dragons who regularly sunned themselves in the same spot each day. "They're both females, right? But they don't have kids. They're always over there chilling. Are they too young to lay eggs or something?"

"Ah, yes, I have observed them. They appear to be a mated pair who are both female."

"Really?"

"Indeed. Sexual diversity is common throughout the animal kingdom."

Duckers cupped his hands around his mouth and shouted "The Bride of Fortune favor you!" at them.

Shortly before Twyla crawled into her tent that evening, Quill intercepted her on her way back from her designated toilet—*toilet* being her euphemism for *the spot where I take care of business and bitterly reflect on how much harder this is for people with my parts as opposed to the people with the other parts.* She was literally thinking, *Hemipenile bulges, my ass*, when Quill popped out of the darkness.

"Ope!" she shrilled.

"Sorry, darl—Twyla, did I startle you?"

"You scared me half to death."

"Ah. Apologies."

"Twy? You all right?" Frank called from the campsite.

"Yep," she yelled before looking to Quill with a mixture of amusement, expectation, and exasperation.

"This is not off to an auspicious beginning." He shuffled his feet, and Twyla was once again struck by how boyish he looked from time to time. Maybe it was the shorts and knee socks. "I wonder if you might accompany me?"

"Where?"

"That would spoil the surprise."

As a general rule, Twyla was not fond of surprises. But she was fond of Quill, so she let him take her hand and lead her along the lakeshore, heading south, away from where the dragons tended to spend their days. Eventually, a romantic scene came into view in the light of their lanterns, a blanket spread on the ground beneath a willow tree. Atop the blanket were a bouquet of wildflowers, a bottle of sparkling wine, and two folksy tin cups.

"I'm afraid wineglasses are in short supply here, but I did manage to smuggle a bottle of Veuf Didier through the portal," he explained as he set down his lantern near the blanket, letting it cast a warm glow over the venue. "I know you do not wish to be amorous while we are inside the Mist, and that is perfectly understandable. But I thought—I *hoped*—that a small date apart from the others might not be objectionable?"

"It's not objectionable. It's thoughtful. Thank you." She sat on the blanket, even though she knew that her knees were going to be killing her by the time she got up again. Amazing how sitting on the ground was now a difficult thing to do.

As Quill popped the cork and poured the Veuf Didier into the undeserving tin cups, Twyla had to ask herself what she was doing, sitting here with this lovely man, when she had been hot and heavy with Frank—*Frank!*—only a few days earlier. Even now, all she could think about was the fact that kissing Frank—*Oh my gods, Frank!*—had felt so much better and more right than kissing Quill ever could.

She'd have to unpack that later. For now, she needed to break things off with Quill. It was only fair to him.

"I think we should talk," she began.

He raised his eyebrows at her, and then his shoulders stooped as he set the bottle down on the picnic blanket. "Ah."

"That was a heavy *ah*."

"I suspect that you are about to tell me, gently yet firmly, that you no longer wish to be romantically involved. With me."

The last two words had been tacked on, as if he thought that she wanted to be romantically involved with someone else. And they both knew who the implied someone else was. Twyla didn't want to think about that particular someone, so she focused her attention on the man who sat beside her. She placed her hand over his.

"I'm sorry, Quill. You're a wonderful man."

"But not the right wonderful man for you."

"I'm afraid not." She squeezed his hand before removing hers. "I owe you thanks, you know."

"For what?"

Twyla took a contemplative sip of champagne. "I've spent most of my life being useful, and when a person has been useful for as long as I have, they come to believe that useful is all they are. But then you came along and wanted to spend time with me, for my own sake. I know this won't make a bit of sense to you, but thank you for helping me see that I don't have to be a chair for all eternity."

His eyes crinkled in amusement. "I think I get the gist. And you are most welcome. Thank *you* for making my time on the island of Bushong infinitely more enjoyable than it would have been without you."

"You're not a fan of Tanria, are you?"

"I wouldn't say that. Where else could you go that affords you the opportunity of near death by glittery saliva?"

Twyla laughed and raised her cup. He clinked his to hers, and they sat together for a long while, drinking sparkling wine and chatting about dragons and marshaling and university life. Eventually, they drifted into a comfortable silence and let the bittersweetness of the moment wash over them.

After some time had passed, Quill gently asked her, "Do you think Marshal Ellis might be the right wonderful man for you?"

"No!" she yelped. The single syllable rang through the mountainous landscape, and the Dragon's Teeth seemed to echo with her guilt and confusion. When next she spoke, she forced herself to sound calm and rational. "I told you, we're friends. Good friends. That's all."

"I don't doubt it. But it seems to me that at least one of those friends is pining away for the other in rather tragic silence."

"I'm not pining for Frank," she insisted. She wondered if she was trying to convince Quill or herself.

"Perhaps."

"I'm not!"

"I believe you," he capitulated, but the urge to wriggle out from underneath his probing gaze spiked inside her. She suddenly felt like a bug under a magnifying glass on a sunny day. She polished off the dregs of Veuf Didier in her cup and rose.

"I should go."

Quill got to his feet as well. "It was not my intention to pry or to make you uncomfortable."

"Don't worry about it."

"If I may…" He reached out as if he meant to touch her, but appeared to think better of it. "I don't quite understand what you meant about not having to be a chair, but I do hope that you will take your happiness where you find it, Twyla. You've earned it."

It saddened her that he thought he couldn't touch her, at least in friendship, so she squeezed his arm with heartfelt affection. "Good night, Quill."

He patted her hand. "Good night, Twyla."

Throughout the following day, Twyla managed to avoid Quill, for obvious reasons, and Frank, too, for reasons that were less obvious to her. She busied herself with gathering firewood while everyone else was eating breakfast. She tidied up the campsite once everyone was out and about—Quill with the dragons, Frank taking care of Mary Georgina, and Duckers out patrolling the sector. Once Duckers returned, she took a tour around W-14 on her own and didn't return until after dinner.

It hadn't occurred to her to avoid Duckers, but it should have, because he had the unfortunate habit of seeing right through her. Case in point, he squinted at her over the evening campfire and declared, "You're being weird today."

"No, I'm not."

"Something is up with you."

She glanced at Quill. She didn't glance at Frank.

"I'm fine."

"Liiiiiiiiies," he hissed.

"Hello-o-o? Mail delivery?"

Grateful for the distraction, Twyla leaped up to welcome the nimkilim into the circle of the campfire's warmth. She sensed Frank's chagrin as she invited Hermia to have a seat with them by the campfire for a few minutes. The hedgehog's short legs dangled from the log bench, and she wound up sliding off with an "Oopsie-doozles!"

Letters went flying through the air, and a few tumbled into the flickering flames of the campfire. Twyla, Frank, Duckers, and Quill lunged, doing their best to retrieve whatever was retrievable, but only Duckers had any success. He handed the smoking remains of four letters to the hedgehog.

"Oh dear," she sighed as she stared at the scorched paper in her sweet little hedgehog hands.

Twyla noticed that one of the burnt envelopes had her name on it. Well, most of her name. It was addressed to *Twyla Bannek*. The rest of the name had been browned beyond recognition, but Twyla had to assume the last two letters were *er*.

"Is that one for me, Hermia?"

The nimkilim held one of the other envelopes in front of her glasses. "No?"

"Not that one."

She stuffed the first letter into her satchel and held up another. "No?"

"I'll help myself," said Twyla, sliding the correct letter out of Hermia's hand.

Quill got to his feet and said to the nimkilim, "One moment, if you please."

"Oh dear, I'm not supposed to..." began the hedgehog, but Quill was already crawling inside his tent. The nimkilim produced a bottle of grape soda from her satchel and took a morose pull on it. As they waited for Quill to return, Twyla opened her letter and read it in astonishment.

It was from, of all people, Wade. She could barely wrap her brain around the concept that her son had actually taken the time to write to her, and yet she held the singed evidence in her fingers. Since a not insignificant portion of the page was burned, some words were illegible, but she got the gist, and the gist was extremely gratifying. He had gone to the insurance office first thing Sorrowsday morning. Since he wasn't the policy holder, he couldn't file the claim, but he'd gotten the agent to start the paperwork at least. And then he'd lined up a contractor to start working on the house as soon as the claim was filed. And he'd picked up Hope and had her installed at his house, and Twyla could share the room with her as long as she liked.

His handwriting had changed very little since grammar school, and some of the words were misspelled, and he apparently had no idea what constituted a complete sentence. And yet, a fierce pride swelled in Twyla's chest. For all Wade's foibles, when push came to shove, he was there to do what needed doing without an air of martyrdom. She must have done something right as a mother, and it gave her hope for the future of the world.

As she refolded Wade's letter, Quill returned with a thick envelope in hand.

Hermia clutched the soda bottle to her heart. "I'm ever so sorry, sir, but you'll have to put it in a nimkilim box. I'm not supposed to pick up the mail. I'm only allowed to deliver. Those are the rules."

"There are extenuating circumstances here," said Quill, extending an enormous tip toward the hedgehog.

Hermia gasped and splayed one wee pink hand over her bitty heart. "Oh, dear me, I can't take a bribe!"

"It's not a bribe; it's a gratuity. This is a report for Chief Maguire. She instructed me to send it with you."

"Oooooh. Okay, I can carry messages within the agency."

The three marshals had all deduced what the report contained, and they watched warily as Quill handed it to the nimkilim. Hermia spilled a splash of grape soda on it with an "Uh-oh" before she stuffed both the bottle and the report into her satchel and tottered off into the Tanrian night.

Quill shuffled awkwardly under the expectant gaze of his companions. A pair of matching dirt stains coated his bare knees from his having scrambled on the ground for loose mail.

"Was that your recommendation to Maguire about what to do with the dragons?" asked Frank.

"Yes."

"Well?"

"I think it best for Chief Maguire to read over it first," Quill hedged.

"Come on," Duckers protested. "What does it say?"

The dracologist looked to Twyla for help, but she wanted to know what the report said, too. "I have to follow protocol on this," he said at last. "Forgive me."

With that, he returned to his tent and stayed there for the remainder of the evening, leaving Frank and Twyla and Duckers to worry over the unknown contents of the manila envelope.

The contents of Quill's report became apparent two days later, when Maguire arrived with three scientists from the Center for Tanrian Biological Research—a zoologist, a botanist, and Dr. Sellet.

"What's going on?" asked Frank, eyeing the new scientists with grave concern as Quill greeted them with chummy collegiality. Maguire pulled Frank to the side while Quill gestured for the scientists to follow him north, presumably so that they could observe the dragons firsthand. Twyla and Duckers glanced at each other and made the unspoken decision to follow Maguire and Frank.

"Good. You two should hear this as well," Maguire said to them when they came to stand with Frank. "Dr. Vanderlinden has recommended setting up a dragon preserve, possibly on one of the uninhabited outer islands, far from human populations. Short of that, he suggests that the dragons be rounded up and placed in zoos that are capable of handling large animals."

"That's ridiculous," Frank objected vehemently.

"I'm inclined to agree with him. Dr. Sellet and his colleagues are here to add their expertise to the matter. This issue is no longer under the jurisdiction of the Tanrian Marshals alone. The Feds are involved now."

"You can't be serious." Frank sounded calm, but Twyla sensed his outrage boiling under the surface.

"I am serious."

"These dragons are harmless."

"They didn't strike me as harmless when I nearly choked to death on dragon spit."

"They were created to live in Tanria. Who's to say they'll survive if they're taken outside the Mist?"

"There's a flourishing pet trade in graps and Tanrian birds outside the Mist. The dragons will live."

"Probably or definitely?" asked Duckers, standing at Frank's shoulder.

"Don't start with me, Duckers." Addressing Frank, she softened. "I know you're attached to Mary Georgina, Ellis, but you need to start thinking about what's best for her."

"What's best for her is to stay in her home!" he shouted before turning away and striding for the lake.

Twyla stared after him in mutual sympathy with Maguire and Duckers. "I'll go after him," she said.

"Hold up. I was saving the good news for last to soften the blow. Guess I should have opened with it. Our lead about Marshal Herd and the illegal mining operation here in Sector W-14 blew open the iuvenicite case. Marshal Fox was able to track Herd's movements in Zeandale days before his death. Turns out he was working with a fence with ties to the Galatian mob. Arrests have been made, and you three are safe to return home at the end of your tour tomorrow. Gods know you deserve the break."

"Great," said Duckers, trying to muster some enthusiasm.

"Thanks, Chief," said Twyla, also trying and failing to muster enthusiasm.

"What's wrong with you sad sacks? I thought you'd be glad to go home without someone trying to kill you."

"My home kind of has a hole in the roof. I'll be staying with my son until it's fixed."

"Stay with Frank. He's got the room, hasn't he?"

"I guess he does," Twyla agreed vaguely. "Let me go talk to him. I'll let him know the good news."

Twyla found Frank exactly where she expected to find him, standing at the lake's edge, watching Mary Georgina swimming near the other dragons. She stood beside him but said nothing, letting her presence speak for itself.

After a time, he spoke. "I'm not going to say it's like losing Lu and Annie all over again, because it isn't. But..." He faltered, struggling for words. "Why can't I seem to take care of my own? I swear I do my best by those who count on me, but I always wind up failing miserably."

Twyla wanted to hug him, to comfort him, but something as simple as a touch had become complicated between them. All she had were words, and words didn't seem like enough. "I can't begin to tell you how wrong you are about that. I count on you, and you've never failed me. Not once."

"You've never failed me either." One corner of his mouth hinted at a smile, and when he spoke again, there was a lightness in his voice, as if Twyla had managed to lift some of his burden for him. "I'm sure your fella is right about what needs doing, but Salt Sea, it does not feel right in my bones, leaving that baby to the care of someone else, not when she's put all her trust in me."

An idea occurred to Twyla, probably a useless one, but it was better than doing nothing. "Frank, what if you were to write up your own recommendation?"

"To who?"

"The Joint Chiefs of the Tanrian Marshals? These scientists? The Assembly of the Federated Islands of Cadmus? Even Quill. He might be the expert on the war dragons of the Old Gods, but if anyone on this earth is an expert on Tanrian dragons, it's you."

He nodded slowly, mulling over her suggestion.

"What would you recommend?" she asked him.

"That they stay in Tanria. They were made for this place; we're the ones who don't belong here. Past that..." He shrugged.

They watched the dragons on the lake. One of the young ones approached Mary Georgina, and the two babies sniffed each other. It was the closest Twyla had seen Mary Georgina get to any of the others. She held her breath, hopeful, as the two little ones swam together, darting in a game of chase on the water.

"Would you look at that," murmured Frank.

"Your girl's growing up."

It was nice to share in his joy, to feel like his friend again. Her heart had been all knotted up these past few days, and this moment was what it had taken to loosen it.

"He's not my fella, by the way. We broke up."

Frank did a double take before schooling his expression into one of sympathy. "I'm sorry."

"It was amicable." She nudged him, her shoulder against his, a blissful sense of normalcy settling over them. "We're good, aren't we?"

"Yeah. We're good." He put his arm around her shoulders, and it wasn't weird or awkward. It was them. It was Frank and Twyla, Twyla and Frank.

"Twy, there's something I need to tell you."

The portentous hint in his voice set her nerves jangling. She looked up into his hound dog eyes. "What is it?"

He opened his mouth and clamped it shut again. Then he said, "I want you to know that I will dismember anyone who tries to make you a chair again."

Twyla gurgled with laughter. "True friend," she said, and as she leaned her head against the reassuring bulk of his shoulder, she told him the good news.

Chapter Seventeen

Zeddie Birdsall and the family autoduck were waiting for Duckers in the West Station's parking lot when the three marshals got off duty, leaving Mary Georgina and a chunk of their hearts behind them in Tanria.

"Fuck me," muttered Duckers.

"Have we talked to him about barnacles and hulls and scraping?" Frank asked Twyla.

"Hey, Z," Duckers sighed as he walked toward his boyfriend.

Zeddie's smile fell into a pissy frown. "Wow. Try to contain your enthusiasm."

"How did you know I'd be out today?"

"I ran into Alma Maguire at Callaghan's General Store. Could you at least pretend to be happy to see me? You know, the guy you're dating?"

"This is not good," Twyla said to Frank.

He was already nudging her inside the station. "Let's wait in the commissary. I don't want to take off without him in case he winds up stranded here."

They grabbed a couple of sodas and sat at a lunch table, waiting to see how things panned out with Duckers's love life.

"When are you expecting Lu and Annie?" asked Twyla.

Frank peeled the label off the sweating soda bottle. He was always nervous before his kids came for a visit. "Late Wisdomsday.

They're driving up after work and staying for a couple of weeks. Thought maybe we could all drive to one of the inner islands while Hope's in town. Wade and Anita and the kids could come, too."

"They'd love that."

"Good thing I don't have a baby dragon attached to me anymore."

"There is a silver lining here." She put her hand over his label-peeling fingers. "No matter what happens, Mary Georgina will be taken care of."

"I hope so."

"And you and Lu and Annie will have a wonderful time together. You always do."

"Gods, I can't wait to see them."

"I bet."

She let go of his hand, and he began to pick at the label again. "You're staying with Wade and Anita while your house gets fixed?"

"That's the plan," she said, making a valiant effort not to melt into a pile of exhaustion at the very thought. The house was going to be cramped with a family of five plus Twyla and Hope.

"You know, you can stay at my place for as long as you need. You and Hope, I mean."

Twyla desperately wanted to accept the offer, but their friendship was barely on the mend, and she didn't want to tempt fate by living under the same roof as Frank for any length of time. "Your kids are coming. And who knows how long the repairs will take. I might look into getting an apartment until the house is fixed up."

"My door's always open to you."

Duckers stepped into the commissary, his head bent. He wiped furiously at his cheeks.

"This is definitely not good," murmured Twyla. She waved to get his attention, and he made a beeline for their table.

"Can I have a ride?" he asked without looking up.

Frank got to his feet, grabbed his pack, and started pushing Duckers out of the commissary. "Yep. Let's get out of here."

"We broke up," said Duckers as they hit the front door of the West Station, his voice cracking.

"We figured."

Twyla wrapped an arm around his waist and tossed her keys to Frank, who hustled ahead to unlock the duck. "I'm so sorry, honey."

"I dumped him," he told them tearfully.

Frank chucked everyone's bags into the hold while Twyla packed Duckers onto the back bench and sat beside him.

"Poor Pen."

"Poor Pen? I'm a dick! Poor Zeddie!" He broke down completely as Frank sat behind the wheel, even though it was Twyla's duck. This was a situation that required Twyla's mom-ness, as Duckers would put it, and they both knew it.

"He was so upset," sobbed Duckers. "He shouldn't be driving."

Twyla didn't know Zeddie Birdsall well, but since he was only a year younger than Hope, she'd seen him grow up. A pang of sympathy for him jabbed her in the heart. But Duckers was beside her, and he needed her now.

"Zeddie's an adult. I'm sure he'll pull over if he needs to." Twyla made a face at Frank in the rearview mirror when he made a dubious grunt of disagreement, and she doubled down on her efforts to comfort Duckers. "He's got his family looking out for him, I promise."

Duckers responded by sobbing even louder.

"Who's up for a beer?" asked Frank.

"That's a fine idea," Twyla answered for her and Duckers since Duckers was crying too hard to answer for himself. They stopped by Hutchins's Sip Mart long enough for Frank to dash in for a case of Ray's Pilsner, and then they headed to his house for beery commiseration.

"I'm through with love," Duckers declared from Frank's sofa, and he was only one beer in.

"Fair," said Frank.

"You know what sucks? Hart Ralston is my best friend on Bushong, but now he's Zeddie's brother-in-law."

"So?"

"So that's going to be weird for him."

"Ralston's a big boy. He knows how to be friends with one man and family with another. Besides, he married Mercy, not Zeddie. If he's a good friend, he'll stay a good friend."

"I hope so."

"I know so," Twyla assured him. Hart was a tough nut to crack, but she got the feeling that once someone had earned his friendship, he was unlikely to turn his back on them. She was certain that included his former apprentice.

"Fuck. I'm going to need to buy my own autoduck now. I'd ask Hart to give me a ride to the sales lots, but he's on his honeymoon. Plus, awkward."

"I don't have anything going on until my kids get here. I'll take you," offered Frank.

"You don't mind?"

"Nah, I don't mind. Saltsday morning work for you?"

"Yeah. Thanks, Frank."

"You bet."

The ease with which Frank did something kind for someone else never ceased to impress Twyla, not when she had spent two decades married to a man who sighed with put-upon exasperation whenever she asked him to do so much as take out the trash.

A few too many beers later, Duckers reverted to his melodramatic mode. "Love is the wooooooorst," he groaned to Frank's ceiling, his head resting on the back of the sofa.

"Cheers," said Frank. Twyla clinked her bottle to Duckers's and took a swig.

Duckers studied Frank, then Twyla, with glassy eyes. "You two are down on love?"

"Yes," said Twyla.

"Gods, yes," rasped Frank.

"But you both seem so emotionally healthy and shit. What do you have against love?"

Frank pointed to himself. "Divorced." He pointed to Twyla. "Chair." He finished his beer and popped the cap off another.

"Chair?"

"Don't ask," said Twyla.

"I thought you were getting it on with Dr. Vandertweed."

"We broke up."

"He dumped you, huh? Sadness."

"I'll have you know that I am the one who dumped him," she informed him with slurred asperity.

"Like I dumped Zeddie?" He started crying again.

Frank handed him a fresh handkerchief since Duckers had depleted his own. "If you're this sad about breaking up, maybe you should be together after all."

"No." Duckers sniffed. "I know I did the right thing. I'm not ready for the kind of relationship he wants. It just feels super shitty."

"To feeling shitty," said Twyla, raising her beer.

"To feeling shitty," Frank repeated.

Duckers kept crying, but he lifted his drink.

As they toasted their romantic miseries, Twyla's eyes drifted to the wall opposite her, to the place where she had tackled Frank and kissed him. And then her eyes followed their path to the left, to the place beside the front door where—

She tore her gaze away. She would have expected to feel any number of things at the memory—regret, embarrassment, even heat—especially since she was tipsy. What she felt instead was a sense of wistfulness, although she couldn't say for what exactly. Did she wish that she could turn back the clock and erase what had happened? Would she have done anything differently the night of the wedding, when a pair of bombs had changed her friendship with Frank in some immutable way?

No, she decided that she couldn't bring herself to regret it. And when her eyes met Frank's, she could see that he didn't regret it either. An understanding passed between them, these two people who knew each other cold. They would weather this storm together, and their friendship would be stronger for it.

"Cheers, darlin'," he said, and he peeled the label off his bottle.

Twyla thought she wouldn't be able to sleep in the same house as Frank anytime soon, but all it took to cure her of that notion were a few beers and a heartbroken twenty-one-year-old in need of tender loving care. She and Duckers had wound up in Lu's old room, giggling about Quill's *ass*-cot like prepubescent girls at a sleepover until they drifted off to sleep. Frank had stuffed them full of sugary oatmeal before they left in the morning, but Twyla was mildly hungover as she stepped outside and gazed longingly at her house next door. It now sported an ugly tarp over the even uglier hole in her roof.

"Where are you staying again?" Duckers asked her as they climbed into the cab of her autoduck.

"With my son."

"The one with all the kids?"

"He only has three."

"But wouldn't it make more sense to stay with your bestie?"

"His kids are coming for a two-week visit on Wisdomsday, and my daughter is already at Wade's house. I'm more worried about you. I hate the idea of leaving you all alone."

"But that's what I want—time to myself in my own place on my own terms. I literally dumped a great guy to get it."

A memory arose like a ghost in Twyla's mind, not of a single moment but of many bound together, of a thousand times in her life when she would have given anything to check into a clean hotel room for one night and order room service and lie there on the bed and do absolutely nothing. Some people dreamed of travel and vacations, but in those days, Twyla had no aspirations of that kind. She wanted only to live and breathe in a room with no one else in it for a few hours. Now that she had her house (mostly) to herself—when it didn't have a hole in the roof or smoke and water damage—she appreciated the value of living on her own terms even more.

She leaned across the bench and gave Duckers a hug. "I have so much respect for you."

"Same to you." He hugged her in return before he hopped out, retrieved his pack from the hold, and climbed the steps to his apartment building.

She put the duck in gear and headed for Wade's house. "Speaking of not having space to yourself," she joked for her own benefit. When she pulled up to the curb, she found Manny and Sal outside, practicing sea polo in the front yard. So far inland, it was always a challenge to adapt the game for play on land, but Bushong kids had long mastered the art of it. In Twyla's grandkids' case, they were riding on bikes instead of equimares, passing the ball around through elaborate formations.

"Wammy!" cried Sal when he heard the door of her duck thud shut. "Wammy's here!" He leaped off the bike while it was still in motion, letting it career toward the garden shed as he ran to Twyla and gave her a hug. He was a rambunctious kid but deeply affectionate. *I'm a hugger*, he'd once informed her when he was all of four years old. It was how he managed to get away with murder.

Manny rode over and took a lap around Twyla. "Want to take a few shots, Wammy?"

The truth was that Twyla could go for a couple more aspirins and a nap, but having been up to her eyeballs in extremely complicated life and career events these past few weeks, she decided that playing with her grandkids would be a refreshing and uncomplicated break.

"You're on," she said, and the two boys whooped in her honor. Sal retrieved his jackknifed bicycle and handed it off to Twyla.

"Ope!" she cried as she pushed down on the pedal and wobbled into motion, teetering on the seat. She knew she wasn't going all that fast, but she was a woman of a certain age, and the bike was too small for her.

"Go, Wammy!" shouted Manny, cupping his hands around his mouth.

"I'm passing you the ball!" announced Sal, and he hurled said object at her face before she could suggest that no, maybe now would not be the best time.

"Oh, shit!" she yelped as the ball came at her. She barely managed to catch it and stay upright.

Manny and Sal dissolved into peals of laughter, yelling, "Wammy said *s*!"

There was only one way to redeem this situation. She pedaled for the rickety goal that Wade had cobbled together last year and gave it her best shot.

And missed by an embarrassing margin.

"Weak!" called a voice that was much deeper than her grandkids'. It was Wade, coming to stand with his boys on the lawn. His children cackled at his joke and parroted him, shouting "Weak!" at their poor, dear grandmother.

Surging with orneriness, Twyla swerved the bike and rode straight at him.

"Oh, shit!" he laughed, darting out of the way in the nick of time.

It was too much for Manny and Sal to bear. They were laughing so hard it was a wonder they didn't pass out. Sal did, in fact, topple theatrically to the ground.

"Language!" came Anita's voice, chastising Wade from the kitchen window as Twyla braked to a stop.

Wade grimaced. "Sorry, honey." He looked to his mother and hissed, "You got me in trouble!"

"Serves you right."

Manny tugged on the sleeve of Wade's coveralls. "It's okay, Dad. Wammy said *s*, too."

"Did she now?"

"Thank you for taking care of my house while I was gone, Wadey."

"Aw, Wadey!" Sal giggled from where he was wallowing in the grass.

Wade toed him affectionately. "Hush, you."

"Are you heading to work?" Twyla asked him, a rhetorical question since Wade's coveralls and boots made it clear that he had a shift at the autoduck mechanic shop on Main Street.

"Yep, if Princess Hope ever decides to get her ass out here since I'm giving her a ride." He raised his voice so that his sister would hear him through the window screens and get a move on.

"Wade! Language! Seriously!" scolded Anita from inside.

"*Ass* is off-limits?"

"Dad said *a*!" shrieked Sal.

"Yes! Gods! Why are you like this?"

Hope stepped out of the front door, tying on her Wilner's Green Grocer apron while her lunch bag dangled from the crook of her elbow.

"Ope! My lunch! Shit!" said Wade, and he sprinted inside the house to get his lunch pail.

"Oh my gods," moaned Anita.

"Sorry, honey!"

Hope hugged Twyla in greeting. "When did you get back?"

"Yesterday evening. We wound up having a few beers, so Frank let me and Duckers stay the night."

"You stayed at Frank's house—with *beer*—and you didn't invite me?"

"I didn't know you wanted to be invited."

"Mom. I am under the same roof as three little kids and *my brother*. This is my idea of Old Hell. Of course I'd rather stay at Frank's house. Are we putting up there until the roof gets fixed? Because I can pack up my stuff real fast before I go to work."

"I don't want to put Frank out. Besides, Lu and Annie are coming this Wisdomsday."

"All the more reason to crash at Frank's! And we're not putting him out. He loves us."

Hope had said the words so casually, and yet the combination of the words *he* and *loves* made Twyla's insides twist with anxiety.

"Go to work," she said, nudging her daughter toward Wade as he stepped outside, this time with his lunch. "We'll talk later."

"Fine." Hope aimed a finger with a neat pink fingernail at Twyla's nose. "But I am not letting this go."

Wade and Hope set off for their respective jobs while Twyla watched the kids so that Anita could run a few errands. She liked spending time with her grandkids, especially if it made her daughter-in-law's life a little easier. At the end of the day (or, in her current situation, at the end of a few weeks) she could go home to her own peace and quiet.

Wade and Hope returned shortly before dinner. Wade impressed Twyla by taking care to remove his greasy coveralls and shoes outside and clean himself up before coming in.

And then he collapsed onto the couch and let the kids run around him.

Hope, on the other hand, hung up her apron and helped throw

together a salad while Twyla set the table with Teo propped on her hip.

"Frank was talking about taking a day trip out to one of the inner islands while Lu and Annie are in town," Twyla mentioned to Hope. "Think you could get a couple of days off from Wilner's?"

"Yeah, I think so."

"The whole family's invited, Wade. You and the kids, too."

He cracked open one eye as Sal body-slammed him. "Oof! That'd be fun. What do you say, babe?"

"I'm in," Anita replied from the stove, where she was stirring a vat of marinara.

Twyla thought this all sounded great until she caught Hope rolling her eyes and blowing a gust of disappointment from her lungs. Her daughter's impatience with Wade and his family grated on her nerves.

Hope disappeared after dinner, leaving the washing up to Anita and Twyla and the two older boys. Twyla went looking for her and found her in the backyard, swaying listlessly on one of the two swings that dangled from the A-frame swing set.

"I wondered where you went."

"It's a small town. There aren't a lot of places to go."

"I'm going to chalk up the sulkiness to missing Everett."

Hope leaned her cheek against the chain and groaned. "It sucks to be somewhere he isn't."

"I remember the feeling." Twyla sat on the swing next to her daughter and was alarmed when her weight made the seat curve painfully tight around her bottom. "Ope! I wonder what the weight limit on these things is."

"I think Wade put this thing together, so I wouldn't put your trust in it."

"You're awfully down on Wade lately."

"All I'm saying is that he's not winning Dad of the Year—or

Husband of the Year, for that matter. He leaves everything to Anita. It's such bullshit."

"Language!"

"What is it with moms and cussing? Besides, you know I'm right."

It rankled Twyla, the way Hope spoke as if she knew better than anyone, when in fact, she knew nothing at all. Twyla had been dreading getting her concerns about Hope's future out in the open. Now, all of a sudden, she found she was willing and eager.

"I hate to be the bearer of bad tidings, but that's what happens when you're the one with the equipment."

Hope snorted. "The equipment? Seriously, Mom?"

"Yes. The equipment. You and Everett want to get married? Fine. But you need to recognize the fact that you're the one who can grow a person inside you. And you think you know what that means before you do it, but you don't. You have no clue until you're already knee-deep. It means never having enough to eat, or never being able to eat, because you're too busy throwing up. It means peeing every five seconds. It means your boobs hurting and your ankles swelling. It means varicose veins and hemorrhoids. It means messing up your back for the rest of your life. It means rearranging everything inside you. It means your body never being the same again. It means being exhausted in ways you never knew possible. And it means dealing with all of that while trying to make it through each and every day like a functioning adult. And Everett, the person with a different set of equipment, won't begin to understand what you're going through."

"I can't believe you're spouting off this Old Gods crap. You, of all people?"

But Twyla would not be waylaid. "And that's only the beginning, because once you push that child into the world in a way that is incredibly hard on your body, not to mention dangerous, you'll be the one with the equipment to feed the baby. Even if you decide to bottle feed, even if Everett promises to do his fair share, you are going to be up to your eyeballs in crappy assumptions from the days of the Old Gods that because you come with the equipment, you are somehow magically endowed with all the knowledge of how to be a parent, how to feed and clothe and diaper and take care of that precious human you put into the world. And that assumption touches everything. *Everything.* You're the one who inherently knows how to navigate doctors' appointments, babysitters, school, homework, when your kid needs new shoes, when your kid needs a hug, when your kid needs help... It will all fall to you—all of it—because you're the one with the equipment."

"I don't even know if we're going to have kids!"

"So? Do you think the lion's share of housecleaning and laundry and cooking and dishes and all of that won't fall to you?"

Hope got to her feet, rigid with offense. "I can't believe this is what you think of Everett! You've known him for years!"

"Everett is a sweetheart. I love Everett. But I also know what it means to be on the losing end of the Old Gods' tug-of-war between This Is Male and This Is Female. It didn't go away when the New Gods won the war, and it didn't go away when the Old Gods took their place on the altar of the sky. And if you think it's not coming for you the second you tie yourself to the person who comes with the equipment that puts him on the winning end of that game of tug-of-war, have I got news for you."

Hope fumed over Twyla like the old God of Wrath. "That's *your* life, the life you chose for yourself, for all of us. You're the one who got married too young. You're the one who had kids when you were still a kid yourself. The whole town is all *Poor Twyla, widowed and alone and grieving for the loss of Doug Banneker*, but I know better. You hated Dad—"

"I did not hate him!"

"Yes, you did, but you stayed with him and made yourself a martyr, and then you blamed him for your misery, and you keep on blaming him, long after he can defend himself. Well, that's not going to be me, because the last person I want to be in this world is you."

In the thick silence that followed Hope's tirade, the image of Penrose Duckers's full-sized crossbow filled Twyla's mind, the heft of it, the tension of pulling the string into the nut, the heady power of the release. If Hope's words were the shaft, then Twyla's pierced heart was the bull's-eye.

Shaking with emotion, she hoisted herself out of the too-small swing. "That's good. Because the last thing I want for you to be in this life is me. But understand this: I am the person who put you into this world and loves you more than anyone else ever can or will, and I don't want to see you making the same mistakes I made. Which is why I'm telling you to think twice before you hand over your birth key to someone who may not cherish it as much as he ought to."

Hope shook her head in fury and disgust. "I can't even look at you right now," she told Twyla before she stomped inside.

Twyla remained beside the swing set as Hope's barb repeated over and over in her mind, shredding her.

The last person I want to be in this world is you.

Twyla needed to run away from those words—to be anywhere but here—but everything Twyla needed was inside Wade's house—her Gracie Goodfist backpack, her duck keys.

Her family.

If she had been thinking clearly, she would have gone to Duckers's apartment and thrown herself on his charity. But she was not thinking at all. She was a giant pile of inarticulate feelings, and her feet took her where her heart, rather than her head, wanted to go.

Chapter Eighteen

Can I come in?" Twyla blurted the second Frank opened his front door.

"Of course." He moved aside so that she could step past him into his parlor. She wasn't accustomed to his short haircut, and aside from his suit and (briefly) his pajamas, she hadn't seen him in anything other than his work clothes for weeks. He looked softer now as he stood in the warm gaslight of his parlor, wearing a clean white undershirt and faded blue dungarees, and since he used the same laundry detergent she used, he smelled like home.

He squinted toward the street through the open doorway. "Where's your duck?"

"At Wade's house."

"You walked here?"

She nodded.

He closed the door and cocked his head at her, his hands on his hips, with his fingertips dipping into his front pockets. It was such a familiar and quintessentially Frank posture that it sent her sailing over the brink. She thought she was all cried out, but here she was, leaning on Frank's favorite chair and bawling all over it. He didn't ask her what had happened. He wrapped an arm around her and whisked her to the sofa and sat beside her and held her hand, and he waited for her to say whatever she needed to say, and it felt the way it was supposed to feel, like a friend comforting a friend.

"I talked to Hope about getting married, and we got into an argument, and she said that the last person she wants to be in this world is me-e-e." She sobbed the last word in a staccato of anguish.

Frank held tight to her hand. "Aw, darlin'."

"And she's right."

"No, she isn't. Hold on a minute." He got up and returned a moment later with a handkerchief.

"She is right," Twyla insisted as he dabbed at her cheeks with the clean linen. "I even agreed with her. I told her that the last thing *I* want for her to be in this world is me. I tried to tell her how hard marriage is, especially when you have kids, and she got so mad at me, and now I can't stay at Wade's house, and there's a hole in my roof, and everything is terrible, and I'm sorry for asking you if I can stay here when I know you're feeling sad about Mary Georgina, but I didn't have anywhere else to go."

"You always have a place with me. You know that."

Twyla wanted more than anything to curl up in his lap and burrow into the solid comfort of him, under his skin, all the way to the bone. The ferocity of that need nearly laid her out flat, not in its bald sensuality but in its enormity. She had the bewildering sensation that she was plummeting into a place far bigger than herself with no idea how far it went.

She buried her face in Frank's hankie and begged herself to get a grip on her life. She needed to blow her nose anyway, since she was a hideous swamp of tears and snot.

"I haven't changed the bedding in Lu's room, so it might smell a little beery after you and Duckers crashed there last night. Why don't you sleep in Annie's bed."

She nodded, not trusting herself to speak in case Frank could hear the roiling confusion of feelings in her voice.

He stroked her hair. "Poor Twy. You don't have your pack or anything? You just hoofed it on over?"

He only meant to comfort her, but his caress made her want to flop over and purr. She had to say something, but when she looked up, his face was much closer than she had realized. She could see his chest rise with an intake of air that didn't seem to come back out of his lungs. He went still, and so did she, and a long, fraught silence settled over them. Twyla's treacherous eyes drifted to Frank's mouth. She bit her lips between her teeth to stop herself from pressing a heated kiss to his. Again.

Frank turned away from her and put his hands on his knees in the universal gesture that announced, *I am about to stand up.*

He stood up.

"Well now, let me see if I can track down a clean toothbrush for you."

She watched him disappear into the hallway, and she heard the door of the linen closet open, followed by Frank's rustling through toilet paper and extra bottles of shampoo and deodorant.

Twyla sat up and wrapped a blanket around her shoulders, the one her mom had crocheted for Frank years ago. Feeling adrift, she let her eyes wander to the house's altar to the left of the front door, a narrow shelf that should have displayed the family keys alongside a bowl of salt water. But Frank had no keys on his altar and, therefore, no reason to set out salt water every day. His estranged father kept his family's keys, and Cora had taken hers with her when she left. Of course, Frank had the care of Twyla's birth key, and she of his—a practical matter, since neither of them had had kids at the time who were old enough or mature enough to handle the responsibility. But since Twyla was alive, it didn't belong on the altar. And when she died, he would give it to her children rather than keep it for himself.

All these years, Twyla had never paid attention to that blank altar by Frank's door, but now it filled her with grief for him, this good man with his generous heart, who had made himself what he was despite, rather than because of, the family he came from.

"Never been used, I swear."

Frank stood where the parlor and dining room met the hallway leading to the house's three bedrooms, holding up a pristine toothbrush in a slim cardboard box.

Twyla gave him a wet laugh and used his handkerchief to dry the tears she had been shedding for him rather than for herself. She walked across the room and took the proffered gift. "What would I do without you?"

"Perish. Obviously."

He was kidding, but she was not.

"It's true. I would."

"Aw, stop it." He ushered her to Annie's bedroom, where he turned up the gas sconce to a dim glow. "Here's a shirt if you want to sleep in something other than what you're wearing. I thought about giving you a pair of my pajama bottoms, but I think you'd drown in them. Need anything else? A glass of water? Something to read? A kitten?"

She decided to latch on to his humor. Humor was what had gotten them through the worst things they had faced together, from fighting the undead to worrying about their children. They'd always found reasons to laugh, and laughing with him now made everything feel normal.

"All I need is a toothbrush and the will to face another day," Twyla assured him, mustering a brave smile.

"And now you have both." He lingered on the threshold of the bedroom, fingering the doorknob. "Twyla, I ought to...uh..." His voice trailed off, but he remained in the doorframe, chewing on something he needed to say. Twyla had no idea if she wanted to hear the words clinging for dear life to his tongue, or if she wanted to run away from them.

"It's nothing," he said at last. "Get some rest. Everything will look better in the morning."

His hand twitched, as if he had nearly reached out to her but thought better of it. He grasped the doorknob once more. "Want this open or closed?"

"Closed, thanks."

Again, he seemed like he might say more, but he only nodded his good night and left the room, shutting the door behind him.

Twyla sat on the bed. As a general rule, arguments and conflict and crying left her a wrung-out sponge of a woman, but as she took the time to think over what had transpired between mother and daughter that evening, an unexpected tranquility strummed through her veins. Hope had not welcomed Twyla's concerns, and Twyla couldn't fault her for that. But speaking her truth had knocked something loose inside her. She was reminded of Rosie Fox banging her fist on the portal at the North Station and somehow, despite the improbability of it, getting it to work again. Twyla's words to Hope were equally inelegant, but they'd needed to be said for her own peace of mind, and she felt better for having spoken them.

Frank's neatly folded undershirt waited for her at the foot of the bed. How like Frank, to offer something she didn't know she needed until he held it in his capable hands. She picked it up and rubbed the soft, worn cotton between her fingers, and before she could think better of it, she held it to her nose and inhaled the familiar scent.

It's laundry detergent fragrance, Twyla reminded herself. And yet, it was also the scent that she and Frank shared, redolent of their friendship, and all the warmth and care and affection that came with it.

Twyla took off everything but her underwear and pulled on the shirt, welcoming the gentle fabric against her skin. Had she been a delicate, petite woman, the shirt would have hung off her like a limp sail. But Twyla was of average height, and her body had thickened over the years, so that Frank's undershirt hugged her breasts and hips before landing in the pale territory between the middle and top of her thighs.

She regarded her body, the one that had kept her on this earth for over half a century, the one that had carried three children and brought them into the world, the one that had worked hard her whole life, the one that had fought the undead beside Frank Ellis.

Frank was wearing a shirt exactly like this one tonight, but how differently it fit him. He had been quite fit when she first met him, when he was nothing more to her than Cora's husband. He was the same strong man he ever was, but with a layer of softness over him now. She wanted to feel the white cotton of his shirt under her fingertips again, the way she had the night they'd kissed. She wanted to let her hands rove from his shoulders to his chest to his stomach. Would he welcome her touch? Would he take pleasure in it?

Yes, she suspected that he would. Of course he would. He was a man, after all, and in her limited experience, it took next to nothing to rev up a man's motor. Doug used to cop a feel every time he happened upon her bending over to sweep dirt into a dustpan, a habit that had made her borderline murderous.

Was Frank ever tempted to touch her in that way? Not when she was bent over a dustpan, but in general?

The memory of their kiss flooded her senses. She remembered his hands on her body, his lips on her lips, his mouth tasting her skin.

So yes, clearly, on some level, he desired her. And now she was grappling with the fact that she desired him in return. But it was more than simply scratching an itch. If that was all there was to it, Twyla could have crawled into Quill's pup tent, and Frank could have taken Liz Brimsby up on her seductive baking.

The problem was that there was no halfway when it came to Frank. With Quill, she could walk away. With Frank, that wasn't an option. Either they were friends or they were lovers, with all the capital-L Love and commitment the word implied. And committing herself to another man, even one as wonderful as Frank, was the last thing Twyla wanted in the time she had left in this world.

Except.

Wasn't there already love between them? Wasn't there already commitment? Hadn't they both demonstrated a hundred times over that they would take a pistol crossbow arrow for each other? Hadn't they been there for each other, time and again, for any and all of life's challenges, large and small?

Hadn't they already crossed the line anyway?

Yes, in fact, they had, so what was the point in trying to go back to how they had been?

Of course, Twyla had no idea to what extent Frank might want her, but she did know that she wanted him. And pretending that she didn't was a lie. How could she lie to her best friend?

Salt Sea, she *wanted* him, and Twyla, who hadn't expected much from anyone since the day she exchanged birth keys with Doug Banneker, thought that maybe, this once, she could ask for something she wanted.

She opened the door and crossed the narrow hall to Frank's bedroom. His door was open, and he sat up in bed, reading a book by the light of his bedside gas lamp. He wore a pair of black half-moon readers, the sight of which inspired a yearning pang of affection inside Twyla's rib cage.

He looked at her over the top of those sexy, adorable reading glasses. "Everything all right?"

She hovered in the doorway, floundering to answer a perfectly simple question. "I don't know."

"Need to talk?"

"No. Can I sit here?" She took a tentative step forward and patted the end of his mattress, next to his blanketed feet.

"Sure."

She knelt at the foot of the bed, facing him.

"Not to be contrary, but it looks like you plan to do some talking," he said.

They'd been this close before at night, on cots in the barracks, but Twyla had rarely entered his bedroom. Now they occupied the same bed, and to her, it was steamier than a sauna.

"That night after the wedding...," she began.

He closed his book. "I think it'll take a bit before it stops feeling awkward, but we'll get there."

"You don't understand. That was the best sex of my life, and we didn't even have sex."

There. She'd said it. The truth was a boulder, and she'd sent it rolling down a hill with no idea of where it would end up. But that boulder had also been sitting on her chest, and she was glad to have wriggled out from under the crushing weight of it at last.

Frank set the book on his bedside table. He took off his glasses and set them on top of the book. Out of things to do with his hands, he spoke without making eye contact. "We didn't exactly *not* have sex either."

The deeper they dove into this conversation, the more certain Twyla was that they needed to have it.

"I'm fifty-three years old, and it's never felt like that. It's never been that good."

Frank stared at his hands on the bedspread, but he was listening and thinking. He hadn't flat out refused her yet, so she worked up her courage to say her piece.

"I've spent my whole life worrying about what everyone else needs, and I've put myself last every day of my adult life. And whenever I do want something, it feels selfish, and I go without.

Well, I want this. For once in my life I want something, and I'm going to ask for it."

Frank's fingers gripped his thighs hidden beneath the coverlet. "Are you asking me to make love to you?"

"Yes." A wave of misgivings crashed inside her, and panicked words flew out of her mouth before Frank could get a word in edgewise. "Ugh, what am I doing? But yes! Fine! Yes, that's what I'm asking!" She slapped the mattress with flattened hands on *yes* and *fine* and *yes*.

She'd rendered Frank speechless. He went on staring at his hands.

"But only if you're willing, obviously," she went on, breathless and dizzy with her own temerity. "I wouldn't force you to do it."

Frank let loose a strained, gusty laugh. "Woman, I couldn't say no to you if I tried. And I have no intention of trying."

He finally looked at her, his eyes smoldering with honest heat, and every inch of Twyla's skin warmed under his burning, truthful gaze. They were friends—good friends, the best of friends—and there would be no more pretending between them.

Frank threw off the bedspread and top sheet and crawled across the mattress to her, stopping only when his face was inches from hers. "If someone's going to put a stop to this, it's going to have to be you. Are you sure this is what you want?"

"Yes, I'm s—"

He pressed his lips to hers, but this kiss was not the desperate passion that flamed up after Twyla had thrown a bomb into his front yard. This was not the lip-bruising, teeth-clashing kiss that had burned itself into her memory. This kiss was deep and slow and savoring. If the kiss after the wedding had set her on fire, this one melted her to candle wax.

He cupped her face in his hands. No one had ever touched her face when kissing her, and the tenderness of the gesture made her whimper.

Frank pulled away suddenly and talked a million times faster than he usually did. "I should have put that better. I meant that we can stop at any time. Just say the word."

"Understood."

"Because I'll stop if you want."

She huffed in exasperation and took the reassuring familiarity of his face into her hands. "Don't stop," she said, echoing her words from the night of the wedding and the bombs. "Do *not* stop." And she kissed him with a raw, open-mouthed desire. He growled, a sound that rumbled straight to her core, and wow, did he stop talking. The pressure of his kiss was exactly what she wanted, the firmness of his lips, the delicate movement of his tongue. Frank's was not the sloppy, tongue-lolling embrace of a teenaged boy; Frank kissed like a man who knew what he wanted and what it took to get it.

Twyla touched him the way she had imagined touching him, starting at his shoulders and stroking her way down his chest and stomach, the thin white cotton of his undershirt stretched taut over his torso, his body hot and solid beneath the fabric. He hummed his throaty approval into her mouth.

Frank's hands followed a similar path along her back, from her shoulder blades, down her ribs, over her hips, all the way to the curve of her derriere. Everywhere he touched her, Twyla felt the loveliness of her own curves.

Until Frank's fingertips brushed the leg opening of her underwear.

Because she was wearing her giant cotton granny panties. Of course she was.

She buried her face in his neck, laughing her embarrassment, even as she took in a fortifying breath of the spicy aftershave lingering on his skin. "I am wearing the least sexy underwear under the altar of the sky."

"You could be wearing a paper bag, for all I care. All I want to do is take off whatever you're wearing."

To prove his point, he ran his hands beneath the waistband of her underwear, seizing her hind end.

"Ope!" she cried in surprise.

"Are we good?"

"We're good."

He smoothed his hands over the skin of her backside, making her feel soft and pretty and feminine. But when he kissed her neck, she shrank away from him in a knee-jerk spasm.

"Ticklish?" he asked with a grin.

"Very."

"I won't kiss you there."

"No, I like it. I just need it softer, I think."

She grasped him by the shoulders, massaging a rhythm into the round strength that matched the slow movement of his hands up her rib cage.

"Like this?" He leaned in again slowly and pressed a gentle kiss against her throat. Incredible how the barest brush of his lips on her skin made the ache building between her legs pulse a hundred times more frantically than if he'd plowed into her, tongue blazing.

"Exactly like that," she whispered.

"You're calling the shots tonight, darlin'," he told her as he kissed a delicate trail along the length of her throat. "I'm doing what you want. Anything you want."

"I definitely want what you're doing right now."

He rewarded her with a husky laugh. She threaded her fingers into his hair as he kissed the hollow behind her earlobe, sending a shiver through her as he swirled the tip of his tongue against the sensitive skin there. He smoothed his hands from back to front, then up and up, under her breasts, then over them and on them, firm without honking her like an old-fashioned Klaxon.

"Still good?"

"So good."

She mirrored his actions, snaking her hands inside his undershirt, his flesh a delicious combination of soft and hard beneath her touch. The desire to burrow into him overwhelmed her. She pulled him against her and captured his mouth in a hot, breathless kiss. He rose to his knees and took her with him, holding her against him with a desperation that matched her own, their bodies flush, his arousal throbbing against her thigh. She brought her kiss to his neck, lightly sucking his gorgeously scented skin.

"Fuck," he gasped, his voice full of hot pleasure, and he moaned when she bit his earlobe. "You're over here worrying over your underwear, when all I want is you, naked in my bed." He tugged at the hem of her shirt. "I'm taking this off you now, and then I'm taking off your underwear so you won't have to worry about it anymore."

She had experienced no little trepidation when Quill had seen her naked for the first time, but here with Frank, whom she trusted more than anyone, she had no qualms. Of course he didn't judge her body harshly as he relieved her of the shirt, revealing her middle-aged breasts and too-soft stomach. Of course he would accept her as she was when he helped her step out of her underwear. She'd gotten off the bed to accomplish the last part, and she was now standing before him as the Three Mothers had made her, while Frank remained kneeling at the foot of the bed, drinking her in with his eyes. When he reached out to caress her breasts and her waist and her hips, his hands told her she was precious to him, and he'd be careful with her.

"I want to see you, too," she told him shyly.

Twyla had no idea that a human being could whip off a shirt that fast, but there was Frank, naked from the waist up, his feet already on the ground opposite hers so that he could wrap her in his arms and hold her skin against his skin, her breasts against his chest. They both sighed with the pleasure of it.

Twyla reached between them to pull on the drawstring waistband of his pajama bottoms. "All of it, Frankie."

"So demanding." His eyes glinted with orneriness, and Twyla wondered how she'd failed to succumb to the sheer sexiness of that glint all these years.

"You said I was calling the shots tonight."

"That's right."

He dropped his pants and boxers in one go and pulled her down with him onto the bed. They twined together, exploring each other in a bubble of timelessness, until Frank put his hand over hers and stuttered, "Stop, stop, stop!"

"Was that bad?"

"No, that was good, way too good. Give me a minute."

He held her hand away from him and closed his eyes and breathed. When he had control over himself, he opened his eyes to burning slits, and he told her, "You don't need to worry about me tonight. This is about you, what you like, what you want. Let me do this for you."

He stretched out beside her and kissed her and held her, his body pulsing with hers as they moved together. She moaned when he suckled her breast, arching against his mouth to bring him closer.

"Aw, you like that," he said, his voice made so husky with hunger that Twyla wanted to bottle every word.

"*Like* is putting it mildly."

"That's good, because I could stay here all night." And stay there he did, lavishing attention on both breasts with hands and lips and tongue until Twyla's feet were twisted in the sheets. When he slid his hand lower and pressed his palm into her growing desire, she writhed against his touch.

"What do you need?" he asked her in a hoarse whisper.

She pushed herself against his hand. "Nothing. This is fine."

"Fine's not good enough. Tell me what you need. Do you want me to taste you here?" He moved his fingers against her, making her ache with the frustration of being close, but not close enough.

"Don't worry about it. I've always struggled with this. I don't have to...you know. I'm enjoying it. Trust me."

He stopped. He propped himself up on his elbow and looked down at her.

"What?"

"Darlin', I'm not going anywhere without you."

"It takes me a while, especially since the whole menopause thing."

"I've got all the time in the world." He fanned his fingers over her stomach and let them drift southward. "All you have to do is tell me what you want."

There was something that would help, but Twyla wasn't sure she could admit to it, not even to Frank. She bit her bottom lip. "It's embarrassing."

"Tell me," he said, convincing her with his soft, delicious kisses and the hypnotic pressure of his hand.

"Um, I usually need, um...mechanical assistance to, you know...get there."

"You mean a vibrator?"

She nodded.

"You use a vibrator?"

She cringed and nodded again.

A slow smile spread across his face. "Twyla Josephine, you minx."

"Stop laughing at me!"

"This is not laughter. This is pure, unadulterated joy. Where is it?"

She grabbed the coverlet and pulled it up to her nose.

"Come on. Fess up. Where do you keep it?"

She tugged the quilt higher so that she was visible only from the eyes up. "Them."

Frank's face lit up.

"Shut up!"

"I'm telling you, I am not laughing. Where?"

"In the drawer of my bedside table, but who knows if they're intact after the explosion."

"Only one way to find out. Don't move."

He rolled out of bed and got into his pajama bottoms.

Twyla bolted upright, clutching the bedspread to her chin, as if Frank hadn't already seen all her business. "You are not going to go into my destroyed bedroom to get a vibrator."

"Vibrators. Plural. And yes, I am." By now, he was fully dressed and hopping on one foot to put on his second shoe.

"You don't have to."

He returned to the bed, bent over, and kissed her so thoroughly that she relinquished the quilt to grab hold of his shirt. He pulled away long enough to say "Be right back" before hustling out of the room with his pajama pants scandalously tented.

Twyla sat against the headboard in stunned silence. And then she burst out laughing. "What in the name of the Unknown God am I doing?" she cackled. This was a disaster. She knew it was. And yet Frank was going to return to this room, armed with her vibrators, and she could not bring herself to put a stop to it. She had wanted something. She had asked for it. And now she was getting it. And if she was being honest with herself—which she was, since honesty was the theme of the evening—she found that she did not have it in her to regret it. Not yet, at any rate.

Frank returned with one of Twyla's pillowcases, her humble collection of vibrators clacking about the bottom. "Your bedside table has seen better days, but these appear to be in functioning order."

Already mildly hysterical, Twyla started laughing again. "This is mortifying."

"Nah, it ain't." He knelt on the bed beside her and opened the pillowcase to reveal its contents to her. "Which one's your favorite?"

"I don't have a favorite."

He gave her a smirk that was both irritating and sexy as all get-out. "It's the glow-in-the-dark green one, isn't it?"

"Yes," she admitted sheepishly.

"Mm-hmm."

He took up the fluorescent vibrator and set the pillowcase full of the rest on the lamp table. After he stared helplessly at the phallic green mechanism in his hand for several seconds, Twyla said, "You have no idea how it works, do you?"

"I've never used one before."

"Mm-hmm."

"Don't you laugh at me, woman."

"This is not laughter. This is pure, unadulterated joy."

He chucked the vibrator to the side and tackled her, tickling her without mercy.

"See?" he cried. "You are laughing at me."

"Because you're tickling me, you jerk," she wheezed. And then one of them kissed the other—difficult to say who—and they were off to the races once more, only more passionate and more frenetic than before.

"Still good?" he asked her when he came up for air.

"Still good."

It occurred to Twyla that in addition to the sex itself feeling phenomenal, she was having fun. She'd had no idea that making love could be as full of laughter and joy as it was of naked bits and passion.

Frank reached across her to retrieve the vibrator. "Can we use this?"

She shrank into the mattress. "Okay."

"We can stop at any time."

"I know. Here." She took the vibrator from him and showed him the tiny key attached to the side, which she inserted into the bottom to crank the internal spring. "Once you pull out the key, it lasts for a good fifteen minutes."

"As long as it doesn't outlast me."

She bit back a snicker, unnecessary since he was kissing her again—languid, heady, drunken kisses that made her feel like she was floating outside of herself. His lips brushed along her jaw and down her throat, soft and sensuous, exactly the way she wanted to be touched there.

"Do you know what I think you like, darlin'?" he asked against the sensitive skin of her neck, his voice low and throaty, his fingers touching her most intimate place. "I think you like a little tenderness with your heat. A little soft with your hard. A little sweet with your salty."

"You're right. You are so right." Twyla felt like she had a spring inside of her, and each movement of Frank's hand and every word that came out of his mouth wound her tighter and tighter. "What about you? What do you like?" she asked him.

He lifted his head and said, simply, "You."

The ridiculous urge to cry swelled in her throat. She didn't know what to do with the notion that someone would want her for her own sake and not for the many services she could render.

Frank picked up the vibrator once more and pulled the key. He took Twyla's hand and wrapped it around the buzzing base.

Her eyes widened. "You want me to use it on myself?"

"You know best where to put it. Go to town." He rushed to add, "If you want to."

Raw vulnerability already rode in the passenger seat of this entire experience; the notion of pleasing herself in anyone's presence but her own nearly shut her down.

Frank must have sensed her hesitation, because he said, "You don't have to, darlin'. It's only that I want you to enjoy what we're doing together, the two of us—"

"I am."

"—and, selfishly, I want to watch you have the mind-blowing, life-altering release you deserve."

His words made her blush, head to toe, as the vibrator buzzed loudly in her grasp. "Oh," she breathed.

He nuzzled her collarbone. "Just saying."

He wasn't wrong. What else was she doing here? What was the point of making herself this vulnerable to Frank if she wasn't going to let him in all the way, if she wasn't going to open all the doors and windows of the house that was Twyla Banneker?

She lowered the vibrator until the tip hovered an inch over where she needed it.

Frank noticed. He stopped his exquisite exploration of her collarbone. "You sure?"

"I think I'd like to have a mind-blowing, life-altering release for once in my life."

She pressed the vibrator against her most sensitive place. The pleasure of it made her close her eyes and press her head into the pillow, inspiring a deeply appreciative huff from Frank. She was stunned to realize that what she was doing wasn't selfish; he wanted this as much as she did. He worked around her, touching her, caressing her, kissing her with the pressure and gentleness and precision she craved. She wasn't on her own; he was with her every step of the way. The spring inside her wound tight before, she came uncoiled at last, spinning and spinning until she was limp.

She opened her eyes, and there was Frank, grinning at her, looking awfully pleased with himself.

"This is the part where you tell me I was right," he informed her.

"I'm calling the shots, so I vote no on that."

He picked up her hand and kissed her knuckles one at a time. *I think you like a little tenderness with your heat*, he had told her, and he was right. Tenderness was exactly what she liked.

Frank is exactly what I like. The words came unbidden to her mind, something she would have to examine more closely later. For now, she turned on her side and reached for him.

"Fuck," he groaned as she took him in hand.

"I think you like a little heat with your tenderness," she told him, wearing the same self-satisfied smile he'd been doling out moments ago.

"You got that right," he agreed, his words cranking through the constricted mangle of his throat.

Tonight, Twyla was calling the shots, not simply asking for what she wanted but receiving it. And she had one more thing she wanted.

"Frank?"

"Yeah?" he whimpered as her touch incapacitated him.

"I want you, all of you." Her hand was more specific than her words.

He swallowed. "You sure?"

"Very sure."

"Thank gods," he sighed, taking himself out of her grasp. "Whew. Give me a minute."

"I've got all the time in the world."

He gave her an *I see what you did there* moue. This was fun, repeating everything he said in a new context. She lay against the pillow with her arms crossed smugly behind her head.

Franks eyes narrowed to smoldering slits. "I wish you could see yourself now, pleased as a kitten with a saucer of milk, lying on that bed like you own it." He opened the drawer of his bedside table and pulled out a box of condoms. "Shit, do these things expire?"

"I hope not," said Twyla, although a part of her was secretly pleased that it had been so long since Frank had cracked open this box that the contents were at risk of expiring.

He took out a foil square and squinted at it, and when he couldn't read the tiny expiration date, he put on his cheaters. As he stood there beside the bed, holding the condom packet up to the lamp, wearing nothing but his blocky reading glasses, an even deeper affection for this man than Twyla had thought possible took hold of her, and she knew it would not be letting go anytime soon.

"We're in business," he declared in triumph, and it was only a matter of seconds before he was in bed beside her again, his body snaking with hers.

"How do you want to do this?" he asked.

"The regular way, I guess."

"The regular way? You mean with me on top?"

"If that's okay with you?"

He cupped her face and stroked her cheekbone with his thumb. "The more important question here is, What's okay with you? Because it's my understanding that ladies sometimes have a better experience when they're on top."

She grimaced. "I was never good at that."

"Was it that *you* weren't good at it or that you've never been with someone who let you make it good for yourself?"

That question was a revelation. Now that she thought about it, Doug had usually grown impatient when she had been on top. He would always take control of the position and the tempo to suit himself.

"Both, probably."

He rolled onto his back, taking her with him so that she was lying flat on top of him. "Try it. Do it for yourself. See what you think."

"Are you sure?"

"You have no idea how sure I am."

So she tried it.

And she was doing it for herself.

And she liked it.

Frank didn't try to take over. He barely moved, save for the clamping of his hands on her thighs and the heaving of his lungs. The only time he adjusted his position was when she asked him to prop himself higher with an extra pillow. *That* had worked miracles.

"You take what you need from me, darlin'," he growled through bared teeth. "You take anything you need."

Twyla, who always struggled to take anything for herself, took what Frank freely offered, and gladly, her core winding tight once more and blissfully uncoiling around him. And when he grasped her by the hips and went rigid beneath her, she was gratified to know that she'd given back as much as she had taken.

Chapter Nineteen

After she cleaned herself up in the bathroom and put on Frank's shirt and her underwear, Twyla dithered in the hallway. Frank, who was also fully clothed again in his white shirt and plaid pajama bottoms, came to his bedroom door in search of her.

"I'm trying to figure out if I'm supposed to sleep in Annie's room or yours," she admitted. No point hiding her fragile emotions from a man who'd seen her wield a vibrator this evening.

"What do you want to do?"

"There you go again, asking me what I want, when I don't even know what I want most days. Who cares what I want?"

"I do."

She rubbed her face with both hands. "You're my best friend."

"And you're mine. That hasn't changed."

"Everything's changed." She dropped her hands and let him see her, all of her, in her stark honesty. She was a house with the doors and windows thrown wide open. Only this house maybe had a hole in the roof and some smoke and water damage. Perhaps this house was no one's idea of a worthwhile house.

"We don't have to borrow trouble. We don't have to regret this." He pushed himself off the jamb and reached out a hand to her, not to touch her, but to offer it to her, if she wanted to take it. "Tomorrow's coming for us anyway. Let's finish out this night together. Come back to bed."

"With you?"

"With me."

She hesitated, staring at that generous hand, and she worried what it would mean if she took it now.

"What's done is done," he said. "Let me hold you tonight."

To hold another person was something people pledged in their wedding vows. It was what Hart and Mercy had said to each other the night Twyla and Frank had taken a step in a new and bewildering direction. It was the promise Twyla had made to Doug and that Doug had made to her, one neither of them had fulfilled to the best of their abilities.

I will hold you in the dark of night.

Twyla wanted to hold and to be held, but she wasn't convinced that it was possible to be held without being held down or held back.

Frank kept his hand outstretched and did not waver. "You'd like that, wouldn't you? To be held, just this once?"

It wasn't as if Frank would ever hold her down or hold her back. His arms weren't a cage. He knew how and when to let go, whether it was his wife or a pink dragon. And the Mother of Sorrows knew Twyla wanted to be held so badly and held by him.

She placed her hand in his. "Just this once."

His fingers closed around hers, and he held her, palm to palm. His calluses matched her calluses; they'd earned them together. He led her to his room, walking backward, as if she'd disappear if he dared to look away.

"Go on and settle in," he told her, nodding toward the mattress.

She gave him a quizzical look as she climbed into the left side of the bed, opposite of where he'd been reading earlier in the evening. "I assume you're joining me?"

"I've slept next to you on tour for the past eight years. I know you sleep on your left side." He walked around the bed and climbed in on the right. "You get comfortable, and then I'll go in for the cuddle."

"'Go in for the cuddle'?" she laughed.

"Yep. Get comfy, Left Side."

It was a lot easier to get comfy when Twyla was laughing rather than worrying. She settled in, noticing that Frank's mattress and pillows were significantly comfier than her own, and maybe she ought to invest in a better sleeping situation for herself since she was going to have to buy a brand new bed anyway.

"You ready?"

"Ready."

He dimmed the gas reading lamp, and then she was surrounded by Frank: his body, his heat, his scent. His arm draped around her waist, pleasingly heavy.

"Sometimes I get hot in the middle of the night, so I might have to scoot away to cool off," she apologized in advance.

"You do what you need to do, Little Spoon."

Already, the warmth and comfort of Frank's embrace was lulling Twyla to sleep. "Left Side. Little Spoon. How many new names do you plan on giving me tonight?" she asked him as her eyes drifted shut.

"As many as you want."

He snuggled her more tightly into him, and it didn't feel too hot or suffocating. She relished the heft of his arm at her waist, the solidity of his body pressed against hers, and it made her fret, because she didn't want to like it quite this much, not when she had come to appreciate sleeping alone.

Frank is not a cage, she reminded herself. *He'll let you go if that's what you want.*

"Twyla?" he said, his bass voice vibrating against her back.

"Hmm?"

"We're going to be fine, okay?"

"Okay," she said, trying to convince them both that it was true.

The same birds that sang outside Twyla's bedroom window every morning sent up a chorus outside Frank's bedroom window, too. She had slept later than she usually did, and was surprised to see how bright the light was coming in through the curtains.

In the books she read, characters often woke in strange beds, befuddled by their surroundings until they remembered the blisteringly hot sex they'd had the night before. Twyla knew immediately where she was and what she had been doing mere hours ago and with whom, and she did not need to wait to plunge herself into a cold sea of misgivings and regret and dread. Their kiss on the night of Hart and Mercy's wedding had been a mistake. This? She didn't know a word for what this was.

She was in Frank's bed. But Frank wasn't in Frank's bed. She was relieved. She didn't think she could face him yet.

She found a note folded in half on his pillow, her name written in his neat, clear cursive. She opened it and read:

Good morning, Twy. I've gone out to pick up breakfast. The coffee's already made, if you want some. Be back soon.

Frank

P.S.—Don't let yourself worry too much.

The paper was small in size, and the postscript was crammed into the bottom margin, as if he had spaced out the original message evenly on the page and had decided to add the postscript at the last minute. It was a short note, but Twyla suspected he had agonized over its composition. She would have. The fact that he knew she would be worrying her fool head off when she awoke stabbed another agonizing shard of remorse into her heart. It was bad enough that she had messed with her own emotions by coming to Frank's room last night; the thought that she had messed with his, too, lashed her.

If she was going to face this day, she would do it in real clothes, not Frank's undershirt. She sat up, and the first thing she saw was her vibrators, three in the pillowcase on Frank's nightstand and the fluorescent favorite, which had rolled against the spine of the book Frank had been reading. Out of habit, she gathered them up to hide them in the drawer of the bedside table, forgetting momentarily that they belonged in *her* bedside table, not Frank's. There wasn't much in the drawer, only the small box of condoms, a scattering of loose change, a couple of pencils, some bookmarks, and a framed photograph.

The photograph caught her attention. Why on earth would he keep it in a drawer rather than on a shelf or table?

Probably an old picture of Cora, she guessed. That would make the most sense. He surely wouldn't feel comfortable keeping a picture of his ex-wife out where anyone could see it, although it had been some time since Twyla got the sense that he was pining for her.

She ought to have respected his privacy enough to leave it alone, but she took out the frame without thinking through what she was doing.

It wasn't a picture of Cora. It was a picture of her and Frank, together and smiling. They were outdoors, on a beach, a picnic blanket beneath them, the sun shining, the sea shushing behind them. The image, of course, lacked color, but she could fill in the brilliance of the blue sky above, the soft gray-green of the ocean, the red-and-white checks of the blanket. She remembered this excursion, five or six years ago, a trip to one of the inner islands with both families while Frank's kids were visiting him for the summer. Frank had given Annie a camera for her birthday, and she had been over the moon, snapping the shutter at anything and everything. Frank must have spent a small fortune on film and development, but then, he would have done anything for his children.

In the photograph, they sat close together, Twyla leaning easily against Frank's shoulder. She was laughing, her face turned toward something outside the frame, while Frank looked at her, smiling, his eyes warm, even in black and white. She had never seen this picture before, but the quiet contentment that it captured made an aching lump swell in her throat. She had no idea why Frank kept it in a drawer, but she knew that she needed to put it back where she'd found it. She was about to do exactly that when she noticed an envelope taped to the backside of the frame, labeled with Frank's tidy hand: *Twyla's birth key.*

Twyla kept Frank's birth key in her safe-deposit box at the bank. She had never thought to ask him where he kept hers, but now that she knew, the lump in her throat grew and throbbed. She returned the picture and the key to the drawer and dabbed at her eyes as she vacated Frank's room, feeling as though she were fleeing the scene of a crime.

In Annie's room, she put on the clothes she had been wearing when she showed up on Frank's doorstep last night. She could almost hear Hope's voice saying, *Good morning, you lucky bitch... How was your walk of shame?* It was fitting, since Twyla had set fire to her relationship with her daughter an hour before she had set fire to her friendship with Frank.

"Grandmother Wisdom, save me from myself," she groaned as she dropped onto Annie's bed and buried her face in her hands. She was tempted to leave while Frank was out, but she knew this was one of those best-to-rip-off-the-bandage situations, as Frank himself would say. Besides, she would never in a million years do something that hurtful to her best friend.

Her best friend who cared enough about her to run next door and retrieve her vibrators so that she could have the mind-blowing, life-altering release she deserved.

"This is a disaster," she cried to any god who happened to be listening, not that it would do her any good now.

There was a knock at the front door. *Frank's* door. She shouldn't open Frank's door, should she?

"Frank! Frank-IEEE! Open up!" Duckers's voice called from the front steps.

"Disaster," she moaned, drawing out the *r* in a long growl before heaving herself to her feet and going to open the door.

"Hey, Twyla," he greeted her, and then confusion knitted his brow. He looked to her house next door, then turned to her. "Did I go to the wrong place?"

"No, I have a hole in the roof. Remember?"

"Right. Is Frank here?"

"No, but he'll be back soon." She smacked herself on the forehead. "It's Saltsday. He's taking you to the autoduck lot."

"Can I come in?"

"Ope! Sorry. Of course." Twyla led Duckers to the kitchen and tried to avoid eye contact without appearing to avoid eye contact.

"So, where's Frank?"

"He went out to get breakfast."

"Did he now?" His tone was an alarming combination of suspicion and smug delight as he took a seat at one of the counter stools.

"Mm-hmm."

"For both of you?"

"Presumably."

Twyla made the mistake of meeting his eyes, which were narrowed to skeptical slits.

"I thought you were staying with your son."

"It was crowded with all the kids, so I stayed here." She reached for the carafe and slapped on a smile. "Coffee?"

Duckers leaned over the counter and met her fake smile with a shit-eating grin. "Give it up, Banneker."

"Fuck," she admitted in defeat. "Fuck, fuck, fuck." She took a mug from the cupboard and poured herself a steaming cup of liquid fortitude.

Duckers hopped off the stool, yanked the dish towel from its hook, and wrapped it around his head like an old-fashioned bonnet. "I swear on Grandfather Bones's pinkie finger," he said in a ludicrous falsetto, blinking his lashes at Twyla. "Frank Ellis and I are friends! Nothing more than that! I have never wanted to jump his bones a day in my life!"

"First of all, that sounds nothing like me. Second of all, I do not wear bonnets made of kitchen textiles."

He took the dish towel off his head and flicked it teasingly at Twyla. "All I know is that someone got lucky last night, and it wasn't me. Which sucks, actually."

"How are you holding up?" She took the towel from him and hung it back on the hook.

"Fucking terrible. I know I need to—wait a minute." He wagged a finger at her. "Don't change the subject. I know what you and your bestie got up to last night, hot stuff, and I want the deets!"

Demonstrating either the best or the worst timing in the history of the world, Frank stepped through the front door, carrying a white paper bag. He froze when he saw Duckers. His eyes went wide as he sent a panicked look to Twyla, who replied with a *we've been busted* wince.

Frank closed his eyes. "Shit. I'm supposed to drive you to the autoduck lot."

"And a good morning to you, too, Frank!" Duckers practically sang.

"Good morning," Frank muttered. He walked to the kitchen and mouthed *Sorry* at Twyla before pouring himself a cup of coffee. Maybe Duckers's showing up was a good thing; dealing with him was easier than dealing with each other in the aftermath of last night.

"Did you forget I was coming over this morning?" chirped Duckers.

"Yep."

"Because you were *distracted*?"

Frank regarded him warily and said nothing.

"With *sexy times*?"

"Fuck," said Frank as he set the carafe on the counter with a portentous *thud*.

"That's what she said."

That earned Duckers a glare from both Twyla and Frank.

"No, really, that's what she said. You two are practically the same person. It's kind of adorable. What's in the bag? Is it doughnuts? Please say it's doughnuts."

Frank rubbed his eyes. "It's doughnuts."

"Fuck yeah."

Twyla watched in dismay as Duckers devoured a cruller in three bites. She hoped there was another one. She was fond of crullers.

"Watch and learn, Marshal Banneker," Duckers told Twyla as he dug another doughnut out of the bag. "Partners who bring me doughnuts earn my undying devotion."

"I'll be sure to mention that to your new partner whenever you get one."

"Ha!" He clapped his hands, as if Twyla had told a good joke. When he saw her tilt her head in confusion, he set down his half-eaten blueberry cake doughnut. "Wait, are you retiring now, too?"

Alarm bells rang in Twyla's mind, but she wasn't sure why. "No, I've got two more years until I'm vested."

"Exactly. So I'm your new partner."

The alarm bells grew louder and more insistent. "Wait. What did you mean, am I retiring 'too'? Who else is retiring?"

Duckers gaped at her before his eyes focused over her shoulder. On Frank.

"You didn't tell her, man?"

Slowly, Twyla turned to face Frank. His posture stiffened, his shoulders hunching ever so slightly, as if he were preparing to take a punch. "Is this true?" she asked him, even though his demeanor answered the question for him. "Are you retiring?"

His lips paled. "Darlin', I can—"

"Don't you *darlin'* me!" she snapped, the force of her hurt and anger hitting her in the gut.

"And that's my cue to leave," said Duckers, picking up his half-eaten doughnut. "Frank, I'll hit you up for a ride tomorrow, if Twyla doesn't strangle you first."

Twyla and Frank remained motionless in the kitchen—Twyla glaring daggers and Frank freezing like a scared rabbit—as Duckers let himself out.

"I was going to tell you," Frank said as soon as the front door shut.

"When?"

"Today."

"Why didn't you tell me before you put in for retirement?" asked Twyla, when what she wanted to ask was *Why didn't you tell me before you made love to me?*

"Well now...," he began, but he floundered, unable to cough up more.

Twyla gripped the edge of the counter and took a breath, forcing herself to talk about things calmly instead of flying off the handle. "It's fine if you want to retire now, but you should have told me. We have a plan. Or we *had* a plan, I guess I should say."

"I know."

"When did you do this?"

"Last Wardensday."

"And you didn't tell me? Maguire knew? And Duckers knew? But I didn't get to know?"

"I had my reasons."

"Care to share them with me?"

He clamped his lips in a thin line.

"Are we still buying a ranch and starting up the bed-and-breakfast?" she pressed.

"I don't know."

"So I'm supposed to go about my business, waiting for you to make up your mind?"

"I don't know."

"Say something other than *I don't know*, because what I'm hearing is that you want me to be a chair, available whenever you need it and forgotten when you don't."

"You're not a chair," he said in a long-suffering way that infuriated her.

"Convince me otherwise."

He opened his mouth, thought better of it, and ran his hands down his face. "What are we doing here, Twy?"

"Arguing!"

"I'm not arguing with you."

"Well, I wish you would, because I am hopping mad right now."

"Go ahead and be mad at me, then. But I need to know one thing: Was it a mistake?"

"Putting in for retirement without so much as mentioning it to me? Yes!"

"Fuck retirement. I'm talking about last night."

He was so calm, so quiet. His tone didn't match the thunder-clap of a question, but that didn't stop the question itself from rattling Twyla, head to toe.

"Did you make another mistake with me?" he asked her again.

Twyla felt like a boat at sea, tossed about by a storm, all unmoored and directionless.

"I'm asking you, was it a mistake?"

This time, his words bore a sharp edge, and Twyla, all cut to pieces, started to cry tears of anger and hurt and confusion. Trapped and resentful of being cornered, she shouted, "I don't know!"

Whatever warmth he had for her leached out of his eyes. His face betrayed nothing. He was a closed door, a locked house. He nodded slowly, then stalked past her on his way to his bedroom.

Twyla had no idea how much time went by while she stood in Frank's kitchen, stunned and baffled and crying, listening to the sounds of his movements in his bedroom. Her knees started shaking, and she thought maybe she'd better sit. She made it to a counter stool and sat there, absently stuffing a cinnamon twist into her mouth since Duckers had taken the one and only cruller.

Last night when he'd held her in his arms, he'd promised her they were going to be fine. How in the Salt Sea was this fine? They'd had sex, and he had retired without bothering to mention it to her. Their friendship—their future—had gone completely off the rails, and what was she doing about it? Eating a doughnut? This was unacceptable.

"Put on your big-girl pants," she told herself, and she went to talk to Frank.

She found him moving between his dresser and his bed, stuff-ing clothes into a duffel bag that lay open on the coverlet.

"You came to me," he said without giving her a chance to speak. "You were the one who started what we did last night. I never would have instigated that."

That. Making love to her was *that* now. Great. She was tempted to remind him that he hadn't put up a fight, but decided the better course of action was to lean against the jamb and hear him out. He did her the courtesy of halting his packing to speak to her face.

"You expect to come and go, in and out of my life, however you please, the same way you walk in and out my door. When you need me I'm here, and when you don't, guess what? I'm still here. And you know it. And you take advantage of it. So you tell me, who's the fucking chair in this relationship?"

"You are not my chair," she assured him, the calm one now that he was the raging emotional storm.

"Could've fooled me."

He zipped his bag shut, a harsh sound in the close space. He made to leave the room, but Twyla stopped him with a hand on his chest, a gesture that, in the wake of making love, took on a far more intimate weight.

I'm losing him, she thought, *in far more ways than one.*

"Frank, this is us. We can talk it out."

"I'm done talking."

He brushed past her, duffel bag slung over his shoulder. She followed after him, all the way to the front door. She nearly grabbed him by the arm to make him stay, but she thought of how Frank's arms weren't a cage, and if she didn't want him to hold her down or hold her back, she wouldn't hold him back either.

"Where are you going?" she asked him.

He paused only to glance over his shoulder. "Haven't you heard? I'm retired now."

"Frank, please don't—"

"You have a key. Let yourself out."

He left and slammed the door behind him.

Chapter Twenty

Duckers wasn't home, which was crushing since she already felt ridiculous seeking solace from a twenty-one-year-old who had his own heartbreak to deal with. She couldn't go home, obviously. She couldn't go to Wade's house, because Hope was at Wade's house. She couldn't wait to get out of Frank's house. Where did that leave her? She had plenty of friends in Eternity, but not the sort who were privy to her innermost secrets. The only person she talked to about her innermost secrets was Frank, and that was clearly not going to work at the moment. Or ever again.

With that depressing thought in her mind and a white paper bag containing three doughnuts in her hand, she walked to All Gods Temple on Main Street. The New Gods surely wouldn't turn her away.

Inside, a lowering sky cast a dim gray gloom through the skylight of the Unknown God. Most people went to temple on Allgodsday, so the place was relatively empty on a Saltsday morning, save for a few elderly folks—mostly women—sitting in various alcoves.

Twyla drifted down the center aisle, trying to decide to which god she should offer up her doughnuts, the doughnuts Frank had gone out to buy for breakfast that morning. A new statue of the Briar Thief had been installed on a small table outside the alcove of the Salt Sea, and already, the hero had begun to collect offerings. It was unusual for heroes to be honored alongside gods, but the Briar Thief's popularity had been in ascendance for some time. The statue was more grotesque than the image in her deck of cards. Now she could stare at the man's agony in three dimensions as he dangled from the briar with the Thorn of Eternal Life piercing his heart. Apt as a barb through the chest might be in this situation, Twyla did not believe in honoring men alongside gods. She moved on.

She thought about taking a seat with Grandfather Bones this morning for the peace and acceptance he brought to his supplicants. She also thought about paying the Warden a visit. As the god of introspection and change, the Warden might have given her insight as to how she had managed to bungle her relationships with the people who mattered most, and how she might move forward from here. But in the end, she made her way to the alcove of Grandmother Wisdom, because if there was one thing Twyla seemed to be lacking in spades, it was basic good sense. She offered up the doughnuts on the god's altar and took a seat.

Closing her eyes and breathing deeply, Twyla thought over everything that had brought her to this crossroads in her life, the events not only of the past twenty-four hours, but of the past twenty-four days and the past twenty-four years, all the experiences and choices that had made her the person she was now, the mother who had discouraged her daughter from getting married, the woman who had sauntered into her best friend's bedroom without truly contemplating how much it might cost them both.

She tried not to cry, but it was useless. And here she was with no purse and no tissues and no Frank to give her a clean handkerchief without having to be asked. The thought of Frank and his handkerchiefs and all the thoughtful kindness those handkerchiefs stood for made Twyla cry harder, and once again, she was having to dry her nose on the shoulder of her shirt.

The next thing she knew, a clean, embroidered hankie appeared beneath her nose, smelling faintly of violets. An older woman had taken the seat beside Twyla and was now patting her back. "There now, sweetie, you blow your nose."

"Don't mind me," said Twyla, even as she took the proffered handkerchief and put it to use.

"If I had a copper for every time I heard a woman say, *Don't mind me*, I'd build my own coin fountain and swim in a pool of my riches. Let's face it, honey, if people minded you more often, you probably wouldn't be in here crying on some old lady's altar. Now, is this a man problem or a kid problem? Because in my experience, it's usually one or the other."

"Both."

"Oh, we'll need snacks for that." The woman opened up her flamboyantly orange handbag and produced a bag of chocolate-covered malt balls, which she offered to Twyla. Of all the things to have hanging out in her enormous grandma bag, what were the odds this woman would be carrying around Twyla's favorite candy? With her life in shambles, Twyla took several. She popped the first in her mouth, savoring the way the chocolate coating melted on her tongue, followed by the sweet tang of the malt underneath it.

"I love these," she said in a watery voice.

"You have as many as you want, honey." The woman set the bag in Twyla's lap. "Now why don't you tell me what's got you crying your eyes out in Grandmother Wisdom's alcove on a Salts-day morning."

Twyla regarded her. With her short spiky gray hair and her cobalt-blue loungewear, the stranger had a robust, ageless quality about her. She might have been anywhere in her sixties or seventies. Twyla had never seen her before, but the woman reminded her of her grandma Eloise, a self-proclaimed "tough old broad," who used to say things like "Watching your children sleep is the

Three Mothers' reward to you for not killing them while they were awake."

Perhaps it was the fact that Twyla had no clue who this woman was, and would probably never see her again, or perhaps it was her Grandma Eloise–ness that put her at ease—but whatever the reason, she decided to open up. She told her about marrying young and her parents' disapproval, especially her mother's, and how much she hated it that her mother had been prophetic. She told her about years of stress and resentment, trying to hold her family together, trying to make ends meet, trying to be a good mother when she felt threadbare. She told her about Hope's getting married and the terrible argument they had had. She told her about Frank and their friendship and their career in the Tanrian Marshals. She told her about going to Frank's bedroom the night before. (She even let the word *vibrator* cross her lips, right there in temple.) She told her about how Frank retired and didn't tell her. All of it came pouring out of Twyla like glittery spit out of a pissed-off dragon, dragons being the only thing Twyla did not spill (since their existence was classified information).

"Let's get one thing out of the way," said the woman when Twyla had finally finished. "You are a good person, a good person who is dealing with the complicated things life throws at you from time to time."

Twyla popped another malt ball. "How could you know I'm a good person? I could be heinous and awful."

"I have a good sense for these things. You're a good person, so you don't need to berate yourself. That accomplishes nothing anyway. What you need to do is figure out what you want. What do you want, Twyla?"

Twyla's brain went blank. If someone had peered inside her ears, they would've seen nothing but a white space where thoughts should be.

"What do I want?" she floundered.

"That's right. What do you want?" The nice old lady in leisure wear chucked a malt ball into her own mouth and chewed thoughtfully on it. Her pencil-thin eyebrows shot up. "Well, hot dang, these things are fantastic! Mind if I have a few more?"

Twyla thought it a bit odd that a woman who carried chocolate malt balls in her oversized grandma purse would be surprised that they were delicious, but who was she to judge? "They're yours. Go to town."

"Let's start with Hope," the woman said through a mouthful of candy. "You warned her against marriage because you want something else for her. What is it?"

"I guess that I want Hope to be happy. No, I want her to be satisfied. I want her to be fulfilled. I want her to be able to live life on her own terms."

"That's what you should tell her, those words exactly."

Twyla considered this over another malt ball. "I suppose that it would go over better than *Don't get married*."

"Of course it would. Of course it will. Think about how annoyed you were with your mother for pooh-poohing your marital bliss. You can have your opinion, but at the end of the day, it's Hope's life, and she's the one who needs to figure out how to be satisfied and fulfilled on her own terms."

"But marriage is one of those things where you don't know what you're getting into until you've already gotten into it."

"That applies to every choice you make in life. Should you get the sweet potato fries or the onion rings with your tuna melt? You might be delighted by the outcome or disappointed or something in between."

"Are you comparing marriage to the menu at the Salt and Key?"

"Am I wrong?" She dug a tube of hot pink lipstick from her bag, glossed it on, and smacked her lips. "Let me ask you this:

If you had your life to do over again—not hypothetically, but in reality—knowing what you know now, what would you do? Would you tell Doug no when he asked you to marry him? Would you walk away and live a different life?"

Twyla forced herself to sit with the question. She tried to imagine how her life might have played out if she hadn't gotten married. What had she wanted when she was nineteen years old, beyond loving and being loved? Not much. The wants and dreams and desires, the different paths she might have taken—they had come after she got married. Maybe she would never have known what she was missing if she hadn't spent so many years of her life putting off what was best for her to make sure everyone else got what was best for them. And if she had never married Doug, she would never have had DJ or Wade or Hope, all of whom were as necessary as air as far as she was concerned. If she hadn't married Doug, she would never have moved to Eternity. She would never have met Frank, much less become friends with him. She would never have joined the marshals. She would never have been to Tanria.

As for Doug himself, there had been good times with him, birthdays and New Year's parties and laughter and even the occasional holding of one another in the dark of night. He had loved his family, and he had loved her, even if he had loved himself more.

"No," said Twyla. "If I had it all to do over again, I'd marry Doug. There's not a doubt in my mind."

Her new friend put her hand over Twyla's, her touch warm and solid. "Spoken like a wise woman. You brought Hope into this world, but her life is hers to live. She'll have her triumphs and her disappointments, same as everyone else. The only thing she needs from you is your support. Does she have that?"

"Yes, of course. Always."

"Then that's settled, which brings us to Frank." She took her hand away to pick up another malt ball from the bag. "What do you want from Frank?"

"His friendship. His companionship."

"How about his love? Do you want that?"

"No! Of course not!"

It was the knee-jerk reaction trained into Twyla from years of people assuming that she and Frank were an item, and both of them having to rush in with the *We're just friends* line.

The Giver of Malt Balls tsk-tsked, pulled an embroidery hoop out of her bag, and got to work, her robust hands working a delicate floral pattern into the weave of the linen. "Not to be rude, sweetie, but I'm not buying it."

"I don't *want* to want his love."

"The problem is that you might already have it. What do you think? Is Frank in love with you?" The woman poked her in the arm with the wooden hoop.

"I don't know," said Twyla. But then she remembered how shaken Frank had been when he thought she had been hurt and the gentle way he'd cared for her in the infirmary.

"Maybe?" she amended. But then she remembered the photograph he kept in the drawer of his bedside table with her birth key attached to it, as if it were something he needed to keep private and hidden.

From her.

The truth left her gobsmacked as it sank in. "Yes. Yes, I think he might be in love with me, now that you mention it."

"Do you love him?"

Twyla didn't have to sit with the question. She didn't have to think about it. She knew the answer. Tears went spilling down her cheeks all over again, and she sopped them up from her face with the old-fashioned hankie.

"So that's a yes?"

"But I don't want to be in love with Frank! I don't want to be in love with anybody!"

"Pretty sure that ship has sailed. Chocolate malt ball?" The woman held out the bag.

"No, thank you."

"Whew, you are in a bad way if you're turning these down." She helped herself to another. "Need a hug?"

Twyla nodded.

The woman set her embroidery hoop on the pew beside her and wrapped Twyla in her arms, the sort of high-quality hug that only a busty old lady who smelled like chocolate and lipstick could give. Twyla wished she had thought to ask her name. It would be awkward to ask now, after a hug and an in-depth discussion of her life that had featured the word *vibrator*.

"What am I going to do?" she cried in the woman's arms. "He took off to gods know where, and who knows if he'll ever talk to me again? How did I mess up so badly?"

"I wouldn't say you've messed up, no more than anyone else. Sometimes you have to really fuck something up before you can fully appreciate it."

Twyla laughed and pulled herself together, giving her cheeks one more pass with the handkerchief before she blew her nose.

The woman picked up her embroidery and got down to brass tacks. "So, let's review the bidding. You're in love with Frank, and you think there's a good chance that Frank is in love with you. But you're friends, and falling in love threatens the friendship, and obviously that's something neither of you wants."

"Yes! That's it exactly!"

"I get it. And there's something to be said for not risking your friendship. But, Twyla." Here, the woman set the hoop in her lap to look Twyla in the eye. "When you're lying on your deathbed someday, are you going to think to yourself, *Good thing I never told Frank how I felt*? Or are you going to regret all the years you spent loving him and not doing a thing about it?"

Twyla leaned back in the pew and said nothing, because she didn't need to.

The woman nodded and picked up her embroidery. "There's your answer."

They sat side by side, one tying off a thread and neatly snipping the loose end with a handy pair of scissors, the other finally seeing her path forward. Frank might be out of the picture for the moment, but Twyla knew where to find Hope. It was a start.

"Thank you," she said, an understatement considering the magnitude of the advice she had received.

"What's a grandma for?"

"Are you from around here? I don't think we've ever met."

"I'm just visiting. Speaking of which." The woman stuffed the embroidery hoop into her bag and got to her feet. "I'd better be off. Someone always needs me. You know how it is."

"I sure do."

The woman smiled at Twyla, her beady blue eyes full of warmth and affection. "Everything will work out in the end, honey. You'll see."

"Goodbye. Thanks again."

Twyla watched her leave, the thick rubber soles of the woman's practical shoes making fart sounds as she made her way down the center aisle and disappeared out of the main entry doors.

Full of lightness and resolution, Twyla considered all that had passed in the handful of minutes in the alcove. She had come here for wisdom, and wisdom had been given in droves, alongside a hankie, a hug, and a bag of chocolate malt balls. She realized that the woman had left her the embroidered handkerchief and the candy, and Twyla hadn't even bothered to learn her name. She gazed at the mosaic of Grandmother Wisdom stretching floor to ceiling behind the altar, where the doughnuts remained, a feeble offering for an incredible gift.

"Thank you," Twyla told the god.

And to the day she sailed the Salt Sea, she would swear on her key and boat that the portrait of Grandmother Wisdom winked at her.

All the air whooshed out of Twyla's lungs. The alcove seemed to spin around her, as if she were drunk. Surely, she had imagined it.

Hadn't she?

She hustled out of the alcove and searched all over the temple until she found Votary Asebedo cleaning up the offerings on the Bride of Fortune's altar.

"Hi, Twyla. We don't usually see you on a Saltsday."

Twyla waved a quick hello and asked, in a rush, "Do you know who that lady was? She said she was visiting family."

"What lady?"

"That woman who was in Grandmother Wisdom's alcove with me."

"You're the only person I've seen at Grandmother Wisdom's altar this morning." The votary shrugged in apology and went about her work as a shaft of sunlight burst through the skylight of the Unknown God, dispersing the gray clouds overhead.

Twyla's entire body started to shake. Her knees gave out, and she dropped onto a pew in the Bride of Fortune's alcove. It was a long time before she trusted herself to walk out of the temple on her own two feet.

Chapter Twenty-One

Hope?" called Twyla as she walked through Wade's front door. She heard rustling sounds coming from the kitchen and was surprised to find her son therein rather than her daughter. "What are you doing home?"

"I work the afternoon shift on Saltsdays." Wade was turned away from her, but the aggressive manner in which he wound the crank and punched down the lever on the toaster led Twyla to suspect that he was angry.

"What's the matter?" she asked.

"Nothing much. My mom stormed off last night and never came home. The usual."

Guilt oozed its way into Twyla's conscience, a familiar feeling but not one generally inspired by her second born. She grimaced apologetically.

"Where have you been?" he exploded, turning for the express purpose of yelling at her.

"I stayed at Frank's."

"Did it occur to you to let your family know where you were?"

"Well...no?"

"I have been worried sick! I stayed up half the night waiting to make sure you got home okay, except you never came home!"

"I assumed Hope would have told you we argued."

"Yeah, but how was I supposed to know that you planned to stay out the whole Bones-loving night?"

The toaster sprang, and two reheated pancakes popped up. Wade plated them, and as he poured a staggering amount of syrup over them, he haughtily informed his mother, "Maybe next time, you can model more mature and responsible behavior for your grandchildren."

"Will do. Did you make pancakes?" The thought of Wade creating anything edible in the kitchen threatened to alter her perception of reality.

"Anita made them before she got the kids off to school and dropped Teo off at day care. She left me these to reheat in the toaster."

"That tracks," said Twyla, relieved that the universe hadn't shifted while she maybe possibly chatted with a god at temple this morning. "Is Hope around?"

A high-pitched keen answered this question. Twyla turned to find her daughter right behind her, red-faced and blubbering.

"I'm so so-o-o-orry!" Hope wailed before grabbing Twyla in a crushing hug.

Twyla tried to give her daughter a comforting pat, but it proved difficult given the strength of the embrace.

"It's okay," she said, although she was finding it difficult to breathe.

"It's not oka-a-a-ay!"

"Honey—"

"I said the most horrible things to you, and I didn't mean them! You're the best mom ever, and I am a bu-u-u-utt!"

"You're not a butt."

"Yes, I a-a-am!"

"You're not a butt, but...can't...breathe."

"Sorry," Hope said wetly, finally relinquishing her mother.

Twyla cupped her daughter's precious face in her warm hands, desperately relieved that all was not lost between them. "You want to talk about it, sweetheart?"

"Mm-hmm." Hope sniffed, and then she turned and snatched the plate and fork away from her brother before following Twyla to the patio.

"Hey," Wade protested in her wake as if he were the one who was nine years younger.

Twyla sat across from her daughter as Hope tearfully shoved a forkful of syrup-drenched pancake in her mouth. "You're not entirely to blame for last night. I didn't do a good job of saying what I needed to say."

"I mean, you did tell me not to marry the love of my life."

"That's not exactly what I said."

"That's pretty much what you said, though."

That was pretty much what she'd said. Twyla cringed at the memory of how badly she had flubbed her big marriage talk with Hope.

"Do you have a problem with Everett?" Hope asked warily.

"No, I do not have a problem with Everett. Everett is lovely. I have a problem with me. I'm my problem." Twyla's stress and her lack of sleep were finally catching up to her. She drooped in her chair. "You were right. I wasn't happy being married to your dad. I wasn't happy being married, period. But I didn't hate your father. He was a kind and decent man, and I loved him. Do you believe me?"

Hope nodded, her face tearstained and puffy. "I'm sorry you weren't happy, though."

Twyla waved this away. "Your dad and I had plenty of good times. Plus, I had you and Wade and DJ, and what could be better than the three of you?"

Hope gave a watery laugh. "I don't know about DJ and Wade, but I'm pretty great."

"You are better than great. You are my heart and my soul, which is why I'm worried that no matter how much you love Everett and no matter how much he loves you, marriage might bring you more sorrow than joy. And the thought of you being trapped in that life kills me."

"But that was your experience. It doesn't have to be mine."

"I know that. I swear I do. But I don't think any woman hands her birth key to a man thinking, *Golly, I hope he turns me into his personal servant.* And yet it happens. All the time. To lots of women. Lots and lots of us. So all I'm asking is that you don't let it happen to you."

"Would it make you feel better if I tell you that I refuse to let that happen to me?"

"It might."

"I refuse to let Everett turn me into his personal servant."

"Promise?"

"I promise."

"Good. I believe you." Twyla reached across the table and put her hand over Hope's. Her daughter's skin was sticky with syrup, as if the universe were reminding her that this young woman would always be her baby girl.

"So you'll be happy for me, even though I'm getting married."

"Whatever and whoever makes you happy makes me happy. And I already love the snot out of Everett, so that helps."

Hope's face crumpled, but in a good way. "Thank you, Mom."

"You're welcome." Twyla came around to Hope's side of the table to hug her. She pressed her cheek to the top of Hope's head and smelled the strawberry scent of her shampoo. "But I'm also going to remind you that you said some awful things to me last night, and I think you need to know how much that hurt me. I freely admit that I'm not winning Mom of the Year, but I did not deserve that."

"I'm so sorry," said Hope as Twyla gently rocked her. "I didn't mean any of it. I was pissy because I thought you were shitting on me getting married."

Twyla straightened and put her fists on her hips. "Honestly, language!"

"You taught Teo how to say *fucking*. He's not even three years old yet. People in glass houses, Mom."

Twyla opened her mouth to fire off a retort, but what could she say? She had, in fact, taught her youngest grandchild how to drop an f-bomb.

Hope remained seated in the black metal chair, but she hugged her mother around the middle and gazed up at her. "You're so badass, Mom. I would be lucky if I turned out like you."

"That's sweet, but I'd say there's plenty of room for improvement. Why don't you turn out like me but better?"

"It's hard to be better than the best."

And now Twyla was tearing up. "Oh, honey, I love you!"

"I love you, too!" cried Hope.

When they finished hugging and dripping sentiment all over each other, Twyla sat again, taking the chair next to Hope, not opposite her.

"So I guess you're not going to marry your cute professor someday?" asked Hope. "You're just going to use him for the hot loving?"

Twyla waved her hand dismissively. "We broke up."

"Oh no."

"And then I . . . made things complicated with Frank."

"As in, you slept with him? In a sexy way?"

Twyla bit her lip and nodded.

"Oh. Oh!" Hope sat up straight and slapped Twyla on the arm. "Ooooooooooh!"

"I can't believe I told you that."

"This is amazing!"

Wade stepped outside, carrying a laundry basket. "What's amazing?"

Twyla turned to Hope with wide eyes. "No, do not tell—"

"Mom finally got it on with Frank," Hope announced to her brother.

"So when you told me you stayed at Frank's last night, you meant that you *stayed* at *Frank's* last night?"

Twyla could feel herself physically shrinking in horror as her children discussed her sex life. "I wonder if this is what Old Hell felt like?"

"Finally," said Hope.

"Took you two long enough," Wade agreed. He walked to the clothesline and began to wrestle with a damp shirt.

Twyla couldn't believe what she was seeing. "What are you doing?"

"Is this a trick question? I'm hanging clothes on the line."

"Someone raised you right."

Hope clicked her tongue in annoyance. "Would you congratulate me or Anita if we were out here hanging up the laundry?"

"Excellent point," conceded Twyla. "Someone raised you right, too."

"Anita left me a note saying that if I didn't do it, she'd kill me." Wade hung the shirt on the line, but it immediately came free of its pins and landed in the grass.

Hope cupped her hands around her mouth and yelled, "Weak!"

"You do it, if you're so smart."

"I am smart, which is why I'm not going to help you. And neither is Mom, because she doesn't need to enable your learned helplessness." Hope shot Twyla a quelling look, as if she knew that her mother was ready to leap up and show Wade how it was done. "It's not rocket science. Let him figure it out. For Anita's sake."

Twyla clutched her chair's arms but forced her butt to remain in the seat.

"Be strong," Hope encouraged her.

"Hello! Mail delivery!" called the cheerily stentorian voice of Eternity's new nimkilim, an elephant named Portia. While she was significantly nicer than Horatio, the former nimkilim, she was also significantly louder and significantly more likely to crush one's garden beds under her massive feet. She stood at the gate, waving a letter in her long trunk and singing "Yoo-hoo!" Twyla was fairly certain that the zinnias Anita had planted last year in that general location were toast. Oblivious to all things floral, Wade went to greet Portia at the gate, which was just as well since he doubtless would have mowed over the zinnias on accident anyway.

"Hi, Portia, whatcha got for us today?"

"Wade, it's the darnedest thing. I reached into my satchel and pulled out this letter, but it's addressed to *Twyla* Banneker, who doesn't even live here. Yet lookie-loo, there she is. Hello, Twyla!"

"Hi, Portia." Twyla joined the elephant and Wade by the gate. "Darling child, will you tip the nimkilim for me?"

"Why do I have to tip? It's your mail."

"My purse is inside, and I gave you life."

"How is anyone supposed to argue with the I-gave-you-life line?" he groused, but he dug into his pocket and handed a coin to the nimkilim.

"Much obliged!" trumpeted Portia before she moseyed away on her mail route, shaking the earth beneath her.

Wade returned to his laundry and Hope's teasing, and Twyla opened her mail. There was no return address on the envelope, and the note inside was composed of words and letters cut from newspapers and magazines and pasted onto the page. It read:

We have Frank. If you ever want to see him alive again, meet us at the following coordinates inside Tanria no later than 5:00 this evening. Come unarmed, and tell no one about this note, or Frank dies. Thank you. Bye.
Latitude: 37.849; Longitude: -106.926

Blood rushed to Twyla's head, and her ears rang. Someone had Frank. Frank was in danger. And Twyla needed to ransom him. Except, was this a ransom note? There was no demand for money, only a request that she show up at a specific location inside the Mist. Twyla gripped the fence post to prevent herself from tumbling to her knees. She could barely hear Hope say "Mom?" through the thundering of blood in her ears.

She reread the letter.

Frank.

They had Frank.

They were going to kill Frank.

"Mom? What's wrong?"

She knew that Wade was speaking to her, but his words didn't register. The only words she could focus on were the ones in front of her, a mismatched jumble of fonts and papers that formed a threat to her neighbor, her partner, her best friend, the man she loved from the depths of her soul.

Hardly knowing where she was going or what she was doing, she walked into the house to get her Gracie Goodfist backpack.

"What did that letter say?" asked Hope as she followed Twyla into the room they were, in theory, sharing at Wade's house, even though Twyla had yet to spend a single night in it. Wade himself hovered at the door, an expression of grave concern painted over his face.

"It's classified," Twyla answered. She had taken next to nothing the last time she went to Tanria, and with her home destroyed, she still had next to nothing. What she did have was a compass and a map, and that was all she needed. She slung her mostly empty bag over her shoulder and made for the door.

Wade hurried in front of her to stop her from leaving. "Mom, what's wrong?"

"I'm sorry, honey. This is Tanrian Marshals business. I have to go."

Reluctantly, he let her slide past him, and both he and Hope watched Twyla hop into her duck and drive off.

As she sped along the highway, kicking up a cloud of dust in her wake, all she could think about was Frank and how on earth she was going to rescue him. Her plan, such as it was, did not include her autoduck breaking down five miles from the West Station.

"No!" she cried as a cloud of steam, or possibly smoke, billowed out from underneath the hood. She managed to pull the duck off the road before it completely died, and she got out to stare at the engine, as if she knew how to fix it. If only she had let Wade come with her. He was a mechanic, for gods' sakes.

The sound of another duck in the distance caught Twyla's attention. She stood in the middle of the highway and waved her hat in the air to flag down the driver and beg for help. The duck came to a stop, its glossy red exterior and white racing stripes blinding in the Bushong sunlight. It must have been driven straight off an auto lot, since the windshield hosted the staggering price tag. The engine growled with power, even as it idled, the sort of vehicle that could only be described as a muscle duck.

The driver's-side window rolled down, releasing the heavy bass of a popular song playing within the confines of the cab, and to Twyla's amazement, Penrose Duckers poked his head out of the tricked-out autoduck.

"Twyla! Need a lift?"

"Duckers?" She could not believe her eyes. Or her luck.

"What do you think? I'm test-driving it! You hear this?" He bobbed his head in time to the music blaring from the autoduck's interior. "It comes with a transistor, so I don't have to listen to you and Frank sing your shitty songs anymore!"

A surge of hope sang through Twyla's veins. If Duckers had made it out to the auto lots today, surely that meant Frank had taken him and the ransom note was someone's sick idea of a joke. "Is Frank with you?" she asked desperately.

"No. I ran into Dr. V. on Main Street, and he offered to take me duck shopping. Have you seen his ride? It's smokin'."

"Hallo, Twyla," Quill called through the passenger-side window.

Despair set in. Twyla fought the urge to lie down on the road and curl into a ball. Curling into a ball wouldn't help Frank, and helping Frank was what she needed to do more than anything.

"Can you give me a ride to the station?" She didn't wait for an answer. She opened the passenger-side door, and since it was a one-bench duck, she set her pack on Quill's lap and pushed him into the center of the bench to make room for her.

"I say," he exclaimed, startled by her behavior, but she didn't care. There were more pressing matters to attend to than Quill's ruffled feathers.

"Uh, okay," said Duckers, turning down the volume of the transistor and putting the duck into gear. "Why are you going to work? You have the next couple of weeks off, don't you?"

"Just drive!" she cried, adding a more subdued "Please" to make him malleable to her needs.

"Is something the matter?"

"Of course not! Nothing's the matter. With me. Obviously there's something the matter with my duck. Ha!" Twyla knew she was talking way too quickly as a fake smile cracked her face.

Quill smiled blandly at her, but she could see that Duckers wasn't buying it. Eager to deflect his skepticism, Twyla turned his attention to the ridiculous autoduck he was test driving. "I think you need to look at something more practical. This thing screams 'breakup duck.' You're better off cutting bangs."

"First of all, this duck kicks ass. Second of all, why do you need to get to the station again? Are you going to beg the chief to take Frank back? Or, shit, are you going to put in for retirement, too? Are you abandoning me?"

"No, I just need to…uh…do a Marshals in the Community thing."

"Ugh. Sucks to be you."

Twyla would have breathed a sigh of relief at redirecting Duckers's perceptiveness if she weren't tied up in knots over Frank.

Duckers nudged Quill with his elbow as he drove. "Hey, Dr. Vanderlectable, do you think Twyla's right? Is this duck too much of a flex? Because, lemme tell you, it handles like a dream."

"What did you call me?" asked Quill, bemused.

"Vanderlectable. Vanderlirious. Vanderlightful. I could go on all day."

"Thank you? I think?"

"You're welcome. So wait, Twyla, if you're doing a Marshals in the Community thing, why are you going to the station? Shouldn't you be, you know, in the community?"

"Or does it have something to do with this ransom note for Marshal Ellis?" asked Quill, holding up the letter that Portia had delivered to Wade's house less than a half hour ago.

"How did you get that?" Twyla demanded, horror-struck.

"It came out of the pocket of your charmingly childish backpack when you set it on my lap and shunted me to the side."

"A ransom note?" asked an incredulous Duckers. "What the fuck? Is Frank in trouble?"

"It would seem so," said Quill, who then proceeded to read the note aloud for Duckers's benefit, finishing with "Who says *thank you* and *bye* in a ransom note?"

"Who cares?" snapped Twyla, although she had wondered the same thing. "I need to get to this place before five o'clock. And I wasn't supposed to tell anyone."

"How will these people know that we found out about it? You should have gone to the authorities."

"I don't want to risk Frank's life."

"Don't be a ninnyhammer. You're risking his life by *not* involving trained law enforcement officers."

"I *am* a law enforcement officer!"

"So am I," said Duckers, "and I'm here to tell you that I agree with the professor. You're being a total ninnyhammer, which is a great fucking word, by the way, and I am using it forever. The point is, we need to tell the chief."

Twyla took a cleansing breath. Frank needed her. She refused to care whether or not Duckers and a man she had dated for two seconds thought she was a ninnyhammer. And, much as she hated to admit it, they had a point (about involving the authorities, not about her being a ninnyhammer).

"You're right. We need all the help we can get. Okay, here's the plan. I'm going to enter Tanria through the portal at the West Station, unarmed. Duckers, you are going to arm yourself to the teeth at the weapons lockers and follow me at a distance, in case they've got eyes on me. You'll be my backup, but don't interfere unless it's absolutely necessary."

"You got it, Twyla."

"Quill, I need you to track down Chief Maguire to let her know what's going on."

"I'm afraid we're supposed to return the autoduck to the lot in thirty minutes," Quill informed her apologetically.

Twyla gaped at him. She was tempted to take him by the ascot and shake him until his tweed unraveled. Fortunately, Duckers piped up and saved her the trouble.

"Pretty sure saving a man's life is more important than a duck, Dr. Vander-lickin'-good." With that, he put the pedal to the metal, sending up a furious cloud of dust in their wake as they blazed down the highway.

When they arrived at the West Station, Twyla went straight to the stable, while Duckers and Quill went into the building to carry out their tasks. She looked over the stalls, and while there were several equimares to choose from today, she knew the stallion for the job when she saw him.

"Time to save Frank, Saltlicker. Do not let me down."

Chapter Twenty-Two

Twyla had the coordinates marked out on her map of Tanria. It was a location in the far northwestern corner of Sector W-7, deep in the Dragon's Teeth, rugged enough that she had to picket Saltlicker halfway up a rocky incline to make the rest of her way by foot. She was usually confident in her orienteering skills, but with Frank's life on the line and her watch quickly ticking toward five o'clock, she was getting nervous enough to be sick to her stomach.

That sick feeling wasn't helped when a man stepped out from behind a boulder, pistol crossbow in hand. A black kerchief hid most of his face.

Twyla put her hands up and prayed that Duckers wasn't far behind her.

"I'll take any weapons you have," the man told her.

"You said to come unarmed."

"That doesn't mean you did."

He kept his pistol crossbow trained on her with one hand and searched her with the other. When he was satisfied that she had no weapons, he tied her wrists together and pushed her through a landscape increasingly shrouded by scrub. Twyla had worked Sector W-7 several times over the years, but she hadn't come this way often. The terrain was treacherous, and since equimares struggled to navigate the landscape, it wasn't an area the marshals patrolled heavily. The logic was that if a marshal struggled to get somewhere in Tanria, a criminal would have an even tougher time.

Apparently not, thought Twyla as the man shoved her into a shepherd's hut she hadn't known existed. It was a two-room shack built at the base of a steep rock face, cobbled together by the sheep shearers who came to the mountains to harvest blue silksheep wool from time to time. It would have been a poor shelter in the days when the undead drudges infested Tanria, a place where a person could be easily trapped with no exit, but the smoke stains on the walls and the detritus of empty cans and bottles indicated years of use.

The main room was dimly lit by one lantern, illuminating Frank, who knelt near the far wall with his hands bound behind his back. His face was bloodied and bruised, and Twyla thought that whoever had done this to him might as well beat her own heart to a pulp. His left eye was swollen shut, but in his right eye, Twyla saw raw agony.

"Gods, no. Twy, why did you come?" he said in a voice made gravelly with pain and exhaustion and terror for what they might do to her now that she was here with him.

"As if I wouldn't come. As if you wouldn't come if it were me." She made to cross the room to him, but the goon held her in place.

"Oh, good, you got my note," said a very sweet and very familiar voice from the doorway to the second room. Disbelieving her ears, Twyla squinted until the speaker came into focus, at which point she was forced to disbelieve her eyes.

"Hermia?"

"Hello," said the nimkilim, stepping into the lantern light with a meek wave.

"*You* sent me the ransom note?"

"I did, and do you know how hard it was to cut out all those letters? The scissors barely fit in my tiny hedgehog hands. I ended up using a pair of nail trimmers, and goodness gracious, it took me ages."

Twyla gawped at the adorable hedgehog with her adorable glasses and her adorable sweater and her adorable blue rain boots with the adorable little clouds on them, and she could not, for the life of her, comprehend what in the name of the Unknown God was going on in this shack. She hoped Quill had found Maguire, and she hoped Maguire would come up with some way to rescue Frank—and also herself, now that she was thinking on it. She was in the process of hoping that Duckers was nearby and ready to help if she needed it when two more goons showed up, one of them holding a full-sized crossbow, the other collaring Duckers into the shelter.

"The lady brought a friend with her," a masked woman holding Duckers's confiscated crossbow informed Hermia. "We probably wouldn't have seen him, but he had this giant weapon that made him easy to spot."

"What did you think you were going to do with a full-sized crossbow in this situation?" an irritated Twyla demanded of her young partner.

"You said 'armed to the teeth'! A full-sized crossbow is as toothy as it gets!"

"I meant the normal stuff! Like *pistol* crossbows!"

Duckers finally noticed Frank. "Dang, Frank, are you okay?"

"Been better."

"Hello-o-o? Excuse me?" Hermia waved her tiny little hand, which was too small for regular scissors but evidently large enough to carry out criminal activities inside Tanria. "Can we get back to the part where I make my demands, please?"

"Hermia, what is going on here?" asked Twyla.

"Well, I was working with Marshal Herd to smuggle illegally

mined iuvenicite out of Tanria in my magical mail pouch for the Galatian mob. But then the illegal miners accidentally woke up the dragons with their illegal fireworks that didn't even work on the rocks they were trying to illegally blow up. And then Marshal Herd died, and the FICBI joined forces with the Tanrian Marshals to bust the iuvenicite crime ring, and where does that leave me?"

"That's...specific," commented Frank.

Duckers shook his head in denial. "Am I seriously going to have to listen to the villain speech of a hedgehog before I die?"

"This is how Frank and I ended up with bombs under our beds," said Twyla, addressing the traitorous nimkilim. "You knew we found the illegal mine, and you told the mob."

"True," said Hermia with a cute little pout. "Sad face!"

Duckers was still deep in his feelings. "I broke Zeddie's heart for this?" he said.

"It was the right thing to do," Twyla assured him, cold comfort though it was.

Hermia held up her increasingly not adorable hand again. "Sorry to interrupt, but I'm having a moment here."

"What do you want with us?" asked Twyla.

"I'm glad you asked. You've always been so thoughtful, Marshal Banneker. Here's my dilemma. I lost my illegal iuvenicite-smuggling operation, but now another Galatian mob family wants in. I convinced them that a real live baby dragon would be worth a whole lot more than a bunch of rocks someone would have to go to the trouble of mining. But now they want *me* to get it for them. *I* can't steal a dragon." She held up her tiny hands as evidence. "And even if I could kidnap a baby dragon, or even an egg, I wouldn't be able to sneak it out of Tanria in my pouch, because we nimkilim can't carry living material in our satchels. And these nice mob people wouldn't be able to catch a baby dragon, because the dragon mommies would attack them. So then I thought of Marshal Ellis, since he's already friends with a baby dragon, and it would be no problem for him to bring her to us. I invited him to join us here in Sector W-7—"

"You carjacked me outside of Callaghan's General Store," Frank corrected her.

"—but he's being super mean about the whole thing, to be honest."

"Go to Old Hell," Frank spat at the nimkilim. One of the mobsters punched him in the stomach.

"Oh dear!" exclaimed Hermia. "But really, you only have yourself to blame for that, Marshal Ellis."

"Leave him alone!" shouted Twyla.

"I'm afraid I can't do that. Since he won't bring me the baby dragon, I need to hold him hostage so that *you* can get it for me."

"Or what? You'll kill him?"

"Goodness gracious, no! I wouldn't hurt a fly." Hermia gestured toward the goons. "*They'll* kill him."

One of the mobsters held up a hand in greeting. "Hiya."

"Don't do it, Twy," Frank begged her, and was rewarded with another punch to the face.

"Okay! Okay! Stop hurting him! I'll get you the dragon," said Twyla.

"No!" cried Frank, but Twyla paid no attention to his protest. She wasn't going to let these goons use him as their punching bag. She decided the best tactic was to agree to the demands but delay as much as possible to give Maguire more time to find them.

"Hermia, why would you do this?" she asked the nimkilim. "What could you possibly stand to gain?"

"Lulu's Grape Fizzy."

A long, heavy pause followed this answer as Twyla tried to make the pieces of the iuvenicite puzzle fall into place.

"What?" she asked completely at a loss.

"It's impossible to find anywhere on the entire island of Bushong! No one around here carries it. My old mob friends kept me supplied with Lulu's Grape Fizzy for months, and all I had to do was smuggle some rocks out of the Mist. But my new mob friends said that if I give them a dragon, they can get me a job delivering Lulu's Grape Fizzy throughout the Federated Islands of Cadmus, and I will have all the Lulu's Grape Fizzy I want!" She clapped her cute little hands with giddy excitement.

"Lulu's Grape Fizzy?" asked Twyla, barely able to form the ridiculous words on her tongue.

"I love it so much."

"The Galatian mob is bribing you with soda pop?"

"Mm-hmm."

"Are you fucking kidding me?" asked Duckers.

Twyla wished her hands weren't bound, so that she could rub away the enormous headache forming at her temples. "I want to make sure I understand you correctly: You betrayed the Tanrian Marshals and the Eternal Order of the Nimkilim for grape soda?"

Hermia, noting the disapproval in Twyla's voice, put her little hands on the approximate location of her little hips. "Have you ever had a Lulu's Grape Fizzy?"

"No."

"Then maybe you shouldn't be so quick to judge."

The goon guarding Twyla jostled her and asked the nimkilim, "Are we killing someone here or not?"

"Salt fucking Sea," said Duckers, "I can't believe that I'm going to die because of Lulu's Grape Fizzy."

Time was running out, and Twyla knew it. Her mind whirred, forming a new plan. "If I get a baby dragon for you, you'll let us go?"

"As long as you don't turn me in for breaking every postal code imaginable. But if you do, I'm afraid that my new friends in the Galatian mob will kill you until you're very dead."

"I think there's only one kind of dead."

"And I don't want to be that kind of dead," added Duckers.

One of the mobsters grabbed Frank by his collar and held a pistol crossbow to his head, making Twyla's heart stop. He looked her dead in the eye. "Are you getting the fucking dragon or not?"

"Yes! I'm going!"

"Twy, it's not worth it," Frank pleaded with her.

Twyla had no intention of declaring her love for Frank in front of four mobsters and a villainous hedgehog, but there was no way she was leaving him without making sure he knew what he meant to her. "You're worth it," she told him.

He closed his good eye, his face painted with pain and regret.

"I'll get you your dragon," she announced as she held up her arms to be cut loose of her bonds.

Hermia slapped her hands on her sweet hedgehog cheeks. "Oopsies! I forgot to mention: You have one hour. If you're not back by then, someone who is not me will kill your friends, all right?"

Twyla had to bite her lip for a few seconds to stop herself from saying all the things she wanted to say to this hedgehog. Her anger wouldn't help Frank or Duckers. She took a calming breath and said, "Goodbye."

"Okay, bye," answered Hermia.

"Bye," said a couple of the mobsters.

"Bye," Hermia said again.

Duckers gave Twyla a knowing wink and said, "Bye, Twyla. Good luck."

"Bye," Hermia said yet again.

Twyla left the shack before she was subjected to any more goodbyes from that fucking hedgehog.

She lost ten minutes simply returning to the place where she had left Saltlicker. "Giddyup!" Twyla hollered at the equimaris as soon as she was situated in the saddle, and then she held on for dear life as the stallion took her at her word. As she raced toward Sector W-14 on the back of a mount that was far too large for her, Twyla found herself questioning her life choices. But there was nothing for it now. She had pushed the metaphorical rock, and now it was rolling down the metaphorical hill.

Twyla had hoped to reach the lake before the dragons made their evening sojourn to their nests, but as soon as she arrived on the lakeshore, they began to take off in groups of twos and threes, the mothers with their babies clinging to them.

"No, no, no," she groaned as she dismounted and took the trouble to tie Saltlicker up extra carefully. She didn't need to lose her equimaris now, and Saltlicker had a reputation for pulling free of his pickets and heading for the nearest body of water. She'd never catch him if he got into the lake.

She spotted Mary Georgina meeping inconsolably between two of the scientists Quill had brought in.

"I know the feeling, honey," Twyla told her as she approached.

Mary Georgina perked up at the sight of her and came to nuzzle her hand.

Chirrup? she chirped in a hopeful, questioning tone, and Twyla knew what she was asking.

"He's not with me." Her voice cracked at the end, and she had to rein in the tears before the scientists noticed.

"Can we help you, Marshal?" asked the zoologist, a blond woman dressed similarly to Quill, but with longer shorts and higher knee socks. And no ascot.

"I'm Twyla Banneker, one of the marshals of record on the dragon case. I need to do a quick check-in. Have they all flown back to the nest for the day?"

"I'm afraid so, all except this one. We think she was the one who imprinted on a marshal."

"Yes, she imprinted on my partner."

"Is your partner here with you?" The botanist glanced over Twyla's shoulder, as if he anticipated the arrival of the marshal who could soothe the pitiful baby dragon.

No, he's not here with me. He's tied up in a shepherd's hut, and he might die if I don't save him. Obviously, Twyla couldn't say that, but since thinking it made her want to sob, she simply shook her head.

"She never goes to the nest, but she seems so forlorn here at the lake once the other dragons leave."

Twyla regarded the small pink dragon who peered up at her with innocent green eyes. Theoretically, she understood that she could trade this life for Frank's, but she knew she could never go through with it, and it wouldn't matter, because Frank would never forgive her if she did. And that left her with her half-formed plan, which ran a high risk of not working.

And which was now running horribly behind schedule.

She crouched down and hugged Mary Georgina, who nuzzled her snout into Twyla's neck. "I'll save him," she whispered. "I promise I will."

She stood and told the scientists "I have to go" before dashing to Saltlicker. As soon as she untied his reins, he fought her, trying to get to the lake when she needed him to go the opposite direction.

The stallion had picked the wrong day to mess with Twyla. She got in his face and seethed. "Frank loves you for no reason I can think of, and if he dies because you decided to be a jerk today, I'm going to turn you into a pair of boots. Is that clear?"

Saltlicker snorted and shrank away from her. Docile as a lamb, he let her mount up without complaint. Twyla heaved herself into the saddle and growled, "Let's go."

And go he did. Twyla was so worried about being hurled out of the saddle that it took her some time to notice a pink blur off to the side. She dared to glance over her shoulder to find Mary Georgina flying beside her and Saltlicker, the scientists left far behind. It was another complication in an already complicated plan, and Twyla allowed herself a good deal of cursing, much good it did her.

Since Mary Georgina was new to flying, Twyla hoped she might lose the dragon en route. But no, Frank's baby stuck with her all the way to the mine, where several federal agents were milling around, looking both official and completely out of place in their dark blue jackets with *FICBI* printed on the back in yellow letters. Standing amid them was Marshal Rosie Fox. The towering, redheaded demigod regarded Twyla's arrival unperturbedly with ruby-red eyes, her appearance so striking that she was the only person present who looked like she actually belonged in the bizarre otherworld of Tanria.

"Hey, Banneker," Fox greeted her, coming to take Saltlicker's reins. "What's the rush?"

Before Twyla could answer, Fox added, "I see you brought a friend."

Mary Georgina landed beside Twyla in a graceless tumble. "Why?" Banneker asked the dragon in a long, beseeching syllable.

Fox, who was one of those aggressively chummy people, slapped Twyla's arm in a bruising gesture meant to be friendly. "Guess you've got to ride like the old God of Vengeance is on your tail to fly with a dragon, huh?"

By now, the FICBI agents had gathered around Twyla and Fox, making polite but stern statements about how Twyla wasn't allowed to be here.

"Mrs. Banneker?" came one incredulous voice from that crowd.

"Nathan! Or, I guess, Agent McDevitt now," said Twyla.

He flourished his FICBI badge to show off. Nathan McDevitt

had been a sheriff's deputy in Eternity before leaving Bushong for a career with the Federated Islands of Cadmus's Bureau of Investigation. He had also been friends with Wade when they were kids. Part of her wondered if she could use the acquaintance to her advantage here, and part of her wanted to throw him over her knee and spank him for calling her *Mrs.* in the middle of Sector W-14.

"It's *Marshal* Banneker," she reminded him as she reached out to shake his hand, the picture of professionalism. She wondered if it flashed across his mind that she made a lot more money than he did. That fact certainly flashed across her own mind.

"What are you doing here?" he asked, and all of a sudden, she was grateful for Mary Georgina's presence.

"Frank Ellis and I have been assigned to the dragon case from the get-go. I'm escorting this young one into the nest."

"You know, it's not safe to go down there, especially when the mothers are in residence."

"I've already been down there while the mothers were in residence. We were the ones who blew open the FICBI smuggling case in the first place."

Another FICBI agent stepped forward, his eyes hidden behind a pair of mirrored sunglasses. "We can't let unauthorized persons into the habitat, ma'am."

"Excuse me?"

"I—"

"I'm a Tanrian Marshal standing on Tanrian soil. I am authorized."

"Oh, I like you, Banneker," said Fox.

Nathan McDevitt turned to his colleague. "It's fine. I went to school with Mrs. Banneker's son, and I can tell you that she is more likely to bring cookies to the temple bake sale than to cause any trouble. Let her go."

Twyla didn't correct him on her title. For once in her life, her invisibility as a middle-aged mother was working in her favor, and she wasn't about to blow it out of pride, no matter how sorely tempted she was to box Nathan McDevitt's ears.

"I don't think—" began Agent Sunglasses, when Rosie Fox intervened.

"I'll go in with her."

"It's dangerous."

"My dude. I literally cannot die. Come on, Banneker."

The marshals did not wait for approval. They descended into the cave, Twyla first, then Fox. Twyla gazed up at the opening and said, "Don't fail me now, Mary Georgina." She gave a sharp whistle, and the dragon's head appeared at the entrance. "Come on, girl."

The skittish baby tentatively lowered her head into the hole.

"You are my cover," Twyla whispered up at her. "We're saving Frank. Now come on."

"Wait, what?" asked Fox.

Mary Georgina took the plunge, landing on the cave floor in another clumsy tumble.

"Is something wrong with Ellis?" pressed Fox as she lit a lantern.

Twyla was already in the tunnel that led to the nests. "Yeah. I need a ride."

Fox hustled after her to light the way. "Why not take Saltlicker?"

"Not that kind of ride."

There was an ominous pause as Fox put two and two together.

"Oh, shit," she laughed, and Twyla sent a prayer of gratitude to the Bride of Fortune for putting Marshal Fox on her side. If anyone would approve of Twyla's outlandish plan, it was notorious troublemaker Rosie Fox.

"I'm in. How are we playing this?" asked the demigod, 100 percent game, gods love her.

"I wish I could tell you that I've thought through everything, but I haven't."

"Best way to go. Act first. Think never. Always works for me."

Twyla decided not to point out the fact that being immortal probably made that approach work far better for her than for people who ran a high risk of dying in dangerous situations.

By now, they'd arrived at the nest of the mother dragon who seemed to have taken a liking to Twyla, or at least to her momness. The dragon lifted her head as Twyla approached, her mate and babies curled in a heap around her.

"Hi, there," said Twyla. In any other circumstance, she would have felt silly or terrified or both. Then again, how often would she need to save Frank from a diabolical hedgehog by communicating with a giant pink reptile? "I know I'm not a god—not by any stretch of the imagination. I'm not even a demigod. But Frank—you know Frank, about this high, deep voice, very pro-dragon—he needs our help. He needs *your* help, specifically, and since he's done so much to keep you all safe, I thought you might be willing to...um..."

She was talking to an animal.

An animal that was blinking her glowing green eyes at her, displaying no understanding at all.

"Not to be a dick, but I'm pretty sure she doesn't understand a word you're saying," commented Rosie unhelpfully.

"If you have any other suggestions as to how I might lure a full-grown dragon out of her nest, I'm all ears."

As if in answer, the mother dragon leaned her head out of the alcove and nudged Twyla's hand, the way a dog might force a person to pet it. She acquiesced, stroking the dragon between the antlers. The dragon made a chirrupy sound and turned her head so that Twyla's hand ran along one of her horns. To Twyla's amazement, the protrusion wasn't bony or rigid. It was soft and pliable, bending under her fingers with ease, the soft peachy fur plush against her skin.

The strangest sensation came over Twyla, a deep calm, a tranquility that came not from within but from the outside. From the dragon.

Twyla kept her hand on the soft, silky antler as she closed her eyes and tried to convey what she needed to her huge reptilian ally.

Mary Georgina rubbed against Twyla's hip, reminding her of her presence. The mother sniffed Mary Georgina, then gently nudged her along until the baby was in her nest, settling beside the other offspring. The father dragon opened one eye and released an annoyed *Meep*, but the mother told him *Meep meep* in a way that sounded, to Twyla's untrained ears, akin to *Deal with it.*

"Oh, I like her, too," said Rosie.

The dragon uncurled herself from the nest and bustled past Twyla and Rosie, heading for the main entrance. The two women looked at each other, then scrambled to catch up. There were shouts of alarm coming from the FICBI agents aboveground as the marshals climbed the ladder. When they surfaced, they found the agents shying away from the dragon, with pistol crossbows drawn.

"Put those away. Y'all don't know how to shoot them anyway," Fox told them, her voice dripping with derision. "Okay, Banneker, do or die."

Twyla wasn't fond of Fox's choice of words, but beggars couldn't be choosers, and she was glad for whatever help she could get.

The dragon crouched low as Twyla approached, to a chorus of FICBI agents calling, "Ma'am! Ma'am, step away from the dragon!"

"Please don't kill me," Twyla mewled as she hoisted herself onto the crook of the dragon's front leg, then hauled herself onto its back. She settled into the depression where neck met shoulder blades as if it were a seat made for her.

"Ope!" she cried when the dragon stood to her full height. The creature extended its antlers toward her, and Twyla, not needing to be told twice, took them in her hands and gripped for all she was worth.

The FICBI agents were shouting to beat all now.

"Whatever you're planning to do, Banneker, do it fast," warned Fox, one hand on the pistol crossbow in her holster.

Twyla had no earthly idea what she was doing, but she did her best to communicate her thoughts to the dragon via the sensitive fur of the creature's antlers. The dragon began to trot, then run, then gallop, gaining speed quickly across the rocky plain as Twyla's hat blew off her head.

"Oh shit!" cried Twyla. "O-o-oh shit! O-O-OH SHI-I-I-IT!"

FICBI agents dove out of the way as the dragon took flight with Twyla screaming on her back.

A profound confidence pulsed through the creature's antlers, up Twyla's arms, deep into her heart, and along with it, a certain sense of irreverent fun. Twyla suspected that if the dragon could speak, it would have hollered a Duckers-esque *Fuck yeah!*

"I don't know how to steer," Twyla shouted over the wind. "That way! Go that way! There's a good dragon!" Doing her best to not look down, she sent directions through the fuzzy, squishy antlers, and the dragon veered toward the shepherd's hut.

The shack came into view in the distance, so small and insignificant from this dizzying angle, and yet there was nothing bigger or more important in the world to her than what was going on in there at this moment.

Twyla wished she had, perhaps, come up with a more detailed plan of action. Instead, she wound up conveying a heaping portion of creative license to the dragon, who once again pulsed a raucous sense of having an excellent time through her antlers. Incoherent screaming was all Twyla could manage as her scaly mount took a nosedive straight at the hut. She closed her eyes and screamed even louder when she thought they were going to go crashing through the janky roof and crush everyone inside. Instead, her stomach swooped as the dragon flew upward once more. Twyla opened her eyes in time for her mount to wing toward the shack at an angle so sharp, she thought she might slide off, but the dragon's shoulder blade heaved upward, keeping her from plummeting to the earth. Now she could see that the dragon had torn the roof off the hut, leaving everyone inside exposed.

"Fuck yeah! Go, Twyla!" cheered Duckers, lifting his bound fists as high as he could.

The dragon turned about again and came in low, landing in a graceful run.

"Ope! Good dragon! Shit!" cried Twyla as the dragon trotted straight for the shack, rattling every bone in Twyla's body. The creature spun at the last minute and used the momentum to swipe through the flimsy walls of the shepherd's hut with her long tail, sending two sides crashing to the ground and making Twyla dizzy enough to see stars.

The diminutive yet deadly arrows of four pistol crossbows began to fly in their direction, but they bounced ineffectually off the dragon's rosy scales. Through the dragon's expressive antlers, Twyla sensed that her mom friend was now seriously pissed off.

Meep-meep-meep-meep-meep!

Twyla recognized the sound, and judging by the way both Frank and Duckers dove for cover, they recognized this particular call, too.

"Oh dear," said Hermia, rolling into a prickly ball a half second before the dragon let loose a thick stream of sparkly, slimy saliva, directing the spray at the nimkilim and her henchmen while keeping it away from Frank and Duckers. The rookie, catching on to the dragon's tactic, lunged for the nearest goon's holstered knife, held the handle between his knees, and began to saw at the rope binding his wrists.

With one last heave of slime, the dragon sent Hermia rolling across the floor toward Frank, at which point she stopped breathing glitter and started picking off the mobsters one by one. While she didn't have the sharp teeth of the battle dragons, she was big enough and strong enough to pick up a grown man in her mouth and toss him several feet to the side. Of the four mobsters in Hermia's company, two ran away in terror as soon as they could get up, one wallowed on the ground, crying in pain, and one huddled behind a flimsy chair, cowering in fear.

Twyla sighed heavily at him, wearing her best *I am so disappointed in you* face.

"What's your name, sweetie?" she asked.

"Alfie," he answered meekly.

"Alfie, you seem like a decent young man."

"I am! I swear I am! Please don't let that thing kill me!"

"It seems to me you've made a few bad choices somewhere along the way. Would you agree?"

"Yes," Alfie admitted in a watery voice.

"I know you're better than this. What would your mother say if she could see you right now?"

That pushed him over the edge. Alfie burst into tears and held up his hands in surrender.

"Dang, Banneker, that Mom Guilt is impressive," Duckers commented as he bound Alfie's hands together with the rope he'd cut away from his own wrists.

Frank managed to hoist himself onto his knees. Twyla was about to dismount to go to his aid, when Hermia uncurled herself at Frank's side and held a pistol crossbow to his temple. Gold glitter oozed over her spines, her Fair Isle sweater drooped low with the weight of dragon spit, and her glasses were fogged and sat crookedly on her button nose, and yet Twyla had never feared anyone as much as she feared this cute hedgehog who threatened Frank's life.

"Excuse me!" she squeaked. "Tell your pet to stand down, or Marshal Ellis gets it in the noodle!"

Twyla put her own hands in the air, releasing her connection to the dragon. "I thought you said you wouldn't hurt a fly."

"That was before you came in here with a nonbaby dragon and messed up my Grape Fizzy dreams!" She stomped her tiny hedgehog foot in its now sparkly gold boot for emphasis.

Frank began to cough, his head bent. And then Twyla realized he wasn't coughing at all; he was laughing. He lifted his head to gaze up at her, his good eye sparkling with amusement and mischief.

"Aw, darlin', if you sitting on that dragon is the last thing I clap my eyes on in this world before I sail the Salt Sea, I'm a lucky man."

He threw his shoulder against the nimkilim, knocking her off balance.

"Oh my goodness gracious!" cried Hermia.

The next five seconds passed incomprehensibly slowly from Twyla's perspective. Hermia pulled the trigger. The arrow blazed a two-inch trail along the top of Frank's scalp before it sailed past him. Duckers grabbed the nearest unglittered weapon he could find—the full-sized crossbow. He hoisted it to his hip, pulled the string into the nut, and took aim at the nimkilim.

Hermia made a run for it, bounding out of what remained of the hut and dashing for the cover of some nearby trees.

"Don't kill her!" Twyla shouted at Duckers, forgetting that the nimkilim were immortal.

"I got this," said Duckers. He pulled the trigger, sending the bolt into Hermia's mail satchel.

"Oh my goodness gracious sakes!" said Hermia as the force of the bolt carried her satchel—and her along with it—to the nearest tree. The arrowhead sank into the wood, leaving the mailbag and the hedgehog dangling several feet off the ground. Letters poured out of the bag, followed by the purple stream of an opened bottle of Lulu's Grape Fizzy.

"Shit, I messed up the mail," said Duckers.

"As if she was going to deliver those letters to the right place without setting them on fire or feeding them to a llama by accident," said Frank before slumping against one of the remaining walls.

"Frank!" Twyla nearly slid off the dragon's back before realizing that she could not simply slide off without tumbling to her doom. Duckers moved toward Frank, but Twyla told him, "No. I'll take care of him. You make sure that twerpy hedgehog doesn't go anywhere."

"That wasn't a very nice thing to say," commented Hermia as she swung from the satchel strap.

The dragon leaned its antlers toward Twyla again. Twyla grasped them and begged her pink companion to help her dismount. This involved sliding down the creature's neck, an act that Duckers no doubt would have found to be a lark but that proved to be fairly awkward and undignified for a fifty-three-year-old woman. Eventually, her feet hit the blessed earth, and she stumbled to Frank on unsteady feet. As soon as she had cut him free, she cupped his cheek with her hand to get a good look at his face.

He put his hand over hers. "I'm sorry to get you mixed up in this mess."

"Shut up, you dolt! You're alive!"

She threw her arms around him and hugged him, making him grunt in pain.

"Ope, sorry!" She let go of him to study his battered face.

"I'm all right."

"You don't look all right."

The scuffle of boots on the rocky terrain announced the arrival of Alma Maguire, a team of armed marshals, and Dr. Quill Vanderlinden panting closely behind.

"The area's secure, Chief," called Duckers as the marshals fanned out, a couple covering the fallen mobsters, a couple helping Duckers keep an eye on the nimkilim, and a couple more eyeing the dragon warily.

"She won't hurt you," Twyla assured the latter two, but they didn't look convinced.

Maguire walked toward the hut, unable to mask her growing bewilderment as she took in the scene.

"What in the Salt Sea happened here? And why is Hermia dangling from a tree?"

Duckers jerked his thumb at the hedgehog. "Turns out she's the bad guy."

"What?"

"Hermia was the go-between in the illegal mining operation," explained Twyla. "She was working with Herd to smuggle iuvenicite out of Tanria in her magical mailbag. The mob paid her in grape soda, and when the FICBI took down the crime ring, she hit up another mob family to see if they'd give her more grape soda if she could deliver an actual dragon instead."

"And I would have gotten away with it if it hadn't been for you meddling marshals and that pesky dragon," cried Hermia from the tree.

Maguire pinched the bridge of her nose. "Ellis, are you okay?"

"Yeah."

"No," Twyla answered for him. "Permission to get him to the infirmary, Chief?"

"Granted."

"We'll have to borrow a couple of equimares."

"How did you get here so fast without an equimaris?"

Twyla glanced at the dragon.

Maguire pinched the bridge of her nose harder. "There is not enough aspirin in the world for this. Go. Both of you. On *equimaris*back."

A loud gurgle came from over the ridge, followed by the equimaris who had made it, a hulk of a stallion, clambering his way into the crime scene. The beast shook out his seaweed mane and slapped one of his front feet on the ground as if to say, *I can't believe you assholes left me out of this.*

"Guess I'll take Saltlicker," said Frank. Judging by the shape he was in, he was going to need help getting into the saddle.

Quill sat on a nearby boulder and mopped his sweating face with his dapper pocket square. "Thank gods it's over. Tweed is not the ideal fabric to be wearing in these rugged environs."

"Short-shorts are way better," agreed Duckers.

Suddenly, the crossbow bolt pinning the nimkilim's satchel to the tree pulled free of the trunk.

"Oopsie-doozles!" cried Hermia as she splatted into the puddle of mail and Lulu's Grape Fizzy below.

Chapter Twenty-Three

There was no one on duty at the infirmary.

"How can no one be on duty at the infirmary?" an outraged Twyla demanded of any god who happened to be listening, but Fern at the weapons counter down the hall overheard her.

"Hiring freeze," she hollered.

"And Maguire can't get permission to fill the opening, and there aren't enough doctors on staff to cover all the hours, and we'll have to go to the hospital in Herington or wait until tomorrow morning. Yeah, yeah," Twyla finished for her.

Fern sucked her teeth so hard, Twyla could hear it from the infirmary door. "Then why are you asking me?"

"I'm fine," Frank told Twyla.

She went on tiptoe to examine the top of his head, where Hermia's pistol crossbow arrow had cut a shallow groove through his hair. "You're bleeding."

"I *was* bleeding. Now I'm not."

"Get in the infirmary, Ellis." She opened the door and gestured for him to go inside.

"Well now, I know I'm in trouble when you start throwing around the surname." He went into the infirmary and obediently sat on the exam table.

"We need to stop almost dying on each other," Twyla said as she plundered the cabinets for bandages and iodine. "Shirt off."

"Agreed, and why?"

She wet a clean towel at the sink. "Why do we need to stop almost dying on each other? Isn't that what they call a rhetorical question?"

"No, I mean, why do I need to take my shirt off?"

Twyla set the damp cloth beside him on the table and put her fists on her hips. "You're going to be shy about this now?"

He hesitated. Given the fact that they had made love the night before and argued this morning, she couldn't blame him. She wondered if this was how Frank had felt when their positions were reversed, when she was the one sitting on the exam table, feeling vulnerable, while he was the one who simply wanted to make sure she was all right.

She softened. "I watched that goon punch you in the stomach, and I don't know what they did to you before I got there."

He sighed his reluctance, but he took off his shirt. She made quick work of checking him for broken ribs and peering at the bruise on his stomach. There was nothing sexy about it, but there was intimacy in her touch. There was tenderness.

"They mostly got my face," Frank said, his voice hushed in the already quiet room.

"They're lucky I didn't get *their* faces."

That earned Twyla a gruff laugh. She motioned for him to put his shirt on, and she set about washing away the blood and dirt from his face and hands.

"At least this comes off more easily than dragon spit."

"I guess, but I prefer dragon spit over getting the shit kicked out of me."

"That makes two of us."

Twyla tossed the towel into the laundry hamper and fetched an ice pack from the icebox. She gently pressed the cold compress to the left side of his face. "Hold this so I can have a look at the cut on your head."

"What do you think? Does it add to my air of mystery and danger?" he asked while Twyla doused a cotton swab in iodine.

"Definitely, although you might want to part your hair on the other side of your head for a few weeks. Hold still."

She dabbed at the cut with the swab, making Frank hiss.

"Sorry," said Twyla.

"No worries."

She worked carefully, doing her best to clean the wound without causing Frank any more pain than was necessary. It brought her comfort to take care of him, especially since she had felt so powerless to do much of anything when she'd seen him bound up and beaten in that shepherd's hut. Now that he was safe, the two of them could figure out what being Twyla and Frank should look like moving forward. Because they were still Twyla and Frank, Frank and Twyla, two people who were meant to be together, one way or another. If she could ride a dragon, she could work things out with her best friend.

Whom she was also in love with.

And who might be in love with her.

She was tossing the swab into the garbage can when Frank started laughing, and he laughed harder when she gave him a quizzical look.

"What?"

"I can't believe you flew to the rescue on a dragon," he wheezed. "Twyla Banneker: the God of Justice."

"More like Twyla Banneker: the Human Trying Not to Lose the Doughnut and Chocolate Malt Balls She Had for Breakfast."

"Gods, you're a gem." He wiped away tears of hilarity with the back of his hand and gazed at her with shining eyes. "Thank you for saving me, darlin'."

"Of course. That's what we do for each other." She put a sterile pad on the cut and wound gauze around his head to hold it in place. "You might need a few stitches up here. Come on. I'll take you to the hospital."

Frank grunted.

"You're retired. What else do you have going on?"

"About that..." He set aside the ice pack and took her hand, the one that wasn't holding a roll of gauze.

Twyla blushed. "It's all right."

"It isn't all right. I should have told you about the retirement thing. I shouldn't have put in for retirement in the first place."

"Why did you?"

"Because..." He licked his lips, wincing as his tongue swiped the cut on the left side of his mouth. "I need to get something off my chest, and I'd appreciate it if you let me get through it before you say anything, okay?"

"Okay." She squeezed his hand to let him know she wasn't going anywhere.

"Here's the thing: I love you. I mean, I'm in love with you, not just in the friend way, but in the gooey, romantic, soulmate way. Fuck, I said that out loud."

He let go of her to grip the edge of the exam table, while Twyla's heart ballooned in her rib cage.

"Frank, I—"

He held up a hand. "I'm not done yet."

"But—"

"Twy."

She clamped her lips shut, even though she badly wanted to tell him how she felt.

His shoulders relaxed, as if a heavy weight had been taken off them. "I love you. I love you, body and soul. I've loved you for years, but I knew—or I thought I knew—that I couldn't compete with a man who died thirteen years ago. And you know what? I was fine with it. I had already messed up my own marriage; I wasn't going to risk what we had—what we *have*—for the slim possibility of something more. Because what we have is good, better than good. I kept my mouth shut, because I had you in my life, and I had you in my future, and that was enough for me. But then you started dating that continental toff in short-shorts and knee socks, and I realized, oh, wait, it isn't that you don't want *anyone*; it's that you don't want *me*."

"Frank—"

"Let me finish. Please."

Twyla's entire body protested, but she kept her mouth shut.

"The night of the wedding when we... You said it was a mistake. And if that's what you thought, then that's what it was, no matter how much I wanted it to be otherwise. Well, I can't stick around to be your mistake, Twyla. Maybe this Quill fella isn't the one for you, but eventually, a good man will come along who is, and I can't watch you falling for someone else. So I went to Maguire that night and told her I was done with the marshals, which I should not have done, not under those circumstances. And I should have told you that I put in for retirement immediately thereafter. I owed you that much. So, yeah. I'm sorry."

"Apology unnecessary but accepted. Can I talk now?"

"Hold on."

Twyla clawed the air with frustration.

"Please?"

If the man ever let her speak, she might end up screaming instead of saying *I love you*. She nodded and gestured for him to continue.

"This morning, I got up before you, because I knew that you'd be upset to wake up in my arms, and I couldn't stand the sight of your regret. But I need you to know that as far as I'm concerned, making love to you could never be a mistake. I'm not sorry, and I don't regret it."

Twyla slapped her hands together, as if in prayer. "Can I please, for the love of the Mother of Sorrows, say something?"

"Yes. No. Wait, can I say one more thing?"

"Ugh!"

"You've never been a chair to me, and you never will be."

All of Twyla's impatience melted away, and she clutched the roll of gauze affectionately. "That's the most romantic thing anyone has ever said to me."

"Well now, that's a sad statement."

"Can I talk now?"

Frank blew out a long breath and nodded.

Twyla kissed him, a soft, sweet kiss on the unhurt corner of his mouth, followed by another and another. His hands came up to hold her face, and she loved that he touched her face when he kissed her. He flinched in pain when she accidentally hit a sore spot, despite her best efforts. She pulled away and stroked his cheek.

"If that's your idea of talking, you can talk to me anytime it strikes your fancy," said Frank.

"Here's my idea of talking." Twyla pressed her hand over his heart. "You are not my mistake. You're the best friend I've ever had or will ever have, and I love you, not just in the friend way, but in the gooey, romantic, soulmate way. I'm sorry it took me so long to figure out what I wanted. It turns out that what I've wanted all along is you."

"Apology unnecessary but accepted." He put his hand over hers and leaned in until their foreheads touched, and Twyla let herself bask in the wonderful newness of what they had become together and what they would be for years to come, if Grandfather Bones and the Warden and the Salt Sea saw fit to leave them on earth for a while longer.

"I've got an idea," said Frank. He slid off the exam table and patted the surface. "You sit here."

"Why?"

"Trust me."

Twyla trusted him, so she sat on the exam table…and watched in dismay as he got down on one knee with a middle-aged grunt.

"What are you doing?"

"Twyla Banneker," he began, taking her hands in his.

"Get up!"

"Will you promise to *never* marry me?"

It took a couple of seconds for the words to sink in, but when they did, Twyla snorted with amusement, the least romantic sound she had ever made in her life.

Frank continued his proposal with an ornery grin on his face, made more wolfish by his purpling eye and swollen lips. "Will you live next door to me and spend time with me when you feel like it and go home when you need to have your own space? Will you let me love you however you see fit for the rest of our lives?"

"Just when I thought I could not possibly love you more." Twyla's smile threatened to split her face in two. "Yes, Frank Ellis, I promise to *never* marry you."

He got to his feet with an "Oof" and kissed her, far less gently than she had kissed him.

"Doesn't that hurt?" she asked against his lips.

"I'd say the benefits outweigh the disadvantages here, darlin'."

"I love it when you call me *darlin'*."

"That's good, because you're going to hear it for as long as I have breath in my body."

She pressed her ear to his chest. "Say it again."

"Darlin'," he drawled, drawing out the word long and low for her so that she could hear it deep inside his chest, right where he kept his heart.

Epilogue

Hi, and welcome to the Federated Islands Park Service's official tour of the Tanrian Dragon Preserve. My name is Lu."

Lu Ellis tapped the shiny silver name badge on his emerald-green uniform shirt and cocked a devastating smile at the tour group. With his slender build and high cheekbones and mane of black corkscrew curls, Lu took after his mother, physically speaking, but his love of the spotlight was all his own, something he put to good use at his job. His folksy tenor, full of authentic Bushong twang, typically won over the tourists within the first five seconds of his spiel, but it didn't hurt that half of today's crowd claimed Banneker as a last name.

"Folks, before we get started today, let me introduce you to some important people. This here is our driver, Annie, also known as my sister. Say hi, Annie."

Annie Ellis gave the crowd a friendly wave from her seat on the driver's box at the front of the coach. Like her brother, she had inherited Cora's cool brown complexion and fine-boned frame, but the features of her face came from Frank, especially the hound dog eyes. Her parents used to joke that she was Frank and Cora's Greatest Hits, and it held true.

"It's a bumpy ride, so hang on to your hats. Here we go!" announced Lu, and Annie gave the reins a shake. The coach lurched into motion as the team of equimares began the ride to the Dragon's Teeth range. Lu kept talking without missing a beat.

"Also joining us today is Twyla Banneker, former Tanrian Marshal and cofounder of the Tanrian Dragon Preserve here at Tanria National Park. Everyone say, 'Hello, Twyla!'"

A significant portion of the tour group said, "Hello, Wammy!"

"How am I doing so far, boss?" Lu called to her where she sat at the back of the coach with her oldest son, DJ, and his family.

Twyla gave him a thumbs-up.

DJ leaned in and whispered, "I can't believe that's Lu Ellis. He was a pimply kid the last time I saw him."

DJ's own son Travis shushed him so that he could listen to Lu with rapt attention. As the coach rolled along, Lu went into the history of Tanria, the invention of the portals, and the evolving role of the Tanrian Marshals, especially now that the Assembly of the Federated Islands of Cadmus had conferred national park status on Tanria—thanks to Frank's proposal.

Twyla only half listened, partly because she'd heard it all before, and partly because, for the first time in years, she was surrounded by her entire family—her kids and her grandkids and her soon-to-be son-in-law—and she didn't want to miss one single precious second of it.

From time to time, Hope jokingly heckled the tour guide, but since she and Lu had known each other from the cradle, Lu happily gave as good as he got.

"Hey, let's give a round of applause to our special guests, Dr. Hope Banneker and Dr. Everett Simms, who are getting married in three days!" said Lu, gesturing to the happy couple and leading the tour group in raucous clapping and hooting and whistling. Hope joined in while Everett grinned in pleased embarrassment.

The coach rumbled along under the steady hand of Annie Ellis, who loved equimares as much as her dad did, and all the while, Lu chatted about flora and fauna and points of interest.

Eventually, they rolled to a stop outside the Vanderlinden Center for Dracological Research, newly built through the generous donation of Dr. Quill Vanderlinden. His book, *Dragons: A Dracologist's Journey into the Heart of Tanria*, was a runaway bestseller, and a percentage of the proceeds went to fund the preserve.

"As you can see, the structure is new, but because New Gods technology doesn't work inside the Mist, all materials and methods used to construct the building were the same as those used during the Old Gods era. The same is true of the marshals' barracks in each of the fifty-four sectors of Tanria."

Except for Sector 28, Twyla thought but decided not to open up that can of worms.

"Hop on out, folks. We have some dragons to visit."

Annie saw to the equimares while Lu ushered the tour group into the Vanderlinden Center and brought the educational displays to the tourists' attention.

"You do plan to have dragons on your dragon tour, right?" asked Wade as Lu finished up a talk about iuvenicite. Anita smacked him on the shoulder, but he ignored the reprimand and encouraged his children—even Teo, who talked nonstop these days—to join him in chanting, "Dragons! Dragons! Dragons!"

DJ joined in, and so did his sons, Travis and Harry.

"Not you, too," reprimanded Twyla. DJ shrugged and continued to chant.

"What's this?" asked Lu, completely game. "You want to see some what?"

"Dragons! Dragons! Dragons!"

Lu put a hand to his ear. "I can't hear you."

"DRAGONS! DRAGONS! DRAGONS!"

"Wade, DJ," said Twyla. "You're turning your own children feral."

"Aw, we're only having fun, Mom," said Wade.

"The kids are practically frothing at the mouth. Tone it down."

"He's honestly the worst behaved out of all of them," Anita murmured to Twyla.

"Don't I know it. I can't believe you married him."

"I blame you. He's your fault."

"Wait until Sal is thirty-four, then come talk to me."

Lu led them out of the Vanderlinden Center to the enormous observation deck that looked out over the lake, with the male-identifying Bannekers at the front of the pack, the non-Bannekers giving them a wide berth, and the female-identifying Bannekers and Everett Simms trailing behind in a feeble attempt to pretend like they didn't know DJ, Wade, Travis, Harry, Manny, Sal, or Teo.

Actually, Twyla might own up to Teo. He was only four. There was hope for him yet.

Ahead of her, Twyla could hear the sounds of wonder as her family and the other tourists caught a glimpse of the dragons on the lake, many of them for the first time in their lives.

"Holy shit," uttered DJ in awe as the rest of the Bannekers caught up to him.

"Language!" Twyla scolded him in unison with DJ's wife, Cecily.

"There are pink dragons swimming around! What else am I supposed to say?"

Twyla thought of her colorful language when she had flown atop Eloise (the name she had given her dragon pal) to rescue Frank, and she decided to let it slide.

They spent some time on the upper deck, with Lu fielding questions, before he led them down a ramp to the north shore of the lake, where Frank awaited the tour with an enormous Mary Georgina sitting patiently beside him.

The sight of a full-grown pink dragon up close elicited a wide variety of responses, as it always did, from Harry sliding behind his father while trying to appear as if he weren't terrified, to Anita restraining Sal so he wouldn't mount up and fly off.

"Folks! Folks! No need to be alarmed! Mary Georgina is perfectly harmless. As a matter of fact, she was raised by humans, because she imprinted on a human when she hatched. She's managed to integrate herself with the dragon enclave, but she prefers to spend her time with people. For that reason, we keep clear of the dragons' nesting site to make sure the babies imprint on their parents, not on Frank Ellis. Speaking of Frank Ellis, here he is in the flesh, our other cofounder of the Tanrian Dragon Preserve. Hi, Dad!"

Frank beamed at him. Frank had not stopped beaming at Lu and Annie since the day they returned to Eternity and decided to stick around to work at the dragon preserve alongside him. Twyla never tired of seeing that particular smile on his face.

"Hi, folks," he said, his deep voice carrying even outdoors. "We're glad you're here today. Your support helps us keep the Tanrian dragons in their natural habitat."

He went through his portion of the tour, with Mary Georgina helping him demonstrate how dragons swam, ate, and flew. Eloise paddled by on the lake and shook out her fuzzy antlers when she saw Twyla. She always said hello in her own way when Twyla was around.

Eventually, the tour wrapped up, with the tourists invited to pet Mary Georgina if they wanted to before they left.

Twyla hugged her family goodbye, even though she'd see them plenty over the next several days, and watched them leave with Lu and Annie. She stayed behind to help Frank close up public access to the preserve for the day.

An hour later, in the parking lot of the West Station, Frank unlocked the passenger door of his autoduck, but before Twyla could take a seat, he reached inside, produced a small gift bag, and handed it to her.

"What's this?"

"Open it."

"You don't have to give me anything."

"I know I don't have to give you anything. I wanted to give you something."

"Oh, Frankie," she said, and she gave him a grateful peck on the cheek. It was sappy, but she couldn't help herself. Then she dug into the tissue paper with gusto.

"Well now, don't get too excited. It's nothing special."

"I'll be the judge of that." Twyla reached into the bag and pulled out a set of white linen handkerchiefs embroidered with violets, similar to the hankie a wise woman had given her at the altar of Grandmother Wisdom, the one she kept in her safe-deposit box at the bank, beside Frank's birth key.

"I thought you might need them at the wedding," Frank told her. "But don't you worry. I have all mine washed and ready to go, just in case."

Twyla was afraid she'd start crying on the spot if she so much as spoke a word, so she kissed him instead. And the kiss was so delectable that she deepened it, then deepened it more, until she realized that they were getting a little too hot and heavy for the parking lot of the West Station.

"I like the way you say thank you," Frank rumbled, low and sexy, making her wish they were already at his house rather than a twenty-minute drive away.

A familiar red muscle duck with white racing stripes came roaring into the gravel lot and parked beside them.

"That is the most ridiculous vehicle on the island of Bushong," said Twyla.

"I would have loved the shit out of that thing when I was his age," said Frank with a twinge of wistful jealousy.

Penrose Duckers rolled down the window and shouted, "Get a room!"

"Aw, young love," his partner chimed in from the passenger end of the bench. From anyone else, it would have sounded sarcastic.

From Rosie Fox, who was older than Twyla and Frank combined, it was sincere.

"See you at the wedding?" Twyla asked them as they got out of the shiny red duck.

"Only if Mary Georgina's invited," said Duckers.

"Smartass."

Duckers gave her a side hug. "You love me."

"Sadly, yes, I do. See you Wardensday?"

"I love a wedding, especially when I'm not in it," said Rosie.

"Fuck yeah," Duckers agreed, and the pair headed into the station to report for duty.

"I'm beat," said Frank, nudging Twyla toward his duck. "Let's go home, by which I mean my house, because DJ and his family and Hope have taken over yours."

"You know, I'm aware that you're never going to pressure me to move in with you. You don't have to reassure me," said Twyla once they were on the road.

"It is one of the many ways I express my love."

"Is that so? How else do you plan to express your love today?"

"I thought I might mow your lawn for you."

"Mm-hmm, go on."

"And maybe I'll do a load of laundry," he drawled suggestively. "Yours and mine. Together."

She fanned herself with a new hankie. "I love it when you talk chores to me."

"You know, darlin', you waving that handkerchief around puts me in mind of a song."

"Oh boy."

"*Honey, I gave you a token of my love,*" he sang, going deep down the bass register on the word *love*. "Come on, Twy, you know the words."

Twyla did know the words, and she sang them with Frank as they drove home to Eternity.

Acknowledgments

Thank you to Priyanka Krishnan, Nadia Saward, and Angelica Chong—editors extraordinaire—and to everyone at Orbit on both sides of the Atlantic, including but not limited to Tiana Coven, Natassja Haught, Tim Holman, Angela Man, Bryn A. McDonald, Lisa Marie Pompilio, Serena Savini, and Ellen Wright. Thanks also to copy editor Janice Lee for saving me from public humiliation.

All hail my excellent agent, Holly Root, and thank you to everyone at Root Literary for your enthusiasm and support.

Thank you to Tanaz Bhathena, Jenny Mendez, and Kathee Goldsich for your friendship and your feedback. And there is not enough gratitude in the world for my Nebulous Dread Cloud compatriots, Amanda Sellet and Miranda Asebedo—I don't know what I'd do without you.

Thank you to Dr. Rafe M. Brown and Dr. Richard E. Glor of the University of Kansas Biodiversity Institute for humoring me. I think we can safely file this under "Emails You Never Imagined That You Would Receive When You Decided to Pursue a Scholarly Career in Herpetology."

Thank you to my friends and family who have cheered me on every step of the way, especially my parents, to whom I have lovingly dedicated this book. Twyla and Frank may not have gotten the whole marriage thing right the first time around, but Alan and Mary Kay Dillingham have been excelling at marital bliss for fifty-seven years and counting, for which I am deeply grateful.

Speaking of marital bliss, an extra special thanks goes to my husband, Mike, for being significantly un-Doug-like. Love you, hot stuff. And to my beloved children, Hank and Gus: Don't you ever turn anyone into a chair. Also, I love you.

Finally, to the truly delightful young person I met at the Raven Book Store in Lawrence, Kansas, on November 26, 2022: You asked me to write a book about a penguin dude named Mary Georgina. I had such a wonderful time chatting with you that I decided to name a character in this novel Mary Georgina in your honor. I'm afraid that my Mary Georgina is a baby dragon rather than a penguin dude, but I'm still holding out hope that you will one day write down the adventures of your own Mary Georgina.

extras

orbit

meet the author

Brian Paulette

MEGAN BANNEN is a former public librarian and an award-winning author of speculative fiction. Her work has been selected for the RUSA Reading List, the Indies Introduce list, and the Kids' Indie Next List, along with numerous best-of-the-year compilations. While most of her professional career has been spent behind a reference desk, she has also sold luggage, written grants, collected a few graduate degrees from various Kansas universities, and taught English at home and abroad. She lives in the Kansas City area with her family and more pets than is reasonable.

Find out more about Megan Bannen and other Orbit authors by registering for the free monthly newsletter at orbitbooks.net.

if you enjoyed
THE UNDERMINING OF TWYLA AND FRANK

look out for

THAT TIME I GOT DRUNK AND SAVED A DEMON

Mead Mishaps: Book 1

by

Kimberly Lemming

Spice trader Cinnamon's quiet life is turned upside down when she ends up on a quest with a fiery demon, in this irreverently quirky rom-com fantasy that is sweet, steamy, and funny as hell.

All she wanted to do was live her life in peace—maybe get a cat, expand the family spice farm. Really, anything that didn't involve going on an adventure where an orc might rip her face off. But they say the goddess has favorites, and if so, Cin is clearly not one of them.

After Cin, in a wine-drunk stupor, saves the demon Fallon, he reveals that all he really wants to do is kill an evil witch enslaving his people. And who can blame him? But now he's dragging Cinnamon along for the ride whether she likes it or not. On the bright side, at least he keeps burning off his shirt....

Chapter 1

I had only two things on my mind: cheese and how to get home. All around me, people danced and sang to the drunken groove of the village baker laying his soul down on his trusty lute while his wife backed him up with her flute. Drums beat to the rhythm of stomping feet as the village came alive with the Hero's Call festival.

It had been a long time since the goddess Myva called upon one of us lowly humans to join the never-ending battle against the monsters trapped behind Volsog gate. As if by some evil clockwork, the gate would weaken every fifteen years. Every manner of myths and monsters would flood through its passage and wreak havoc from our glittering coasts to the deep harsh mountains of the North, where only the maddest of men lived.

None of that, however, was why we were celebrating. No. The reason for our village-wide riot was the fact that we would finally be rid of the uppity brat that was chosen. Priscilla was a fine girl, if a little full of herself. Until her face appeared in the sacred chalice during the Great Calling. Each time Volsog gate opened, the goddess will shine a light into each of her four temples to call forth her chosen heroes to fight back the demons and close the gate once more. A high honor, to be sure. But everyone loved to conveniently ignore the minor issue of our heroes not always coming back.

It was an honor that I had NO desire to be a part of. I was fine with letting Priscilla and those other fools go off and die. *I'll stick to selling my spices, thank you very much.*

My self-preserving habits made me a bit of an outlier with the other girls in town. "Who wouldn't want to go off on a grand adventure with a bunch of hot heroes also chosen by the goddess?"

Me, bitches. No, thank you.

Biceps were nice, but so was not having my guts eaten by an orc.

Nevertheless, the promise of finding love with a handsome hero from another village was more than enough incentive to get many women praying for the day they'd be chosen as Myva's "lucky" winner. Maybe we all just grew up reading too many fairy tales.

Priscilla was one of them. Soon after the chipper blond was presented with her new role, no one could hear the end of her bragging until it was time to kick her ass out of the village, sword in hand.

Bye.

The image brought a sting of the memory of my ex leaving town for similar reasons. My lack of desire to be eaten by orcs was a turnoff, and the bastard needed a more adventurous woman. Weeks of crying later, a dear friend came over to slap me out of my sad-girl routine to remind me that "he ain't shit."

Who needs him? Or any man! Love is for people with not enough wine in their hands!

extras

With an equilibrium entirely hampered by my love of wine, I stumbled out of the dancing crowd into the food stalls in my daring quest for more cheese. My trusted nose locked on to the smell of aged cheddar and the race was on. With a mighty step over a passed-out blacksmith, followed by a not so graceful stumble past empty wine bottles, I found myself at the glorious cheese stall owned by my best friend and cheesemaker, Brie. Brilliant name for a cheesemaker, I know. Her mother thought herself wildly clever for that one.

"Brie!" I hollered over the music, slumping my body over the counter. "Brie, my goddess of cheese! Bring me that sweet, sweet Gouda!"

The tarp leading to the back room of the stall opened, revealing my amused friend. Her light pink hair flitted loosely past her shoulders as she stuck her hands on her hips. Her pink locks sent my mind into a stupor until I realized we had agreed to dye our hair pink that morning.

"Cinnamon Hotpepper, you are drunk as a skunk!"

OK, so maybe my mom thought she was terribly clever with names as well.

"Pfft, you look like you dunked your head in a pile of snap-dragon," I laughed, eyeing her hair.

She wiped her hands on her apron and fixed me with a glare. "Says the woman who came up with this brilliant idea. What was it you said, O wise one? 'Let's dye our hair pink now that the goddess finally chose her sacrificial lamb.'"

"I may have said something along those lines." I mean, it was true. Brie grabbed one of my pink braids and flipped it out of my face to emphasize her point. "You can't say it didn't work, though. Neither of us was chosen; now we can party!" My friend had always been the logical sort who shared my disinterest in danger and death. We dressed in plain clothing and tried not to stand out in the village to avoid being picked.

It was common knowledge that Myva loved her pretty things. The heroes' party was always made up of two men and two women. Each one was always some beautiful flamboyant nut, not necessarily the best for the job. Sometimes I wondered if Myva just picked them to be entertained. But hey, I'm no goddess, so what do I know?

"Enough with that sour face. Gimme some cheddar to go with this wine and come drink with me!" Far too impatient to mind manners, I grabbed a slice of cheddar and bit a sizable chunk. Its sharp taste danced across my tongue in time with the baker's lute as I took a swig from my wine glass to help wash it down.

"Cin, my sweet girl, that was a whole-ass mood and not in a good way." She shook her head at me disapprovingly and snatched the glass from my hand. "You're done, hun."

"Lies! I have not yet begun to drink!"

"From the looks of it, you began to drink about four glasses ago. Go home, Cin. I won't be done manning the stall for a few more hours anyway. But tomorrow, it's my brother's turn. If you manage to survive the blinding hangover you're going to have in the morning, then I promise we can make a mess of ourselves for the last day of the festival." My stalwart companion paused her motherly ribbing to package up a few slices of Gouda before handing it to a customer to my side.

"You pr-promise?" I hiccuped.

"I swear on the temple itself. So go home for tonight and sleep it off." Her heart-shaped face turned severe and her coal eyes danced with delight. "For tomorrow, we have two things to celebrate. Freedom from the choosing... and freedom from Priscilla's constant... Priscillaness."

A mug slammed on the table, making us both jump. "Hell, I'll drink to that!" The source of our fright was the blacksmith, John. He was undoubtedly another victim to the princess of self-importance, as he had been tasked with making a suitable weapon for her journey. "If I ever get another request for a periwinkle sword that 'can't be too heavy, but not too frilly' again, I will retire on the spot!" he hollered.

Maybe John had it a little worse than the rest of us.

I gave the older man a pat on the back. "But what a beautiful blade it was! I'm sure it will get our heroine to Goldcrest City without fail."

John smiled and nodded his head in pride. "It is a fine blade if I do say so myself. It took me two entire months to make it." The blacksmith was a gruff fellow but never passed up the chance to talk about his creations.

As much of a pain as our little heroine could be, all of us still wanted her home at the end of her journey. Maybe with a handsome hero in tow. Picturing her getting the fairy-tale ending she always wanted was easier than thinking about her not coming home at all. The chosen heroes had never failed in their quest before. In the end, most of the crazed demons had been killed off or pushed back behind the gate. But I couldn't help but wonder: if the goddess was powerful enough to banish all demons when she first came to this land, why did she need heroes to repeat the action every fifteen years?

Suddenly, an enormous boom shook the earth, knocking us off our feet. Near my family's farm, a gigantic dust cloud plumed in the air off toward the East. The crowd fell silent, aside from a few startled screams. "What in the three hells was that?" John slurred. I scrambled back on my feet, looking around wildly.

"Is everyone OK?" I yelled.

"I'm g-good," Brie stammered.

All around me, villagers looked around worriedly as they dusted themselves off. The baker's booming laugh cut through the thick silence as he helped his wife back on her feet.

"What's all this worry?" he began. With a pat on his lute, he began playing once more. "Can't you lot see? It's our mighty heroine doing her damned duty already! Kill all those damn demons, I say! By the time that firecracker gets to the castle, there won't be any left for the other heroes!"

"Yeah, that must be it. Give 'em the wrath of our goddess, Priscilla!" another man roared, eager to push the thought of terror away. Soon the crowd erupted in cheers of affirmation as the dust settled. All sense of danger dissipated as the other musicians resumed their playing.

Brie looked at me with a worried expression. "I sure hope that's all it was. The smoke cloud looked close to your farm. Is your harvest going to be alright?"

I waved her off with a grin. "Don't you worry about us. We've already brought in most of the fall harvest. If it hit the fields, there's not much left."

"That's good to hear," she said with a sigh. "Still. I think you should head home. You're still looking a bit too sloshed for your own good."

"Yes, mother," I teased, bidding my companions farewell with one last bite of cheese, and heading out of the festival toward home. I grabbed one of the backup torches at the festival entrance and lit it. It was way too dark to travel home by moonlight.

Thankfully, my family's farm was close enough to the village that I could stumble my way back with enough booze in my system to kill a moose.

I know; I've done it a dozen times or so.

Food stalls and lantern lights gave way to winding trees and glittering night stars. The spirited music died off in the distance. A bit creepy, honestly. All I could hear were my footsteps crunching the leaves beneath my feet and the crackle of fire from the torch. It was so quiet I could hear myself think. Which is not ideal. Thinking leads to worrying and worrying leads to—

"WHAT THE GINGER WAS THAT SOUND?!"

I whipped around to see a squirrel darting up in a tree. The little critter stopped to eye me for a moment before skittering up into the trees above. "Oh. Of course, it was just a squirrel. What else would it be?" The all-encompassing crunch of the leaves resumed as I swallowed my paranoia and kept going. My home was only a two-mile walk. The blast from earlier probably just fried my nerves a bit.

As if on cue, some twat in a black tartan and a matching scarf to cover his face jumped out before me.

Clearly, the gods had favorites, and I wasn't one of them.

if you enjoyed
THE UNDERMINING OF TWYLA AND FRANK

look out for

THE HEXOLOGISTS

by

Josiah Bancroft

The first book in a wildly inventive and mesmerizing new fantasy series from acclaimed author Josiah Bancroft, where magical mysteries abound and only one team can solve them: the Hexologists.

The Hexologists, Isolde and Warren Wilby, are quite accustomed to helping desperate clients with the bugbears of city life. Aided by hexes and a bag of charmed relics, the Wilbies are well acquainted with the weird, and they never shy away from a challenging case.

393

But when they are approached by the royal secretary and told the king pleads to be baked into a cake—going so far as to wedge himself inside a lit oven—the Wilbies soon find themselves embroiled in a mystery that could very well see the nation turned on its head. Their effort to expose a royal secret buried under forty years of lies brings them nose-to-nose with a violent anti-royalist gang, avaricious ghouls, alchemists who draw their power from a hell-like dimension, and a bookish dragon who only occasionally eats people.

Armed with a love toughened by adversity and a stick of chalk that can conjure light from the darkness, Iz and Warren Wilby are ready for a case that will test every spell, skill, and odd magical artifact in their considerable bag of tricks.

1

THE KING IN THE CAKE

The king wishes to be cooked alive," the royal secretary said, accepting the proffered saucer and cup and immediately setting both aside. At his back, the freshly stoked fire added a touch of theater to his announcement, though neither seemed to suit what, until recently, had been a pleasant Sunday morning.

"Does he?" Isolde Wilby gazed at the royal secretary with all the warmth of a hypnotist.

"Um, yes. He's quite insistent." The questionable impression of the royal secretary's negligible chin and cumbersome nose was considerably improved by his well-tailored suit, fastidiously combed hair, and blond mustache, waxed into upturned barbs. Those modest whiskers struck Isolde as a dubious effort to impart gravity to a youthful face. Though Mr. Horace Alman seemed a man of perfect manners, he sat with his hat capping his knee. "More precisely, the king wishes to be baked into a cake."

Looming at the tea cart like a bear over a blackberry bush, Mr. Warren Wilby quietly swapped the plate of cakes with a dish of watercress sandwiches. "Care for a nibble, sir?"

"No. No, thank you," Mr. Alman murmured, flummoxed by the offer. The secretary watched as Mr. Wilby positioned a triangle of white bread under his copious mustache, then vanished it like a letter into a mail slot.

The Wilbies' parlor was unabashedly old-fashioned. While their neighbors pursued the bare walls, voluptuous lines, and skeletal furniture that defined contemporary tastes, the Wilbies' townhouse decor fell somewhere between a gallery of oddities and a country bed-and-breakfast. Every rug was ancient, every doily yellow, every table surface adorned by some curio or relic. The picture frames that crowded the walls were full of adventuresome scenes of tall ships, dogsleds, and eroded pyramids. The style of their furniture was as motley as a rummage sale and similarly haggard. But as antiquated as the room's contents were, the environment was remarkably clean. Warren Wilby could abide clutter, but never filth.

Isolde recrossed her legs and bounced the topmost with a metronome's precision. She hadn't had time to comb her hair since rising, or rather, she had had the time but not the will during her morning reading hours, which the king's secretary had so brazenly interrupted, necessitating the swapping of her silk robe for breeches and a blouse. Wearing a belt and shoes seemed an absolute waste of a Sunday morning.

extras

Isolde Wilby was often described as *imposing*, not because she possessed a looming stature or a ringing voice, but because she had a way of imposing her will upon others. Physically, she was a slight woman in the plateau of her thirties with striking, almost vulpine features. She parted her short hair on the side, though her dark curls resisted any further intervention. Her long-suffering stylist had once described her hair as resembling a porcupine with a perm, a characterization Isolde had not minded in the slightest. She was almost entirely insensible to pleasantries, especially the parentheses of polite conversation, preferring to let the drumroll of her heels convey her hellos and her coattails say her goodbyes.

Her husband, Warren, was a big, squarish man with a tree stump of a neck and a lion's mane of receded tawny hair. He wore unfashionable tweed suits that he hoped had a softening effect on his bearing, but which in fact made him look like a garden wall. Though he was a year younger than Isolde, Warren did not look it, and had been, since adolescence, mistaken for a man laboring toward the promise of retirement. He had a mustache like a boot brush and limpid hazel eyes whose beauty was squandered on a beetled and bushy brow, an obstruction that often rendered his expressions unfathomable, leading some strangers to assume he was gruffer than he was. In fact, Warren was a man of tender conscience and emotional depth, traits that came in handy when Isolde's brusque manner necessitated a measure of diplomacy. He was considerably better groomed that morning only because he had risen early to greet the veg man, who unfailingly delivered the freshest greens and gossip in all of Berbiton at the unholy hour of six.

Seeming to wither in the silence, Mr. Alman repeated, "I said, the king wishes to be baked into a ca—"

"Intriguing," Isolde interrupted in a tone that plainly suggested it was not.

Iz did not particularly care for the nobility. She had accepted Mr. Horace Alman into her home purely because War had insisted one could not refuse a royal visitor, nor indeed, turn off the lights and pretend to be abroad.

While War had made tea, Iz had endured the secretary's boorish attempts at small talk, made worse by an unprompted confession that he was something of a fan, a Hexologist enthusiast. He followed the Wilbies' exploits as frequently documented in the *Berbiton Times*. Mr. Horace Alman was interested to know how she felt about the recent court proceedings. Iz had rejoined she was curious how he felt about his conspicuous case of piles.

The royal secretary had gone on to irk her further by asking whether her name really was "Iz Ann Always Wilby" or if it were some sort of theatrical appellation, a stage name. Iz patiently explained that her father, the famous Professor Silas Wilby, had had many weaknesses—including an insatiable wanderlust and an allergy to obligations—but none worse than his fondness for puns, which she personally reviled as charmless linguistic coincidences that could only be conflated with humor by a gormless twit. Only the sort of vacuous cretin who went around asking people if their names were made-up could possibly enjoy the lumbering comedy that was the godless pun.

Though, in all fairness, she was not the only one to be badgered over her name. Her husband had taken the rather unusual step of adopting her last name upon the occasion of their marriage. He'd changed his name not because he was estranged from his family, but rather because he'd never liked the name Offalman.

extras

Iz had been about to throw the royal secretary out on his inflamed fundament when War had emerged from the kitchen pushing a tea cart loaded with chattering porcelain and Mr. Horace Alman had announced that King Elbert III harbored aspirations of becoming a gâteau.

His gaunt cheeks blushing with the ever-expanding quiet, Mr. Alman pressed on: "His Majesty has gone so far as to crawl into a lit oven when no one was looking." The secretary paused to make room for their astonishment, giving Warren sufficient time to post another sandwich. "And while he escaped with minor burns, the experience does not appear to have dissuaded him of the ambition. He wants to be roasted on the bone."

"So, it's madness, then." Iz shook her head at War when he inquired whether she would like some of either the lemon sponge or the spice cake, an inquiry that was conducted with a delicate rounding of his plentiful brows.

"I don't believe so." Mr. Alman touched his teacup as if he might raise it, then the fire behind him snapped like a whip, and his fingers bid a fluttering retreat. "He has long moments of lucidity, almost perfect coherence. But he also suffers from fugues of profound confusion. He's been discovered in the middle of the night roaming the royal grounds without any sense of himself or his surroundings. The king's sister, Princess Constance, has had to take the rather extreme precaution of confining him to his suite. And I must say, you both seem to be taking all of this rather in stride! I tell you the king believes he's a waste of cake batter, you stifle a yawn!"

Iz tightened the knot of her crossed arms. "I didn't realize you were looking for a performance. I could have the neighbor's children pop by if you'd like a little more shrieking."

War hurried to intervene: "Mr. Alman, please forgive us. We do not mean to appear apathetic. We are just a bit more accustomed to unusual interviews and extraordinary confessions than most. But, rest assured, we are not indifferent to horror; we are merely better acquainted."

"Indeed," Iz said with a muted smile. "How have the staff taken the king's altered state of mind?"

Appearing somewhat appeased, the secretary twisted and shaped the points of his mustache. "They're discreet, of course, but there are limits. Princess Constance knows it's a secret she cannot keep forever, devoted as she is to her brother."

"Surely, you want physicians, psychologists. We are neither," Iz said.

The secretary absorbed her comments with an expression of pinched indulgence. "We've consulted with the nation's greatest medical minds. They were all stumped, or rather, they were perfectly confident in their varying diagnoses and prescriptions, and none of them were at all capable of producing any results. His condition only worsens."

"Even so, I'm not sure what help we can be." Iz picked at a thread that protruded, wormlike, from the armrest of the sofa.

The secretary turned the brim of his hat upon his knee, ducking her gaze when he said, "There's more, Ms. Wilby. There was a letter."

"A letter?"

"In retrospect, it seems to have touched off His Majesty's malaise." The royal secretary reached into his jacket breast pocket. The stiff envelope trembled when he withdrew it. The broken wax seal was as sanguine as a wound. "It is not signed, but the sender asserts that he is the king's unrecognized son."

Warren moved to stand behind his wife's chair. He clutched the back of it as if it were the rail of a sleigh poised atop a great hill. Iz reached back and, without looking, patted the tops of his knuckles. "I imagine the Crown receives numerous such claims.

No doubt there are scores of charlatans who're foolish enough to hazard the gallows for a chance to shake down the king."

"Indeed, but there are two things that distinguish this particular instance of blackmail. First, the seal." Mr. Alman stroked the edge of the wax medallion, indicating each element as he described it: "An *S* emblazoned over a turret; note the five merlons, one for each of Luthland's counties. Beneath the *S*, a banner bearing the name Yeardley. This is the seal of Sebastian, Prince of Yeardley. This is the stamp of the king's adolescent ring."

"He identified it as such?" Iz asked.

"I did, at least initially. Of course, I like to believe I'm familiar with all the royal seals, but I admit I had to check the records on this occasion. Naturally, there is much of his correspondence that His Majesty leaves me to open and deal with, but when something like this comes through, I deliver it to him unbroken."

"The signet was no longer in the king's possession, then?"

"No, the royal record identified the ring as lost about twenty-five years ago, around the conclusion of his military service, I believe."

"That's quite a length of time to sit on such a claim." Iz reached for the letter, but the secretary pulled it back. She looked into his eyes; they glistened with uncertainty as sweat dripped from his nose like rain from a grotesque. "What is the second thing that distinguishes the letter?"

"The king's response to the correspondence was...pronounced. He has thus far refused to discuss his impressions of the contents with myself, his sister, or any of his advisors. He insists that it is a hoax, that we should destroy it, though Princess Constance won't hear of it. She maintains that one doesn't destroy the evidence of extortion: One saves it for the inquiry. But of course, there hasn't been an inquiry. How could there be, given the nature of the claim? To say nothing of the fact that the primary witness to the events in question is currently raving in the royal tower."

"The princess wishes for us to investigate?" she asked. Though Isolde held little affection for the gentry, she liked the princess well enough. Constance had established herself as one of very few public figures who continued to promote the study of hexegy, touting the utility of the practice, even amid the blossoming of scientific discovery and electrical convenience. Still, Isolde's vague respect for the princess was hardly sufficient to make her leap to her brother's aid.

Mr. Alman coughed—a brittle, aborted laugh. "Strictly speaking, Her Royal Highness does not know I am here. I have taken it upon myself to investigate the identity of the bastard, or rather, to engage more capable persons in that pursuit."

"I'm sorry, Mr. Alman, but what I said when we first sat down still holds. I am a private citizen. I serve the public, some of whom come to me with complaints about royal overreach, the criminal exploitations of the nobility, or the courts' bungling of one case or another. I don't work for the police—not anymore. Surely you have enough resources at your disposal to forgo the interference of one unaffiliated investigator."

"I do understand your preference, ma'am." The royal secretary rucked his soft features into an authoritative scowl. "But these are extraordinary circumstances, and not without consequence. The uncertainty of rule only emboldens the antiroyalists, the populists, and our enemies overseas. You must—"

Isolde pounced like a tutor upon a mistake: "I *must* pay my taxes. I *may* help you. Show me the letter."

Mr. Alman tightened like a twisted rag. "I cannot share such sensitive information until you have agreed to assist in the case."

"There is another way to look at this, Iz," Warren said, returning to the tea cart. He poured water from a sweating pitcher into a juice glass and presented it to the dampened secretary, who readily accepted it. "You wouldn't just be working for the Crown; you would be serving the interests of the private citizen who has come forward with the claim...perhaps a *legitimate* one." The final phrase made Mr. Alman nearly choke upon his thimble swallow of water. "If the writer of this letter shares the king's blood, and we were to prove it, I don't think anyone would accuse you of being too friendly with the royals."

Isolde bobbed her head in consideration, an easy rhythm that quickly broke. "But if I help to prove that he is a prince, I'd just be serving at the pleasure of a different sovereign."

"True." Warren moved to the mantel to stir the coals, not to invigorate them, but to shuffle the loose embers toward the corners of the firebox. "But if you don't intervene, our possible prince will remain a fugitive."

"You think we should take the case?"

"You know how I feel about lords and lawmen. But it seems to me Mr. Alman is right: If there's a vacuum in the palace and a scramble for the throne, there will be strife in the streets. We know who suffers when heaven squabbles—the vulnerable. Someone up on high only has to whisper the word 'unrest' and the prisons fill up, the workhouses shake out, the missions bar their doors, and the orphanages repopulate. And when the dust settles, perhaps there'll be a new face printed on the gallet bill or a fresh set of bullies on the bench, but the only thing of real consequence that will have changed is the number of bones in the potter's field. Revolution may chasten the rich, but uncertainty torments the poor."

Isolde patted the air, signaling her surrender. "All right, War. All right. You've made your point. Mr. Alman, I—"

A heavy, arrhythmic knock brought the couple's heads around. The Wilbies stared at the unremarkable paneled door as if it were aflame.

Alman snuffled a little laugh. "Do knocking guests always cause such astonishment?"

"They do when they come by my cellar," Warren said.

The door shattered, casting splinters and hinge pins into the room, making all its inhabitants cry out in alarm. It seemed a fitting greeting for the seven-foot-tall forest golem who ducked beneath the riven lintel.

Its skin, rough as bark and scabbed with lichen, bunched about fat ankles and feet that were arrayed from toe to heel by a hundred gripping roots. Its swollen arms were heavy enough to bend its broad back and bow its head, ribbed and featureless as a grub. The golem lurched forward, swaying and creaking upon the shore of a gold-and-amethyst rug whose patterns had been worn down by the passage of centuries.

"A mandrake," Iz said, tugging a half stick of chalk from her khaki breeches. "I've never seen one so large. But don't worry. They're quite docile. He probably just got lost during his migration. Let's try to herd him back down."

With hands raised, Warren advanced upon the mandrake, nattering pleasantly as he inched toward the heaving golem that resembled an ambling yam. "There's a sport. Thank you for keeping off my rug. It's an antique, you know. I have to be honest—it's impossible to match and hard to clean. I haven't got one of those newfangled carpet renovators. The salesman, wonderful chap, wanted three hundred and twenty gallets for it. Can you imagine? And those suck-boxes are as big as a bureau. I have no idea where I'd park such a—"

The moment War inched into range, the mandrake swatted him with a slow, unyielding stroke of its limb, catching him on the shoulder and throwing him back across the room and violently through his tea cart. Macarons and petits fours leapt into the air and rained down upon the smashed porcelain that surrounded the splayed host.

The mandrake raised the fingerless knob of one hand, identifying his quarry, then charged at the royal secretary, who sat bleating like a calf.